LINDSEY N. RHODEN

A BOND OF DARKNESS & DISCORD

BOOK 2

For anyone learning to accept the love they deserve.
You are worthy.

Content Warnings

A Bond Of Darkness And Discord is book 2 in an adult dark fantasy series that contains strong language, mention of self harm, suicidal ideation, strong themes of anxiety and depression throughout, scenes of torture/violence on page, primal play, bondage, CNC/forced orgasm on page, and mention of miscarriage/infertility. Some of this content may be triggering to individuals and should be taken into consideration before reading. If you are struggling with anxiety, depression, or suicidal ideation, please don't hesitate to reach out to one of these national mental health agencies, or find an agency local to you for those not in the US.

Your mental health matters and you don't have to suffer alone.

988 Suicide & Crisis Lifeline-free and confidential 24/7 support to people in suicidal crisis or emotional distress

Call or text 988 or chat 988lifeline.org

MHA Crisis Text Line-free, text based support 24/7

Text MHA to 741741

The Trevor Project-national 24 hour, toll free

Confidential suicide hotline for LGBTQ youth

Call 1-866-488-7386 or text START to 678678

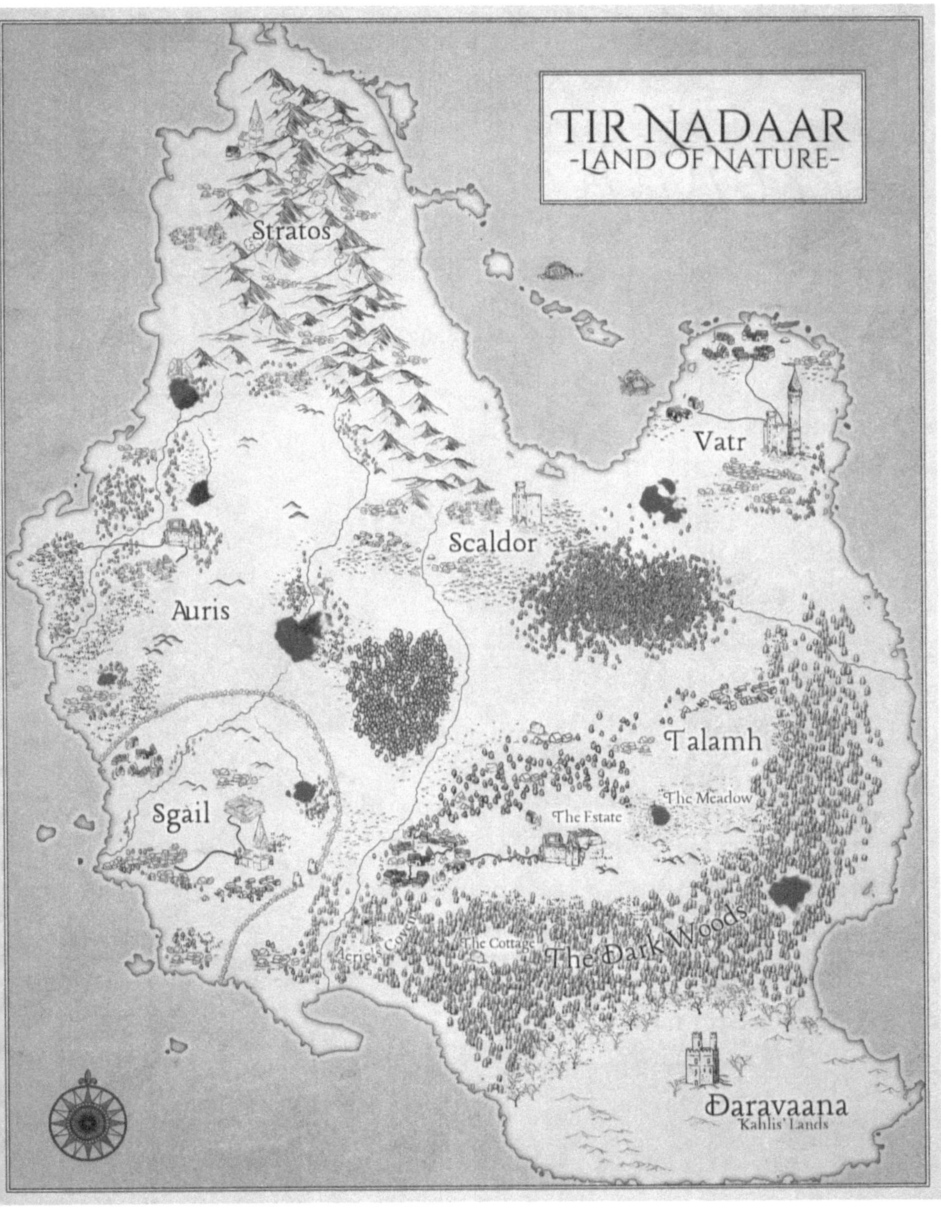

TIR NADAAR
-LAND OF NATURE-
Stratos
Vatr
Scaldor
Auris
Talamh
The Meadow
Sgail
The Estate
Coscur
Acrie
The Cottage
The Dark Woods
Đaravaana
Kahlis' Lands

Pronunciation

TIR NADAAR	TEER NAH–DAHR
TALAMH	TALAV
SGÀIL	SGAːL
STRATOS	STRAH–TOHS
VATR	VAH–TER
SCALDOR	SKAHL–DOR
AURIS	AWR–IHS
KAHLIS	KAH–LEES
HAZLENN	HAZ–LIN
AERMIDH	AIR–MIHD
KIRWAN	KEER–WINN
MIRREN	MEER–EHN
CAILLEACH	KALʲəX
DAEOMI	DAY–OH–MY

*SOME WORDS HAVE BEEN *INSPIRED* BY THE GAELIC LANGUAGE AND CELTIC FOLKLORE/MYTHOLOGY. PRONUNCIATIONS HAVE BEEN PULLED FROM LEARNGAELIC.SCOT/INDEX.JSP FOR APPLICABLE WORDS, HOWEVER THIS IS A WORK OF FICTION AND NOT ALL PRONUNCIATIONS WILL BE THE SAME AS THEIR CELTIC INSPIRED COUNTERPART. IF YOU HAVE ANY QUESTIONS ABOUT FURTHER PRONUNCIATION, PLEASE FEEL FREE TO REACH OUT TO ME VIA EMAIL OR ON INSTAGRAM.

Playlist

- ▶ **BAD DREAMS**
  TEDDY SWIMS
- ▶ **HYMN TO VIRGIL**
  HOZIER
- ▶ **MAN OR A MONSTER**
  SAM TINNESZ, ZAYDE WØLF
- ▶ **FAIR TO YOU**
  VINCENT LIMA
- ▶ **SLOW DANCE SLOW**
  THE WEATHER MACHINE
- ▶ **LIKE YOU MEAN IT**
  STEVEN RODRIGUEZ
- ▶ **SAVING YOUR SOUL**
  DAVID KUSHNER
- ▶ **GIVE**
  SLEEP TOKEN
- ▶ **TRAUMA**
  NF
- ▶ **START A WAR**
  KLERGY, VALERIE BROUSSARD
- ▶ **HALF OF FOREVER**
  HENRIK

PART 1: DARKNESS

CHAPTER 1
HAZEL

A scorching heat lit my veins, rippling in waves of agony and torment. I screamed out at the sudden burst, as if my very core was being split in half. I fought desperately to piece it back together, following my natural instinct of self-preservation. I didn't understand what was happening to me, but everything within me was screaming to make it stop.

I looked down at my hands, clawing at my skin to put out whatever invisible fire was burning there. To my shock, it wasn't my own hands that came into view. In place of my too-pale skin, I found the rough, sunkissed arms of my fated mate, Vander. I recognized the intricate roots inked onto his skin from his tribal magic, a mark of the gift that had been passed down through his bloodline.

Suddenly, the ink shifted, another mark taking form in the snare of twisting black. I gasped in pain. It burned like fire from the Depths—a bottomless, never-ending inferno. It would tear me apart—tear Vander apart—if I didn't stop it.

Too slowly, I realized what this was. The moment Vander earned the Mark of the Grimm.

There was nothing to be done, no time left to talk him out of this deal. Only nightmarish memories of the pain and heartache he experienced all those years ago. The same pain he still experienced here in his dreams.

I reached out through the tether, begging him to wake. The pain was too much to bear. Hot, bitter tears slid down my cheeks as I felt what he'd sacrificed to save me, what he sacrificed every day because of the choices I'd made.

The world around me cascaded into a void of suffocating black. I worked to break the surface, to find consciousness and return to the world I belonged to. It was too slow, like trying to run through wet sand or treading water during a rageful ocean storm. I would never be free. He *would never be free.*

I awoke, heart beating hard and skin still searing from the pain of my dream. Of Vander's pain... *Vander's* dream. I looked to where he'd fallen asleep at the foot of my bed in his wolven form, expecting to find him in a similar state as I was now. Instead, I only caught the slightest glimpse of that midnight tail as he slipped past the door and into the hallway beyond. I exhaled hard, sucking down the familiar air of my bedchamber as I tried desperately to rid my lungs of the toxic darkness of that bitter memory.

I swiped a hand across my face, pushing damp ruby strands of hair away as I scrubbed at my eyes. Dreamwalking still felt so strange to me. I still hadn't learned how to master it, rather than letting it master me. This was the third night in a row that I'd accidentally slipped into Vander's dreams. And the third morning in a row he'd left before I could even bring it up.

I knew we should talk about it, that avoiding it like this would only lead to more issues, but the message was clear: this was something Vander would not discuss. Not yet. Even the tether between us appeared closed in those few hours following our waking—until Vander later reappeared with a newfound sense of calm and control over whatever he'd been feeling.

So much had happened since I'd closed the Rift. Since Arlo...

And at the same time, nothing had happened at all. Vander was here; Arlo was gone. But it turned out things weren't that simple. Beginning things with Vander—or perhaps, *restarting*, was the better word—had proven more challenging than I had expected.

I let out a sigh as I swept my legs off the bed and sat on the edge, trying to settle my racing heart. I looked around the room, grounding myself with the reality I now occupied and pushing out the wretched visions of the past. My eyes caught on the ethereal, golden dress hanging against the bathing chamber door on the other side of the room, my stomach plummeting as I remembered what day it was today.

Sol Litha. And my birthday.

I'd tried so hard to convince Aerie that it wasn't necessary to hold Summer Solstice festivities, in light of everything that had happened in the past two weeks. It felt wrong to celebrate anything after the loss we were all still mourning. Mirren's absence within the estate was more than evident. The rooms felt empty, stripped of their warmth and joy, as if even the house itself was crying out for her to return.

But Aerie and Bastian insisted the solstice was a ceremonial acknowledgement of the Divine's return, a monumental phenomenon that deserved recognition. And seeing the small window of reprieve this celebration was bringing Aerie made me eventually let go—despite my deep desire to escape the attention. So few things brought Aerie joy these days, and despite the heartache I knew she was drowning in, she was still here. Still trying. And it warmed my heart to see how deep her love for me went. She'd already lost so much, and if she could find some distraction and excitement in the planning of these festivities, then I'd deal with the discomfort they caused me.

I shook my head, pushing myself off the bed and forcing myself out of the circling thoughts. I grabbed some simple clothing from the wardrobe, dressing in a hasty manner as I knew Aerie would be waiting in the kitchen with breakfast. It would do no good to worry about these things—the fear and panic of letting everyone down, not living up to the expectations the tribespeople must have of me, either from my past life or the title I now held as the Divine. I'd put on a brave face for Aerie. Aerie, who'd taken me in as one of her own, who'd never given up or doubted my power, and who even now expected nothing from me despite that power she could sense in my veins. Aerie, who'd lost so much and who was battling a kind of grief I knew went deeper than what I currently understood.

She needed this, and no matter how badly I wanted to run and hide from the events of today, I'd give her this.

My bare feet padded lazily on the floorboards as I turned away from the wardrobe. I stopped in front of the dress, running a hand down the delicate fabric. The layers of the dress shifted, flecks of gold catching in the early morning light. The color was surreal, the hue of the sunlight flitting through the window. Not merely a dusty orange or a golden fabric, but sunbeams and daylight itself between my fingers. I loved every detail of the gown... I just couldn't imagine *me* in it. It felt too elegant, too regal. When I'd tried it on, the shimmering fabric braided and cascaded in an intimate wrap around my body, showing off far more than I'd ever been comfortable showing off before. Dread clenched in my stomach as I thought about having to don the outfit in front of the entire earth tribe in just a few short hours, forcing me to drop the fabric and step away.

I moved over to the vanity, picking up the crown Aerie had made for me as well. I'd never held something so beautiful and valuable in my hands and they shook just touching such a thing. Clear and golden-hued crystals carefully accented the headpiece, with sunbursts and gilded, handmade adornments filling the spaces in between. Its intricate beauty was a true testament to the labor

Aerie had poured into this piece. I carefully set it back down, making sure not to let it clank against the surface of the vanity.

It was all so beautiful, so extravagant. And simultaneously a delicate, intimidating responsibility to navigate.

Aerie had prepared everything as a kind gesture, a way to ensure I didn't have to worry about having no memory of their—of *our* traditions. But the more plans were made, the closer the day came, the more I realized how crippling it would be. So many eyes on me, so many people who seemed to know me from a past life I still couldn't remember, or from ancient legends and tales I still didn't know.

I folded my arms over myself, wishing Vander was here to talk about all of this. I'd follow through with tonight's festivities. I couldn't let Aerie down. But between the guise I would hide behind tonight and the disconnect between me and Vander, I felt too uneasy. The world around me felt rocky, unstable—like so much of my reality was too far out of my control. Tendrils of Vander's dream snaked their way back into my mind, whispering disconcerting thoughts and tugging on those dark corners of my mind. It was a not-so-subtle warning, a foreboding reminder of how fragile everything seemed—how one wrong move could bring everything around me crumbling down.

CHAPTER 2
HAZEL

I shuffled through the Estate, rubbing the sleep from my eyes and trying my best not to worry about Vander. I knew I wouldn't find him amidst these walls. He'd be out in the Dark Woods, as he often was when faced with uncomfortable moments. That was his retreat, his safe haven—no matter how demented the idea of the Dark Woods offering anyone safety seemed.

I entered the kitchen, overwhelmed by the flurry of movement within. Staff and merchants from the nearby town were working hurriedly, filling the space with the most decadent smells. Every available countertop was overflowing with freshly baked pastries, cakes, and roasted meats. Exotic fruits I hadn't ever seen before were piled high on polished silver trays, accompanied by wheels of rich, creamy cheeses layered on intricately carved wooden boards.

I strolled over to the side of the kitchen, out of the hustle and bustle, and snagged a piece of cheese from a particularly delicious looking stack. I leaned against the table, watching in awe as the staff worked in harmony to bob and weave around one another—a pristine dance as they kneaded dough, prepared pies, and filled platters. The kitchen was fuller than I'd ever seen it before. And yet my chest ached as I remembered the one who wasn't there. The one who should have been. Mirren would have been so excited for Sol Litha, would have been right there in the mix, doing as much as she could to help.

Someone cleared their throat off to my right. I forced my gaze away from the crowded room as I was pulled back to the present.

Aerie stood in the doorway leading to her greenhouse just beyond the Estate. She didn't speak, just gestured for me to follow. As if she knew exactly where my thoughts had gone. She offered me a small smile, but there was no light behind her pale blue eyes. There hadn't been since Mirren...

I pushed off the table, forcing my body to follow even though it was screaming at me to turn the opposite direction and run back to the solitude of my room. I ducked into the greenhouse, making sure to latch the door behind me. The quiet barrier offered a sudden wave of relief. I sighed, closing my eyes for a moment to soak it in.

"I thought we'd meet in here today." Aerie's soft voice filled the room. "Given the chaos that's ensuing in there." I looked up in time to see her gesture back towards the kitchen, surprised to find Bastian leaning on the table behind her. I saw it in her eyes, the same pain I'd felt while standing there, looking for someone who'd never arrive.

I swallowed hard, trying to will my mouth to speak, but nothing came out. Instead, I simply took my seat at her table as she slid a fresh plate of food in front of me.

"Eat up," she instructed, walking around the other side of the table. She laid a hand on Bastian's chest, pausing beside him for a moment before taking her seat with a palpable sort of exhaustion. I noticed the books spread out around her, the jars of herbs and bits of spellwork littering not just the worktable but all of the greenhouse. I had never seen it in such shape, as if it was too much effort to keep up with it.

Bastian worked dutifully around us, sweeping the wooden floors. This had become his custom as of late; he barely let Aerie out of his sight. I think the image of Kahlis standing against her at the Rift had jarred something in him. Or maybe it had been watching Mirren's death... My chest tightened for what felt like the millionth time today as those haunting images flashed through my mind over and over again. Something that had become a pattern for me apparently, never truly being able to find escape from them.

I rolled my shoulders, using the motion as an excuse to look back at Bastian and focus my mind elsewhere. It was sweet, the way he looked after Aerie. He was so attentive, so present with her. Something that I wish I could say was reflected in his brother. But I felt as if Vander was more distant than ever after everything.

It seemed these days he took any opportunity he could to go hunting in the Dark Woods or run off with Lennox and Kirwan to go after some new threat. I knew there was much to be done:

wards to fix, borders to protect... and the attack from Kahlis had left too many of his creatures loose within our realm.

But it felt like we were regressing. And my heart was so heavy right now, so full of pain and grief, and I didn't know what to do with that. There was no one I wanted to lean on more than Vander. And yet, I felt as if he was the furthest one away from me.

I pulled my plate towards me, picking at the pieces of my still-warm breakfast as I watched Aerie across the table. She lit a candle and pulled out a thin strand of leather. She tossed the knots and braids of her almost white hair over her shoulder, digging through her strands and adornments until she found an untouched section.

Her fingers worked in steady rhythm as she wove the sections together. Her eyes remained closed, guarded, as she retreated to some distant world. It was hypnotic watching her fingers work over her hair. An energy filled the room that I couldn't quite explain, but I quickly understood that this was a ritual, an intimate moment to which I was merely an outsider, an observer. She finished the end of the braid, tying it off with the strand of leather, fastening a small bead along with it.

"What is it for?" I asked, gesturing down to the ceremonial items she'd set up. She ran her fingers over the new plait before tucking it back amongst the rest of her hair.

"A memorial." Bastian's voice rang through the greenhouse, his tone strong and booming. He leaned the broom against the wall, coming up beside her and placing a kiss against her cheek. A tear I hadn't noticed lingered there, and Bastian wiped it away before letting his hand fall to the freshly braided section of her hair. "For Mirren." His voice was lower now, rougher, as he ran the pad of his thumb over her white strands.

He pulled up another stool, dropping onto it heavily. He turned his back to Aerie as she began weaving a small section of his deep brown hair. Aerie's hands worked quickly, fastening Bastian's braid with another strip of leather and a matching bead. When she finished, she let the braid fall against his back. Her fingers lingered there, sweeping through the strands and admiring her work.

She paused, eyes snagging on something before her fingers dove into the tresses and reemerged with another, practically identical, braid. "Bastian..." she breathed. It sounded like a reprimand, but her voice was full of sympathy as she laid the braid she'd discovered against his shoulder. He reached up to her hand, looking down at the braid as both of them held it for a moment.

He stood abruptly, pulling a dagger from his belt. In one swift motion, he drew the other braid out from his head and lifted the dagger to it, slicing through the hair.

He held the severed plait in his hand, looking down at it with an air of remorse. "With everything that's happened, I haven't had time to cut it out." His eyes caught mine, sad and heavy, before dropping his gaze and stabbing the worktable with his dagger.

"Here." He jutted his hand out toward me, unable to hide the emotion in his voice as he ushered me to take the lock of hair. "Burn it." He nodded down to the candle on the worktable between me and Aerie.

"Why? If it was meant to be a memorial…" I looked up at Bastian, brows furrowed.

"That one wasn't for Mirren," he explained, his free hand fisting by his side. He swallowed hard, unshed tears shimmering in his chestnut eyes. When I didn't move to take the braid, he laid it on the table before me.

"For me?" I whispered. He gave a small nod.

I inhaled sharply at the hard truth. If a braid was a memorial for the dead then this meant he'd at one point given up hope of ever finding me again. I didn't blame him. Looking back, I sometimes wish Vander had given up too. They had all suffered so much through their efforts to find me, Vander most of all. My dreamwalking this morning was a testament to that. Perhaps if he'd lost hope as his brother had, he could have avoided the Mark, avoided the pain I sense from him—even still.

"It's an old tradition my sisters taught me." Aerie's words broke my thoughts. "We knot our hair for those we've loved and lost. Hair holds memories, and braiding it helps ensure their memories live on with us. Even once their spirit has moved on to the realms beyond."

My eyes fell to Aerie's hair with a new awareness. It was riddled with similar braids and knots. I couldn't help but wonder how much loss she must have gone through in her lifetime to earn them all. And which of them were meant to symbolize her beloved sisters.

"But leaving this one intact is a bad omen," Bastian continued, motioning down to the table. "You're not a memory. You're here.

And I was foolish for leaving it for as long as I had, foolish for being so hasty in my grief back in those days when you were gone." He swallowed hard, eyes downcast on the braid as his fingers thrummed idly against the table. "Burning it banishes the negative energy, and hopefully the omen along with it."

I nodded, lifting the lock of hair carefully and dragging the candle over the uneven surface of the table. Slowly, I held the braid over the flame, watching the way the flame grew to meet the hair and burned brighter as it swallowed the braid completely. Aerie offered me an empty bowl to drop the now burning plait in. I did as she instructed, and she took the bowl back. Reaching into a nearby jar, she grabbed a handful of dried herbs and sprinkled them over the bowl. The herbs met with the remnants of the fire, crackling and sparking to life in the air as we sat in silence and watched. The fire died out a moment later, releasing us from whatever spell we'd been trapped in.

Bastian cleared his throat, turning to the rest of the greenhouse and looking to tidy up some of the mess as Aerie turned her attention back to me.

"Are you ready for the festivities today?" she asked, thumbing through a journal of delicately kept notes.

"Mhmm," I hummed, rubbing my arm as I looked back towards the kitchen I knew was still bustling with energy just beyond the greenhouse door.

Aerie's hands stilled over a newly blank page, setting the book down. "Hazel, I know this isn't exactly how you planned to spend your birthday. And I'm so sorry. But I do think it's important for the tribe to celebrate this day together. There's been so much grief, not just in our family, but throughout the tribe too."

I looked down at my plate of food, feeling suddenly shameful. Aerie reached out a hand, lacing our fingers together and pulling my gaze back to her kind eyes. The soft blue hue twinkled with something like love, the corners of her eyes creasing as she offered a small smile.

"We need to rely on each other. We need community now more than ever. Even if there's some growing pains at the start."

She was right. The tribe had been through its own hardships and it deserved its leaders. Ever since my return I felt like I'd been consuming all of Aerie and Bastian's attention. I knew there had been other attacks on the tribe, other family members and loved ones lost to Kahlis' violence. We weren't the only ones grieving.

As afraid as I felt, the Divine's power within me had instilled a new, stronger urge to protect the tribe. Not just Talamh—*everyone*. The lands beyond, the creatures big and small. Burning under this new wave of power was a love and compassion for every living thing so deep I wasn't sure I could ignore it.

There was still a lot of darkness, still a lot of doubt and pain lurking in the hidden recesses of my mind—but Aerie was helping me work through it all. She was also persistently explaining that they would probably always be there, on some level. That we all have our secret battles we must learn to live with. The key was not to be rid of them, but rather to learn how to manage life alongside them.

I lifted my head, taking a deep breath and deciding in the moment that I would choose love over darkness. I would be there for the tribe just as Aerie and Bastian had been here for me over the past few weeks. Because Bastian had been right, I was not just a memory. I was here, living. And no matter how terrifying it felt to fill this new role I found myself in, it was a path forward—hopefully one filled with love, and light, and healing.

CHAPTER 3
VANDER

I stood back and watched the twins circle the most recent Daeo-mi they had caught within the Dark Woods. Two identical looks of anger and revenge ravaged their features.

The boys had shown up at the Estate today, cutting it rather close for Sol Litha, but had quickly agreed to help me fortify the warding for the celebration. I had made it my own personal mission to restore the tribe's wards. I was desperate to do anything that would keep Kahlis away from Hazel.

Now that we knew he was her father, the threat felt more impending than ever. There was no way to determine if Kahlis knew we'd discovered this information, but I wouldn't take any chances. Not when it came to her.

On our last pass around the Estate triple checking the spellwork Aerie had given us, we'd spotted a Daeomi lurking in the Dark Woods. The warding seemed to be doing its job, but I wouldn't take any chances by letting the fucker go. And I knew the twins Kirwan and Lennox—or Nox to those who knew him well enough—wouldn't either.

They had pinned him to one of the towering Hemlocks, Nox's enchanted blade protruding from the spot where they'd secured his hands above his head. Blood dripped continuously, painting the Daeomi in a thick black coat.

They'd taken turns questioning him, gathering what information they could for why he'd been here and what Kahlis knew about tonight's festivities—exploiting any upper hand they could find to exert their vengeance for their sister's brutal death.

I knew without prodding that exacting this kind of violence was more about finding somewhere for their anger to land. Truly, getting intel on Kahlis was just a convenient cover-up. We'd had enough experience with the Daeomi at this point to know they wouldn't give up their leader. No matter how much pain and suffering we put them through.

Nox prowled forward, reaching up to twist the blade that pierced flesh and bone in place above him. The creature grunted, trying to stifle a scream.

"Give us something, you piece of shit." That was Kirwan now, leaning over and landing another blow against the creature's already swollen face. "Tell us why you're here."

The Daeomi sniggered, spitting blood as he raised his head again to the twins. He mumbled something, causing Kirwan to lean in and motion for him to repeat himself.

"Suck. My. Cock." The Daeomi broke out in husky laughter as Kirwan landed another blow against his split cheek. The noise did nothing but spur Kirwan on, beating the Daeomi down into a pulp. Lennox intervened, pulling his twin off the sadistic creature.

"What the fuck are you doing?" Kirwan yelled, desperate to get back to the Daeomi. "Let me kill him!"

"Not yet, brother." Nox's words were ragged with the effort it was taking to hold Kirwan back.

"He doesn't deserve to live!" Kirwan's eyes burned with an unyielding rage. I debated stepping in, but this wasn't my battle to fight. They needed this. And I needed to let them work it out for themselves, rather than let the Mark take over and handle the situation… even if it had been itching to be set free since the moment we'd captured the Daeomi.

"He deserves to fucking die, Lennox! Get the fuck off of me and let me end him!"

"You don't think I know that?" Nox spoke through clenched teeth as he shoved Kirwan back, hard enough to send him flying through the Dark Woods and onto his ass.

Both brothers paused for a moment, breaths heavy and eyes wild.

"You don't think I want to rip him apart just as badly as you do?" Nox's voice was raised now, the closest thing to yelling I'd ever heard from him. He threw his hands up, turning to walk away but then spinning back on his brother within an instant, storming up to where he still sat amidst the muck of the forest floor. "You're not the only one who lost her, Kirwan. She was my sister, too. You don't get to be the only one grieving, nor do you get to collect that revenge alone."

With one last downcast look, Nox stormed back in the direction of the Estate.

Things had been tense between the brothers since their return, and there didn't seem to be enough time in the day to address it. They hadn't spoken much about their time away, but something told me there was more that happened there than they were letting on. A stronger Daeomi presence at the borders was keeping us all busy enough, without digging up our own demons.

Just as I noticed the tension between them, I knew Hazel was seeing the same in me—how she could see through all my walls. Hazel's newfound power had made the tether less stable, harder to control. And her dreamwalking had become more frequent, which unfortunately put me in a rather vulnerable position. I'd gone from being able to hide anything I wanted from her, to her seeing my most stripped down, raw moments of fear and pain.

So until I figured out how to get a handle on the tether, or until I figured out how to keep her from dreamwalking to me, I needed to minimize contact between us. Which was proving to be earth-shatteringly painful. Because there was nothing I wanted more than to watch that pretty little face come undone as I worshipped her body over and over again.

My cock twitched in response to where my thoughts had wandered, bringing my attention back to this moment here in the woods with the beaten and bleeding Daeomi and the two pissed off brothers that needed to be dealt with.

I flexed my fists, cracking my knuckles as I made my way over to where Kirwan still sat on the forest floor, dusting off his hands.

"He always has been able to beat your ass in a fight." I chuckled low as I stuck a hand out to offer him help. Kirwan's irritated gaze found mine, stalling for a moment while he processed what I'd said. He scoffed, slapping my hand away and jumping to his feet.

I bristled, slightly taken aback by how personal he was taking everything. Giving each other shit had always been our coping mechanism. Nonetheless, he glared at me as he passed.

Okay, so humor wasn't going to get through to him this time around. Duly noted.

I caught up to him, making our way back over to the Daeomi who'd been watching with wicked amusement. Well, as much as anyone could watch through blood soaked and swollen eyes. Kirwan grabbed another enchanted dagger from the sheath strapped to his side, poising himself to lay into the Daeomi. Bleeding them dry was the way to kill them—at least, the only way we'd figured out so far. The enchanted blades slowed their healing long enough to let us deplete them before they could repair themselves or replenish their blood. I held out a hand, grabbing Kirwan's wrist midair.

"Don't you think we should wait for Lennox? He made it pretty clear that he wasn't happy with you claiming this kill alone."

"Fuck Lennox." Kirwan spat.

I raised an eyebrow at him, waiting for him to explain. When he didn't, I pressed him further:

"I take it this was a frequent argument between you two while you were gone?"

Kirwan looked away, swallowing hard. I let out a gruff sigh, dropping his hand and scrubbing mine over my face.

Everything had gone to shit. Things between me and Hazel couldn't have been more complicated, the twins were all out of sync. Even Aerie was losing that usually annoying twinkle in her eyes. But who could blame her? A light had been extinguished in all of our lives.

Mirren was the only person Lennox and Kirwan had besides each other. She'd been a bright light of joy in the piercing darkness of all of our lives for so long now. Fuck, Aerie had practically raised her. Visions from the night Aerie and Bastian had snuck into the woods to be joined under the full moon flashed through my mind. I had barely made it in time, had barely convinced myself to go after everything that had happened between me and Bastian at the time.

Mirren had been the only other soul there, aside from the priestess who bore witness to their union. I closed my eyes, feeling the wind blow through the trees of the Dark Woods. Tears threatened to spill behind my eyelids, feeling almost as if I was back in that moment, and I'd open my eyes to see Mirren playing at my feet.

But when I did open them, all that I found was a piece of shit Daeomi and a sulking Kirwan waiting for my say-so to bury his blade in the creature and coat his grief in another layer of bloodshed.

I sighed again, unsure what the right answer was here. The vile beast deserved to die. There was no argument about that. But I worried for Kirwan. I recognized the self-deprivation in his eyes, knew that this violence was nothing more than an attempt to make up for the guilt he felt for losing Mirren.

I didn't want to see him go to that same dark place I went to after Hazel's disappearance. It took me years to find my way back to this side of okay. And I couldn't have done that without Hazel. I feared Kirwan would just keep burying himself and wouldn't have anyone to help pull him back out, especially with how things were between him and Lennox right now.

My heart hurt for the pain I knew he felt, but it broke for the path I saw him going down—and knowing there was nothing I could do to stop it. But I wasn't one to deny a kill, especially when it was one he was owed. And if it would help satisfy that hunger, even momentarily—I'd let him have it.

I dropped my gaze, shaking my head as I motioned him forward. That was all the permission he needed as he lunged, tearing into the Daeomi mercilessly.

CHAPTER 4
HAZEL

I adjusted the crown resting atop my head for what felt like the hundredth time as I stared at my reflection in the mirror. Adorned in every last embellishment Aerie had arranged for me, I felt like a whole different person.

The female I saw in the mirror was no longer the frightened, confused stranger who could remember nothing of this land; nor the skeptic with trust issues who didn't know how to believe in herself, let alone anyone else.

No—she was something else entirely. As I stared into the emerald eyes of the female in the mirror, I knew it was a goddess who stared back. The Divine in all her glory, clothed in gold and adorned with a crown made from her own creation. Just as I'd felt it earlier in Aerie's greenhouse, a sort of weight settled over me, a gentle reminder of the new responsibilities resting on my shoulders. And with the new powers beside it.

A soft rap at the door pulled my attention away from the mirror, turning just as Vander opened the door and stepped into my room. My breath hitched at the sight of him, shock melding into something sweeter, warmer, as I let my eyes pore over his dressed up form.

I knew my dreamwalking had been affecting him. But looking up at him now, it was as if all of that had melted away to make room for this new version of Vander, complete with a velvet black, collared vest and matching silk tunic. My eyes caught on his chest, admiring the way he left the tunic unfastened to show off the tanned skin and rough, cut muscle beneath.

Vander stopped short, no doubt as shocked by my appearance as I was to see him in something besides his typical plain tunics. Or in his wolven form. Heat crept into my cheeks as my thoughts turned from the view of him before me to the memories of him shifting, and those blessed little moments when he revealed the full extent of his mortal form.

He must have sensed my thoughts through the tether because he prowled forward, a growl low in his throat.

"You keep looking at me like that, little spitfire, and I don't think we'll even make it to the celebration." He closed the distance between us, lifting his hand to run a finger over the low-cut neckline of the gilded gown.

The boldness of his actions had me short of breath, especially when he'd been so distant and distracted the last couple of weeks. I'd missed him. I rested my hand against his chest.

"I thought Sol Litha was all about celebrating the summer sun. You know, golds and dusky oranges and yellows. This outfit choice doesn't seem very festive."

Vander brushed an errant curl from my cheek, my heart thrumming at the touch.

"But how are we to appreciate the sun if not for the reminder of darkness that the night brings? It's impossible to acknowledge one without the other, is it not?" He raised an eyebrow at me before grabbing my hand and twirling me around the room to get a better look at my gown. The sun and moon inked onto my palms warmed with my magic in recognition, two sides of the same coin.

I couldn't suppress the giggle bubbling within me as Vander finally slowed our motion and pulled me to him once more. He looked down at me, hunger and admiration burning in his dark eyes. I'd learned to check their color, recognizing the way they grew a deeper black when the Mark became too taxing, and longing for the golden swirl that meant it would be a good day for us.

They were a mix of both now, though I had no time to question its meaning, as he pulled me closer and lowered his face to mine.

My chest tightened with a mixture of confusion and excitement as I waited for him to keep going, urging him with gentle desperation not to stop. A smirk settled across his lips, a sure sign that I still hadn't mastered blocking him out of my mind—despite Aerie's continuous lessons with me. But I couldn't find the energy to be bothered as he closed the remaining breaths between us, pulling my lips to his in a warm, inexplicable moment. I savored the burn of sunbeam whiskey on his breath, his tongue gently parting my lips, testing and teasing.

The world melted away as I fell apart in his arms. I lost myself in that kiss, the simple gesture feeling like home. We had been through so much, *suffered* so much. Every logic and reality should have separated us.

And yet here we were, losing ourselves in one another like two old lovers. It was the best birthday gift I could have asked for.

Too soon, he was pulling away.

"Um, Aerie... she sent me to tell you it was time." Our ragged breaths filled the air. He swiped a thumb and forefinger over his lips, as if he had to do something to keep himself from kissing me again.

I chewed on my own lip, averting my gaze as I tried to process the storm of emotions threatening to overtake me. I wanted to be back in his arms. To push this further and see where he'd let us take it.

I shook my head instead at the mention of Aerie's name, trying to remember how important today was. "I... just need a moment," I said, the nerves evident in my voice.

"Take your time, goddess."

I blushed at the title. Something about the way it rolled off his tongue felt like it was dripping with wicked intent.

Flustered, I turned back to the mirror, readjusting the crystal crown once more and returning things to order. As a final touch, I pulled my long braid over my shoulder so Aerie's handiwork would accent the braided ropes of the gown.

I turned back to Vander and gave him a nod.

"Alright, I'm ready."

He held out a hand as he pulled the door open. I stepped past him into the hall, doing my best to put on a brave face for the members of the tribe that waited beyond.

Vander was at my back, his fingers wrapping around my elbow to slow my steps as we emerged into the sitting room, already full of people. He leaned in close, planting one last soft kiss to my ear as he spoke through the tether.

Don't worry, you're going to be amazing.

CHAPTER 5
VANDER

Sol Litha was beautiful. But no one would have expected anything less of Aerie. Tribe members filled the Estate, both within the house and beyond, fluttering about as they greeted distant friends and relatives. Staff members gracefully weaved in and out of the crowds with food and drink. The sounds of fiddles and flutes intermixed with laughter as people danced and sang. And as the soft daylight settled into sunset, Aerie's gentle voice called the tribe's attention out toward the day's final spectacle.

Bastian had chosen the perfect spot for the summer solstice ceremony, building an altar on one of the higher hills of the Estate. It offered a pristine view of the vast land beyond our home and the open sky above. It was perfect viewing for the sunset, the sky burning bright with rageful hues of reds and oranges that soon gave way to the softer calm of periwinkles and lavender.

From behind the hand-carved wooden altar, Bastian and Aerie thanked the earth for the season of growth and sunlight. They lit candles and rang out songs and chants. Aerie mixed herbs into sachets to hand out to the tribe, encouraging them to sprinkle the blend over the lands. A symbol of a prosperous harvest come autumn and safekeeping for Talamh's borders. At one point, Aerie even invited Hazel up to the altar to offer a token of her magic, which was mixed in the herbs handed out to the tribe.

Hazel *glowed* as she stepped up to the altar, backlit by the setting sun. The most beautiful thing I'd ever seen. Pride radiated from me as I watched her take her place, calling her magic forth with ease. She'd grown leaps and bounds in just a few short weeks.

I had to force my gaze away as a wave of dark magic rose within me, the Mark calling out violently for me to claim the light flowing from her. The sheer force of power had my skin going cold. I crossed my arms over my chest in an effort to hide my clenching fists, pouring every bit of my strength into controlling the darkness inside me. As I rolled my shoulders, the power within me subsided.

Bastian stepped up again, taking the lead as both Aerie and Hazel stepped back. Without even trying, he seemed to command respect. A natural born leader and defender. I was grateful to him and Aerie for filling this role—not just because I couldn't, but because they were meant for it. Bastian defended these families in a way I never could. And Aerie was all too perfect a match for his leadership, caring for each and every tribe's member as if they were her own flesh and blood.

Bastian closed out the ceremony with a prayer to the land and to the Fates just as dusk fell. As the Estate staff made their way around lighting the gardens, Bastian and Aerie drifted off to mingle with the tribe. Hazel lingered awkwardly by the altar, surely overwhelmed with the prospect of socializing. I made my way over to her, slipping my hand around hers. Her body stiffened momentarily, unused to the amount of affection I was giving her tonight.

I wasn't sure what had changed. The time between her closing the Rift and now had been full of challenges to overcome. It was a difficult time, full of trepidation and worry. Neither of us wanted to push the other too far, not sure what this new evolution of our relationship fully meant. But tonight, seeing her as the living embodiment of the power that flowed through her veins and the namesake she'd claimed for herself, wrapped in confidence and dripping with bewitchment... It was doing something to me. Pushing me over the edge.

I couldn't get enough of her. Her taste—which still lingered on my tongue no matter how much I ate or drank. Her smell. The way her body moved in that gown. Despite my silent battle to keep the Mark in check, I knew I wouldn't be able to prevent myself from keeping close, her shadow through the night. I thanked the Fates she let me, grazing her with my touch as we eventually gave into the merriment of the solstice.

As the night deepened, bonfires were lit throughout the Estate. Each fire provided its own hub of entertainment. Dancers and music, performers and tricksters. And endless tables of food and drink. We ran from one set of flames to another, dancing the night away under the magic of Sol Litha. She was an enchantress, filling the air with her intoxicating allure.

I filled my cup with endless servings of sunbeam whiskey, taking the opportunity to tell Hazel of the backstory for my brother's and my favorite indulgence. It seemed an appropriate time to tell her of the wonders of the Auris Tribe. Hazel was enthralled enough with our Sol Litha traditions, but her eyes grew wide as saucers as I explained the way the sun tribe spent a whole week in celebration of this sacred day.

After snagging a bottle of whiskey, we found a seat beside one of the fires, watching a troupe of dancers move to the beat of a low vibrating drum as I explained to her the magic the sun tribe harnessed, capable of suspending the sunset for days at a time. Their people would set up entire villages outside for the week, eating and sleeping and fucking beneath the perpetually glowing, setting sun. I chose to leave out the more scandalous details, but judging by the heat creeping up her neck, she caught my meaning.

"It is truly such a beautiful tribe," I whispered as I leaned into her scent. "If only we could go there now—spend your birthday tucked away in a distant land where no one could interrupt us." I leaned in, murmuring close to her ear. "Who knows what watching you glow in that endless sunset might do to me."

She giggled, no doubt feeling the effects of the whiskey now running through her veins. "That's the twins' tribe, right?"

I nodded, running the back of my hand over the curve of her shoulder.

"Nox told me about it once. The way he described his home, his mother. I could tell it must have been a really special place."

I hummed, thinking back to the twins' spat earlier today. The reminder was sobering, killing the buzz that had been running through my body. I grabbed the bottle of sunbeam whiskey at my feet and refilled my cup. Another breathtaking detail Aerie had arranged special for today: cups carved out of citrine that practically glowed golden. Aerie had to barter with a local merchant, eventually giving up a whole vault's worth of silver for such a luxury. But it was worth it. I held the now full cup up to the flames for Hazel, appreciating the way it glistened and glittered in the light of the flames together.

The buzz returned as I drained the glass, offering another pour to Hazel. She giggled again, tucking her cup behind her back as she leaned into me.

"I think you've had enough for the both of us, Vander. I could get drunk simply off the smell of your breath."

I narrowed my gaze, bringing my mouth closer to her. "Oh, little spitfire, I can think of a much more effective way to get you drunk off me."

The hint of amusement fell from her face, turning to a much more wicked yearning. I closed the distance between our lips, kissing deeply as I let her taste the remnants of the burning whiskey on my tongue.

A roar of laughter and clapping broke us from the moment, forcing her to pull away as the dancers took a bow. I gritted my teeth, cursing under my breath as Hazel politely joined in the clapping.

My head spun, looking around as an idea hit me. Fueled by drink or perhaps something darker, I grabbed Hazel's hand and pulled her up.

"Follow me," I urged, whisking her away. Her cries of protest quickly turned to fits of laughter as I pulled her deeper into the darkness of night. We slipped behind the tree line, wandering into the shadows of the Dark Woods.

"Vander, where are we going?" she pressed, her head turning back towards the festivities to track just how far away I was dragging her. My lips curled up as I tracked the path through the woods, having walked it no less than three times today. I knew exactly where the border for the warding ended, and consequently just the place for us. Perfectly safe, and even more perfectly hidden from view of the party. Before she could ask any more questions, I pulled Hazel into the shadows of a low-hanging hemlock and pinned her between me and the rough bark. Fear shone in her eyes, her head on a swivel as she watched the trees around us.

"Is it safe to be out here?" I could hear the panic creeping into her voice, the way it wavered as her tone reached a higher pitch.

"What's the matter, goddess? Scared of being alone in the Dark Woods with the Shadow of the Grimm?"

I leaned my weight on my arm above her, looming so I'd be the only thing she'd see. Her eyes locked on mine, her fear settling as she watched me, waiting to see what I would do.

I ran my other hand up her leg, her warm skin in my palm contrasting the cool silk of her gown as it grazed over my knuckles. I had dreamt of ripping the delicate fabric off of her all night, and my fingers twitched as the thought overtook me once more. To my surprise, she lifted her leg to follow my hand, and I landed behind her knee, cradling the soft flesh as I leaned down to her neck and inhaled deeply.

Her scent was lethal, intoxicating in the best way. She'd claimed I had drank enough for the both of us, but it was her scent that had done this to me, forcing me to toss my faculties by the wayside and drag her out into the Dark Woods.

"Vander," she whispered as I buried my face into the crook of her neck. I hummed in response, enjoying the honeyed taste of her warm skin against my lips.

"Why now?"

Her words stilled me, my lips hovering at that sensitive spot below her ear. She was voicing the same question I'd been asking myself all night. And I still didn't have an answer. I'd told myself it was because I'd finally gotten a hold on the Mark for the first time since she'd claimed her power. But the familiar building of dark magic in my veins told me that was the farthest from the truth.

When I didn't answer, she pressed on:

"Don't get me wrong, I'm happy. Thrilled, even." She pushed lightly against my chest, moving me back so she could see my eyes. "But I've been waiting, desperate for you, for this, *every* day since the Rift. And you seemed to only be pushing me farther away."

I growled, trying desperately to decide between the instincts coursing through my body. One told me to pursue her further. To ignore the question and prove to her how badly I wanted this by lifting her up against this tree and finally fucking her till the only word left on her lips was my name.

The other instinct told me to pull away, to shut this down before it went too far and I lost control entirely—claiming her and our bond without a second thought. Even as I forced more distance between us, that dark desire was taking over. Consuming me.

I pushed off the tree, head in my hands as I tried to calm the raging storm threatening to take over. I *needed* her. But I needed to protect her more. And I would be damned if after everything we'd been through, I would be her downfall.

"Vander, I didn't mean for you to stop—" She sighed, stepping forward and trying to pull me back to the moment. "Please, we don't have to talk about this right now. Let's just forget about it."

I pulled my hand out of hers, a gasp sounding from her at the sudden movement.

"I can't forget about it, Hazel. It's what I think about constantly. *You* are what I think about constantly."

"So what's the issue then?" She was on me again, tugging at my vest and pulling us back against the Hemlock. She pulled my lips to hers, desperation building.

Everything in me was begging to give in. To push her back and grab her face hard as I pushed my tongue in her mouth and kissed her as if I was a starved, lovestruck animal.

Instead, I pulled away.

"The issue," I shouted, raising my voice louder than I'd meant to. I could see it all happening. The way I was losing control over not just my words but my power too. The forest darkened around us, the night going silent. I tried to shut it down, tried to walk away. But it was as if something else took over me, speaking for me. Shadows rose, wrapping around her and shoving her back until she slammed into the tree. They pinned her in place as I bent over her, grabbing her chin to force her wide gaze to mine.

"Is that if I let myself have what I truly wanted—truly let myself claim you as I want to…" A noise barreled through my chest, something desperate and hungry, as I flicked my gaze over her nearly trembling body, inhaling her fragrant scent, now spiked with the presence of her fear. "You'd be left fucked and frightened on the forest floor."

CHAPTER 6
HAZEL

Fear should have been coursing through my veins—between the way he was looking at me now and the words that just came out of his mouth. Yet all I wanted was for him to be true to his word. To show me all the things he wanted to do with me. *To* me.

This had been the most honesty I'd gotten out of him for weeks. But even as he said it, I could see him receding, shutting it down and pushing space between us. I understood Vander needed space. That he was struggling through his own grief and confusion. It was just as hard for him as it was for me to understand what it meant that I was back—and with these newfound powers. But what hurt more than the distance was that he kept giving me these moments just to take them away. To give my desire hope, just to smother it.

We stared at each other, trapped in this moment of uncertainty. Waiting for the other to make the first move. I raised my hand slowly to his cheek, daring to break the spell that held us here in an effort to reassure him I wanted this.

"Let's go." He growled, grabbing my wrist before it found its target and pulling me back through the woods.

"What are you doing?" I argued. I fought his grasp as he dragged me back towards the festivities. I could barely hear the music with how far out he'd taken me. This forest was the kind of place to fear. Not the place to get *fucked*, as he so eloquently put it. Yet it did nothing to deter the desire swirling low in my belly, spurring me to fight him harder to stay within the trees.

He'd reminded me of the power he held here. The way others shrank in his presence. The power his name possessed as the Shadow of the Grimm. He was the monster stalking these shadows—the thing to be feared in the Dark Woods. And he wanted me.

But the more distance we put between us and that spot in the woods, the more that dream crumbled in my fingertips. He didn't slow, didn't explain. Just charged forward in stoic, vicious silence, ignoring my protests and gripping my wrist tighter when I tried to break free.

The festivities carried on around us, the noise of celebration suddenly too much to bear in the face of everything that had just happened. Vander continued to drag me back to the fire, seating me in the same place we'd been just moments ago.

"Stay here," he mumbled under his breath.

"Vander." His name was a curse on my tongue. "Where are you going?" I reached out for him as he turned to walk away.

My voice cracked, my own emotions betraying me as tears sprung to my eyes. "Please. Don't leave me here. Not today."

He paused for only a moment, looking back over his shoulder through pitch black hooded eyes and gritted teeth.

"I'm needed in the Dark Woods."

No other explanation, no offer to talk about what had just happened between us before he stalked back into the shadows of the trees and was gone.

We'd had a connection, a real, genuine moment together. I could feel it through the tether, the way he was allowing himself to stay open. Perhaps it had been the spirits impeding on his judgement, or perhaps it was meant to be a gift for this special occasion—whatever the reason, I'd been grateful.

Until he stopped long enough to think about what he was doing.

He'd shut me out so fast, pushing me away yet again as he ran off to do Fates knows what. He'd left me here. To spend my birthday alone, amongst strangers. After all the fears I'd shared with him about this day.

I pushed off the ground, making my way back to one of the tables Aerie had set up with refreshments. Grabbing another citrine cup, I filled it to the brim with sunbeam whiskey. Turning back to the fire, I drank deeply, watching the flames dance before me—mimicking the burn of the whiskey as it slid down my throat.

With each bit of distance Vander put between us, I built up a wall to shut him out. I didn't want him spying on me when he'd made the choice to walk away. If he didn't want to be with me in that way then he wouldn't get *any* part of me, including the privilege of the tether.

The whiskey flooded my system, bringing heat to my cheeks and melting the tension away from my fight with Vander as I ventured from fire to fire. At first I just watched, each new performer bringing a bit more amusement to my tense body. But then the music grew louder and the others around me joined in, pulling me along with them. Before I knew what I was doing, I found myself dancing with the strangers, letting the beat of the drums guide my movements.

I lost all sense of time, the world around me becoming a blur of flames and grass and strange faces I didn't recognize. I spun and spun as the night grew on and the faces ran together until I couldn't differentiate one from another. They were all the same, all curious onlookers, strangers fascinated by the dancing goddess before them.

If that's what they wanted, I would happily deliver—enjoy the Divine in all her glory, drunk off her ass with sunbeam whiskey and a broken heart. Alone on her own birthday.

A familiar face finally swam into my view, slowing me as I stumbled into her arms. Rather, both of their arms.

Aerie smiled, letting me lean on her as she stepped away from the dance she was sharing with Bastian. I mumbled out something that was supposed to be an apology, bursting out into a fit of giggles as I heard the ridiculous sounds that were meant to be my words.

"Hazel, where's Vander?" Bastian asked, setting a hand on my arm to steady me.

"Oh, you know. Out with his one true love."

Bastian furrowed his brow, or at least I thought he did. It was so hard to focus on his face with the world spinning around us.

"The Dark Woods!" My voice grew louder than I meant, catching the attention of several of the nearby tribe members. "He decided it was more important to spend this special day with her, rather than with me. Which, why wouldn't he? We're only fated mates. It's not like he *has* to be with me. He can do whatever he damn well pleases."

"Alright," Bastian said, throwing his arm around my waist to support me as he turned me back to the Estate. "Let's get you inside and get some coffee in you."

"No, no." I swatted him away, my attempt futile as Bastian was practically three times my size, and apparently not intoxicated. "I have to wait for Vander. He told me to stay here."

I stumbled, losing my balance as I tried to find my way back to the fire Vander had left me at. I squealed as Bastian wrapped his arms around me, this time lifting me and cradling me across his body as he started off towards the Estate.

The movement was jarring, sobering me as a wave of embarrassment overtook me. I shouldn't need Bastian to be here, shouldn't need anyone to carry me back to my home. I shouldn't have been foolish enough to drink as much as I had, to act the way I did. I could practically hear Vander's taunting voice telling me my actions weren't very becoming of a goddess. Only, he wasn't here to ridicule me. If it had to be anyone, it should have been Van- der—wrapping his arms around me and taking care of me tonight.

I clung to Bastian, tears pricking my eyes. Aerie followed in our wake, finding my gaze over her mate's shoulder and offering me a reassuring nod. They had me, like they always did. And a brand new dose of guilt filled my chest as I realized I was once again taking them away from the myriad of people that needed them more—a whole tribe full of souls more deserving of their time.

All of these thoughts swirled in my head, spinning along with the world around me as Bastian carried me away from the celebration. But there was one thought that kept blasting through the storm raging in my mind, coming up again and again like the waves of nausea I was trying so hard to push back down. It pelted against my mental barriers, still somehow in place, trying with all its might to break them down, break me down, until there was nothing left.

Vander left me. Vander left me. Vander left me.

I awoke the next morning, not in my normal room, but in Aerie's greenhouse. It took a moment for the memories of last night to flood my mind, what bits and pieces I could actually remember. I pushed myself up, digging the heels of my palms into my eyes, hoping that if I tried hard enough, all of those embarrassing moments would go away, before slowly raising myself off the bed and heading for the bathing room.

I ran cold water over my hands and face, hoping the shock to my system would prepare me to face everyone after last night. I stopped for a moment longer, staring into the mirror and letting myself take my fill of the pathetic creature staring back. *A goddess*, I thought. Utterly ridiculous.

I scoffed, the sound bringing a sharp pain through my head as I turned back towards the daybed and sat on the edge.

A knock sounded on the doorframe as Aerie slipped quietly into the greenhouse, a fresh mug of coffee clutched in one hand.

"Rise and shine, beautiful." Her voice was too chipper for the burden my body was carrying. I groaned in response, burying my face in my hands out of pure mortification.

"Now, now, Hazel. It wasn't that bad." She set the mug down on a small bedside table before taking a seat on the edge of the daybed.

"Wasn't that bad?" I repeated. "I ruined yours and Bastian's night because I couldn't handle my whiskey." I scooted back on the bed and wrapped my arms around my knees, tucking them into my chest as I refused to meet her eyes.

"Oh please." She scoffed. "You did not ruin our night. Bastian and I had plenty of time with the members of the tribe and we even got some much needed time to ourselves as well. Besides, you're family. Looking after each other is what we do."

"I'm not convinced that sentiment is truly a family trait," I replied bitterly, huffing out a frustrated breath. Aerie didn't comment but offered the mug to me, encouraging me to take a sip. Reluctantly, I obeyed. The bitterness of the coffee on my tongue was a welcome feeling, already working to tame the nausea fighting with my body.

"Do you want to talk about it?" Aerie asked when I'd taken several more sips of the blessed liquid.

I laughed. "I don't even know what there is to talk about. Vander..." I trailed off. I couldn't find the words. Vander loved me but didn't know how to show it? Vander had changed his mind about what he wanted? Vander was more concerned about his duties as the Shadow of the Grimm than he was with our relationship? The last thought had me stifling another bitter laugh, the word *relationship* feeling like grit in my mouth.

"I know things between the two of you are difficult right now. New relationships are hard enough as it is, without all the added pressure of things like split souls and dark curses."

I hummed, smiling at her attempt at a joke, trying to lift my spirits. She grinned, her own breathy laughs filling the greenhouse.

"I just thought—" I shook my head, running my hands through my hair. "When he told me that we were fated, I thought it would make things simpler. That it was black and white. If the Fates bound us together, then why does this feel so hard?"

Aerie pursed her lips in thought, giving herself a moment to consider her response.

"Things are so complicated right now," she answered finally. "Not just with you and your bond, but with everyone. There's so much uncertainty going around, so much grief." Her face fell at the word, a wave of pain trying to break through. "Just—try and be patient with him. And with yourself as well. You both deserve the time and space to figure out what you want, fated or not."

I knew she was right, as always. There were so many other things happening, between the impending threat of Kahlis, the new power I apparently had, and Vander's own monsters he was wrestling with. Even with being fated, it was a wonder we'd made it as far as we had. And this was probably the last thing we needed to be focusing our time on. But not being with him, knowing what I know now... It was like trying to survive with my heart outside my body. And I wasn't sure how long I could go on existing like this.

"Okay," I answered at last. I finished off the last bit of the coffee before setting the mug back on the bedside table. It didn't matter how I felt, it didn't change anything that had happened last night, didn't change how Vander felt about me. So for now, the only thing I could do was listen to Aerie and move forward. "Can you do me a favor and not mention last night to him? I don't need him making a bigger deal out of all of this than it is."

Aerie sucked in a breath, throwing her gaze back over to the Estate that lay beyond the closed greenhouse door. "Well, I promise I won't say anything, but I think it may be a little late to warn Bastian."

My blood went cold, following her gaze. "Oh no," I groaned, pinching my eyes closed. "What did he do?"

"Oh, he's just giving Vander a bit of brotherly advice." Aerie tried, and failed, to stifle her smile. A new round of embarrassment ran through me as I imagined how that conversation would go.

"I'm sure it will be fine," Aerie added, patting my leg. "But I do have a bit of news for you. I received a tip from one of the attendees at last night's festivities. A possible lead on information about Kahlis." Her eyes slowly found mine, no doubt noticing the way I sucked in a breath at the mention of my father's name. "We didn't have time to discuss further but she did invite me to a meeting to go more in depth. Now under normal circumstances, I would consider traveling to discuss such things further, knowing how important a lead like this could be for us. But I'm not sure right now is a good time for you to—"

"No," I interrupted, cutting her off. "If there's something that could help us end this, we need to go."

Aerie watched me for a moment, brows furrowing. "Hazel, I know this battle is important. I want to bring Kahlis down just as much as you do, to find a way to protect our tribe from his reach once and for all. But let's take a moment to think about this. Are you really sure you feel up to traveling right now? Not even a full moon cycle has passed since our return from the last exhausting journey. And while we were successful... it was not without loss."

A heavy silence fell between us as I averted my gaze, shaking my head. "I know," I whispered, though the words came out rough, scratchy.

Aerie closed her eyes briefly, taking a deep breath. "Leaving the borders of the earth tribe is no small thing, especially with the amount of warding surrounding you here and the uptick in attacks from Daeomi. This may be important, but your safety is more important than any piece of information against Kahlis could ever be."

I swallowed hard, nodding my head even as dread clenched in my stomach, even though I couldn't agree with the sentiment. "We have to go, Aerie. I would never forgive myself if I kept us from something that could be a key to this battle. A key to using my powers against him."

Aerie sighed, clearly at odds with my urgency to leave. But she didn't argue further. Instead she pushed off the bed, rising to her feet. "Okay," she said at last. "In that case, we have to get some things in order before we leave. Because we're journeying to the moon tribe."

CHAPTER 7
VANDER

I made my way towards the tree line, body ragged and bloody after a night as the Grimm. I'd stayed away for as long as I could, trying to work out the unscratchable itch the Mark had left me with, when I'd stupidly brought Hazel into the Dark Woods last night.

What a fucking idiot.

I'd lost my control, letting the Mark push me too far with her. I needed to be more careful, because what almost happened last night couldn't happen again. Everyone had begun to accept the existence of the Mark, it would seem—trusting that I'd defeated its hold and were no longer scared of me losing control of it. And while I had learned to subdue it in certain settings, I could feel its instability grow whenever Hazel was near. And last night... Last night it had threatened to overtake me completely. The more I danced on that dangerous line, the more it wanted to unleash itself. Yes, there'd be pleasure, relief, at first. But the aftermath…

I shuddered, turning my course and pacing the tree line. I didn't regret my actions. I needed to put distance between me and Hazel for now. But I knew she'd be angry with me. I'd tried to reach her through the tether and was surprised, and a little proud, to see how well she'd blocked me out.

I could have forced my way, could have shattered her walls without lifting a finger. But I thought better of it, knowing she must have already been furious with me. And her mental blocks were stronger than they had ever been before, so I let them be.

"Hey!" Bastian's voice called out across the Estate grounds. I paused my pacing, rolling my eyes as the fool stormed his way towards me, all red and huffy.

"Bastian, I—"

Bastian's fist collided with my jaw just as I turned to answer him. I reeled back, the tinge of blood filling my senses. I lifted my hand to my face, my fingers soaked in crimson as I pulled them back.

"What the fuck?" I called out.

"Damn right, Vander. What the fuck."

He charged at me, throwing his weight against me and knocking us both to the forest floor. Instincts kicked in as we sprawled out amidst the muck. He'd had the element of surprise, but before long the Mark was taking over and fighting back.

Shadows stretched out around us, pushing him off me as I landed a few blows of my own, making sure not to hit anything too vital.

"What were you thinking?!" he yelled as he got a lucky shot to my ribs, pinning me briefly beneath him. "You're going to end up losing that girl. I can't decide if you're too stupid or just too arrogant to even see it coming."

I locked his legs against mine, rolling us both through the dead leaves and roots of the Dark Woods until I was on top again. I scoffed, looking down on my brother with a sense of pity as he struggled beneath me.

"I *can't* lose her. Or have the stipulations of being fated changed since the last time I checked?"

"Fine, smart-ass. Keep believing that and see where it gets you. My guess? The lonely solitude of the bloody Dark Woods with nothing but the bottom of a bottle of sunbeam whiskey to keep you warm." He leveraged his feet between us, kicking hard and sending me backwards. I shuffled, adapting to the change in my momentum and using it to my advantage. Within a moment I was back on top of him.

"Bastian, enough!" I pinned his arms down with my shadows as I sucked down hungry breaths. Bastian looked as ragged as I knew I did, both of us beaten and bloody. When I watched the anger in his eyes recede a little, I let him loose and fell back against a nearby hemlock for a moment of recovery.

"What the fuck is going on?" I spit a mouthful of blood to the side, massaging my torn up knuckles and willing some of my magic over the wounds.

Bastian sighed, shaking his head. "You stormed off, Vander. You left her alone on a night when she needed you. On her fucking birthday. What were you thinking?"

Fuck. I'd forgotten in the heat of the moment that the celebration was for more than just Sol Litha. My hand absent-mindedly flew to the breast pocket of the velvet vest I still wore from last night, checking to make sure the box with her present was still tucked safely inside. I'd really fucked this whole thing up.

"You're pushing her away. Storming off every chance you get, stalking the Dark Woods at all hours with no explanation for what you're doing or when she'll see you again. She deserves better than that." At my growl of indignation, he raised his hand. "I will always be your brother first, but I'm not going to stand idly by and watch you hurt her over and over again. Not after everything we did to get her back."

Bastian pinched the bridge of his nose, letting his head fall back against the tree behind him in an effort to slow the torrent of blood coming from his face. "You need to get your head out of your ass and figure out how to be there for her like she needs or you might as well just kiss her ass goodbye."

"You don't think I know that," I sneered. I leaned back against my own hemlock, letting the rough bark bite into my scalp. I forced my magic back down, refusing to let it heal the rest of my body. I didn't deserve it. I needed to feel the pain.

"So if you know it then why are you acting like this? *Do* something about it." Bastian chucked a rock towards me, missing by a long shot.

"It's… complicated." I grimaced, knowing my brother couldn't begin to understand the hold the Mark had over me, nor would he be able to sympathize with the desires it had for Hazel. Truly dark, detestable desires I had no intention of ever letting her see.

Bastian scoffed, shaking his head as he stood up, dusting himself off.

"Whatever, I've said my piece. But just know that if you continue to treat her like shit, I won't hesitate to continue beating your ass."

It was my turn to scoff this time. Even a chieftain was no match for the Mark. I didn't argue, though. I let him go, wholly aware that if I kept him here, I'd only be doing so to bring myself more pain.

"Figure out a way to work through your own shit without distancing yourself from her. She's your mate, Vander. You know how much that shit hurts. And no matter what fucked up shit you're going through, she needs you right now."

I let my head hang, incapable of meeting his gaze when I knew his words held truth. If I didn't figure out a way to work through this with Hazel by my side, I was going to lose her forever. Fated or not.

Bastian huffed in frustration, giving up on waiting for a reply. "Aerie has some big lunch planned for us. You need to go get cleaned up."

"I'm not particularly in the mood for a family lunch," I bit out, still refusing to meet his gaze. My shame was too heavy to look in his eyes now.

"Well, that's too damn bad, brother. You have an hour."

After a tepid bath and a fresh change of clothes, I made my way into the dining room. The midday light flooded the space, making me feel entirely too exposed in front of everyone. The table was already partially full, Bastian, Lennox, and Kirwan all having found their seats.

"Fun night?" Nox asked, louder than necessary as he threw me a wink. I grimaced. Somebody must have told him what happened. I shot him a crude gesture back, not finding his sense of humor all that amusing at the moment. He sniggered, an annoying glint in his eyes as I passed through the dining room and into the kitchen beyond.

Aerie and Hazel were busily working to prepare lunch. Aerie must have given the Estate staff the day off, because they worked alone. Hazel met my gaze, eyes going wide as she took in the sight of my injuries from my outing to the Dark Woods last night, not to mention what few shots my brother got in before I returned this morning. I hadn't allowed myself to heal them fully, the pain somehow keeping the Mark at bay.

I nodded carefully over my shoulder for her to follow me and she muttered to Aerie, excusing herself to the privacy of the adjacent sitting room. I turned back to face her when we'd retreated far enough, looking over her shoulder to make sure we were out of earshot.

"Vander, are you okay?" she asked, her brows pinched together in concern. Given different circumstances, I would have found her worry endearing. But I knew the current state between us was fucked. I'd put myself in tricky territory, trying to keep her at an arm's length while simultaneously trying not to hurt her.

"I'm fine." I wrote her off too quickly, seeing the concern turn to irritation as she folded her arms over her chest.

"What do you want?" Her words were cold, indifferent. Whatever I'd seen in her a moment ago was gone now, hidden behind a mask of protection.

"I uh—have something for you," I said, clearing my throat. I pulled the small package from my pocket, fumbling with it for a moment before sticking it out towards her in a stiff, awkward gesture. "It's a birthday present."

I sounded like a fucking idiot, stating the obvious as she stared down blankly at the gift, then back up to me.

"I meant to give it to you last night..." My voice trailed off. I pushed a hand through my hair as she just continued standing there and staring at me. "Open it," I urged, shoving it once again towards her when she still hadn't taken it.

She took it hesitantly, tearing at the wrappings as if they were venomous snakes, poised to strike. The wrappings finally fell away and she opened the box, a small gasp escaping her lips. She lifted the necklace out of the box, holding it between us—a small, obsidian crescent moon on a delicate silver chain.

"How did you—" She choked on her words, the faintest bit of emotion leaking into her voice.

"Aerie noticed you looking at it when she took you and Mirren to the market a few weeks ago. I snuck back the next market day in hopes that it would still be there."

She nodded, but didn't say anything.

"Do you like it?" I asked, voice low as I reached out to take the necklace. I motioned for her to turn as I draped the jewelry around her neck.

"I love it," she whispered.

I fastened the necklace in place, my fingers brushing faintly against her skin. My muscles stiffened, feeling the electricity in the accidental touch. I longed for more, to find ourselves lost in one another. But, as if on cue, the Mark sparked to life beneath my skin. Too soon, my hands fell away, dropping her hair back in place. I stepped back abruptly, clearing my throat.

She turned to look at me, pain and confusion on her face at the space I'd placed between us. That I wished wasn't there, but *needed* there. Even now, I was still fucking this up. I knew this wasn't enough, that a simple gift like this wasn't capable of making up for all the wrong I'd done to her. I wanted to tell her how sorry I was, how I wished I could give her more.

I opened my mouth, waiting for the words to form on my tongue, but nothing came.

"Let's get a move on, you two. Some of us are hungry!" Bastian's voice boomed from the dining room. Hazel looked at me one more time, those emerald eyes filled to the brim with something akin to hope, or maybe desperation. Searching. But she dropped her gaze and backed away, turning silently to join the others for lunch.

I watched her leave, scrubbing a hand over my jaw. "Fuck," I muttered to myself, knowing that nothing about that interaction went according to plan. I should have waited, should have fucking stayed with her at the festivities last night. But even as my shadows unfurled around me, filling the sitting room, I knew why I hadn't. Why I couldn't.

I let out a low sigh as I tensed my body and attempted to rein in that power before making my way back into the dining room and taking my seat beside Bastian. My head pounded with the remnants of whiskey still trying to work its way out of my system and I slumped over in my chair, head leaning against my hand.

Aerie had already started to set trays of food out on the table, and Hazel had disappeared into the kitchen to help her finish bringing out the last few remaining items. When she returned, I waited for her to take the open seat beside me, but to my surprise, she took the seat next to Nox instead. Nox's eyes brightened for a moment before finding mine and giving me a wicked smirk. I rolled my eyes, sitting up and grabbing at the platters of food without waiting for permission to dig in. I didn't know why I expected anything different. I needed there to be space, needed her to keep her distance. But it still angered me that she was occupying Nox's space. Not mine.

Lunch droned on, the conversation superficial and tedious. Hazel kept her gaze off me and I kept mine on Nox. With every laugh, every touch between them, my anger grew. I gripped my fork in my hand, knuckles white as I stabbed at the roast beef Aerie had made.

Lennox had always been a flirtatious motherfucker, but even he had to know this was crossing a line.

"So love, I hear you had quite the night." Nox's voice broke over the other conversations, purposefully making himself loud enough to cut everyone else off. My brow furrowed as I finally allowed myself to look over at Hazel. Her face had gone beet red, eyes darting between Nox and Aerie.

"No," Hazel finally responded. "Nothing noteworthy."

My hackles rose in response. Something must have happened after I left.

"That's not what I heard," said Nox, pushing back. "From what I understand the light of Sol Litha, the very Divine herself, was left crying at her own birthday party."

"I wasn't crying," muttered Hazel bitterly.

Kirwan nodded along, interjecting: "Hazel was having a grand time! You should have seen her, Vander. Dancing and drinking the night away. Although, she may have single-handedly caused a sunbeam whiskey shortage amongst the earth tribe." Kirwan's gaze cut to mine, a coy smile playing on the edge of his lips. "We'll have to restock our supply, Vander. I think her performance last night gave you a run for your money."

"Oh, we will definitely have to replenish our stock." Nox's lips smacked as he scooped bites of meat off of his plate. "I only caught the tail end of it—but damn, she must have communed with every being at the party." His fork hovered in front of his mouth as he added, "Male and female."

"Lennox," Bastian warned, his voice low.

"On second thought." Nox set his fork down, wiping his hands on a napkin before tossing his arm over Hazel's chair and leaning into her. "It's probably better he didn't see, right, love?"

"Fuck you, Lennox," I seethed, rising to my feet as my shadows grew around me. The bastard had the audacity to smile at me, as if my power was the farthest thing from a threat to him. It had my blood boiling, my shadows reaching through the room to wrap around his throat.

"That's *enough*." Aerie stood at the head of the table, hands out, magic at the ready. "Both of you are behaving like children. Now sit down and drop it. We have other matters to discuss."

I fixed my stare on Nox, slowly calling my shadows back as I sunk into my chair. I tested the tether, finding Hazel's walls up. I pushed a little further, sending a series of cracks through her reinforcements, in an effort to test her boundaries. She stiffened across the table, concentrating as she rebuilt her mental blocks—still refusing to meet my gaze.

Fine.

I leaned back, crossing my arms over my chest as I watched my best friend and my mate from across the table, evidently being iced out.

"Now," continued Aerie, "last night presented an opportunity to speak with some of the visiting members of Sgàil, the moon tribe. They believe they may have some resources that could help us get a better idea of how to stand against Kahlis." The mention of his name was a burden none of us were ready to feel. Bodies stiffened, attention at the ready. "Hazel and I have decided to go. To see what information they have to offer us."

Bastian's brows rose in surprise, mirroring my own as I looked between Aerie and Hazel. Both females sat up straight, shoulders squared as Aerie shared their plans.

"I mean, it's an interesting tactic, utilizing the moon tribe's extensive archive." Bastian lowered his mug of coffee. "Not to mention their divination skillset. But would they even grant you access to such things? They tend to be rather closed off to other tribes."

"And is it worth the risk of leaving Talamh's wards?" I quipped, my eyes landing decidedly on Hazel as I reached for my own mug of coffee.

"From what I was told, I believe they have already agreed to do so. And as for risks"—she cut a scolding glance towards me—"I have already been working on some spells to take with us for added protection. Plus Sgàil's borders are supposedly some of the most secure in the continent. And for all intents and purposes, Kahlis seems to be hiding back in Daravaana. No attempts or even inklings have been felt from him since Hazel came into the Divine's power."

I watched Hazel carefully as she flushed but didn't back down. Aerie shared the truth: Kahlis had been neither seen nor heard since our battle at the Rift. I knew it as fact, for no other reason than because Hazel had been dreamwalking to me since we'd returned. And while I hated the sensation of having her in *my* nightmare, it soothed something inside of me to know she was not currently being pursued by that monster in hers.

But his Daeomi were still attacking, which had me doubting how scared the Dark One truly was. And every part of my being hated the idea of Hazel venturing outside the earth tribe's borders. I straightened in my chair, ready to voice as much, but Aerie held up a hand.

"You can save any further arguments, because the matter worth discussing is not *if* we are going. It's who's going with us. Or rather, who's not." She paused, sighing at the obvious tension. "Our tribe has been suffering from the Daeomi attacks and weakened wards. We cannot leave it unguarded as we did when we went out to the Rift. Especially now as we are unsure where Kahlis is or what he has planned after..." Aerie's words trailed off. I grimaced, cutting a careful look across the table to Nox and Kirwan, both expelling anger.

She cleared her throat as she pushed on. "Hazel and I have already decided. We're going. She's the closest tie we have to Kahlis, and therefore the obvious choice to visit the moon tribe. And she's going to need someone that has some knowledge of the Old World to help her decipher whatever information we find, which would be me."

"Then I'm going as well," Bastian answered.

Aerie pursed her lips, preparing for a fight. "Bastian, our people need someone here in case Kahlis attacks again. We cannot leave them unattended."

"I'm not sending you off alone. Vander can stay behind."

"Fuck that," I answered. "If Hazel's going then I'm going, too."

Shit. Everyone's gaze turned instantly towards me, Hazel's eyes sparkling with the smallest bit of hope. I couldn't bear the idea of her traveling that far from me, unprotected at that. But the not-so-subtle purr of the Mark beneath my skin at the look in her eye had me averting my gaze, refusing to give her hope affirmation. I could be near her, protect her. But for the Mark's sake, I would not let myself have her.

Aerie let out a sigh, rubbing her forehead with her hand. "Yes, how very chivalrous of you both, but the problem remains that someone needs to stay behind to look after the tribe."

A beat of silence passed.

"Well, if all we need is one of us to stay behind, then problem solved!" I turned my head to Nox, raising an eyebrow as I waited for him to explain. "Kirwan can stay." He slapped a hand against his brother's back, Kirwan grimacing at the motion. "And the rest of us can be on the road within—how long did you say, Aerie? Two days' time, yes?"

When Kirwan didn't argue, Bastian inclined his head towards the twin. "Are you okay with that, Kirwan?"

Kirwan nodded reluctantly, clearing his throat. "Yeah, I suppose. If you're okay leaving the tribe in my hands. If I'm being honest, I could use a break from all the Daeomi slaughtering."

"And if I'm being honest..." Nox's enthusiastic voice boomed through the room. "A little road time with my love sounds like exactly what I need." His arm was around Hazel again, winking at me as he caught my attention. "Oh, and I guess, Hazel, you can be there too if you want. It's just been forever since Vander and I have had any one-on-one time, if you catch my drift."

Bastian rolled his eyes, rising to his feet and clearing his plate. "Nox, you're an idiot. Shut the fuck up and come help me with the dishes."

"Yessir." Nox grinned as he pushed his chair back, grabbed his and Hazel's plates, and planted a kiss on her cheek before running off to the kitchen.

I stifled the urge to growl, eyes tracking Hazel's movements as she did everything she could to not meet my gaze. Despite that, her cheeks reddened with her embarrassment, bringing my power to the surface without a second thought. A journey alongside her in my current condition was truly a terrible decision. But the more time that passed since her return, the more I was beginning to understand how difficult of a balance this would be—to maintain my distance while simultaneously ensuring her safety. My desire to fix things with her was consistently clashing with my need for space as I figured out how the fuck to get ahold of the Mark's call for her.

I sighed, pushing off my chair and excusing myself from the table. If I was going to make it through this trip in one piece, I'd need to feed the Mark extensively beforehand. Which meant retreating to the Dark Woods. Again.

CHAPTER 8
HAZEL

I tossed my rucksack on the floor of the small horse-drawn wagon, circling the large wheels to see Brigid harnessed at the front. I patted her chestnut coat, leaning my head against her muzzle. Bastian had given her to me upon my return to Tir Nadaar. Since then I had found comfort in my frequent trips to her stable, ensuring she was fed, watered, and groomed daily.

Something about her calmed me, and I found it reassuring she'd be the one to guide us on this journey. I reached in the pocket of my cloak, producing an apple I'd swiped from the kitchen on my way here. I patted her forelock, moving the hair out of her eyes as she chomped away at the apple in my hand.

"About ready?" Nox slid up beside me, paying his own respects to Brigid before the journey ahead. It made me smile, seeing him show the same kind of reverence to this magnificent creature as I had.

I had spent the last two days by Nox's side, trying with all my might to avoid Vander. To my relief, Vander hadn't even tried to come to my room the past two nights. However, hearing his wolven form pacing just outside my door all night had interfered with my ability to get much sleep.

I knew Nox understood what I was doing. And even though he had yet to bring it up, I was more than grateful that he was playing along as he guided me up to the wooden bench within the wagon, settling in beside me.

Aerie and Bastian finished loading their things in the back of the wagon before climbing up into the box seat together as Bastian readied the reins. Vander was the last to join, throwing his small rucksack in the back. He circled to the side of the wagon, grabbing onto the wood as his eyes caught me and Nox sitting side by side.

His grip on the wood tightened as he ground his teeth, letting out a low growl. Nox threw an arm over me as he smirked at Vander.

"Ready to get all cozy, brother? I've got an extra blanket and a satchel of road snacks with your name on it."

"I'll walk," Vander gritted out, pushing away from the wagon and starting off down the path.

"Get in the damn wagon, Vander. We have a long journey and I'm not going to slow down so you can keep up with us."

Vander ignored his brother, continuing down the path ahead. Bastian made a clicking noise and Brigid started towards Vander, leading away from the Estate. We caught up to him easily, Bastian slowing to let him climb up into the wagon.

Vander ignored the gesture, rolling his shoulders. I'd come to recognize the moments before his shifts, the little mannerisms he had as he prepared to let the wolven form through. Heat crept up my neck. He wouldn't shift here in front of everyone... would he?

"Don't worry about trying to keep up with me, Bastian." He threw one more look over his shoulder, his eyes finding mine for a brief moment. "We'll see who gets there first." He broke out in a run, pulling his tunic over his head and tossing it to the wayside.

"I hope you brought more clothing, jackass. Because I'm not stopping to pick up after you." Bastian called out, slowing to scoop up the discarded clothing anyways. Vander made it three more strides before his wolven form took over. Midnight fur replaced tanned muscle, his steps transitioning from two to four. I wanted to pull my gaze away, wanted to find anything else to occupy my vision. But I couldn't. And despite my mental blocks still wholly in place as they had been the last two days, a deep, vibrating chuckle crept through the tether—letting me know he was fully aware of the effect he had on me.

I grunted in frustration, throwing every bit of my concentration into working on my mental blocks as we started on our journey.

Hours passed in contented silence as we traveled further away from Talamh. Aerie gave me a brief explanation of precautions we needed to take to ensure Kahlis wouldn't sense us. The potion she'd made me with Daeomi blood had worked well since closing the Rift. Either that or my newfound power as the Divine was somehow protecting me from his reach.

But I'd be lying if I said I wasn't a little worried about traveling outside of the warding of Talamh. Each tribe was responsible for their own borders, each chieftain having their own rituals and magic for how to guard their land. I didn't know how diligent the moon tribe was, but I was grateful to Aerie for having thought to take extra precautions.

I also couldn't recall a time I'd ventured so far from the tribe's borders. If I had visited other tribes before, the memories were lost in a life I couldn't remember. My stomach tightened in trepidation of what I'd find beyond the tribe I called home. But despite the fear, I found myself hoping deeply that there'd be answers for me there—whether they be in reference to our battle with Kahlis or my power as the Divine.

My fingers played idly with the crescent moon charm sitting against my chest. I fiddled with the delicate chain, sliding the onyx stone back and forth. It had surprised me, Vander's sudden gift. After our interactions at the Sol Litha celebration, my frustration with him had grown tenfold. But the sudden softness of his gift, the way he fumbled over his words as he tried so hard to be vulnerable for the briefest of moments.

It was almost cute, almost enough. But he'd held back, relied solely on the gesture of the necklace to repair the pain he'd brought me. And while it was a thoughtful gift, it did little to change my mind about my plans moving forward. All he'd proven to me was that he *was* capable of being what I needed. He was just simply choosing not to.

I fixed my eyes on Aerie and Bastian before me, watching as she leaned into him, settling in for the journey ahead. Bastian wrapped an arm around her, tucking her in against him as he held the reins in his other hand. My lips tipped up, enjoying the view of my two guardians so beautifully in love.

"So, are we going to talk about it?" Nox whispered in my ear, jarring my thoughts as I blinked, turning to face him.

"Talk about what?"

Nox stalled, looking down on me with one of those, *Are you really going to make me say it*, looks. I sighed, rolling my eyes and turning my head to look out at the woods to my left.

"Is it really that obvious?"

"Hazel, love. I'm flattered, truly. But I'm not that big of an idiot to believe you've spontaneously abandoned your mate for a sudden interest in me."

I bit down on my cheek, nerves twisting in my gut.

"No matter how beautiful or charming I may be, even I don't have the power to break a bond like yours."

The wagon trotted along, the sound of the wheels rolling against the rock and dirt of the well-worn path, filling the awkward silence.

"I'm sorry," I whispered finally.

"Hey, I didn't say I'm not enjoying it. You have nothing to apologize for. Fucking with Vander happens to be my favorite pastime." He leaned over, planting a kiss on the top of my head. "I just want to make sure you're okay."

"I'm okay," I reassured him, looking up as he pulled me under his arm.

"If you say so. Just know, despite all the fun we're having, you will have to actually talk to him at some point."

I sighed again, letting my eyes fall back to the trees surrounding us. Without meaning to, I realized I was looking for his wolven form in their shadows.

"I know," I whispered.

I dozed off, resting against Nox's chest. The gentle sway of the wagon was too enticing a rhythm to ignore, and it lulled me into a deep, dreamless sleep. When I awoke, Bastian was guiding the wagon through a great stone archway. I looked up in wonder as we passed below, turning around to get a closer look as we rode on.

"Sgàil's border." Nox answered my unspoken question. The stone continued on in either direction, forming a low wall as far as the eye could see. A slow-moving mist covered the mossy ground just past the archway, unsettling my stomach as we entered it.

"It's their method of warding. The moon tribe is a bit more... *eccentric* than the earth tribe." The thickness of the mist settled as we pulled through the other side, the feeling in my belly slowly subsiding. "The stones offer protection for their borders, reinforcing their warding. And the mist is a form of shadow magic. It doesn't let any pass through that may have ill intentions towards the tribe."

"How do you know so much about their practices?" I asked, sweeping my gaze across the enchanted land surrounding us and back up to Nox.

"It's in my lineage, remember." He looked out at the path before us, his eyes darkening. "My father belonged to the moon tribe."

Nox had spoken so much of the sun tribe, so much of his mother and the warmth of her people, that I'd forgotten Auris was only half his lineage. I was about to ask him to elaborate, to tell me all he could about the mysterious tribal traditions, or why they never seemed to come up in our conversations, when Bastian pulled the wagon to a stop. He jumped down, offering a hand to Aerie and then me, before turning to Brigid and offering her a treat for a job well done.

I stretched my legs, walking a few paces from the wagon as I peered out to what I could see of the tribe before me. From what little I knew about the moon tribe, it was where the Priestesses for Tir Nadaar resided. Their practices and traditions were somewhat guarded, still a large mystery to me. But I knew the kind of magic that originated from here had been tied to seers and oracles for the tribes, as well as recordkeepers.

The air seemed different here, heavier, the stifling fog around my arms and legs sending waves of gooseflesh up my skin. Just barely, through the fog and quickly setting sun, I could make out the humble round stone structures that made up their austere homes. I couldn't imagine what kind of people lived here, what kind of lives or traditions they'd lead in a land like this. Not only that, but the land before me seemed eerily empty, devoid of souls, sending a chill up my spine at the utter stillness stretching out in every direction.

I turned back to the wagon, my muscles tensing as I saw Vander make his way out of the mist, still in his wolven form. He prowled up to us, seemingly cocky despite the fact we had indeed beat him here. I folded my arms over my chest, ready to turn away and continue with my plans to ice him out when his flash of movement stopped me in my tracks. He shifted back to his mortal form, striding right in front of the lot of us to grab his clothing out of the wagon.

"Fucking Fates," Bastian grumbled, tossing the clothing at Vander.

My eyes went wide, trying hard to not drag my gaze over his naked form. I chewed on my lip, heat stinging my cheeks.

"I love when he shows off for me," Nox boasted from inside the wagon, clasping his hands behind his head and letting out a low whistle as Vander pulled his clothing back on.

I turned, my face surely an unruly shade of red as Aerie rolled her eyes and laced her arm in mine, blessedly guiding me away from the wagon and into the tribe beyond.

"Ignore them," Aerie called out. "They're clearly too occupied competing with each other to be worthy of our attention."

I grinned, covering my face with my hand as I tried to rub away the color still burning in my cheeks. I thanked the Fates for Aerie's insistence on accompanying me on this journey.

Just as we stepped up to one of the odd stone structures, a shadow stepped out of the low mist.

"Bastian! Lady Darroch! It's so nice to see you again. It's been too long!" The form stepped forward, slowly revealing himself as he strode up to Aerie. The male's umber arms wrapped around Aerie, pulling her in for a welcoming hug and planting a kiss on each of her cheeks before turning to Bastian and offering the same.

His attention turned to me, stunning me slightly as he greeted me just as fondly. As if we'd been lifelong friends and not total strangers. His long ashen hair surrounded me, filling my senses with that smoky scent I'd come to know from Aerie's greenhouse. The remnants of earthy incense calmed my nerves, helping me to lower my guard as I returned the hug.

"Hazel," he hummed, pulling back just far enough to look me over. His eyes matched the hue of his long, wiry tresses—almost milky in their appearance. They swirled with shades of grey and black and sparkled with something bright and distant. Like a sea of stars in the Cosmos.

"I'm so glad you were able to make the journey, my girl. I have a feeling this visit will reveal much to you." He let go of my arms, finding my hands and patting them as his eyes locked on mine.

"Hazel, this is Vesper." Bastian stepped forward, breaking the odd enchantment between us. "Chieftain of Sgàil, the moon tribe."

"Ah yes, forgive me," Vesper replied. "It's difficult to remember that not everyone sees things as I do. We may be strangers now, but to me we have met in a multitude of lifetimes." He offered me a kind smile, dropping my hands as he turned to Bastian. Judging by the shade of his hair and the wisdom I'd noticed in his eyes, I got the vague impression that Vesper was much older than he seemed. But there was a certain playfulness about him, the way he moved and spoke, that contradicted itself.

"Thank you for accommodating us on such short notice." Bastian continued on as they strode off towards the stone buildings beyond.

"Of course! These are trying times indeed. Anything we can do to help one another must be done. The sooner we can get you lot settled in, the sooner we can start showing you what we've found."

Aerie laced her arm around mine, urging us forward.

"What did he mean, we'd met in a multitude of lifetimes?" I whispered to Aerie.

"The moon tribe believes in reincarnation. The idea that a life lost is simply a new life reborn."

"And you?" I asked, peeking over at her through the wine-colored strands that had fallen free from behind my ear.

She paused, absent-mindedly raising a hand before her. Her fingers danced through the mist, almost as if she was playing with its magic. "I think it's a beautiful concept, that our loved ones live on, renewed with life and opportunity. A new journey for them to embark on. But I will not pretend to understand the inner workings of the Cosmos."

I sighed, raising my eyes to the sky above. The weather had turned, the hazy clouds promising an oncoming storm. There were no stars to be found, despite the twilight hour. Perhaps the presence of the mist was something more than just the magical warding of the moon tribe, an omen for darker things to come. I rubbed my hands over my arms, feeling suddenly eerie about our presence here, the threat of Kahlis ever constant in my mind.

"I trust Vesper." Aerie cut a sidelong glance at me. "I'm not going to tell you what to do. You need to make your judgments for yourself. But the moon tribe knows more, sees more, than all the other tribes combined. They hold much wisdom in their borders. And they are a kind people. I trust Vesper and I would not have brought you here if I thought for even a moment you'd be in danger."

I swallowed hard, looking ahead to where Bastian and Vesper had disappeared into the mist. I could barely make out the door of the stone structure they must have ventured into.

"Okay," I finally answered, taking a step forward. "I trust you. And if you trust them, then so will I. Just... stay with me okay? For now?" I looked back towards the wagon where Vander and Nox were still gathering the rest of our belongings in strained silence. I wasn't ready to let Vander back in yet, but I knew this journey would be a heavy one. And the thought of facing it alone was nearly crippling.

Aerie followed my gaze, seemingly understanding where my thoughts had turned. She pulled me forward, nudging me along as we left the boys behind in the thick air of the oncoming storm. "I'm always here for you, Hazel. You won't have to face any of this alone."

CHAPTER 9
HAZEL

The stone structure was surprisingly large on the inside. The mist must have clouded much of the building as we'd approached it. Now that I was within its walls, I couldn't help but look on in awe as the tall stone walls stretched into a grand, generous foyer.

The hallway ahead was full of warm torchlight, casting dancing shadows onto the paintings and tapestries covering the walls. To my left, a never-ending, spiraling stone staircase was tucked against the shadows of the foyer, leading up to the domed stone ceiling above. To the right was a grand sitting room, flanked by long gossamer curtains draped delicately across the ceiling and pristine velvet sitting chairs placed precariously throughout. Vesper and Bastian's voices drifted from down the hall, pulling Aerie and I further into the chieftain's home.

Aerie led us into a den, a fire blazing in an intricately carved white stone hearth at its center. Bastian was relaxed against a low-sitting sofa, a drink already in hand.

Vesper, standing by the fire, raised his own glass to us as we entered. "Ladies, come! Join us!"

He ushered us over to another sofa across from Bastian. I took my seat, letting my hands run over the velvet cushion, and took a look around the room. The walls were lined floor to ceiling with books, encased in obsidian shelves. It reminded me so much of the library back home.

"Can I get you anything to drink?" Vesper's words pulled my gaze over to him. His voice was thick with a hypnotic accent, rich and luscious and somehow captivating, regardless of what he was saying. It made me want to push him to keep speaking, so I could sit and listen and feel the tension of the world melt away.

He raised a decanter to me, full of a dark red liquid, waiting for my reply. I blinked, trying to find my voice.

"I think a bit of wine would do us both some good," Aerie answered for me.

Vesper bowed slightly, turning back to the ornamental cart behind him, filled with fresh glasses and spirits of every color.

Aerie rested her hand upon my knee, patting gently. The motion helped clear my mind from the wonderment Vesper's residence had to offer. It was overwhelming being here, my senses flooded with too much to see, too many scents. My head felt funny, light and buzzing with the unfamiliar energy.

The heady scent of frankincense took me back to Aerie's sessions, where her earthy incense would aid me in retreating to the dark recesses of my mind. The same sensations flooded me as the steady tendril of smoke swirled around the room. I tried to fight the lull, forcing my mind to stay present rather than retreat within myself. It was a painstaking process, fighting my body to do the exact opposite of everything Aerie and I had trained it to do. The well of emotions I often experienced in those beginning moments of our sessions started circling, threatening to pull me under.

I blinked and Vesper was before me, holding out matching glasses of a deep burgundy liquid. I took mine, raising the glass to my lips and drinking deeply.

"Careful there, Hazel. Our wine is unlike your spirits back in Talamh. It may take some getting used to." Vesper winked at me, turning back to the sofa Bastian occupied and taking a seat beside him.

I lowered the glass, swallowing hard as the smooth, fruity taste danced on my tongue. It was definitely unlike the sunbeam whiskey Vander and Bastian preferred. Where that was all fire and bitterness, this was sweet and inviting. I could have easily drained the glass without a second thought.

But even as the fruity taste slowly faded away, leaving my mouth parched for more, I could feel just how strong the wine was. My head spun faster than it had before, the light of the fire feeling brighter as the room seemed to glow and dance with the shadows of the flames coming to life around me. I leaned over to the short table separating us from where Bastian and Vesper sat, setting the glass down decidedly. I didn't need any more reason to lose my faculties in this mystical place.

The faint sound of bickering voices drifted down the hall, letting us know that Nox and Vander had found their way inside. A third voice joined them, something low and almost sultry, mimicking Vesper's smooth accent. All heads turned in their direction, my fists clenching around the fabric of my tunic pooling in my lap. The last thing I wanted to see right now was Vander, especially with the odd hold either this dwelling, or Vesper—or *both*—had on me.

"I've arranged for one of the priestesses to show them to your chambers," Vesper explained, waving a hand in the direction of the disgruntled voices. "I figured the boys could get you settled while we caught one another up."

His swirling grey eyes found mine, offering a knowing look as the corner of his lips tipped up briefly. I didn't know how he'd noticed the tension between me and Vander, if he even did at all. But I was thankful for a longer reprieve from his presence.

"Speaking of the priestesses, one of them shared something with us at our Sol Litha celebration. That you may have some information on Kahlis that could prove useful?" Bastian set his own glass down, now empty.

Vesper sighed, running one finger along the rim of his own glass. I noticed the length of his nails, the sound of their pointed tips tapping lightly against the glass, ringing in my ears.

"I'm aware of what my priestess shared with you. We have indeed been consulting the Cosmos—in various ways—ever since Bastian informed us that Kahlis was growing bolder in his attacks against Tir Nadaar." He sighed, finally letting his eyes meet Bastian's. "Talamh hasn't been the only tribe to experience attacks." The chieftains nodded slightly towards each other, each recognizing the pain of loss the other had endured.

"And," Vesper continued, "we've had to take precautions to guard our archives. Kahlis getting his hands on the wealth of knowledge we guard here could be catastrophic to not only our tribe, but to all of Tir Nadaar."

Vesper stood, grabbing both his and Bastian's glasses, and strolled over to the cart next to the fire, lifting the decanter to fetch them both a second round. "Being a bordering tribe, though, I have no doubt that you are receiving the bulk of Kahlis' attention." He offered a glass back to Bastian, raising his own in silent tribute to the earth tribe's loss.

I lowered my gaze to my lap, shame suddenly blooming in my chest. I was the Divine, with unique healing powers, somehow still helpless to fix the situation with my father. Whatever information the moon tribe had, I prayed to the Fates it would help me understand my powers.

"However, I'm sorry to say that my priestess spoke out of turn." Vesper leaned against the hearth, rather than taking his seat back on the sofa. "I fear she may have unintentionally misled you."

My heart dropped, my hopes dying fast.

"So you don't have any information to share?" Aerie asked, perplexed.

"Exactly." Vesper pointed at her before raising his glass to his lips—taking a deep pull from the wine before running his tongue over the corner of his mouth to catch whatever liquid remained there. "But that in and of itself holds promise."

"What do you mean by that?" Aerie pressed, scooting forward against the sofa.

"Rest assured, our priestesses are working tirelessly to discern an answer from the Cosmos. Being skilled in the art of divination, there is not much the moon tribe cannot at least inquire about. The future is typically unclear, more like a web of possible paths that we have to work at to see what path will lead where." Vesper reached his hand out as he spoke, weaving it through the air as if to untangle invisible pathways around us. "It is a delicate process that requires careful consideration and the most skilled mystics. And while we may not have any answers yet, we've found something quite... interesting." Vesper's gaze drifted off, as if leaving the room for a moment and venturing somewhere unseen.

Bastian set his glass down with slightly more force than necessary, snapping everyone's attention his way. "You're being intentionally elusive, Vesper. You yourself just insinuated you understood the importance of such a topic, how the longer we go without answers, the more loss we are subjecting our tribes to at Kahlis' hand. Get to the point, if there is one, and stop teasing us with these Cosmic games of yours."

Vesper bowed his head slightly, in an effort to hide a hint of a smile. I hated the way he seemed to be enjoying himself. As if these stakes weren't high. As if this was all some sort of carefully constructed game that he loved playing a part in. "We have nothing to share yet... because our divination is bringing up no possible paths."

"What," Aerie gasped, her hand flying to her chest. "No future at all? There's *always* multiple paths."

Vesper nodded. "Which means something is unique about this. Something is being shrouded by the Fates. Or perhaps the Cosmos themselves. A destiny so vital it can't be gambled on." His eyes found mine as his voice crept through the quiet room, sending a chill down my spine. "No death. No destruction. No end—and no peace."

Vesper excused himself when one of his priestesses interrupted, needing his assistance. He left us with a steward to see we got dinner and to our rooms safely. Aerie and Bastian quickly elected to take their food in their rooms while I politely declined. The way my stomach had soured at the small amount of wine Vesper had offered me, I wasn't sure I'd be able to eat anything. Despite their concern, I insisted Aerie and Bastian go ahead, claiming I needed a moment alone. I could tell Aerie was tired and I didn't want her fussing over me.

Despite Vesper's reassurance, I found it oddly unsettling that whatever powers were at work—the Cosmos, the Fates, whoever—were refusing to give us the opportunity to utilize the moon tribe's magic. It felt like a slap in the face after the hope that had built within me during our journey here. After everything that Kahlis had put us through, after all the vile, evil, things he had done... I couldn't understand why the Fates wouldn't afford us this one advantage.

I made my way down the hall after a fair amount of time had passed, having made sure to get directions from the steward before he'd retired too. I stumbled my way through the darkness and up the stone steps, despising the way their windy nature caused my head to spin and my stomach to turn.

The stairs broke off in one direction, providing a small landing for the floor beyond, before continuing up to the higher levels. I veered off their path, making my way down the second floor hallway. I counted the doors as I moved through the dimly lit space. When I reached the door I believed to be mine, I pushed against it. It didn't budge at first, calling for several more shoves before finally falling open as I stumbled through the doorway.

Firm hands caught me on the other side, both of us stunned by the other's presence.

"It's called a lock, love." Nox laughed, helping me back to my feet. I looked around the room, seeing Nox and Vander's belongings spread out on two parallel beds.

"I, uh," I said, pushing my hair out of my face as I turned back to the dark hallway. "I thought this was my room." I let my eyes scan the space quickly, suddenly worried I'd stumble into Vander next.

"Relax," Nox whispered, coming up beside me and patting me on the shoulder. "Our pup decided he needed a moonlit stroll to get acquainted with Sgàil's lands." Nox guided me out of the room, my head still spinning. He led me to a door one down from theirs, pushing the solid wood open and pointing to my rucksack waiting on the bed. "This one's yours."

I nodded, stepping in. The room suddenly felt too quiet, too isolating. I sucked in a few rapid, shallow breaths, trying to calm myself. It was just a simple guest chamber, clean and well equipped to house whatever guests may be visiting the Chieftain of the Moon Tribe. Yet, on my own—without Vander here—each shadow, each corner of the empty room had me on edge.

I spun back to Nox, who was leaning against the doorframe and watching me with a raised eyebrow.

"Will you—" I sputtered, cutting myself off and shaking my head. I needed to get a grip on myself. Nothing here was inherently wrong, everything looked fine, and this was *just* a guest room in the home of Aerie and Bastian's friend. A chieftain no less. I was safe.

"What's that, love?" Nox asked.

"Nothing. Nevermind."

I shifted nervously, waiting for him to leave so I could close the door and lose myself within the privacy of my own chambers. Instead, he stepped forward, taking my hand.

"Hazel," he chided. There was a shade of amusement in his voice, but when I looked into his eyes, there was nothing but genuine concern. "If you need me to stay with you, all you have to do is ask."

"No, I can't ask that of you, Nox. I'll be fine, I promise."

He looked down at my fingers in his grasp, shaking even as I lied to him.

"Come on, let's get a fire going in that hearth of yours. You know, I think this one is twice the size of mine and Vander's." He guided me into the room and over to the edge of the bed, before moving to start a fire. "I'll have to have a word with Vesper about that. Can't have him playing favorites on us, now. Even if you are a goddess, or whatever."

Within moments, Nox had a fire roaring to life. He stood, dusting off his hands as he turned to face me. The firelight bathed the guest chamber in a warm glow, somehow chasing out the shadows—and my panic along with them. I let out a sigh of relief, feeling suddenly silly for having had such an absurd and sudden fear take hold of me.

"Thank you, Nox, but really, you can go now. I'll be fine."

Nox disregarded me, striding over to the bed I sat on and carefully unpacking my rucksack for me. He set the changes of clothes I'd brought in the nearby wardrobe, made sure the bottles of Aerie's potions and elixirs were set up on the small vanity, and even brought me a dose of the potion she'd concocted to help guard Kahlis from my mind.

"Open," he ordered as he let the drops fall on my tongue. "Can't be forgetting this one," he joked. He returned the stopper, setting the bottle down next to the bed, before taking a seat beside me, doing nothing more than occupying space as I felt the final waves of panic recede.

"Thank you, Lennox." My voice sounded odd in the otherwise silent room. Like it was intruding on the space, an unwelcome, eccentric visitor in an otherwise peaceful environment. "You didn't need to do all of this."

He smirks, nodding slowly.

"Hazel, let me ask you a question."

My stomach dipped, my face cringing. I wasn't ready for more discussion, not with the way my mind still felt muddled and my eyelids drooped heavy with exhaustion.

"Do you think I'm a bad individual?"

The question made me do a double take as I whirled on him. Had I given him that impression? My brain ran wild, quickly replaying any of our interactions that I could remember—trying to think of what I'd done to make him believe I thought that of him.

"Nox, I never—"

He held up a hand, cutting me off. "I know I haven't had the cleanest past. There's things I've done that I'm not proud of. Things that haunt me." He pursed his lips, his jaw feathering. "My time as tribal spy did not come without its scars. And now, after... I just need you to answer the question."

I closed my mouth, taking a deep breath through my nostrils before shaking my head. "No, of course not."

He nodded, considering for a moment. "Then why does it shock you so much to see me show up for you? My love for you is genuine. Mine, Aerie's, Bastian's... damn, even Vander's, when he can get his head out of his ass long enough to do the right thing."

I huffed out a breath, wordlessly agreeing with Nox's assessment.

"We show up for you because we love you. Not because we owe you something or because we want you to owe us. We're *family*, love. And after..." He took a deep breath, his eyes pinching shut. "After losing Mirren," he gritted out, "I care about nothing more than making sure the little bit of good I do have left in this life is cared for."

"Mirren wasn't your fault, Nox," I breathed, my voice cracking slightly with emotion. If anything, the guilt of her death belonged to me—the reason Kahlis was there in the first place. Me, the supposed Cosmic being who couldn't muster up the ability to use her magic to save her friend.

He swallowed, nodding beside me. "I know. I may not fully believe it yet, but I'm getting there." Tears stung the back of my eyes as I looked over to him. His two-toned eyes glistened, his throat bobbing with the effort to swallow his grief. "But I need you to understand this, Hazel. This group we have here? This is my home. And I've vowed to protect that home in a way I never have before. I can't lose anyone else."

He laid his hand tenderly against my knee, squeezing once. "I will continue showing up for you as long as my body walks this realm. It's why I won't leave you here alone when you're very clearly working through some things, why I'm always here to check in on you when I can. Fuck, it's why I've played along with your little scheme to make Vander mad."

My cheeks went crimson. I turned my face away instantly, dropping my gaze to my feet as a wave of embarrassment washed over me.

"Do you think… Vander knows what I'm doing?"

Nox chuckled, a breathy sound that somehow made the heat in my face burn even brighter as his hand slipped off my knee.

"Love, a rock could have picked up on what you're trying to do. Vander knows." Nox paused, wrapping his arm around me and leaning down to my ear. "Despite how thick he may be."

I smirked, surprised by my own amusement despite the heaviness I felt in my chest. Nox straightened, leaving his arm around me. "Have you considered taking a more conventional approach? For instance, perhaps just try talking to him?"

I rolled my eyes, scoffing as I pushed his arm off my shoulder. It plopped onto the bed with a bounce and I folded my arms over my chest, fixing Nox with a leveled stare. "If Vander has an issue with the current circumstances, then he can come talk to *me*. I'm done trying to reason with him."

Nox just laughed and shook his head, rubbing a hand over the back of his neck. "You two really are a fated match. I couldn't think of two more stubborn souls to be twined together for all eternity."

"What's that supposed to mean?" I bit out.

"Oh, just that as much as you're trying to get his attention by flirting with me, he's trying to get your attention by being the big brutish idiot he so often is."

I pushed back onto the bed, kicking off my boots as I scooted up to the headboard. "He is not," I argued, tucking my knees against my chest. Nox stood, circling the bed to my other side and tucking himself beside me, against the headboard.

"That boy is so hopelessly consumed by you, it isn't even funny."

"Then why can't he show it?" I barked out. I turned to face Nox in the heat of my response, my eyes wide with frustration and unspoken rage. Nox watched me for a moment, evaluating.

"I don't know, love. There's so much Vander doesn't share, even with me. Things changed with him from the moment he made that deal and bore the Mark. Most days he's still the same Vander I know and love, but sometimes... sometimes he's something else entirely."

I fell back against the headboard, wrapping my arms around my knees once more as I stared straight ahead, into the dancing flames of the hearth. I'd seen that version of him, stared into the eyes of that monster countless times. And yet, I hadn't turned away. So why wouldn't Vander accept that? Accept me?

"But I do know, despite whatever secret trials he faces, he does love you. Hopelessly." Nox nudged me gently, an effort to pull me out of the shell I felt myself receding into.

I focused my gaze harder on the flames, refusing to turn back to Nox. I wouldn't argue, not when I knew on some level he was right. It didn't change the fact that Vander refused to give himself over to that love. I gritted my teeth, pain and guilt and rage bubbling up. I bit back tears, begging them to go away.

"Hazel." Nox leaned in, wrapping his arm around me. "Good guy, remember? Talk to me." He tightened his hold—pulling me into him, despite my indifference.

I'd been fighting this wave of emotion since entering Vesper's home, something about this place making everything within me harder to control. There was only so long I could keep that gate sealed. Tears broke past my lashes, the feel of them on my cheeks suddenly making me come undone. I turned into Nox, burying my face into his chest as he wrapped his other arm around me.

"I just don't understand," I whimpered into his chest, incapable of holding back the raging emotions crashing through me.

"Understand what, love?" His voice was softer, tender. Too kind. I thought about what he'd said about us being family and how he'd always be here for me, asking for nothing in return. But the question he'd asked echoed through my mind, refusing to be let go. Why was it so hard for me to accept their support? Even now, after everything we'd been through together. After closing the Rift and discovering my power, after finding my place amongst their tribe and accepting this as my home.

Deep down, I knew why.

It was always there—that dark, hidden thought in the recesses of my mind that I always acknowledged but hadn't figured out how to deal with yet. And it was the same reason that Vander's refusal to let me in stung so badly.

I clung to Nox's tunic, a deep, unrelenting ache coursing through me as I finally voiced the one dreadful thought that refused to let me be:

"Why am I not worthy of him?"

CHAPTER 10
HAZEL

I awoke in the morning, suddenly aware of the emptiness in the bed. Nox had held me while I'd cried myself to sleep last night. He didn't argue with me, didn't fight to tell me I was wrong or that my mind was lying to me. He just held me and let me cry until my body was utterly exhausted and sleep pulled me under.

I'd half expected him to stay the night, half expected to wake up to find Vander there instead—in his wolven form at the foot of the bed. But waking up to find neither of them there... I let out a sigh as I cupped my face in my hands, the pain and panic of last night slowly creeping back in.

There had been a time in my life that this had been my normal. Living with the constant fear and crippling panic—it was all I knew. But I'd grown so much since those dark days. I'd worked so hard to pull myself out of that life. And I hated how it felt like I was reverting to that older version of myself, someone less composed, less sure of herself. Definitely someone unbefitting for the powers of a goddess.

I pushed back the covers, getting off the bed and padding over to the small wardrobe. I grabbed a change of clothes from the things Nox had unpacked for me, pulling on a simple deep blue skirt and matching corset in exchange for the tunic and leggings I'd donned for the journey here.

I checked myself in the vanity mirror, hastily pulling at my hair in an attempt to tame the wild tresses. I fumbled with the braid I'd started, anger bubbling inside of me as the task proved to be more difficult than I'd expected.

On the third try, I dropped the tangled mess, bringing my hands down hard on the vanity and letting out a stifled cry of frustration. I focused my eyes on the table in front of me, my hands shaking even now. No amount of sleep, no amount of tears, could stop last night's confession from circling in my mind.

Why was I not worthy of him?

I knew it was nonsense, utterly untrue. I'd seen how deep his love for me ran. But when push came to shove, when I was breaking down in my room with not a soul in sight, the doubt crept in. Not that he didn't love me, but that all along, maybe I had never done anything to deserve all of it—all of him.

A knock from the door snapped me out of the vicious cycle of thoughts running through my mind. I spun to face the door, stunned to see Aerie standing in the open frame, seeming to have opened it long ago without my noticing.

"Morning." Her voice was quiet in the early morning hour, soft enough that I wondered how much of that breakdown she'd just witnessed. She crossed the room on near silent feet, turning me back to the mirror.

"Let me," she said, pulling my hair back over my shoulders and picking up a nearby comb.

I sat in silence as she braided my hair back, eyes downcast and cheeks hot with embarrassment. Her hands worked effortlessly, weaving my dark red strands into an elegant design. I shifted uncomfortably in my seat as our eyes briefly met in the mirror's reflection. I was starkly reminded of her experience in such matters, how many other braids she'd done in her lifetime—how many other females she'd comforted in their times of need.

It was intimidating sometimes, being in the presence of someone as wise and caring as Aerie. Especially when all I could think about was how I had nothing to give back to her, no skillful braiding nor wise advice. Not even a smile, my mood so low. I wrung my hands in my lap as I waited for her to finish.

"There," she said at last, leaning down to look at us in the mirror, side by side. "Beautiful, as always." She squeezed my shoulder, but didn't press me to open up, or ask if I was okay. She already knew the answer to that.

Instead she grabbed my hand and pulled me up into a hug. Tucked sweetly against my ear, she whispered, "It's a new day, yes?"

I nodded, though I couldn't bring myself to agree with the sentiment.

"There's much to be discovered here, a new land of opportunities to explore, answers to be found. And I'll be here beside you the whole way."

She released me, too soon if I was being honest. But she fixed me with a reassuring gaze, making sure to breathe with me as she did so. "Remember our lessons, alright? These emotions are a part of you. Acknowledge them and then let them go. Don't let them control you."

I nodded again, retreating into that mental space we so often visited during our lessons. I felt the pain, the panic, the fear of being unworthy. I let each one roll through me like the swell of a storm, but even as I tried to let them go, they lingered within my mind—spreading slowly through me like an infection.

When I opened my eyes, Aerie was watching me steadily. "Vesper has requested our presence downstairs. He's scheduled time for us to meet with some of his priestesses in the archives, to discuss what they may be able to find in regards to the Divine."

I swallowed, nodding as I sidestepped her to break away from her penetrating eyes. I straightened, pushing back my shoulders and lifting my chin as I let the facade slip in place, praying it was enough to keep Aerie's questions at bay. "Then let's not keep the chieftain waiting."

Vesper led us from his home through the grounds of the moon tribe's main village. Despite the early hour, I was shocked to find it as dim and dreary as the night before. Nox had explained a bit about their magical mist, and it struck me that it may in fact stretch throughout the whole of the tribe's land.

It felt odd, not being able to see the sun overhead. I pulled my cloak high around my neck as I peered into the deep grey clouds.

"As you can see, our people tend to not be early risers," Vesper called out as he led us through a sea of simple stone structures and deep green grass. Moss covered the dwellings, making them nearly invisible until one was practically on top of them. Between the nearly invisible homes and the neverending fog, this land felt so isolating, so eerie.

I squinted, looking around us and realizing how empty the land was. Not another soul passed us as we walked through the grounds. I moved a touch closer to Aerie, ensuring myself that she was in fact beside me, that I wasn't alone.

Vesper continued talking as we ventured further from his home, telling us about all the intricate details of their tribe—their routines, rituals, and customs. I let the information work as a distraction from my racing thoughts, losing myself in his explanations of their near nocturnal schedules and how it aided their communication with the Cosmos. We slowed as we came upon a grand stone structure. Chills crept over my skin, taking in the sheer size of it. Thick, solid pillars of white rock loomed over us, lining the entrance.

"This is the home of Sgàil's archives," Vesper breathed, looking up in reverence. He turned back to us, his features shifting from the poised, sultry male I'd come to know him as to reveal something heavier, more serious.

"Entering our archives is an honor not bestowed upon many," he explained. His eyes drifted from Aerie to me. "But it is not our place to deny the reincarnation of the Divine from our connection to her Cosmos. We are merely keepers of knowledge; we do not feign authority over it."

He bowed his head slightly towards me, throwing me off guard. I shifted awkwardly, unsure how to respond.

"That being said," he continued on. "I will ask that you treat the artifacts and information within with the same amount of reverence you'd show the Fates, the gods, or the Cosmos above." He lifted his hands in front of us, head tipping back as he looked up at the clouded sky. "And lastly, I ask that you speak of what you see to no one. There may be things you come across in your research, things too sensitive to be released into the world. And I need your assurance that you will respect the laws laid out by the Cosmos themselves before I let you embark on this journey."

I stood stunned, looking past him to the towering building. It suddenly felt so much more intimidating than it had a few moments ago—and it had already felt pretty damn scary.

Aerie nudged me slightly, returning Vesper's bow as she stated her agreement. I mimicked the movement, bowing my head as I agreed to his rules.

Vesper smiled, his easeful charm slipping back into place as he led us up the steps and through the front doors. Two priestesses were there to greet us, taking our hands and bringing us forward. They covered us in white robes, similar to theirs, and anointed our heads with a fragrant oil. When Vesper had finished watching over the ritual, he bid us goodbye and left us in the hands of the priestesses to venture into the depths of the archives.

The priestesses led us forward, the space before us cast in pitch-black darkness. The only light came from the torches each of them carried.

"I'm Delphine," the priestess holding my arm whispered. "And that's Ophelia. I take it Vesper shared with you the laws of our archives?" She spoke in such hushed tones, I almost couldn't hear her.

"Yes," I whispered back. "Where are we going now?"

"Wherever the Cosmos guide us," Ophelia responded. Both priestesses looked across us and giggled quietly, before turning a corner and leading us down another hall. We eventually stopped in front of a copper door, barely visible through the shroud of darkness. I looked to either side of me, wondering if there were more doorways we'd passed. I hadn't seen any. However, it was impossible to see more than a few paces in front of me, even with the torchlight, and I found myself suddenly wondering how many wards or glamours were being held over a place like this.

"This will be your room while you are visiting the archives." Delphine pulled a key from the folds of her robes, unlocking the door with surprising ease and pushing it open. She touched the torch to something within the black space, igniting a fire that traveled down the length of the room before turning a corner and heading back in our direction.

Aerie stepped in first. I trailed behind, spinning in a slow circle as I took in the odd energy of the room.

"What about the books?" I asked, feeling entirely foolish for asking such an obvious question. The priestesses giggled to each other once more.

"We will bring you what the Cosmos desire you to see." Ophelia lifted a pale, lanky finger to point at the table behind us. "It seems they have already supplied you with your starting point."

I turned back to the table, mouth agape as I saw a small stack of ancient looking tomes appear.

"If you need anything," came Delphine's voice, a little distant and faded, "knock on the door and Ophelia or I will be here to assist you."

Before I could ask how they'd done that, they had disappeared into the darkness of the hallway, the door closing behind them and the lock clicking in place.

"This is... odd. Right?" I half whispered to Aerie. She nodded, slowly turning back to the table and pulling out a chair.

"Each tribe has their own customs. I'm sure some of ours would seem just as odd to them, if the roles were reversed." She took a seat, letting out a low breath as she grabbed the first tome off the top. "The moon tribe has always been known for their... eccentric behavior. But they are also the most trusted tribe in Tir Nadaar. Out of all the tribes, only the priestesses have freedom to roam between borders without invitation."

She patted the chair beside her, cracking open the tome and waving her hand over the cloud of dust that rose into the air. "I assume working so closely with the Cosmos would lend to some... adverse reactions. Like I told you before, I don't pretend to understand the inner workings of such power. Let's just play by their rules and see what we can find. Because at this point, we don't have an alternative."

I nodded, letting out a small breath and taking my own seat. Grabbing the next tome off the stack, I brushed a hand over the cover—the cracked and peeling leather catching against my skin. I couldn't read the title, the language being something I was unfamiliar with. But even as I opened the tome and peered at the contents within, I could feel some foreign part of me stirring inside. And for the first time since arriving here, I started to feel hope again.

CHAPTER II
HAZEL

I sat beside the fire in the den, staring into the burning logs as they crackled and broke under the heat of the flames. I'd retreated here after dinner, helping myself to another glass of Vesper's red wine. I'd decided to take my chances with the strong drink after the overwhelming events of today.

Aerie and I had pored over everything the archive offered to us, but it felt more like an endless, futile pursuit as time went on. When the priestesses had come back for us near dinnertime, releasing us out into the open air, I nearly cried with relief. Being locked up in the archives was suffocating, full of that old, dusty air and never-ending darkness. We hadn't found much of anything after our first day—and I longed for the feel of the sunlight on my skin, the wet dewy grass beneath my feet. Unfortunately, the fog hadn't cleared and I'd had to settle for the thick, wet air.

I let my drink dangle in one hand as I turned the opposite palm up. The ink of the sun etched onto my skin caught in the firelight, and I let my vision focus there, imagining its warmth.

"I bet you miss it." Vesper's voice surprised me, my eyes flitting up to find him standing beside me. I looked back down at the inked sun, running a finger over the length of its rays.

"I can't remember the last time I went this long without the feel of sunlight on my skin," I replied. It was a lie. I could, but returning to those haunting, dark days with Arlo was a journey I didn't feel like embarking on at the moment.

Vesper nodded, strolling over to the cart and pouring himself a drink before taking a seat across from me, closer than I'd expected. "I apologize for the mist. Usually our lands are quite beautiful. That isn't to say there's not a certain beauty to find within the fog, it just typically looks... different than it does now." He took a sip from his glass, eyes trained on me.

"So it's not always like this?" I asked, pointing to nowhere in particular.

Vesper shook his head, laughing briefly. "No, it's a precaution we take whenever outsiders visit. Which, if I'm being honest, isn't often."

He leaned in, lowering his voice. "You'll forgive me for the skepticism? It's not a lack of trust, but rather an abundance of caution during these uncertain times we find ourselves in."

He gave me a wink, as I paused to consider his words. Part of me felt insulted, if only on behalf of my company. Aerie and Bastian were the most trustworthy souls I knew. And while I didn't quite know where I landed with Vander at the moment, I knew he and Nox would never do anything to hurt Tir Nadaar.

I supposed I understood Vesper's perspective, though—the more I thought about it. Kahlis was a powerful individual. And despite our pure intentions, it was a risk for Vesper to accept any outsiders into this sacred space. Kahlis had been able to attack me, despite being tucked safely behind Talamh's borders—his only weapon being my own mind.

"Of course," I answered at last, returning his wink with one of my own. I sat back, taking my own sip of the alluring wine. The taste of honeyed berries danced on my tongue, coating the back of my throat in its sweetness. It seemed to be fueling my confidence, somehow working to tame the nerves that had been a constant since we'd arrived yesterday. I took several more sips, draining what was left in the glass in hopes that the wine would smother the nerves altogether.

"Did you and Aerie enjoy your time within the archives?" Vesper asked as he reached out for my glass, offering to fill it again. I shook my head, discarding it on the low table in front of the sofa.

"I'm not sure 'enjoy' is the right word," I hummed. The whole experience had been jarring, sending a chill down my spine that had yet to fade. "However, it was... interesting."

"But not telling? No helpful information you've stumbled across yet?" Vesper set his glass down beside mine, settling back against the sofa and—to my surprise—draping an arm around the back.

"Not yet." I shook my head, only too aware how close his arm was to slipping over my shoulder.

"Give it time. The Cosmos work in mysterious ways." Vesper smiled at me. His eyes caught on mine, the two of us exchanging the briefest of glances. The room was silent, the crackling of the fire acting as an incantation to hold us in the moment.

Vesper's presence was so captivating, something about him pulling me in—making it hard to tear myself away. In my heart, I knew I was fated to Vander. But after the confusion of the last few days, the last few weeks... I was starting to wonder if that meant much of anything anymore. Vander had once told me he'd suspected our fate for quite some time, but knew it to be true when I was taken from him. Before he'd made the decision to split his soul. I swallowed hard, a distant sort of grief building in my throat as I thought of Arlo, every good and wholesome piece of Vander. Perhaps... Perhaps splitting his soul as he had and letting Arlo sacrifice himself for my sake, rather than finding a way to piece Vander back together, had done something to disrupt the tether, to alter our fate. Had doomed us.

Vesper stood abruptly, breaking the spell and offering me his hand. "Come, I have something I wish to show you."

I eyed his outstretched hand carefully, pulling my own to my chest.

"I promise, you're safe with me." A hint of a smile played at his lips as he edged his hand forward.

I blinked, momentarily taken aback, but for whatever reason I couldn't muster up any dismay. Vesper had shown himself to be shrewd, knowing just how much of a boundary to give or hold—a power I was still trying to hone myself. Instead of being disappointed in being viewed as an outsider by him, I respected how he protected his people. It gave me a reason to trust him, fueling my body to move as I accepted his offer—willing my heart to not hold back. He pulled me off the sofa, turning out of the den and pressing further down the hallway before leading me up a stairwell I hadn't noticed before.

After climbing for what felt like an eternity, he pushed open another door. He stood back, offering me passage through. I stepped hesitantly, unsure what would greet me on the other side.

My feet moved forward, pushing me out into the open night air. I looked up, awestruck at the view before me. The clouds had cleared, allowing me to see the sky above.

Stars sprinkled over a deep purple tapestry, dancing and swirling to the magic of their own little world. The moon sat low amongst them, full and shining bright with a secret sort of power. It was the same sky I'd seen a million times over, but in this moment, above this land, it was something else entirely—an exquisitely painted canvas close enough to reach out and touch.

"I figured if I couldn't let you see the sun during your time here"—Vesper stepped out to join me, letting the door close behind him—"I'd at least let you experience one of the wonders of Sgàil."

I let out a breathy laugh, incapable of pulling my eyes away from the masterpiece above us.

"The moon shines just a bit brighter for us here. It's not a sight I get to show many. But it would be a waste for the Divine to miss such an enchanting phenomenon."

The name pulled my attention back to him. I folded my hands against my stomach, my thumb rubbing absent-mindedly against the moon inked on my palm. I turned to that same celestial body in the sky, closing my eyes and soaking in its beams dancing over my skin.

"Thank you for this," I heard myself saying. My voice sounded distant, as if my soul was floating up towards the Cosmos while my body remained firmly planted on the ground.

"Anything for the Divine," Vesper answered in a low tone. I pursed my lips, uncomfortable with the title, but he pressed further: "May I?" He moved closer and reached out for my hand, waiting for me to give permission before he cradled my palm in his own. He ran his fingers over the markings of the moon, his eyes sparking to life as he took it in. His touch felt foreign, scandalous. And I was suddenly aware of the distance between us, or lack thereof.

The motion made my own magic come to life, the moon glowing in my palm. I tried to hold back a gasp, jumping a little as the energetic feel of my magic skittered through my body, powerful and eager. It felt like I was just scratching the surface, a whole store of power untapped. I stared at my now glowing palm, a warmth swirling inside me that was hard to deny.

I forced my eyes back up to Vesper, conflicting emotions battling to overrun my mind.

"Vesper, ever since I arrived here—"

"You want to know why you feel such a pull between yourself and this place." He motioned to the sky before us. "Between us," he added, bringing my open palm into our view and running his soft fingers over the glowing ink once more.

I nodded, turning over the question in my mind. I didn't want to admit it. What I'd been doing with Lennox, it was innocent. Harmless. We both understood that it was nothing more than a way to mess with Vander. But this. This was starting to feel entirely the opposite of harmless. I turned away, pulling my hand to my chest as I stepped carefully towards the balcony edge in an effort to put some distance between us.

"Ever since we entered your borders, I've felt so odd. Something about this land has such an effect on me, an enchantment I can't seem to break."

Vesper joined me at the balustrade, respecting the space I'd forced between us. When I met his gaze, twin galaxies of silver and black swirled back to me.

"Your magic is unique, Hazel. Tribal magic... it is a gift from the land. Nature's way of ensuring balance remains amongst its inhabitants. But yours. Yours comes from the Cosmos themselves." He turned back to the sky, leaning on the balustrade and admiring the beauty above. "And while most chieftains take on a seed of their magic from the earth, the chieftain of the moon tribe must learn to harness something different." His eyes cut to mine, glowing brighter than before. "Something stronger."

He lifted his hand, reaching out to the stars as he plucked one out of the sky. I gasped, my hand flying to my mouth as I watched, spellbound. He offered it to me as it glowed in his palm.

"It is tradition that each Chieftain of Sgàil take on the power of a star. It is a burden we consume so as to keep the tribal magic alive. Something we pass down, generation to generation."

I watched as the star danced in his grasp, swirling and jumping from finger to finger, a trail of stardust following in its wake. I gawked in wonderment as it jumped from his hand to my own before settling into the ink of my moon.

"You feel this way, Hazel, because your power recognizes its own. In this tribe. Under these stars. Within me."

I looked into his eyes, watching as the glow of starlight receded from them.

"I imagine you'll feel the same way with the Chieftain of Auris, if you ever have the pleasure of meeting him." He gestured to my other palm where I felt my sun warm at the mention of the tribe who worshipped it.

Vesper offered me his hand once more, squeezing it delicately in his grasp as he continued, "The others could never understand what it's like to feel the Cosmos within your bones, as we do. They still see you as the mortal you never were, and not the goddess you so clearly are. The pain and conflict you must feel, to yearn to be both..."

I nodded, realizing the truth in his words. As if he could read my very soul.

"I was truthful when I said I'd known you in a different lifetime. Not me in this body, but the power I harness as chieftain. It recognizes you, worships you."

I tensed at his words. He chuckled, letting my hand go as he raised his own to tuck a loose strand of hair behind my ear.

"We've been waiting quite some time for your return, Caelliach." A ripple of light passed through the sky above, as if in answer to his words. I leaned closer, my hands gripping the balustrade as I stared up at the stars.

I didn't feel all that different than I had before this power claimed me. The Divine felt like a separate entity still. There was me and my power, and then there was the power of the Divine—sitting somewhere deeper within me. Disjointed. Confused.

Vesper must have sensed where my thoughts had turned, because he shuffled beside me, laying his hand atop my own.

"I don't mean to make you feel uncomfortable." He leaned in, whispering in my ear as his fingers stroked the back of my hand lightly. "I only mean to help you understand the power that now inhabits you. I..." His words faltered, a husky laugh warming my neck. "I understand what it feels like to feel utterly helpless while being viewed as all powerful. To have the weight of a tribe—even of the whole of Tir Nadaar thrust upon your shoulders. And have to harness a Cosmic spark within. That kind of power... it is as beautiful as it is terrifying."

I looked at him over my shoulder as he closed his eyes for a moment, letting the moonlight pour over him.

"I see a goddess in you, Hazel, lost and scared as you are. Something in me—that part which worships the Divine in all her iterations—is desperate to help you find your power." He opened his eyes, narrowing his gaze at me. "To help you know your worth."

I sucked in another breath, my body suddenly breaking out in a cold sweat.

I wanted to tell him how wrong he was, wanted to scream it since the day they all had told me what these symbols on my palms meant—that I wasn't the Divine. That everyone had it all wrong. He was right, I was lost and scared. But that only served to solidify in my mind that I couldn't be the goddess they all hoped for.

"You are her." Vesper answered my unspoken thought. "Even if it doesn't feel like it yet. You are her, Hazel. You're you, flawed and beautifully broken. An earthly being, to be sure. But you are also her, powerful and perfect and full of divine magic."

"I'm not," I scoffed, completely astounded that he'd somehow been able to read my thoughts. I turned to face him, trapping myself between him and the balustrade. I watched him for a moment, debating if I should build my mental blocks. But something told me it would make no difference.

"I'm not her," I repeated, shaking my head slowly. "I don't even know who *she* is."

"But that's why you're here, yes? To discover who she is, who you truly are. How do you expect to do that if you can't even accept you and the Divine are one in the same?"

A tear fell down my cheek, this conversation somehow stripping me down to my most vulnerable self. I didn't know how he'd done it, how he'd seen me for who I truly was, my deepest, darkest insecurities. Nor did I know how he could see all of those and still call me a goddess. But he had. And somewhere, somehow—I wanted to believe him.

He watched me for a moment, a smile growing across his face as I processed his words. He nodded, recognizing the power I could feel radiating through my body. It traveled down my arms, my legs, swirling in my chest and burning behind my eyes.

He hummed his approval, giving the stars behind me one last glance before taking my hand and pulling me away.

"I think that's enough for tonight. Let's get you to bed, goddess."

I didn't want to leave. I wanted to stay here forever, to sleep beneath the stars and let their confidence, *his* confidence, in who I was radiate through me until it was all I could feel. So that it would never leave me.

But there were still battles to be fought, information to find. I couldn't abandon the rest of them to focus all my time on the Cosmos. They needed me—the souls in this world, the elements of creation here. I didn't know what for yet, but I knew they needed me to accept this power, this namesake. They'd been waiting for me.

When Vesper pulled me back into the darkness of the stairwell, I felt the weight of my world return to my shoulders. My hand still glowed in Vesper's as he led me back through his home and walked me to my room, but with each step I felt that confidence slip away. Gone was the surety of what he'd shared with me.

But I couldn't deny the way he'd made me feel—as bright as the moon above, as powerful as the Cosmos that fueled an entire tribe's magic. Nor could I deny the power that had radiated through my body for the briefest of moments, no doubt inspired by the idea of someone who wanted me, who accepted me, and wasn't afraid to pursue that desire.

Vesper pushed open my door for me, stepping back so I could pass through. I turned back at him, prepared to thank him for whatever he'd done tonight—and to insist it could never go further.

He held up a hand. "That balcony is yours for as long as you choose to stay with us. Return to it as you wish, so long as you promise not to forget the strength the stars give you when you leave."

His lips tipped up, mirroring my own as a silent conversation passed between us. He reached out, placing his palm against my cheek and brushing his thumb over my skin.

"I will be here for the Divine, however she needs. Close or far—in this lifetime or another." He brought my cheek to his own, his lips brushing against the sensitive skin. I flushed, confused by the feeling sparking within me. "But for now, dear Hazel, I bid you goodnight."

Before I could respond, he was off, strutting down the hallway to his own private chambers tucked somewhere within the home. I stood there wide-eyed, clutching a hand to my cheek as I tried to process everything that just happened. It was all a whirlwind—being in his presence, experiencing his power. Seeing for myself the very Cosmos above reacting to my own.

Vesper had revealed myself to me in a way I wasn't sure anyone else would ever be able to. His power spoke to mine, recognized mine. And somehow that had helped me understand my role in all of this.

I let out a breath, trying to bring myself down from the high of it all. I placed a hand on the door, turning to retreat into the quiet sanctuary of my room, when my eye caught on something looming at the other end of the hallway.

I stopped, chest tight, breath gone as I watched him step forward. His eyes were narrowed, the deepest shade of black. His presence filled the hallway, shadows growing to snuff out each stream of torchlight as he prowled forward. The heat left my body, my skin crawling with fear as I whispered his name into the ever darkening space between us.

"Vander."

CHAPTER 12
HAZEL

"V ander, where—"

A cold wave of shadow rushed past the open doorway, silencing me.

"What." Vander's form stepped up to me, only a mere breath of space remaining between us. "The fuck." He closed the short distance, backing me into the room with no true effort. "Was that?" He raised an arm, pointing his finger back to the hall where Vesper had just left me.

I swallowed hard, an argument forming on my tongue. I had seen Vander in so many ways, so many temperaments—but this was different. True, raw anger radiated off him. He was nothing but pure, territorial instinct. And he'd just seen another male walk me to my room. Kiss me goodnight. Knowing his shadows, they hadn't hesitated to fill him in on the secret longings Vesper had mentioned before he left.

I hadn't realized I was still moving until the back of my legs hit the edge of the bed. Vander raised a hand, sending a wave of shadow to slam the door shut. Its resounding echo through the dark room reverberated through my bones.

"It's not what you think." I tried to explain. "Nothing happened..." The argument died on my tongue as I stared up into his deep black eyes, knowing that was a lie.

"Really, little spitfire? Because from where I'm standing, it looks like a whole lot has happened."

He leaned over me, pushing me further back still. I cowered onto the bed, not stopping until I felt the sturdy support of the headboard behind my back. It was a short-lived reassurance, as I turned my attention back to Vander to find him kneeling on the bed before me. He leaned against the headboard, both arms on either side of my head.

"Vander, I would never—"

Vander's shadows exploded around the room, even as he pushed himself away.

"Don't sit here and lie to me, Hazel. Not when I can feel your emotions, when I know what you are capable of." He took to pacing before the bed, hands flexing as he tried to reign in the darkness reverberating around us. "You're tethered to me, don't insult my intelligence by assuming I can't feel when your desire sways."

I shook my head, even as I knew his eyes weren't on me. "No, Vander," I pleaded, desperate to explain to him, as well as myself, what that desire had meant. "I'm sorry, I—"

"I said *don't* lie to me!" He was on me again, caging me against the headboard.

I was shaking, a swell of emotion battling behind my tongue. I'd relished in the feel of Vesper's attention, rejoiced at the faintest hint of emotional companionship. Something I couldn't seem to pull from Vander, no matter how hard I tried. But now that I was face to face with his wrath, I wasn't sure what to do. If I pushed further, as I'd done the night of Sol Litha, he could retreat again, run away and abandon me in this moment. But if I remained quiet, guarded, I wasn't sure how deep his wrath would run. Some small, distant part of me almost begged to test it.

"You want the truth? Fine. Perhaps I was interested in Vesper's notice. Perhaps it felt nice to have someone see—" My words stopped short as I saw the rage in his eyes grow, the way his jaw ticked as he tried to hold back the shadows lapping at my skin.

"It was just nice to feel noticed," I added carefully. Tentatively. "Like I wasn't some sort of afterthought or obligation."

The headboard creaked behind me, Vander's knuckles going white with the force of his grip. I dropped my gaze, letting loose a breath and praying to the Fates that he'd stay here, like this. Revealing himself to me.

Vander gritted his teeth, turning his head away for a brief moment—as if to allow himself a moment to tamp down on the power of the Mark. "So there's nothing? With Vesper?" he asked through a locked jaw. I shook my head slowly.

"No, of course not." My voice had dwindled to nothing but a mere whisper, seemingly snuffed out through the thick fog of his darkness.

Vander closed his eyes. A war was waging inside him, something hidden that I couldn't see. But I could sense it through the tether, his logical side fighting hard to overtake his primal, territorial anger. Fighting with the sway of the Mark.

"You are the only one for me, Vander." I reached out, attempting to brace my palm against the side of his face. He was faster though, his hand catching mine before it could land its aim.

"How can you claim as such when another male's scent still lingers on your skin. Another yet, amongst your sheets?" he seethed. "I'm not a fool. You don't think I know what you've been doing with Nox? Your little ploy to get a reaction out of me?"

He turned his gaze to me at last, his eyes swirling with that dark, forbidden power.

"Well, you have my attention now, goddess. Congratulations."

He was faster than my eyes could follow. One moment he was hovering over my body, the next he was back at the foot of the bed, grabbing my ankles and pulling me flat on my back.

I cried out in surprise, confusion lacing through my mind as I tried to process what he was doing. He pushed back my cobalt blue skirts, exposing my legs to him as he ran his hands slowly up their length. I squirmed beneath his touch.

"I know the games you're playing, but I've grown tired of watching you beg for my affection. I know there was never any *real* danger of you going elsewhere to fulfill your... desires." His eyes flicked up to mine. "After all, how could you when it is *me* that you need. It's not just lust, not just release you seek. It's ecstasy at *my* hand." He pulled one of his hands away, holding it for me to see as tendrils of shadow danced between his fingers. The sight of it had my imagination running—picturing what it would feel like to have those fingers elsewhere, shadows and all.

"Still," he went on, lowering his hand back to its path up my leg. "Certain acts cannot go unpunished. And you showing attention to another male..." His hands paused, his eyes darkening as his fingers dug roughly into my thighs. I squealed in response, sure the pure strength of his grip would leave bruises there, come tomorrow. "*Any* male... well, I'm afraid I cannot let you get away with that, goddess. No matter how *seen* they make you feel. I don't share."

Panic gripped my chest, even as desire stirred lower. It was a conflicting storm of confusion, such contrasting sensations swirling together to create something new, something strong within me.

"I'm sorry, Vander," I whispered again. I wasn't sure I truly meant it. Despite how wrong it had felt to tease him with Nox, it had proven to be successful, if his current intentions were any sign. The same with Vesper. The attraction to him, how he responded to me and my power, had been something totally unexpected. And while part of me truly was apologetic for hurting Vander through it all, I couldn't help the small piece of me that was grateful for an opportunity to wound him as he had wounded me— after everything he had put me through.

I bit my lip as he growled, digging his fingers once again into my legs.

"You forget how easily I can read you, Hazel. How easily I can access those little thoughts of yours." His hands were gone from my legs in an instant, leaving behind a haunting and painful chill in their place. He rose up, sitting back on his heels as he watched me for a moment.

I tried to sit up, but his shadows shoved me back down, grabbing my wrists and twining around the headboard until I was held securely in place. Their bitter cold bit into my skin, but I didn't shy away from it.

"Do you have any idea"—he snarled, moving forward to grab the tie at the bust of my corset—"the torment you put me through last night?"

I pulled my eyes away from where his fingers worked, cocking my head to the side.

"I'm sharing a room with the bastard. You really didn't expect me to notice his absence all night?"

Understanding dawned on me as his fingers kept working at the corset tie. Perhaps on some level I had realized asking Nox to stay with me last night would affect Vander. Perhaps that's why I'd thought to ask in the first place. I couldn't help but imagine him, alone and brooding in the room next to mine—his imagination running wild with jealousy as he waited to see if Nox ever returned.

I bit down on my lip in an effort to hide the smile attempting to peek through.

I shouldn't be smiling, not when the Shadow of the Grimm had me pinned beneath him—bound in his shadows and fully at his mercy.

"And then seeing him step out of your door the next morning. Sensing your *arousal* at the hands of that fucking chieftain tonight." Vander's body shook with rage, his shadows tightening around my wrists. "You must have a death wish."

I opened my mouth to argue, but no sound came out. Maybe he was right. Why had I thought it would be a good idea to tempt Fate and play with Vander's emotions like this? He was unstable at best, a chaotic storm of darkness at worst. Yet here I was, practically melting beneath his touch and the threatening way he was speaking to me, treating me.

"So you have nothing to say for yourself?" He finally freed the chord of leather holding my corset in place, throwing it to the side so the corset fell away on either side of my body. He shoved up the cream-colored shift beneath until I was fully exposed to him, looking down in admiration of his work. Another growl slipped from his lips as he ran a rough hand down the center of my chest, the air vibrating with his power.

"Well, I have something to say to you, goddess." He leaned over me, caging my head in again with his tan, corded arms. He nudged my face to the side with his chin, forcing me to turn my ear to him. The Mark on his arm filled my view, the magical ink snaking around his skin, as if it was alive—as if it was calling for me.

His breath heated the shell of my ear, sending shocks down to my toes. His voice was low, rough, dripping with rage:

"You are *mine*, Hazel. Mine. And I will not sit idly by and watch you throw yourself at other males to get my attention." He bit at my ear, bringing a cry from my lips. "Do it again, and I won't hesitate to spill their blood."

I couldn't help the scoff that sounded from me. I bit down on my tongue immediately, cursing myself for testing his patience further.

His chest rumbled as he let out a low laugh against my neck. "You think I don't speak the truth? Let me make this perfectly clear."

He sat up, his shadows rushing over my body, teasing, tasting, exploring. His eyes locked onto mine, his hand wrapping slowly around my throat. I could feel each of his fingers constrict, their weight settling against my pulse.

"It does not matter who he is. Chieftain, friend, brother. There is nothing—*nothing*—in this world I care about more than claiming you as my own." His hand tightened, making my eyes go wide as I realized the truth in his threats.

"So let me repeat it again, in case you were not listening." He lowered himself to my center, letting his hand fall from my neck only long enough to grip my hips. He pulled my core to his mouth, hovering close enough that I could feel the heat of his breath fan over me. His eyes locked on mine over the plane of my exposed body.

"You are *mine.*"

Every part of me screamed to bend to his will, to obey without question. But something deeper, something foreign, pushed me to fight back, to keep going:

"Then prove it."

I hadn't even been sure the words had come from me, hadn't been sure I'd even uttered them out loud. Everything about Vander told me he was about to take whatever this was further than we ever had before, but I couldn't risk him walking away again. He could end it all here and now; I could agree and he could walk out that door without ever truly touching me. But I couldn't let us go back to the awkward space we'd fallen into, somewhere between strangers and lovers. No matter how many threats he spewed at me, no matter how much blood he spilled, no matter how rough he got, I refused to let us settle back into that place. I would take his darkness over that half life any day.

He chuckled at my challenge, his breath skittering over my most sensitive parts. I squirmed in response, desperate for him to touch me.

"Oh, goddess," he purred, a sadistic smirk on his face. "I plan to."

He didn't wait for permission, didn't waste another moment before he buried his face against me. I cried out, far too loud for the fact that others were mere rooms away. But I couldn't help the noises escaping me. His tongue didn't just lap and taste.

Vander *devoured* me.

He showed me no mercy, gave me no rest. My release came fast, tearing through me in a violent storm of sensations. But he didn't stop. Even as my body started shaking and I pleaded for his mercy, his forgiveness, he refused to stop.

My body quivered from the overwhelming feel of his tongue against me. Even as my mind begged for more, my body fought to be free of his touch. He tightened his grip on my hips, holding me in place as his shadows clamped down on my wrists. More trailed up my body, wrapping around the peak of my breasts and tightening until I was nearly screaming from the sensations ravaging my body.

I could feel Vander chuckle against my core, the vibrations from his mouth only pulling another release from me as his relentless tongue consumed me.

"Fucking Fates, Vander," I ground out, even my jaw shook with the overstimulation wrecking my body. Tears pricked my eyes, my back aching with the way it arched off the bed in response to his motions.

Vander pulled away at last, letting his thumb replace the punishing strokes of his tongue. He looked to me, face glistening with my desire.

"Do I need to keep going, goddess? Or are you ready to obey?"

I gritted my teeth, a wave of defiance coursing through me. He raised an eyebrow before tracing maddening circles over my clit. His shadows still clinging to my breasts tightened. I cried out, more tears falling from my eyes as I watched him torture me. I couldn't take any more. He'd destroyed me, wholly and truly. I'd broken for this male. My mate.

"No more," I whimpered, caught somewhere between torment and bliss. "You win."

His thumb picked up in rhythm, my body jolting with each punishing stroke.

"Hmmm," he purred. "I don't think I heard you properly." The smug look on his face was maddening. If I had the ability, I would have smacked it from his lips. My wrists fought against their bindings in response to the thought, the shadows holding strong despite my protest. Frustration brought more tears to my eyes, spilling past my lashes in hot, angry trails.

"I'm yours," I muttered, trying to scoot away from his touch. A finger plunged into me without warning. His name was a curse on my lips, a desperate plea. I wasn't sure if I was asking him to stop or begging him to keep going. Need coiled low inside me, a third release winding me impossibly tight. He added another finger, crooking them forward as his thumb continued its persistent rhythm.

"Say it, Hazel. Scream it for this whole fucking house to hear. Because they will. They will know whose you are before this night is over."

I gave into the desire, riding his hand as if it was the only thing I had ever craved. His touch, his attention. I needed it all. He was merciless and celestial, something otherworldly, and I knew I needed this for every moment of the rest of my life.

"I'm yours, Vander," I cried out as I came undone around his fingers. "I'm yours, fully and explicitly yours."

My body quivered as he lingered inside me, letting the last waves of my orgasm radiate through my body. I melted around him, falling apart as I curled in on myself and sobbed.

He pulled back his shadows, letting me go as he lay down beside me and pulled me into him. His hand stroked my hair gently, his voice in my ear. "Such an obedient little goddess." Gone was any inkling of the dark fury he'd entered my room with. All that was left was adoration. He wiped away my tears, but never urged me to stop, to hold them back or shut them down. He let me cry as I released the last few weeks of pent-up emotion in his arms.

I didn't need to speak them into existence. I could feel his presence in my mind, experiencing each and every one with me. Still, he didn't shy away. He didn't leave. He just held me as they washed over me, one after the other.

"Sleep, little spitfire," he whispered into my ear after my cries had finally died down. He leaned in, his lips pressing softly against mine. I could still feel the hard length of him against my back and it had me chasing after him for more.

I leaned in, kissing him intentionally and exploring his taste as I prepared to experience him fully. He shook his head slowly, pulling away.

"Not tonight, goddess." He didn't give me an opportunity to argue as he rose off the bed, finally ridding my body of the skirts still bunched around my waist. He raised me in the crook of his arm, lifting my hands above my head as he gingerly pulled the shift off before lowering me back to the bed and tucking me into the covers. He planted a soft kiss against my forehead, then padded over to the hearth to light a fire.

I watched him through hooded eyes, the pull of lust-filled bliss lulling me to sleep. I blinked slowly, his form suddenly walking back towards my bed. He pulled his clothing off. The last thing I remember seeing was the length of his arousal as he set his pants on the floor next to the bed before shifting.

My eyelids fell closed, too heavy to open after the events of the evening. But I felt the warmth of his fur as he curled against me, letting my fingers twine in it as I drifted from consciousness.

CHAPTER 13
VANDER

I sat at Vesper's dining room table, eyes trained on Hazel as she helped herself to the platters of food one of the priestesses had set out for us this morning. I'd filled my own plate with eggs, fruit, and bread. However there was only one thing I had an appetite for right now.

My cock strained against my pants, my body revolting for not being allowed to find release last night. It had been one of the most difficult nights of my life, controlling myself as I had. Or rather, controlling the Mark. It had screamed for her, scratching at my restraint until I was a raw, bloody mess. Metaphorically speaking.

But it had been worth it, the momentary surrender to my desire. I could still taste her on my mouth. I rolled my tongue behind my teeth in answer. She was every bit as decadent as I knew she would be. Seeing her ride my fingers, hearing my name on her lips as I made her come over and over again. It was an ethereal experience, my own personal form of worship.

"Morning, all." My face fell as Nox's voice boomed through the room. He was still on my shit list, even if I hadn't believed for a second there was anything going on between him and Hazel. He knew exactly how to fuck with me where it would count and I planned to thoroughly beat his ass. It wouldn't change anything, He'd still fuck with me for the rest of our lives, and I'd keep beating his ass. Those were the roles we played with each other.

Still, my body bristled at the sight of him.

He saddled up beside Hazel, grabbing his own plate and filling it with piles of food. I watched her carefully, enjoying the opportunity to prove she'd learned her lesson.

"Morning, love," Nox chirped, planting a peck against her cheek. Hazel tensed, cutting a quick glance to me. I raised an eyebrow at her, an offering to let her decide for herself what she'd do next.

Hazel gave Nox a tight-lipped smile, stepping a smidge to the side to urge more distance between them.

Good girl, I purred through the tether. Her head dipped, trying to hide the heat in her cheeks.

"So that's how it is, then? One night with him back in your bed and it's all *Nox who?*" Nox shook his head, looking over to me. His contrasting eyes shone with amusement, despite his condescending tone. "What'd he threaten you with then, love?"

Hazel went pale, her gaze darting between me and Nox. I bowed my head, giving her permission to speak.

"Not me," she answered at last. "You." Hazel finished making her plate, a smile playing on her lips as she took the seat across from me.

Nox broke out in a laugh. "Oh, you dirty dog," he hollered. "Well, I'm happy for you. Truly. It was about time you fucked out whatever was going on between you."

Hazel choked on the bite of egg in her mouth, her fork clanging against her plate when she dropped it. I raised my middle finger to the bastard, but a smirk curled across my lips nonetheless.

"Lennox, that's enough," Bastian chided as he strode into the room, glancing momentarily at me before dropping his gaze pointedly at Hazel. I could sense an air of contempt as he disregarded us and made his way to his seat. I was sure there was more he was dying to say, opinions he wished to share and advice he thought I needed. But I didn't want to hear it. For the world's smallest moment, things felt manageable between us. Even if it was a facade, it was one I refused to tear down just yet.

Nox sniggered, filling his plate with more food, but his eyes caught mine once more, genuine approval shining in them. I bowed my head slightly, a silent nod of thanks for taking care of my mate while I worked through whatever bullshit had been infecting me these past couple days. He returned the subtle bow before sauntering to his seat.

Vesper was next to enter, alongside two of his priestesses. His presence had the Mark sparking to life beneath my skin. The anger of last night returned without a moment's hesitation, seeing the male that had put his hands, his lips, on *my* mate.

The more logical side of me told the Mark to settle, that he was simply curious about Hazel's new namesake and a little too eager in his interest. It wasn't all that surprising for a member of the moon tribe to be forward during one of our visits. The tribe as a whole was rather free in their beliefs about love and intimacy. During the few visits we'd made in our lifetime, Bastian and I had both been invited to partake in their extracurricular activities, and I'd be lying if I said I hadn't accepted once or twice, in my younger years. But the more primal side of me felt the challenge of another male showing too much attention to my mate. A chieftain, no less. It wanted to make him pay for ever even thinking about touching her.

A growl slipped through my lips, my shadows unfurling around me and stretching through the room. They slipped across the floor, wrapping around the table. Wood splintered as the table creaked with their force, pulling Hazel's attention up from where she sat across from me.

Vander, she warned through the tether. I cut a glance her way, my eyes narrowing on her emerald eyes as I tried to dispel my magic. It did little to settle me.

"Ladies, I regret to inform you I cannot accompany you to the archives today." Unfortunately, Vesper seemed completely oblivious to my little slipup as he addressed the room. Or purposefully chose to ignore it. "I have some business to attend to along the border. Something I was actually hoping your boys could help me with."

I rolled my eyes, tightening the hold on my fork. I opened my mouth to argue my utter lack of interest in helping Vesper with anything, but Bastian cut me off—seemingly knowing where my thoughts had turned.

"Of course we'll help. Anything we can do to be of service while we're here."

I gave him an irritated look, to which he served one right back. Bastian shoveled a fork full of eggs into his mouth and rose to his feet. He leaned over and gave Aerie a kiss on the cheek as he swallowed his eggs, before coming around the table and pulling me out of my chair.

"Fuck, Bastian, I don't need a babysitter."

"Debatable," Bastian hummed, snapping his fingers at Lennox to follow along. "I'm not leaving either of you alone unsupervised in someone else's tribe."

Nox scoffed, feigning offense with a hand to his heart, but then shrugged and stood to his feet. "Fair point," he joked as he strode towards the dining room entrance.

Vesper chuckled, slapping a hand on Bastian's shoulder in thanks. "These two do seem the type to get into trouble. However, I'm sure I could trust them." His eyes cut over to mine, almost too quick to catch. "If needed."

My muscles flexed in annoyance as Bastian continued to push me out the doorway.

"My priestesses will take you back to the archives today. If you need anything at all, just let them know." I looked over Vesper's shoulder to where Hazel still sat at the table, suddenly in the company of strangers rather than under my careful watch. Bastian refused to give me a minute longer as he shoved me down the hall and out the front door. I growled, louder this time to ensure he could hear me, my shadows creeping out over his body in response.

"Fuck off, brother. Put your power to use and be helpful for once."

I shoved off him, anger bristling within me. The distance calmed me somewhat, and I rolled my shoulders as I looked back at the chieftain's home behind us. I hesitated a moment, debating if I should defy his orders and take my chances going back in. But I knew Bastian and he would stop at nothing to prove our tribe cooperative. He was a new chieftain, in comparison to Vesper, and he was desperate for a chance to prove himself. Besides, with each step in the opposite direction, I could feel the swell of dark magic settling within me. As if the more distance I put between myself and Hazel, between myself and the developments of last night, I was regaining control over the Mark.

I turned away from Vesper's home, stomping through the thick grass and moss to catch up with the other males several paces away. Perhaps this would give me a moment to settle the score with the chieftain of the moon tribe, if nothing else.

"Where the fuck are you taking us, Vesper?" I called out as we trudged through yet another small village. This was the third one we'd passed since leaving the chieftain's home. *Village* was probably a stretch, but I wasn't sure what else to call these groupings of stone dwellings. Every hour or so of walking, another group of them popped up.

"Vander, I wouldn't have taken you for one to complain about a walk out in nature," Vesper called back. I bared my teeth in response, the Mark jumping to life. I wasn't complaining because I couldn't keep up, I was complaining because I wanted to be doing quite literally anything besides helping the male that was seducing my mate just last night.

"Just ignore him," Nox responded for me. "He's just bitter because he wants to be back home brooding about his love life beneath the trees of the Dark Woods."

Vesper turned around, walking backwards for a moment as he raised an eyebrow at me. "The Dark Woods, eh? Quite a sinister place from what I hear. What in the name of the Fates would make you want to spend your time out there?"

"Haven't you heard, chieftain?" Nox chirped again. "The hemlock trees are his dearest friends!"

I rolled my eyes, raising a middle finger to Nox as he broke out in a chorus of laughs. Vesper joined him, though not as enthusiastic in his amusement.

"You'll have to excuse them, Vesper. They are unfamiliar with using appropriate behavior around company." Bastian grunted in disapproval.

Vesper slowed his movements as we approached the stone wall that acted as a physical border for the moon tribe. "No excuses necessary, Bastian. I quite enjoy the camaraderie between them. We could all do with a healthy dose of fun during these dark times."

As if on cue, Vesper stopped short and turned our attention to the stone border, evaluating.

"So what seems to be the issue?" Bastian asked, stepping up to the stone and placing a hand atop the wall. The stacked stone only came up about knee-high, less of a physical deterrent and more of a marking for the wards. I knew from tribal lessons as a boy that each stone was handpicked and placed by the first chieftain of the moon tribe. It had been a meticulous undertaking, the entirety of the wall taking years to complete, but the magic embedded in the stone was strong because of it.

"We've been experiencing some attacks recently. Nothing too terrible, mostly just depthhounds here and there, but recently they've figured out a way to weaken our warding."

"I don't know how helpful we can be," I replied, stepping up beside my brother and assessing the wards for myself. "Your borders are the most secure out of all the tribes. Far superior to Talamh's wards."

Bastian raised an eyebrow at me, surprised by my readiness to participate or perhaps my knowledge. I scoffed at him, trying to ignore the look of incredulousness, or the fact my brother expected so little of me. As if I hadn't been the one groomed to take over for our father as chieftain.

"True," Vesper agreed, taking a seat atop the low-rising stone wall. "But as you now know, the priestesses and I have been communing with the Cosmos, looking for ways to strengthen not only our borders, but our powers as well. This ongoing battle with Kahlis has left everyone a bit on edge, I'm afraid." His eyes found Bastian's. "My people are scared, Chieftain. Which has driven me to look for solutions amongst the stars."

Bastian nodded in understanding. "So what is it you've found?"

Vesper's lip tipped up in a smile, his head turning towards Nox. The oblivious fool paid Vesper no mind, his boot toeing a rock stuck in the ground.

"I've been waiting for an opportunity to test my findings, and was pleasantly surprised when I saw you brought young Lennox with you," Vesper quipped after a moment of silence.

"Who, me?" Nox said with astonishment once he'd noticed Vesper's pointed look.

Vesper nodded, laughing slightly. "The Cosmos have advised me to rely on those whose power transcends tribal borders. That divided power can only generate more division."

I looked from Bastian to Nox, understanding Vesper's meaning. Nox was born into the moon tribe; in many ways, this was his home. However, his mother had belonged to the sun tribe, Auris, and now he himself to the earth tribe, Talamh. His magic was strong, pulling from so many tribes at once. There was no doubt about that.

Vesper raised to his feet, stepping towards Nox with outstretched hands. "Would you mind if we tried a bit of magic gifted from the Cosmos? To utilize the uniqueness of your power in an attempt to strengthen our borders?"

"You know me," Nox called out awkwardly, stepping up to Vesper. "Always happy to help."

"Is it safe?" I spoke up, a wave of concern passing through my mind for Nox. Discrediting Vesper was just an added bonus. "This is something new, yes? Experimental even? Who's to say it won't hurt him, drain him? Let alone work to strengthen the border."

Vesper nodded thoughtfully, agreeing with my speculation and looking out into the invisible warding. "There is always risk when venturing into the unknown. But I'm sure you would know all about that, wouldn't you Vander?"

"What the fuck is that supposed to mean?" I asked on a growl, advancing towards the moon tribe's chieftain.

Vesper turned to face me, dropping his hands from Nox's. "You know, Vander. I have heard rumors."

I paused, glaring at him.

"Tales of a dark being that frequents the Dark Woods. A protector of Talamh's border."

"Vesper," Bastian warned as he stepped between us. Vesper raised a hand, cutting Bastian off as his eyes found mine.

"The magic that runs through your veins is dark, my friend. Dark. But powerful. And not without its risks, as well." His eyes flicked down to the Mark on my forearm. He paused, watching the ink dance over my skin for a moment as he chose his next words. "Sgàil would be lucky to have the services of such a being to protect its borders. I suppose I'd hoped you wouldn't mind sharing a morsel of that power while you were here, as well."

Vesper extended a hand, a peace offering between us. "That perhaps all of you could work with me, testing this new discernment from the Cosmos. That of all the tribes in Tir Nadaar, one made up of diverse, complex magic would be the one to aid in these new strides of unification."

I thought about it for a moment, making him itch as his hand hung midair for just a moment too long. I reached out finally, clasping his hand in mine and giving it a firm shake. I still didn't like him, and I sure as fuck didn't trust him. His interest in Hazel would forever be a stain on his reputation in my eyes. But anyone who could sense the power in me and still have the balls to ask for my assistance was deserving of it.

Vesper let out a sigh of relief as he shook my hand, returning my grip with the same amount of fortitude I showed him. His eyes met mine, and I couldn't help but stare into the galaxy within them. I knew Vesper was a seer, his well of magic deep and confusing. He couldn't have been the Chieftain of Sgàil without some sort of massive mystical power.

But as I stared into his eyes while he refused to drop my hand, I was hit with the overwhelming feeling that there was far more playing within his mind than he was letting on.

CHAPTER 14
HAZEL

A new stack of books awaited us in the archives, the priestesses leaving us with a wink and a giggle in the same unsettling manner as yesterday. I was still all over the place from breakfast, flushed and confused by Vander's fluctuating behavior. Last night had felt like a step in the right direction, only to find him once again on edge and distant in the daylight. Arriving at the archives hadn't helped much, my mind jumbled even more by the chill of the eerie stone structure, and the somber ritual the priestesses performed again before allowing our entrance.

"So," Aerie mused as we took our seats and examined the newly delivered books. "I take it you've patched things up with Vander?" Her eyes didn't leave the books as she started dividing them between us. My cheeks reddened.

"Does the entire house know of our activities last night?" I groaned, scrubbing my hands over my face.

Aerie looked up this time, a breathy laugh on her lips. She reached out, patting my arm. "It's hard to hide such things when we're in such tight quarters... especially given how *vocal* things seemed to have gotten between the two of you."

I hunched into myself, burying my face in my hands. If it was possible to disappear, I would have.

"It's nothing to be embarrassed of, Hazel." Aerie laughed, swatting at my arm. "I'm glad you're both figuring out how to be there for each other."

I peeked an eye through my fingers to find her still looking at me.

"Well..." I took a deep breath, dropping my hands from my face. "I'm not so sure we've figured out how to be there for each other... exactly."

Aerie tilted her head to the side. "What do you mean?"

"I mean..." I sighed, messing with the parchment on the table before me. "That he refused to take it there. Refused to *let me* take it there."

"So you didn't—"

"I did," I answered slowly, heat burning in my cheeks. "But he didn't."

"Oh," Aerie answered, *"OH."* I could practically see the wheels spinning in her mind as she read between the lines. This was so embarrassing. The last thing I wanted to do was talk about my intimate life, even with someone like Aerie.

"Did he say why?" Aerie asked.

I shook my head, pausing mid-motion. "Things did get a little emotional... after. And Before. And then today it felt as if he was retreating again, distancing himself once more."

"Hmm." Aerie fiddled with the pages of the tome in her hand. "Perhaps he still needs some time then. But felt as if he needed to make his feelings clear in some way before he did more harm than good."

"Maybe." I agreed, pausing as I tried to build up the courage to divulge the rest of last night's affairs. "There's something else I didn't tell you about last night." I sat up, chewing nervously on my bottom lip.

"What's that?" Aerie asked, not looking up from her work.

"Vesper spoke with me last night. He... was filling me in on some things about my magic. How it connected me to, well, all the tribes really, but especially the moon tribe."

Aerie nodded absent-mindedly. "That makes sense. The power of the Divine is creation. I'd assume that would connect you to all elements of nature. Not just one."

I swallowed hard, pushing forward to the other detail I'd still neglected to mention. "Yeah, that's essentially what he said. Before he mentioned his desire for the Divine and kissed me goodnight outside my room."

Aerie paused her skimming, looking up at me. "Was this before or after Vander visited your room?"

"Before." I cringed as I remembered his wrath when he found me in the hallway. "Like, right before. Vander sort of stumbled upon us."

Aerie sucked in a sharp breath, the book in her hands long forgotten. "Hazel, I didn't say anything when you and Lennox were having your fun. Mostly because I know Lennox and Vander have a special kind of relationship. And part of me had hoped it would jostle Vander out of whatever mood he's been in. Plus I trust Lennox to not push things too far. But Vander finding you with another male—it's no wonder he made such a move last night."

"But it's not like I was pursuing Vesper. He didn't even do anything, really!"

"I know," Aerie consoled, leaning over to take my hand. "I know you didn't instigate this, but regardless, it does give insight into Vander's actions. Fated males can act foolish at times. Territorial. Especially when the bond is incomplete and... unstable. As yours is. Vander is most likely feeling threatened by Vesper's advances. It's not surprising to hear he made his interest known. The moon tribe has a reputation for their freedom with such activities, but I would have thought Vesper wiser than to make advances towards a fated female. Especially when her mate was under the same roof and unaware of his intentions."

A mixture of emotions flooded my system. "Vander doesn't *own* me, Aerie." I was suddenly overwhelmed with the feeling of being stuck, trapped in this in-between void of being fated while simultaneously having no mate at all. I hated to admit how isolating it felt.

"You're right, Hazel. But you must admit there's a bond between the two of you. No matter the state of that bond currently, it's there, and it's going to have repercussions when outside forces challenge it. Just as you felt them during the Sol Litha festival, Vander is feeling them here, now."

I kept my eyes trained on the tome in front of me, refusing to look at Aerie as I processed everything she was saying. No matter how little I wanted to admit it, it made sense. I felt firsthand the effects of our bond, the heightened emotional responses when Vander had rejected me on my birthday.

I nodded slowly, accepting the truth she was giving to me. "So what do I do?" I asked at last.

"There's nothing much to do," Aerie sighed. "Until Vander is willing to face whatever is keeping him from accepting your fate and decide for himself if he's going to stop fighting the bond, these kinds of heightened reactions are unfortunately going to be rather common, I'm afraid."

"Great," I groaned, burying my head in my hands once more. I had hoped last night was a turning of a page. But it seemed it was less about Vander making an intentional decision forward, and more about his innate reaction to Vesper's advances. Another primal response, followed by a wave of more distance. Another round of me questioning how I got here, and what I could do to fix it.

Aerie offered me a sympathetic smile. "Relationships are hard, Hazel. Being fated doesn't make them any easier. It just makes them more intense."

I huffed at her words. *Intense* was a delicate way of putting it. I had never felt this kind of visceral reaction to anything before. I wanted to rip him apart nearly as much as I needed him to rip into me. I needed him, his presence, the feel of his hands on my skin. I didn't think there was anything I needed more in this world. But he also infuriated me—his actions, his stubbornness. And I found myself fighting the urge to do everything in my power to rile him up, just to see what sort of reaction it would elicit.

But even as Vander had finally crossed some line with me last night, he'd still refused to accept me fully. He'd stopped himself. Again. Proving once more that he didn't think I was worthy of his bond. My fists tightened against the parchment I was holding, a wave of shame building inside me.

I let the conversation fizzle out as I turned to the book before me. I pushed the struggles with Vander to the back of my mind, forcing myself to focus solely on our purpose here in the archives. If this was the one chance we had to find information against Kahlis, I wasn't going to mess it up by allowing myself to be distracted. I didn't know how long Vesper would grant us access to the archives, but we'd already spent a whole day within these walls, with little to nothing to show from it. I couldn't let whatever problems Vander and I had keep my attention from where it should be.

We worked in silence, each flipping through the pages of our respective books and jotting down any notes that felt worth re-membering. When I reached the end of the first tome, having found not a single piece of noteworthy information, I slammed it closed and tossed it to the side in frustration before picking up another one.

Aerie finished flipping through the pages of the book in front of her before doing the same and discarding it to the stack of fruitless tomes beside the worktable. The stack had grown to quite an exceptional height after just one day of searching, reminding me of how frustrated I'd felt after we left the archives yesterday. Aerie stood, stretching her back as she made her way around the table to better assess the stacks of books the archives had left for us.

"Still nothing?" I asked with a hint of disappointment in my voice.

Aerie shook her head. "Unfortunately these topics aren't ones with an overwhelming amount of useful information. Fae magic in and of itself is rare. Finding things we can use against a powerful fae king like Kahlis—if it were easy, we would have already taken care of him."

I sat back, crossing my arms over my chest. "I wish they'd let us peruse the archives for ourselves." I couldn't help but feel like we were being intentionally kept in the dark. Like the information we needed was just beyond that door and if I could simply go looking for it, I'd find it with ease. Aerie hummed her agreement. I watched her for a moment as she sifted through the rest of the tomes, trying to decide which to start with next. "And what of my magic?" I asked after several moments of silence had passed.

Aerie pulled her eyes off the pile before her. Her fingers tapped idly against a cracked leather spine. "That, I'm afraid, is proving to be even rarer a topic." She let out a slow breath, no doubt watching disappointment creep over my features. She pulled a stack of tomes into her arms, moving around the table to drop them in our workspace. I rose to my feet, helping her sort the pile and choosing which ones I felt more inclined towards. "We'll get there," she reassured me as we both took our seats again.

I hummed my agreement, knowing we had no other choice. The more time we spent digging through these tomes and records, the hungrier I got for the information we were chasing. I knew we were close, that the Fates had led our path here for a reason. And despite the discouraged feeling growing in my chest, I could also feel the subtle buzz of my power within my veins. As if the Divine herself knew we were close, and was pushing me to not give up.

I pulled titles off the stack, discarding book after book until I found one that caught my eye. It was smaller, less impressive than the massive texts we'd prioritized. The leather was old, the engraving patchy and hard to read. I squinted in the firelight, flipping open the delicate cover and letting my eyes roam over the scribbled handwriting at the beginning of the book.

From the archives of the Keepers of Time, Wisdom,
and Destiny

There are moments in time where even we cannot predict how dark things will become. All we can say is we regret the things that were asked of us, the depth of the darkness we had to find in order to reclaim peace for this world. It was too high a price to pay. And for that, we will do whatever is necessary to ensure that peace remains. As a testament and reminder of the

*price that was paid, we've collected and arranged a
firsthand account of our sins against the Deities, may
they rest in peace. Let this story live as a reminder of
the blood that was shed and the sacrifices made.*

May we never have to relive that darkness.

The story of Death and the Divine.

"Aerie," I breathed out, letting my fingers dance over the last line. "I think I found something."

"What is it?" she asked, leaning forward in her chair to get a closer look. I didn't move, my eyes fixated on the Divine's name on the parchment before me.

Aerie gasped beside me. "It can't be." She reached out tenderly, taking the tome from me even as my body screamed to not let it go.

"Do you know what it is?" I asked, finally tearing my eyes away from the pages to look at the shock ravaging her face.

"It's a story I'd long forgotten," was all she answered. She closed the book, rising to her feet. "We'll have to ask the priestesses if we can get permission to bring it back to Vesper's home. We need to show the others."

Aerie made her way back to the door, knocking three times to summon the priestesses. I sat and watched as she spoke in hushed tones to the one who had come to answer. My mind reeled, thinking about the possibilities that lay in her hand. We'd finally found something, a mention of the Divine—and with any luck, a useful guideline for how to proceed accordingly. It was a rush of emotion, an energy buzzing within me. Suddenly, I understood how the priestesses could stay locked within this living tomb, chasing the high of digging for whatever snippets of knowledge the archives or the Cosmos deemed us worthy of.

Even as Aerie ushered us to leave, I found myself anxious to return, to keep pushing, keep pursuing. Because I had inquired with the Cosmos, and despite my desperation, despite my doubts, they had answered.

The priestesses were adamant about staying with the copy and accompanied us back to Vesper's home. They would only allow us to keep it there for long enough to discuss it with the others, at which point they would return it to the archives and we could spend our time reading it there. This seemed to irritate Aerie, but my heartbeat picked up at the idea of getting to return to the archive and continue our pursuit for more information.

Aerie made us some food back at Vesper's home as we waited for the others to return, despite my protests. I was in no mood to eat, not when I still didn't fully understand what the book contained.

She gave me small details, but wanted to wait for Vesper before divulging more.

I was picking at a mostly uneaten plate of roasted vegetables in the den several hours later, when I heard the boys trample through the front door. My eyes went wide, finding Aerie's and jumping off the sofa. Aerie held up a hand, a request to give them time to get settled as they made their way through the halls.

As if on instinct, Vesper led them directly to the den. His eyes met Aerie's, that annoying twinkle dancing in their depths. "You've found something, haven't you?" he asked. Although, judging by the way he was looking at us, I suspected it was more a formality than an actual question. Somehow, he'd already known.

Vander trailed in last, finding my eyes quickly and letting his gaze roam over my body, as if to make sure I was okay. His sudden attention on me was jarring, and I shifted my weight between my legs as I tried to ignore the feeling.

"We did," Aerie responded excitedly. She motioned for the priestesses to bring her the tome. They hesitated, but Vesper nodded his approval and they produced the old, black leather book.

"Have you ever seen this before?" Aerie asked Vesper. Vesper closed the distance between them, taking the tome delicately in his hands as he invited everyone to find a seat.

"I can't say that I have, but our archives are rather extensive. Even I have not been able to put eyes on every piece of knowledge acquired over its lifetime."

"Well, I've seen it." All heads turned to Aerie. "This book, it was something my sister once owned. Something she read to us often during my time with her coven."

Bastian pulled on Aerie's hand, guiding her down beside him on the sofa opposite where Vander, Nox, and I now sat. I inched forward, excited to hear more about this mysterious text.

"I just don't understand how it would have shown up here. How I could have forgotten it all this time, until it revealed itself to me again." Aerie's brows were pinched together in concentration, as if she was sifting through her memories.

"That's the magic of the archives." Ophelia stepped forward from her spot tucked within the corner of the den. "Records and stories acquired by it are often forgotten by those who've previously held their knowledge. It protects our tribe from outsiders trying to claim what they wrongfully believe to be theirs."

"So the magic of the archives just acquires things randomly and distorts others' memories of its previous existence?" I shook my head, not understanding how such a thing could exist. "How?"

"We are not ones to question its methods," replied Delphine. "We simply accept the knowledge it deems us worthy to receive, when it comes time to receive it. The archive knows what knowledge it must protect."

Vesper nodded, turning back to Aerie. "Which means the archive deemed the knowledge this book holds as something worth protecting. But it must have some sort of connection to you. A deep, personal history, if the archive decided to pull it for you and remind you of its knowledge. I can't say how it made its way here, but it knew it needed to find its way back into your hands."

Tears shone in Aerie's eyes, as they often did any time the topic of her sisters arose. My heart hurt for her. Seeing the pain she was clearly in, I wanted nothing more than to reach out and comfort her.

"May I ask where you came across it, originally?" Vesper flipped delicately through the pages. I leaned forward slightly, desperate to peek at the knowledge that lay within its pages.

"My sister, Flora—she used to read it to us while we bundled herbs." Aerie's glance darted my way, just for a moment. Something like trepidation flashed in her eyes, but she pressed on regardless. "It's the story of Death and the Divine. One version of it, at least. One I hadn't heard before or anywhere since."

Vesper's eyes widened slightly as he skimmed the pages, but a mask of composure slipped easily over his features. "I see. A rare find indeed."

"I never believed it to be true. Maybe some parts of it, but I thought it was just a folktale, an embellished story of what had really taken place. Nothing more than a fictional retelling written by someone with a creative imagination and a romantic heart."

Vesper closed the tome, handing it carefully back to Aerie. Her hand lingered on his as she took it. "Do you think it could be true?"

Vesper was quiet for a moment, lost in thought as his eyes swirled with silver. As if he was looking elsewhere, assessing something far from this room.

"It's possible," he answered at last, letting his hands drop from the tome. "Folklore, afterall, is typically birthed out of a grain of truth. But we must remember to tread carefully. The Fates are a deity worthy of reverence. They have been for as far back as our history extends."

Aerie bowed her head in agreement, a small sign of respect at the invocation of their name.

"But—" Vesper leaned forward, lowering his voice slightly. "The Cosmos wanted you to see this, to remember this, for a reason. And that cannot be ignored."

"Can someone tell me what *it* is?" I broke out, my eagerness fighting to take over.

Both Aerie and Vesper turned to face me, something akin to pity radiating from both of them. It only made me grit my teeth harder as I waited for them to answer.

"This tome," Aerie finally responded, holding up the decrepit book between us. "It's a story about the old gods. Creation, Power, Love, War…" Her eyes cut over to Vander, his body tensing as if he understood what was coming next. "And Death. I know it well, having been read its contents countless times. But had I for a moment been able to remember its existence, I would have mentioned it, Hazel. Please believe that."

I tried to sift through her words, to determine what she was saying. "Why is this so important, why does it matter?"

"Because," Vesper took over. "It's a recollection of the Divine's power. Her life and—her death. At the hands of the Fates."

CHAPTER 15
HAZEL

Aerie had given me an overview of the text, a captivating explanation of the schemes and deception the Divine had faced at the hands of her counterparts. The love she'd found in Death. And the gutwrenching ending she'd found at the edge of an enchanted blade. Having read a decent amount about the Fates upon my return to Tir Nadaar, I was shocked to find such a story existed, its claims feeling so drastically opposite the deities I'd learned to revere. The small details she shared with me felt like lightning against my skin, striking something distant but profound within me. It was hidden beneath so many layers of confusion and intrigue, but it was there. I could feel it, the connection to my namesake, the familiarity within the legend being shared. Not my story, but the Divine's beside my own.

It wasn't everything. We still didn't know how to access my powers or how to fight Kahlis. But it was something—something more than we'd had before.

I left Vesper and Aerie in the den to dive into deeper discussion and speculation, retreating to my room as my head buzzed with energy from our discovery. Or perhaps it was just this place, the magic that seemed to fill every crack and crevice having such a physical effect on me.

The solitude of my room was a welcome feeling, and I let out a sigh of relief as I entered its walls. Vesper had agreed to let the tome stay with Aerie, so long as he and his priestesses could wrap it in extensive warding before we left. I appreciated the gesture. Seeing the joy in Aerie's eyes as she clutched the book to her chest was a welcome sight.

I had every intention of diving into the tome for myself right away, but Aerie had insisted I wait. She needed time to discuss with Vesper, and for whatever reason seemed hesitant to let me see the book in its entirety. Which only made me more anxious to get my hands on it.

A knock sounded at the entrance of my room and I spun to find Vander leaning against the open doorframe. He must have followed me upstairs from the den. "Mind if I come in?" he asked, his tone indifferent.

I nodded hesitantly, eying him as he made his way over to the beverage cart in the corner of my room. He poured two glasses of the rich, red wine, sauntering effortlessly over to me and handing me a glass.

"Thanks," I breathed, thrown off by his close proximity to me. Our night together had left me feeling somehow more distant than ever from my mate. And now he was here, in my room once more. I took the glass, raising it to my lips and letting the spiced liquid ground me.

"I can't believe we found that tome." I backed away, drawing closer to the hearth and pacing within the fire's reach. "I was worried it would take us much longer to find something of so much value." I turned, stunned as I almost ran into Vander. I arched my back to look up at him. "But we did it, we found something that may actually prove to be useful with my power." I was absolutely giddy with the discovery, despite the weight in my stomach at what Vesper had revealed about the story's ending.

I pushed that thought away, refusing to let anything dampen my joy in this moment. I was already planning out my next trip to the archives, hope renewed with the promise of a tangible piece of information. Vander smiled down at me, but it felt forced. Something was troubling him still.

"What's wrong?" I asked, brow furrowed.

"Nothing, little spitfire," he whispered into the space between us. He reached out, tucking a strand of hair behind my ear. I leaned into his touch as his palm cupped my cheek, the attention surprising me. "I hope this proves to be as helpful as you're expecting it to be. I'm just prone to pessimism, is all."

I closed my eyes, sighing deeply as his hand fell from my face.

His absence was a weight on my soul; my eyes fluttered open quickly to find he'd taken a seat beside the hearth. I followed him, taking the seat beside him on the sofa.

"I just want to make sense of this power I now hold." I set my glass down on the floor, resting my hands in my lap and opening my palms to reveal the inky sun and moon etched into my skin. "To find out what it all means."

I knew he understood, the Mark on his arm causing his shadows to grow around us just as I mentioned my own magic. But where my magic seemed to be tied to light, his was tied to darkness. I understood why he'd chosen to stay ignorant, why he wanted to know nothing about the origins of his own power, and why he had some trepidation about me learning the origins of mine.

"I see you're still wearing that necklace I gave you," he said, changing the subject.

I straightened, giving him a second look. "Yeah," I agreed, thrown off by his abruptness. Embarrassment crept up the back of my neck and heated my cheeks.

"Good." He took a sip of his wine, eyes trained on the piece of jewelry resting against my collarbone. "It's a fitting piece for a creature as strong as you."

Chills ravaged my body, his words feeling eerily familiar. I inclined my head towards him, trying to break through his shields and read whatever cryptic thoughts were circling in that mind of his. But as always, he remained closed off, guarded, unrelenting.

"What are you doing here, Vander?" I almost didn't voice the question. Almost made myself shut up because I didn't want to give him a reason to walk away. But I couldn't help the curiosity taking over me. He'd been all over the place as of late, by my side one minute, gone the next. Moody as ever, but this side—the one here where he was just almost letting himself exist beside me, with me—it was so hard to keep watching it recede.

He looked at me like he could read every single one of my thoughts. Maybe he could. There was practically nothing I could keep hidden from him, if he wanted to know it. Which made it that much harder to understand why he kept doing this. Why, if he knew how it made me feel, he kept choosing to hurt me.

"It's been a long day," he said after a beat of silence. He averted his gaze, his jaw feathering in the firelight as his throat bobbed. "And you need some rest." He rose suddenly, my body practically falling forward at his sudden absence on the sofa.

Endless questions circled in my mind, begging me to keep pushing, to not let him walk away again. But the wine was clouding my thoughts, swirling in my belly and making my limbs feel too heavy. And with each passing moment he was retreating, forcing that ever-present space between us. I couldn't find the will to argue, trapped in a daze as I rose from the sofa and made my way over to the bed.

He didn't follow, just stayed beside the fire and watched as I tucked myself into the warmth of the covers. I watched him for a moment through hazy eyes, as he settled into an armchair opposite the sofa. He picked up a book from an end table, flipping it open and pretending to read.

"You know," I called out, my words slurred with either the effects of the wine or my own exhaustion. "One of these days, you're going to have to learn to actually sleep beside me."

He hummed from his spot beside the fire, eyes trained on the book as he flipped through its pages. I drifted between worlds, falling into unconsciousness as the sight of his glowing skin in the firelight drifted through my dreams. His presence crept into my mind, mixing and melting with the dancing flames and growing shadows as I ventured into a different realm entirely.

Somewhere in that half-sleep I could feel the tether loosening, opening, as if Vander could let his guard down finally. Just at the edge of unconsciousness, before the black overtook my being, I heard his voice echoing in my mind.

You deserve more than I can give, little spitfire.

I awoke with a start, remnants of a nightmare clinging to my skin. My breath was heavy as I looked around my room, trying to orient myself. Vander was curled up by the fire in his wolven form, sound asleep.

I forced slow, deep breaths into my lungs as I reminded myself I was safe and it had just been a dream. Despite all my training so far, and the clear terror I felt whenever Kahlis infiltrated my dreams, I could never shake the eerie uncertainty that he had somehow been there, watching. I pushed off the bed and took an extra dose of Aerie's potion, just in case.

I looked to where Vander still lay fast asleep, and decided to not wake him. It was so rare for him to truly get a moment of rest. Between his hunts in the Dark Woods and looking after me, he deserved all the rest he could get.

I pushed the bedroom door open, slipping out into the hallway before letting it latch softly behind me. My lack of appetite during the previous day had left me absolutely famished tonight. I made my way softly down the hallway and to the floor below, in hopes that I'd come across some sort of late-night snack to hold me over till morning.

The lighting was dim on the first floor, the rest of the house having gone to bed hours ago. I must have been the only one awake. The thought was comforting, knowing I'd escape any prying eyes.

I tiptoed into the kitchen, making quick work of finding a bit of bread and jam and some hard cheese. I made myself a small plate, then snuck through the darkness to the den across the hall.

"Oh," I called out, louder than I'd intended to. A figure sat tucked away at a small tea table in the corner of the den, shuffling what appeared to be a deck of cards. "I'm sorry, I didn't mean to disturb you. I figured everyone would be asleep at this hour." I backed up a step, preparing to take my plate back up to my room.

"Nonsense," the melodic voice called out. "Join me, won't you?"

I hesitated a moment, dread filling my gut at the idea of sitting with an absolute stranger in the dark recesses of an unfamiliar house. But something drew me in, my feet moving of their own volition as I found a seat beside the alluring creature.

In this close proximity, I could see them a bit clearer. They were draped in cloth like the priestesses were accustomed to wearing, but there was an air of familiarity about them.

"I see that piece found its way to you, after all."

I tilted my head, peering into the darkness to get a better look at them. My hand absent-mindedly went to the new weight against my neck, my fingers outlining the crescent moon.

It clicked into place all at once. The vendor from the market, the one Vander must have purchased the necklace from. The one I'd spoken to that day, who'd told me the necklace was meant for me.

"You're a priestess?" I asked, astounded.

She hummed her agreement, continuing the steady rhythm of shuffling the deck of cards in her hand. She gathered the cards in both hands, bringing them down against the table.

Tap. Tap. Tap.

Then raised them again, bending the two sides of the deck together until they folded into a new order in her hands.

"I enjoy jewelry making, and Vesper has allowed me to travel to nearby villages to sell my creations on market days. When I have a collection to share, that is."

Tap. Tap. Tap.

She leaned forward, lowering her gravelly voice. "It allows for the opportunity to gather gossip. Happenings in other tribes and other towns. And Vesper is nothing if not a glutton for gossip." She threw me a wink, one I could barely distinguish beneath the shadows of her hooded robes, and leaned back in her chair as she shuffled the cards once more.

"While you're here—" *Tap. Tap. Tap.* "Would you like me to do a reading for you?"

I watched her shuffle the cards once more. I'd read of the tools the moon tribe used for their mysticism. But I had never experienced them firsthand. Did I want her to look into my future? To see my fortune? Something about the impending information had me on edge.

Still, there was a certain layer of intrigue. Just as there had been when Vesper had shown me the Cosmos the previous night. Just as there had been in the archives today, after finding the book about the Divine. Something about this place, their magic: it drew me in, made me incapable of turning away.

I nodded wordlessly, anticipation building in my gut.

The priestess' mouth curled up into an unsettling grin.

Tap. Tap. Tap.

She broke the cards into three even decks, placing them before me and motioning for me to take a card off each. I did as she instructed, laying the cards out on the table between us.

"Ah, the Goddess." She picked up the middle card, holding it out for me to see. A painting of an ethereal being stared back at me, her palms outstretched, her body levitating above the ground as her robes of silk flowed in the air around her. She looked powerful, intimidating. "But then again, we already knew this, didn't we?" Magic sparked in her eyes, a sudden silvery glow beneath her hood, causing me to stifle a gasp.

"Your magic is powerful. I knew it from the first time I laid eyes on you." She tapped her nails idly against the card as she turned it over in her hand. "But it would do you well to keep in mind that you are not the first of your kind. The magic that courses through your veins is ancient, cloaked in scandal and history. It is to be respected. Tread carefully as you explore the limits of your power... or lack thereof."

I swallowed hard. As much as I wanted to discover these powers, it was also terrifying. That level of power, of responsibility, it shook me to my core trying to imagine how to tame such a thing.

She moved on to the next card, turning it around to look at it for a minute, humming in mindful consideration. She turned it back to me at last.

"Discord," she stated simply, showing me the creature painted on the card. Deep red eyes stared back at me, surrounded only by a mask of bone and shadow. Two long horns adorned its head, twisting skyward in a sickening fashion. Disjointed and broken limbs surrounded the being, making my stomach turn with their obscene appearance. Its head was canted to the side, as if the creature was taking me in through the painting. I shivered under its scrutiny, forcing my eyes away from the card.

"A monster worse than death. Death is final, definite. Discord, however... Discord is an entity that is ever-changing. It haunts and possesses, ruining the purest of intentions and paths." She laid the card down next to the goddess, her fingers lingering as she watched me carefully. "Be careful, my goddess. For the Cosmos are warning you."

I folded my arms over my chest, rubbing my bare skin to chase away the chill that refused to settle. I was feeling suddenly regretful for giving her permission to do a reading. I'd been right to be weary. But there was one card left, and something in me remained spellbound, as if my soul was stuck to the chair when my physical body wanted to leave. I needed to know what came next.

"My, my," she chirped, the sudden uptick in her low voice making me jump. Her eyes drifted from the card to me; they crept over my body in silent assessment.

"What is it?' I asked, my impatience growing unbearable. I peered across the table, trying to get a glimpse of the card tucked between her fingers.

She waited a moment longer, clicking her tongue as she set the card down at last.

"The Match."

I took in the image on the card, divided directly across the middle. One side depicted a bright shining sun, full of golden rays, set against a vibrant blue sky. The other side was plunged in the darkness of night, a deep purple, crescent moon sitting against a black velvet sky, a scattering of stardust shining brightly in its beams. I sucked in a breath. The likeness of the image to the ink marking my palms was uncanny.

"This card is often depicted as a sign of mates, mistakenly known as *the Lovers*." She paused, her eyes watchful. "But more skilled readers know it can have many different meanings. A match of power, of purpose. The card shows two equal sides of the same coin."

"But that seems like it would be good, right? A match means you've found your counterpart." I tried to make sense of what she was saying, to explain away the dread building within me.

"Correct," she went on, laying the card down amongst the other two I'd drawn. "But as pure and beautiful as a true match can be, it can also be a curse. The realms' history is littered with tragic stories of creatures meeting their true match, and time and time again history has proven how devastating those stories can be."

My stomach plummeted, my body breaking out in a cold sweat. "But why? If they are a true match, why would it end in tragedy?"

"That kind of unchecked power can only end two ways." She pulled another card from the deck, an image of a path diverting in two different directions. "It's seen as a threat to the rest of the world, a threat to both entities involved. And while that kind of power can manifest into something beautiful"—she pointed to one of the paths on the card—"it can also become the opposite." Her boney finger slid over the card to the other path, tapping carefully against it. "Power isn't always a blessing, my goddess." She bowed her head in apology.

"No, that can't be true. There has to be a way to make it work." I took in the cards lying before me, desperation choking my words. "Right?"

"Of course," she hummed. "There's always the possibility of balance." She drew another card; this time an image of a perfectly balanced golden scale greeted me. "A perfect match can only succeed in total balance. Take your dear friends, for example."

I narrowed my gaze on her, trying to understand who she meant.

"The chieftain and his lovely fae wife. They are an example of perfect balance. Fated mates who understood how to meet their match and make it work, how to balance power and respect and love."

I breathed a sigh of relief. I had always known their love was something special, something to be sought after. But the differences between Vander and his brother were striking. Panic crept into my chest as I worried if Vander and I would ever be able to find that balance... if we'd ever be able to achieve what Bastian and Aerie had. Or if we were doomed to a lifetime of tragedy.

The priestess reached out, patting my hand and offering me the Match card.

"It will be fine, my goddess. The Cosmos would not write your story into existence if they did not have a purpose for it. Take this as a warning, a reminder of what could come to pass. But also as hope for the happiness you could be destined to find as well, should you take heed."

She rose to her feet, her thick robes swaying around her as she gathered the rest of the deck and moved to leave the den. "Remember," she said, laying a hand against my shoulder as she passed. "A true match is a powerful phenomenon. Don't take it lightly and don't take it for granted. As long as you follow your heart, I'm sure you will be fine, my dear."

And with that she was gone, the only sound through the house was the swaying of her robes as she made her way down the hallway.

I sat for a long time, staring down at the card she'd left for me. The Match. It had to mean something that its depiction was the exact images inked onto my palms. I laid my hands on the table, palms up to compare the images. It was too similar to be a coincidence. Too haunting to not mean something more.

It was motivation, inspiration to find out who I was. To make things work with Vander. Because now that I was staring down at the possibility of our future, the two paths diverging before us, I understood the weight of our bond. And the possible repercussions if we continued on the path we were on.

"Hazel." My head snapped up, bewildered to find Vander rushing into the den, Bastian quick behind him. "Thank the Fates, I didn't know where you'd gone."

Vander stopped short as I stood, as if holding himself back from wrapping me in his embrace.

"I'm fine, Vander," I promised as I looked over his shoulder to Bastian. Both he and Vander looked crazed, wide-eyed and worried. "I just couldn't sleep. What's wrong?"

"Vesper needs us," Bastian answered for him. I looked back to Vander, searching his face in an attempt to understand the worry ravaging his features.

"There's been an attack on one of Sgàil's bordering villages."

CHAPTER 16
VANDER

I threw Hazel's rucksack into the back of the wagon, ushering her in quickly. Aerie followed, the girls tucking in close together in the darkness of the night. Nox took his place at the box seat, after assuring Brigid had everything she needed to make the journey home swiftly.

"I still don't like this," I grumbled as Bastian climbed into the wagon, securing Aerie's own rucksack beside her and lifting the hood of her cloak over her head.

"Nor do I, brother," he called down to me. "But if Kahlis' creatures are here, the safest place for them to be is back within our borders—within the warding we've fortified for Hazel."

My eyes cut momentarily to my mate, her head dipping in shame. We'd barely been able to discuss her connection to Kahlis—how her mother's diary had revealed him to be her very own father. Such a revelation was shocking, especially after all the pain and torment she'd experienced at his hand. But it wasn't like I'd exactly been present with her lately, making myself available to discuss such things. And now his creatures were here and I was having to send her off into the night without my protection.

I gritted my teeth, feeling her shame radiate down the tether. I'd been so foolish, focusing on my own issues these past couple weeks rather than being there for her as she processed everything. I'd failed her. Again. It seemed to be a regular occurrence lately, despite that I was doing all of this *for* her.

I turned away from the wagon, clenching my fists as the Mark roiled against my skin and shut out her emotion. I needed to silence it before it consumed me and I followed them into the woods with unmovable determination, abandoning Vesper and my brother to fight on their own.

"We'll be fine," I heard Aerie reassure Bastian behind me.

"I'll guard them with my life. I promise." There was no usual tone of humor in Nox's words, which only made my dread deepen. Nothing about this felt right. Not Hazel and Aerie leaving, not us staying to help Vesper. I couldn't give two fucks about the moon tribe. Not when it was separating me from Hazel. Not when it meant I had to choose between protecting them or protecting her.

The wagon shifted behind me as Bastian climbed out. I turned around, searching desperately for a reason to make them stay.

Aerie leaned forward, planting a kiss on Bastian's temple. "Be careful," she whispered, loud enough that I could hear it too.

Lennox cracked the reins and Brigid started off in a slow trot. I followed the path of the wagon, reaching my hand out to find

Hazel's at the last minute. She quickly grabbed it, squeezing hard before letting my fingers slip through hers as the wagon picked up speed. She kept her eyes on me, looking over her shoulder until she disappeared into the night.

"Come on, brother. Keeping those Daeomi distracted is the best thing we can do for them now. Vesper is waiting for us." Bastian turned back to the chieftain's home.

I stayed a moment longer, watching the path the wagon had traveled, staring hard at the spot it had disappeared into the fog. I wanted to send my shadows after them, let them follow her home and wrap her in their safety until I returned. But with this kind of distance, I knew it would be futile.

The wind shifted around me, forcing a growl from my throat as the Mark sensed Kahlis' presence further south. I ground my teeth together, shutting down any feelings of fear or trepidation as I turned to follow Bastian. Bitterness took over me, rage and hate filling the void that was left in my mind.

Maybe we didn't know how to stop Kahlis once and for all, but I didn't mind experimenting on his Daeomi when they were foolish enough to sneak over Tir Nadaar's borders. I'd let them know the pain of crossing the Shadow of the Grimm.

I caught up to Bastian as he pushed hastily into the barn behind Vesper's estate. The moon tribe chieftain was indeed waiting for us, along with a handful of his priestesses. They appeared different from the priestesses we'd met before, seemingly well trained in combat and ready for battle. They still donned variations of the typical white robes, but theirs acted more as cloaks, draping over their shoulders and leaving their limbs free to fight. Harnesses were strapped to each of their chests, containing an assortment of daggers, and a broadsword hung against each of their hips. I made eye contact with the one closest to Vesper, grunting in approval as I took the reins of the horse Vesper held in his hand.

We wasted no time with small talk as Vesper gave Bastian another horse, quickly mounting and riding out together. Vesper had explained when he'd woken us that his scouts had reported to him in the midst of the night, claiming the distant village was under an unusual black smoke. They'd heard muffled screams, and rode back immediately for reinforcements. I hated feeling like we were entering the situation blind, as if this was some sort of trap. But I could sense Kahlis was close—knew he was near. And I wouldn't waste an opportunity to show him just how much hatred there was in my soul for him.

It didn't take us long to arrive, affirming in my mind that sending the girls home was most likely the better alternative. Knowing how close they'd been to Hazel... I was just grateful they hadn't discovered her presence here.

Vesper was silent on the ride, revealing a part of him I hadn't been willing to accept before. In this light, he reminded me so much of my brother. Despite his decades of service to his tribe, he was still a terrified chieftain, hurting for his people. The thought had me turning my head back to the path before us, my mind at war as I tried to continue justifying my hatred for the male.

"It's just ahead," Vesper called out. He slowed his horse as another grouping of stone dwellings became visible through the thick fog. This one seemed a bit more sparse than the others had been, laid out on both sides of the border and scattering into the forest beyond.

There was a shocking lack of movement, an utter silence as we entered the village. My shadows reached out, sensing the energy. My hackles raised as I surveyed the land. Bastian was beside me in an instant, doing the same.

"Something's not right," he said under his breath to me.

Vesper joined us, dismounting from his horse as his warrior priestesses waited for his command.

"I don't understand. My scouts said there'd been an attack, but the village looks untouched." Vesper stepped towards the first row of stone dwellings.

"Vesper, wait!" Bastian's words broke out across the air, too loud for the eerie silence in the village, but I understood his warning immediately.

A thick, black mist appeared, creeping along the mossy ground towards Vesper. He looked back at us, tilting his head in confusion, only to scream out in agony as the mist grasped his legs.

Bastian and I dismounted immediately, followed by the priestesses, but too late. The mist overtook Vesper, raising his body in the air. His back arched, his arms splayed wide as it ravaged him, plumes of the mist wrapping around his body and constricting him. Inky black veins slithered over his exposed skin. His eyes went black and empty as the mist possessed him, claimed him.

And the darkness in me smiled.

It was the briefest of moments, a surge of excitement at seeing the male that had touched my mate being overcome by something so evil. Though I had little time to consider its meaning as my instincts took over, my shadows growing around me as I raised my hands and called my power forward to fight the mist. Bastian did the same, calling on his tribal power to raise rock and root in an attempt to suppress the obsidian smoke.

I could feel its energy, its darkness as it recognized my own. It lashed out at us, licking at our hands and dancing around our feet as if taunting us—unimpressed and unthreatened by our power. I sent a new wave of shadows into the mist, suffocating the magic and expelling it into the ground below.

It just kept coming, growing thicker and angrier the more we fought. It wanted Vesper, and would stop at nothing to claim him fully.

One of the priestesses came up beside me, pushing back her cloak and calling upon her magic. "You keep fighting the mist, covering us. We'll focus our energy on the chieftain."

I nodded, cutting a quick glance to Bastian to make sure he'd heard. He nodded his agreement, kneeling low and thrusting his hands into the thick moss below. The ground shook in answer, rumbling with the power and reverence due to a tribal chieftain of Tir Nadaar.

I turned my attention back to the mist, closing my eyes for the briefest of moments as I called on the power of the Mark. I felt the darkness spark to life within me, taking over my control fully. My shadows grew tenfold, hungrier and darker than before.

Bastian and I attacked in unison, our magic cutting through the mist where it still grasped Vesper. The priestesses raised their hands towards their chieftain, focusing their power on him. Vesper's eyes shot open, a silvery glow overtaking the empty black.

We fought together, my brother and I pushing forward with each blast of our power. Vesper cried out once more, fighting with his own power to break the mist's hold on his body and mind. Bastian shouted to him, urging him to keep fighting.

Three more blasts of power, of my shadows strangling the mist and forcing it down to be swallowed by the earth below, and Vesper was free. His body fell to the ground, lost in a fit of coughs and cries as he regained control over himself, forcing out the last of the mist that had possessed him.

We were beside him in an instant, along with his priestesses, providing him cover as he scrambled to his feet. I tried to assess his state, to see what kind of damage had been done, when more mist broke forth. My arms strained with the strength of my power flowing from my palms. Wave after wave of shadow stretched before me, wrestling with the mist in an effort to keep it from touching us.

"Any ideas here, Bastian?" I called out.

"Get down!" Vesper shouted, rising to his feet in the midst of our makeshift circle.

"What?" I shouted, turning to throw an incredulous look at the chieftain, who was barely able to hold himself up. Power began radiating from him, bright blinding light surging from his fingertips, his chest, his eyes.

"Get down!" he repeated, enunciating the syllables as he stretched his arms out. "And close your eyes!"

I barely had time to obey, crouching as low as I could and throwing an arm around my brother to force him to the ground.

Vesper's power exploded, drenching the mist in the blinding light of the Cosmos. I forced my eyes shut, the light overtaking all within its reach. Even my shadows were extinguished, angering the Mark as it felt the challenge to its power. I peeked out carefully, ensuring the blast was ebbing. Silver sparks rained down from the stars above, as if the sky itself was answering his call.

Then his light dimmed, darkness falling back over the village as the ground swallowed up the power.

I rose to my feet, head on a swivel as I evaluated the area. Any sign of the mist was gone; not even a tendril of its power remained. The others stood, all aghast at the sheer amount of power the chieftain had expelled.

Bastian let out a small chuckle, breathless from the fight. "Well, I'll be damned, Vesper. You're going to have to tell me how you learned to do that little trick."

Vesper laughed along with him, ragged and clearly exhausted. He reached out a hand, patting Bastian on the shoulder. "I'll tell when you do. I'm well aware of the tricks the earth tribe has up their sleeves, and I've been desperate to figure them out."

Bastian smirked, snapping open the harness that sheathed one of his battle axes. He tossed the axe in the air before catching it and holding out the blade for Vesper's inspection. "I'm sure we can think of a couple secrets worth bartering."

"Bastian, I think this is going to be the beginning of a beautiful friendship." Vesper eyed the blade, clearly impressed by the magic he sensed in the etchings.

They draped their arms around each other in camaraderie, breathless in the aftermath of the victory. I rolled my eyes, utterly uninterested in their newfound friendship. Instead, I turned my attention back to the village, peering out into the darkness.

"Not to be the bearer of bad news," I called out. "But I wouldn't start celebrating just yet." I took a step forward, assessing the scene before us. "This is meant to be a village, correct?"

"Obviously," Vesper chuckled, dropping his arm from Bastian's shoulder.

"With people?" I asked, gesturing to the still empty state of the dwellings.

Vesper caught my meaning, all sense of amusement dropping from his eyes. He stepped up beside me, looking through the dark village and noticing the same thing I had. Despite the lack of the mist's presence, the sounds of our battle, no villagers had made an appearance.

"Spread out," Vesper ordered to his priestesses. "Search the dwellings, the grounds."

They did as he said without a moment of hesitation, slinking into the darkness in near silence. Vesper sprinted to the nearest dwelling, throwing open the door and disappearing inside. Bastian and I followed him, but he was recoiling back through the doorway before we could enter.

"What is it?" Bastian asked.

Vesper stumbled past us, turning to the side and folding at the waist before unloading the contents of his stomach onto the mossy ground. I didn't wait for him to collect himself enough to explain. I pushed past Bastian as he pivoted towards Vesper, pushing open the door and peering into the dark room within.

My eyes went wide at the carnage I found. The dwelling itself was no more than a single open room, a hearth and stove on one side, several pallets laid out on the other. But as my eyes adjusted to the dark, I realized the family that slept atop the masses of blankets and pillows wasn't asleep at all.

Their eyes were open wide, infected with the same black that had claimed Vesper's in the mist. Their skin was overtaken with the inky veining of the sinister magic, limbs jutting out and bent in sickening directions. Silent, frozen screams were affixed on their faces, capturing their final moments of agony as the mist overtook them.

I stepped back, breath heavy as I looked down at the ground before me. My mind was reeling, my anger growing with each breath I took. I turned and ran to the next stone dwelling several feet away, pausing a moment as I laid my hand against the doorknob. My jaw stiffened as I pushed the door open, knowing I'd find the same haunting scene within.

I moved onto the next, and the next. Each house infected by the mist, each family lost to its power. It made no discrimination as it overtook the village. The elderly, the innocent, the too fucking young to have experienced such a terrible fate. They were all gone.

The Mark pounded behind my eyes, rage boiling my blood as I returned to where Bastian was aiding Vesper.

"They're all gone," I huffed out, realizing a second too late how my words might affect Vesper. "We have to find the priestesses," I urged, turning to look for any that may have returned. "This is a trap."

A slow clap pierced through the silent village. I hunched down, ready to attack.

A tall, slender form slunk through the shadows between dwellings, revealing himself to us. In his mutated form, he stood a whole head taller than the three of us, his oily pitch-black skin glistening under the starlight, stretched too tight over his bony frame.

"Well done, Grimm," he praised, smiling wide to reveal a row of razor-sharp teeth. "I thought perhaps you'd be the difficult one to fool. These others were too easy to bait out here."

He stopped a few paces from us, several more of his kind appearing with the priestesses trapped in their grasp.

"But not you." He wagged his long finger my way.

"Let them go," Vesper called out. He wiped the back of his hand over his mouth, straightening and readying his power. But I could tell his reservoirs were more than drained after the effort it took to expel the mist and break through its hold.

The Daeomi must have sensed it too, his tongue clicking against his teeth in a tsk-ing noise. "Now, now, chieftain. It seems as if your power is dwindling after that whole debacle." The Daeomi waved his hand towards the air where Vesper had been strung out just minutes ago. "Such a shame."

"I have more than enough remaining to take out you and your friends," Vesper shouted, angling his body to charge the Daeomi. Bastain laid a hand against his chest, holding him back.

The Daeomi laughed, catching the motion with his penetrating obsidian eyes. "I'm not sure your counterpart agrees with you!"

I stepped up to make myself even with Vesper, in an effort to help Bastian hold him back.

"You, however..." The Daeomi leveled his gaze at me. "You may actually present the most delicious kind of challenge."

I sneered, letting my shadows unfurl from my palms. "You'll be wishing you'd taken on his threats by the time I'm done with you."

The Daeomi stopped, piercing me with a soulless glare. "I think I'd rather take on that little plaything you've been hiding from my master."

My muscles bristled at the threat, primal instinct threatening to take over.

Bastian's hushed voice brought me back. "Vesper and I will go after the two behind, freeing their hold on the priestesses. On my count, okay?"

"Rumor has it she shares blood with the Dark One." The Daeomi continued his taunting. "She'd been so enticing before, when my brother sliced into her upon her return and the call of her magic rang through our fold. Now that we know the master's blood flows through her veins? His magic? She's fucking irresistible."

Memories of a different day floated slowly back to me, of another Daeomi encounter—one where I'd barely made it to Hazel in time. The day she returned to me, and the day Kahlis had been lucky enough to collect her blood for whatever dark magic he'd performed against her, to ensnare her mind.

The Daeomi must be connected, then. I cursed as the realization hit me. With as expendable as they were to Kahlis, it made sense. They were nothing more than a hoard of darkness. Cattle being led to the slaughter, easily replaced when need be. But they were connected, a detail we had yet to realize. When one felt something, they all felt it.

I deepened my stance, readying myself to fight and praying to the Fates that their pain echoed through the horde, not just their pleasure. Bastian adjusted his grip on his battle axes, finally letting go of Vesper.

The Daeomi licked his obsidian lips, the white of his fanged teeth glinting in the bits of moonlight that broke through the clouds. "I can't wait to *taste* it when I rip into her flesh."

Fuck Bastian's count.

I lunged forward, throwing myself against the Daeomi. He laughed as I tackled him to the ground, summoning his claws and thrusting his fist towards me.

"Fucking Fates, Vander," I heard Bastian swear from somewhere behind me. He and Vesper rushed forward, on the other two Daeomi instantly. "I thought I said wait for my count!"

Still on top of the Daeomi, I grabbed his wrist as he tried to attack again and snapped the three pronged claws from his knuckles. Black blood sprayed my face, coating me in the foul, sticky liquid. I sprang to my feet, stomping hard on his throat before cutting a look over to Bastian who had landed a battle axe directly in a Daeomi's skull.

"Count faster next time," I shot back, tossing the claws still in my hand to the side. The Daeomi's wails turned to hysterical laughter. A wave of his magic knocked me backwards in my momentary distraction, his wings unfurling to lift him to his feet before me.

He lunged at me, his claws having already regenerated from the fist I'd ripped them from. I cursed under my breath as I rolled to the side and scrambled to my feet, assessing the others. Bastian and Vesper had been successful in freeing the other priestesses, their sheer numbers quickly taking over the rest of the Daeomi.

"Drain them!" I called out, reminding Bastian of the one sure way we knew to defeat these creatures, before returning my attention to the Daeomi before me, circling him. His features screwed up in hatred as he watched my movements, waiting for his moment to strike.

"I should have given you more credit." The sound of his voice was as slick as oil. He spit a mouthful of black blood to the dirt below, dragging a hand over his lip from the blow I'd landed. "How did you learn that little trick?"

"This isn't the first time your kind has threatened my *mate.*" I smirked. "Turns out being territorial has revealed some advantages. Like finding out ways to claim your life."

I urged my magic forward just as he pushed off the ground. His wings unfurled again, but my shadows were faster, wrapping around the expansive area and shredding the delicate, thin flesh.

He tumbled in the air, falling to the ground as his cries of agony broke through the small village. But it only spurred him on as he advanced again, his wings dragging in ruins behind him.

"I will gut you for that, fucking dog!" His fist shot out, claws bared as he swept across my body. I dodged backwards, missing the first blow. But his other hand was right behind, catching me off balance from the first attempt. His claws sliced into my arm, ripping through flesh and muscle. I roared in pain, grabbing at the wound.

My eyes narrowed on him, shifting to their primal form. Blinding rage overtook me as he laughed, watching me fight against the monster always hidden within.

"That's it, *Grimm*, show us who you really are. Tell me, does your mate know all those dirty little thoughts that slink their way through your mind?"

I jutted forward, trying to attack with my one good arm. He dodged it easily, sniggering as he watched.

"Does your family know how deep that well of darkness within you really is? You're no different from us, *dog*. I can sense it, sense your darkness. My own recognizes it, festering inside of you. The only difference is I know how to own it. And you refuse to." He reached out, letting more of that black mist snake forward. "Which gives *me* the upper hand."

The mist bit at my feet, wrapping around my wound and seeping into my skin. I shook my head, fighting its hold as I lunged forward again. I landed my blow this time, shoving the creature before me to the ground. Still, his mist wrapped around me.

"Vander," Bastian called from somewhere behind me. "Hold on, I'm coming."

"No!" I shouted, my voice sounding more wolven than mortal. "He's mine. No one touches him."

"That's what I like to hear." The Daeomi smiled up at me, his sinister grin reaching from ear to ear. "Show me what all those rumors speaking of the Shadow of the Grimm are really about. Prove them right."

I took his bait, letting the Mark take over fully. The dark power was a rush of relief through my veins as it worked to heal my arm and fuel my power. I took several steps forward, feeling the shift in my bones as my primal form came to life.

I let out a guttural sound as my body morphed from mortal to wolven, my vision homing in on the bleeding and crumpled form on the ground before me. I attacked, leaping onto his body without a second thought. My vision went white with rage, hearing his laughter and nothing else. It surrounded me, penetrated me, as the mist fought to possess me.

But the Mark welcomed its darkness, pushing it out and turning it on the very creature that had summoned it. He fought hard, but I fought harder, unleashing every bit of rage and anger shoved deep within me onto his form. My teeth tore through black, oily flesh. The rotten taste of Daeomi blood flooded my senses.

Still, I pushed further, tearing limbs from his body and letting my own claws rip through what remained of his wings, his stomach, his throat. I let the Mark fuel me, accepting its influence and leaning into its darkness—deeper than I ever had before. Anything I could thrash and tear and make bleed, I did. Every slash, every bite, it was for those innocent lives he'd taken tonight, for my own tribe members I'd lost in this war, for my mate, who'd been subjected to a lifetime of terror at her father's hand.

My world became nothing besides hot, black blood.

I bathed in it, becoming one with the Mark as I shredded the creature beneath me and let my darkness drink its fill.

"Vander." Bastian's voice broke through my trance, but the anger within me was so strong, possessive in its own right. I didn't want to listen to my brother. I didn't want to stop.

"Vander," he tried again. His presence was closer, his power reaching out steadily to try and ease my own. "It's okay, brother. It's done."

I clamped my muzzle around the Daeomi's neck, tearing his throat out at last, before stumbling backwards.

Bastian caught me, my body transforming back into my mortal form. I looked around the village, wild-eyed as I recognized the others around me.

The priestesses looked shocked, terrified. I could only imagine the image I had given them, was still giving them now as my naked form faced them, soaked in the thick, black blood of my enemy.

I brushed off Bastian's grasp, spitting out a mouthful of blood and flesh and tendons.

My breath was ragged as I looked at the Daeomi bodies littering the ground. Vesper and Bastian had taken care of the others, with the help of the priestesses. Bodies splayed out in pools of the deep black blood. But entirely whole. I looked back to the Daeomi I had claimed. He was unrecognizable. An absolutely demolished pile of blood and bone and battered, shredded flesh.

I closed my eyes, letting out a deep sigh as I felt the Mark retreat to that distant place I always kept it hidden.

"It's alright, Vander." Bastian laid a hand on my shoulder. I brushed it off again, turning around and taking the cloak he offered with an outstretched hand.

"I know it's alright," I spat back, using the cloak to wipe my face before letting it fall to the ground. "He deserved every bit of what he got." I strode past Vesper and the others, pausing momentarily to lock eyes with him. "You wanted to see if the rumors were true? How are we feeling now, chieftain? Still want this monster protecting your borders?"

Vesper watched me for a moment longer, darting a glance back at the pool of remains behind me, considering. "Your services, though unorthodox, have saved my tribe." He reached out a hand, though more tentative than when he'd offered it before. "And you saved my life. For that, I owe you my eternal gratitude."

I grunted, brushing past him, refusing to return the handshake.

"It's been an honor," he called out after me. His words gave me pause, stalling my footsteps. "It's been an honor to fight alongside the Shadow of the Grimm."

I looked back, just enough to see him put a fist to his chest as he kneeled before me. The priestesses followed the motion immediately, despite the fear still laced in their eyes. I cut a look over to Bastian. His eyes were heavy with somber understanding. He straightened his shoulders, bowing his permission for me to leave.

I gritted my teeth, uncomfortable with the darkness I'd just revealed, before shifting to my wolven form and taking off into the early twilight of dawn.

CHAPTER 17
HAZEL

Aerie and I sat opposite one another on the sofas in the sitting room, a fire blazing in the hearth despite the warm weather outside. Aerie's magical fires always seemed to keep the room at the perfect temperature, burning brighter in the colder months and calmer in the heat of the summer.

Nox had done as he'd promised and returned us home, safe and sound. Both he and Kirwan were just outside the Estate, keeping an eye out for anything suspicious. Nox had been thorough to make sure we weren't followed during our journey home, but I could tell he was still concerned. With the threat of Kahlis feeling so tangible, all of us were on edge.

Kirwan had been waiting for us, already aware of the threat at hand—thanks to their odd twin magic. He informed Nox that he'd gone around double-checking all the warding and sent word to the tribe members to be on high alert.

Nox had ushered us inside, instructing us to stay there and wait for Bastian's return. They'd keep watch outside and make sure no other visitors made an appearance.

We settled into the sitting room for the night, reading in quiet silence. Aerie held the tome Vesper allowed her to bring back with us. She went over it in great detail, referencing one or two other books she'd grabbed from the library upon our return.

I'd grabbed my mother's diary from my chambers before taking up my spot on the sofa. I'd already read the whole thing front to back at least six times, and aside from the bit about Kahlis being my father, there wasn't a whole lot of useful information within its pages. Mostly just a lot of cryptic apologies from my mother and explanations for her ability to fall for such a vile male. I didn't care for her reasoning... but seeing her handwriting, reading of her thoughts and feelings during my younger years, always eased something within me.

Aerie had offered to make us some food, but neither of us had much of an appetite. Unable to admit to one another what we were waiting for, we sat together as the dread built within each of us and the hour turned later and later. I looked out the window of the sitting room, unsure of the time. The early morning light was chasing away the darkness of the night. I told myself their journey would be a long one, that the hour meant nothing in terms of their safety.

Aerie's movement pulled my attention from the window as she made her way over to the far side of the sitting room. A wall of inset shelves lined the other side of the hearth and she perused them quietly, letting her fingers trail over each trinket until they landed on what she was looking for. She plucked a small golden box off one of the lower shelves.

Making her way back over to the sofa, she opened its lid gingerly and wound the key on the back several times. She set the box down on an end table as a steady stream of music filled the room.

"I hope you don't mind." She offered a small smile. "It just felt too quiet in here. I'm afraid my nerves are getting the better of me."

I returned her smile, looking in wonder at the small music box I hadn't noticed before.

"It's beautiful," I said, having completely abandoned my reading to take in the soft music.

"It's always reminded me of something my mother used to hum to me." Aerie closed her eyes, as if drifting off to some far away world.

Aerie rarely spoke of her past life. Even less of a mother. I wanted to ask more, to take advantage of the small window of opportunity she'd given me. But watching her in this peace, I couldn't interrupt it.

A few moments passed with nothing more than the delicate melody drifting between us.

"I didn't know her," Aerie finally offered. I scooted closer to where Aerie sat, leaning in to listen as she told me her story. "My father was a cruel male. He took her from me at such a young age. Once she'd given birth to me, I suppose she'd served her purpose. I still don't even know what happened to her. But every now and then, little streams of memories find their way to me—from that brief time we had together."

Her body swayed as she let the music envelop us. "Her scent, the caress of her hand on my face." Her eyes drifted open as she looked down to the music box. "And this one song she used to hum to me as an infant. Any chance she could get."

I leaned back, mimicking her movements as I also closed my eyes and soaked in the melody filling the space. In utter awe of the way it stilled the panic within me.

"Sometimes, I pull this out when I'm overwhelmed with the pain of all I have lost." Aerie's voice flowed with the melodic sound, only acting to complement it as she spoke. "You'd think it would make me upset, the reminder of her loss. But it doesn't feel like that. It feels like a reminder of the love and light that can live on—long after loss."

I knew now that we weren't just talking about her mother. Maybe on some level we were, but I couldn't stop my thoughts as they turned to Mirren. As if she sensed the shift, she added, "I would play this often for her, when she was a child. It was one of the only things that calmed her on those long, restless nights. She must have used it recently, because I found it tucked away in her room when I..." Her words trailed off, her eyes fluttering closed.

She didn't have to finish them. I knew she'd been going through Mirren's things, tidying up the room to remove those personal belongings so it would be ready for another, if necessary. I couldn't imagine the pain she felt while cleaning up the last few remnants of Mirren's existence in this world. Her last mark of the joy and peace that had radiated through her.

I sat up at the abrupt sound of the side door in the kitchen. Bastian emerged, his sudden presence in the Estate startling me. I'd been so distracted with Aerie's voice and the music that I hadn't even heard them return. He made his way into the sitting room, over to where Aerie sat. He was covered in splatters and stains of a black substance, and exhaustion ravaged his features. But from what I could tell, he was whole.

His movements were slow, on time with the melody of the music, as if he understood its significance. Tears now stained Aerie's cheeks, but she didn't move to turn off the music box, didn't move to wipe them away. She sat with her grief, letting every thought and every emotion wash over her. Welcoming it.

I sat motionless, in awe before her.

Bastian nodded to me, kneeling beside where Aerie sat. He took her hand in his and reached his other out to cradle her face. She didn't flinch at all at the motion, but rather leaned into it and let out a shuddering breath—as if she'd known of his return without even opening her eyes.

He pulled her up, swallowing her in his embrace. His broad arms held her as she continued to let her grief be felt. I could hear her cries now, the pain and care and love and endurance in each soft sob and ragged breath. The music played on and Bastian swayed with its notes, dancing with his mate as she broke in his arms.

Bastian crooked his head to the side, motioning to me that Vander was just behind him. I closed my eyes as relief flooded my system—tears threatening to spill past my own lashes.

I set my book down tenderly as I moved to leave them in this intimate moment, wanting to give them space. I looked back at Bastian as I approached the edge of the sitting room. He nodded to me once more, as if to say *I've got her*. It was all the confirmation I needed as I padded down the hall, letting the drifting music carry me further into the Estate.

The soft melody rang throughout the house, as if propelled by Aerie's magic. Before I knew where I was going, I found myself within the library. Its sight was a welcome comfort as I felt the weight of grief burdening me. I wanted to go find Vander, to feel him beneath my touch as confirmation that he was okay and thank the Fates for keeping him safe. But despite that desire building deep within me, I wanted to make him come to me—to prove he was ready.

For me, for this. It felt necessary to have him make that call.

I wrapped my arms around myself, circling the space as my eyes roamed the vast library shelves.

Not circling, no. *Dancing*. The melody moved through my body, igniting my bones as I pictured the joy on sweet Mirren's face any time she listened to the music box. Our trip to the moon tribe had been a momentary relief from her memories, but now that we were back within the Estate's walls, it had all come rushing back.

Damn, I missed her.

It wasn't fair that she'd been the one taken from us. This wasn't her fight. Every day since I'd watched Kahlis take her life before me, I couldn't help one singular thought echoing through my mind.

It should have been me.

That day haunted me. Watching helplessly as Mirren's pain-filled screams rang out through the Dark Woods. Sensing Arlo's presence disappear into the Rift as he let go of my grasp. Yet, it had been me Kahlis wanted. Still wanted. All of them were putting themselves in harm's way, risking so much, just to protect me. There had been so much loss, so much confusion that day. There was still so much I didn't understand. Still so much violence and pain ravaging all of Tir Nadaar. And I couldn't help but feel like it was my job to stop it somehow.

My head began to spin with the weight of it all, my body twirling of its own accord as the music filled me. I could feel it wrestling with the grief in my mind and my heart—trying to snuff it out and overtake it. But I didn't want to let it go. I didn't want it to disappear. I wanted to feel it, because I didn't deserve to be rid of its burden. All of this was my fault and letting go of the grief meant letting go of the guilt. And I couldn't bring myself to do that.

I spun into something solid, unrelenting. Firm, warm hands wrapped around my arms. When I lifted my head to look up through tear-filled eyes, I found Vander's deep golden ones staring back at me.

It's not your fault, little spitfire. His voice was a blanket of calm over the battle waging war in my mind. He didn't let go, didn't allow any space between us. He just held me firm as he fixed his gaze on me. As if to insinuate that he wouldn't relent until I acknowledged his words.

I nodded, turning away as shame heated my cheeks. Still, he wouldn't let me go. Instead he wrapped his arms around me, just as Bastian had for Aerie. He swayed to the music somehow still playing as he held me, letting the steady melody carry us around the library.

Moments passed. Or maybe it was hours. But with each motion, some small part of me healed. Just a little bit. It wasn't perfect or skilled, but it was magical. Him here with me, holding not just me but my grief. I let myself be vulnerable in his arms. Let myself feel every bit of guilt that wracked my mind, every thought of fear and hurt and confusion from my connection to Kahlis. I didn't understand how I could be the daughter of such a vile creature, someone so willing to inflict pain and violence. How my mother could have ever loved such a thing. Why the Divine's magic chose me when I'd come from such a monstrous line of fae power.

Vander's hands skimmed over my skin, the rough feel of his calloused fingers somehow grounding me. I wrapped my arms around him tighter, clinging to him as if my own life depended on it. As if I couldn't let go or he'd be lost to me forever. He planted a soft kiss on my forehead and tucked his chin over me so that my cheek rested against his chest. We danced to the slow rhythm, entirely in our own world.

I realized eventually that the music had long since faded and we moved through the library to some silent melody of our own creation. I slowed my movements, pulling back far enough to look up into his dark, gilded eyes. He was covered in dried blood splatter as well, worse than Bastian had been, and tunic-less. But I could sense no injury from him, no pain other than his usual.

Seeing him here—coated in bloodshed but wholly here and un-harmed—it made everything between us seem somehow so super-ficial. All the bickering and discord we'd been experiencing, none of it mattered now. Some part of me had hoped, had known, he'd make it home to me. His power was too strong to be taken down by a simple Daeomi attack. He'd faced them countless times before, and I knew he'd face them again. But a deeper sense of fear had overcome me, convinced me there was a possibility I'd never see him again.

And now that he was here, I just wanted to push past all the troubles we'd faced. I wanted to have him and for him to have me. To relish in whatever time we had together. Because too much loss had happened already to continue taking for granted what we had. And I'd be damned if we'd waste any more time without one another.

I went up on my tiptoes, stretching to reach his lips as I kissed him. It was soft, intimate. A silent thank you for being here to hold me when my world felt like it was falling apart. For coming back to me when some part of me had feared he wouldn't.

He didn't move, didn't return my gesture with strokes of his own, but he didn't push me away, either. I wondered to myself if it was an invitation to keep going, the small gesture stirring a darker desire low within me. He went eerily still as he let me explore the planes of his face and neck. I pressed more kisses into his heated skin, trailing up his jaw and to his ear, nipping slightly at the tender flesh there.

I would have given anything to know what he was thinking, to feel his response to my movements. But as he so often did, he'd shut me out from the tether. My advances fumbled slightly, my confidence ebbing as I noticed the way he was blocking me out. But I doubled down, refusing to let this go. Perhaps his resolve would break if I kept going, and he'd finally decide to let me in.

I found myself back at his lips, kissing harder and deeper than I had the first time. His taste flooded my senses and I was greedy for more. I clung to him, tightening my grip as he parted his lips for me. His hands had hooked around my waist and I could feel them bunching the material there, clinging for some semblance of control. Behind my closed eyelids, I could sense the room darkening—his shadows growing along with his desire. I could feel his composure was close to breaking.

I reached out through the tether, stroking a soft, subtle hand along the length of the obsidian wall blocking me out. A shudder ran through his body at the motion—his shadows reaching around me instinctually, now working to find somewhere to land. I welcomed the feeling, desperate for more of him in any way I could have him.

He broke away, pulling back so abruptly that I practically stumbled forward. He was across the library in a matter of seconds, his shadows unfurling and stretching in his wake. He was mad—no, he was furious.

I'd gone too far, overstepped. I'd thought perhaps, after everything that happened within the moon tribe, his walls would finally come down. But as he reinforced those boundaries he'd previously set, I found myself scrambling to hold onto what small shed he'd finally exposed.

"Vander I—I'm sorry. I didn't mean to—"

He threw up a hand without meeting my gaze.

"Stop. You have nothing to apologize for, Hazel."

I moved through the library, making my way towards him. But I was met with a black wall of resistance. He was keeping me away, forcing space between us.

"What is it, then?" I hated how desperate my voice sounded, how small and scared it was.

He just shook his head, keeping his eyes trained on the same invisible spot in front of him. His body was rigid, his knuckles turning white with the amount of force he was using to clutch his fists closed. I knew that look, knew it meant he was trying desperately to tamp down on the dark power writhing beneath his skin.

"Vander," I pleaded again, trying to step through the wall of shadows. "Let me in." I wasn't sure if I was speaking to him or the shadows themselves, but I could feel the ever growing familiar thrum of power in my chest as I spoke. Vander's concentration broke momentarily as he gaped at the shadows parting to let me through. They'd only ever answered to him, and I could feel their resistance at bending to the will of someone besides their master. But I would let nothing, not even the Mark of the Grimm, keep me from my mate.

Deep black vibrated around him, off of him, raging and roiling to new heights as I closed the distance between us. He was a midnight storm, a force of nature. He was beautiful. I laid a gentle hand on his chest.

"Talk to me." My words pulled him out of his mind slightly, his eyes at last finding mine. I barely managed to stifle a gasp at what I saw.

The usual golden swirls in his eyes were gone. Only pure black was left behind. They were desperate with a powerful kind of hunger, a look I didn't think I'd ever seen on him before. The longer I peered into them the more I noticed the underlying pain there, the regret and fear that ravaged him. But why?

He moved to release my grip, to turn away yet again. I brought my hands to his face, holding his gaze to mine—a quiet insistence that he stay.

"Vander. What happened out there?"

Moments passed in utter silence. I waited and waited for him to explain what this hidden storm raging within him was. Why it seemed to be cresting, today of all days. But he refused to answer.

I took a deep breath, fighting the urge to grind my teeth in frustration.

"You've been holding back, I can feel it. Every time you get close to me, you shut me out—shut down the tether. Why?" If he wouldn't tell me what was going on, then I'd just have to be the one to unearth the issue—to shine light on the shadows. "What are you keeping from me?"

He grimaced at my words, eyes darting down and jaw set in stubborn determination.

"Vander," I scolded softly. "We have to address this." The priestess' words returned to me, the haunting energy of the discord card she'd drawn for me before. I knew the two paths that lay before us, and the looming possibility of us going down the wrong one. I'd do everything in my power to keep us from that fate.

"You once asked me to keep fighting, to not give up. Well now I'm choosing to fight for us. You hold me in my pain." I tipped my head back to where we'd been dancing just moments earlier. "Let me hold you in yours. Tell me what's going on. Please."

His breath fell over me in a shuddered release, the effort it took to control his power weighing heavily against him. I dropped my hands from his face, taking a step back to give him some room to process—when he reached out a single, firm hand, wrapping his fingers around my wrist in a swift motion that held me in my place.

"I can't," he whispered into the quiet of the library. I shook my head, brows furrowed. Before I could argue back, he continued:

"I can't control it when I'm with you. When we're... *together*. I can barely control it at all other times." He shook his head, grimacing. "But with you, it overtakes me. I'm helpless to the curse, the darkness within."

I looked around the room, at the dark shadows evergrowing and changing. They enveloped us, swallowing us and snuffing out any light the library may have once offered. Perhaps what I'd sensed earlier was not a fear of letting me in, but rather a fear of what he'd do to me if he did.

"It's okay." I tried to reassure him. I wasn't afraid of him anymore, not like I had been at one time. The idea of the Mark, of the animal he could so easily become, had once terrified me to my bones. But now? Now I couldn't imagine a world where he'd ever harm me.

"It's not *okay*." A new ripple of darkness danced around us. It was impossible to miss the way his grip tightened around my wrist.

"I've done so many dark things, Hazel. Truly detestable things. As recent as last night, even." He leaned in, the planes of his face hard, cold. "I am a *monster*. I can't be with you, *fully* with you, without losing control of that side of myself."

My heart cracked, tears threatening the back of my eyes.

"It feels unnatural to shut you out, especially in that intimate space when we're together. But I don't know how else to keep the darkness from you. If I let you in, it's not just my thoughts and emotions you will feel. I can't control the Mark and open up the tether at the same time. Not in those moments."

I closed my eyes, grateful that he was at least talking to me. Even if what he said sent a chill down my spine. I'd felt the Mark several times before. But Vander had always made sure to keep a stronghold on it, to not let it grow too large a presence in my mind.

"It's okay," I repeated on a shaky breath. He moved to argue, but I shook my head, cutting him off. "I knew this day would come eventually. You weren't going to be able to tamp down on that power forever."

"You don't understand." His voice sounded strained, rough. "It's not just a matter of controlling this power." He gestured to the storm of shadows writhing around us. "The Mark has desires, things it wishes for me to do to you. It calls for you, Hazel, and I'm barely strong enough to hold it back."

A shiver crept over my skin at his words, at the thoughts they insinuated. Warmth pooled at my core, despite the haunting threat in his voice. I was desperate for his touch, more than curious about the things he'd pictured us doing together—of the things the Mark called for him to do to me. It didn't spark fear, didn't upset me, even if it should have. Instead it fed into that desire swirling deep within me, pushing me to move closer to him.

He stepped back at my movement, still firmly holding onto my arm—like he didn't want to get too close but couldn't stand to stay away.

"I don't want to hurt you, Hazel," he pleaded.

I looked up into the eyes of the male I loved, weary and darkened with the magic coursing through his veins. He could never hurt me. Not truly. But this crossroad we'd come to, it could destroy us if we didn't find our way through it. He wouldn't be able to shut me out forever. I could see now just how much holding control was wearing him down, how grating it must've been for him to not let that power go. And I didn't want him like this, a fraction of the male he was, constantly guarded and offering only the pieces he felt were safe to reveal. That wasn't love. That wasn't trust.

I put my other hand out, an offering for him to accept. He hesitated, his jaw clenched as he looked at it like it was my very heart and blood for him to take. To my surprise, he took it delicately and allowed me to step towards him.

"You," I said, making sure his eyes were on mine as I spoke, "will not hurt me."

I punctuated each word with a sort of finality. I needed him to see that I believed it. Enough for the both of us. I needed him to see that I trusted him, Mark or no Mark.

"You've always believed in my strength, why stop now? Let me in, Vander. Let me see you and feel you. The real you. Because I don't think I can last another second without it. No matter what monsters lurk within you. No matter what dark desires the Mark has. What dark desires *you* have. I want to be with you, darkness and all."

His eyes fluttered shut as he turned his face away from me. Cords of muscle strained along his neck and jaw. He was fighting it even still, letting the power roll through him as he tried to keep control. All that pent-up darkness and rage was building to unprecedented heights. He would kill himself trying to keep it all sheathed. All for the sake of protecting me. Because he didn't think I could handle what he wanted from me.

"You are goodness and light, Hazel. A goddess for fuck's sake." He shook as he spoke, finally dropping my wrist to run a hand through that beautiful midnight hair. "This Mark is vile, *I am vile.*

You were right about one thing. I *won't* hurt you. I won't allow myself the opportunity."

My heart dropped hearing his confession. He was everything to me—my light, my love. Yet he thought so lowly of himself, couldn't even be his true self when he was with me. It cracked something inside me, bringing tears to my eyes. I knew that pain—knew what it was like to try and hide your true self for fear of rejection, to feel like you were unworthy of the person you loved.

"I don't want to corrupt you." His words were like ice. *Corrupt.* Was that what he thought he'd do to me? Couldn't he see that I wanted this, wanted him no matter what that entailed? Maybe even *because* of what that entailed?

"It's not corruption," I argued softly as I stood tall in front of him, straightening my shoulders and facing him head on. I cradled his jaw against my palm when he refused to look at me, turning his eyes back to mine. He would see my strength. And he would see my authenticity. He grimaced, ready to shut down or fight back. I pressed on, desperate for him to hear my words.

"It's not corruption to show the one you love the deepest desires of your being. It's not corruption to want dark things—to want dark things with me. And it's not corruption to share those desires with the one you love." I took his hand once again and put it against my heart, showing him the steady, calm rhythm there. "It's not corruption, Vander. It's trust."

Something shifted within him, his eyes clearing slightly as he took me in—looking at me in a new light. He stayed like that for so long that I thought perhaps he wouldn't say anything at all, wouldn't ever respond to what I'd said, leaving the library behind like none of this ever happened. After minutes of painful silence, with his hand on my heart and the shadows palpitating around us, he finally spoke:

"So you think you can handle my darkness?" His tone was weary, unbelieving and unconvinced. I nodded anyway, sure he saw the motion.

"I need to hear you say it, Hazel." He'd gone so quiet, so desperately still.

I didn't hesitate as I voiced my response with a power only matched by his own, praying to the Fates that he would actually believe me. "I don't *think* I can handle it, Vander. I know it. I *want* it. I want to be with you, fully be with you. And I want you to be who you truly are when you're with me."

He let out a shuddering breath as he dropped his hand from my hold and grabbed the back of his neck, rubbing at the tension building there. He paced a few strides away, returning his gaze to that invisible spot it had been boring into before. When his eyes finally found mine again, it was impossible to miss the shift in demeanor. The shadows stilled, somehow feeling as if they'd turned all their attention on me. He narrowed his gaze, no trace of the pain and the fear that had been there before. All that remained was lush, dark desire and a threatening kind of hunger.

"So this is what you want," he taunted, his voice dropping to a deep, vibrating growl as he gestured to the shadows around us. "You *want* to experience my darkness?"

His words, full of promised pleasure and laced with dark intent, stole the air from my lungs. Unable to speak, I nodded in response as I watched him stalk forward. He was so close to me now that I could feel the rise and fall of his chest as he leaned in. His whispered words skittered against my ear as his breath heated my skin.

"Then get on your knees, little spitfire."

CHAPTER 18
VANDER

I watched with bated breath as her eyes widened, betraying the fear I sensed creeping up inside her. She wanted to act tough, to put up a strong facade, but it was impossible for her to hide her true emotions from me. It wasn't the fear of my typical prey, full of dread and agony as I stalked them through the Dark Woods. This was different. This fear was edged with excitement and nerves, coated in desire of the unknown. And the power inside me cried out at the sight of it.

Painfully slow, she sank to her knees. I felt my cock twitch at the sight. This goddess, *my* goddess, on her knees before me. I swallowed hard, still struggling to keep all that power clawing beneath my skin at bay. She wanted to experience my darkness? Against my better judgment, I wondered if perhaps it was time to oblige. At least to the extent that would show her exactly what it was she was asking for.

Tearing apart that Daeomi in front of my brother, Vesper, and the priestesses... it had done something to me. I'd seen the shock on their faces, the fear. But neither my brother nor Vesper had backed down—neither had passed judgment. It had unlocked some understanding within me that perhaps there was a way to work around these boundaries I'd placed—some sort of delicate balance between the two sides of myself that I could maintain. If I was careful.

But even if I was willing to take on this venture, I had to make sure the Mark understood my intent—her intent. She wasn't just another soul for the taking. She may have been mine to have, but I wanted to ensure there would be more of her left to give after this moment together.

She looked up at me through those emerald eyes, the ones that I knew shone brighter when filled with tears, and I almost lost control completely. I wanted to be the one making her cry, wanted to be the reason she was choked out and fear-filled. The sight of her agitated the dark magic coursing through my veins. The shadows around us snaked closer, in answer to the Mark's call. Every single part of me loved this, wanted this, needed this. And she was so desperate to please me, so obedient to my command. I felt the Mark call out within me, a push to see just how obedient she could be.

I circled her, shadows trailing in my wake, as I assessed every angle of her perfect little form—the way her deep red hair spilled over her bare shoulders, the ease in which her dress pooled around her legs as she knelt, and that tantalizing ass perched so sweetly atop her heels.

I hummed in approval as I made my way back around her. She didn't even so much as move as she waited for me. I pulled up one of the oversized, cushioned armchairs of the library, making sure to stay in her view—eyes trained on hers.

I leaned back in the chair, my pants feeling suddenly, unbearably restricting. I wanted her here—wanted that ass in my lap, those lips around my cock as I watched those eyes gleam with tears.

"Such an obedient little goddess," I mused.

I worried my words would break the spell, would shake her out of whatever daze she was in that had both of us losing our minds, pushing these boundaries. Instead she dipped her chin, *bowing* her fucking head to me. I sucked a breath in between my teeth as my shadows closed in on her involuntarily. I watched as they twined around her feet, her stomach, and up to her arms before curling around her middle and ripping through the bodice of her dress. The torn fabric flitted through the air and fell around her waist, releasing her breasts and exposing them to the chill of the library air, nipples pebbling instantly as more shadows snaked around them to play.

She took it all with no hesitation, no arguments. Each action of obedience eased my troubled mind, soothing over the rage and bitterness that still lingered after my fight with the Daeomi. Countless times I'd questioned the Fates decision to bring us together, after everything we'd been through, after the beings we'd now become. I'd called out to them, prayed, torn apart the earth until I was red in the face, trying to decipher why she'd been cursed with this Fate. I hated to admit the thoughts I'd had, the things I'd considered—the things I was still considering—to save her from this.

But sitting now, before my goddess, I couldn't help but admit this felt right. Her response to my desires felt like cool water over a fresh burn. The heat in my blood became slightly more bearable as I watched her. She truly wanted this, wanted *me.* I saw it in the way she arched her back towards me, desperate for my touch—could sense it through the tether as each second caused her desire to deepen.

She wasn't scared of this.

Of me.

But she didn't know what she was asking for.

I leaned forward, settling my elbows on my knees as I clasped my hands below my chin and took in the sight of her wrapped in my shadows. It wasn't enough, this small sliver of darkness I was letting through. She needed to see more, to feel that fear amplified deeper, so she'd finally understand why this wasn't an option. Sure, she'd been afraid, but it wasn't real, wasn't bone deep. I needed to see that *real* fear. The kind only the Mark could invoke, the kind that it called for, lived for—*killed* for. As if in response, the Mark lashed out, the shadows around her pushing her forward, making her get on all fours.

"Let's see just how obedient you can be."

She looked up at me from lowered lashes, hesitant to make a wrong move but desperate to have her eyes on me. I watched her a moment longer before giving her my next command:

"Crawl to me."

She paused for a moment, showing her first real hint of uncertainty. It was a sigh of relief to my bones, the key words to shut down whatever was happening here. I began reining in the power I'd started to let loose, caging the monster once again.

Before I could conceal my power, she reached one hand out, followed by the other. She closed the distance between us in a steady, captivating rhythm, never taking her eyes off mine. Her hips swayed with each stride she made, the bare skin of her breasts glowing in the lamplight of the darkened library.

I didn't think it was possible for anyone to make crawling look so beautiful, so powerful. When she reached my feet, she settled back on her knees and let her hands fall to my legs. I watched her measured movements as she slid those punishing fingers up my calves, to my thighs, landing finally at where my pants were fastened.

She paused, waiting for my permission before continuing. I raised an eyebrow at her, impressed and slightly surprised at her confidence and willingness.

"Did I tell you to fucking stop?" I couldn't help the words as they rolled off my tongue, so impatient with the playful manner she was moving in. The excitement I saw skipping across her features had my hands twitching to reach out and grab a fistful of that silky hair, to smother those feelings until there was nothing left besides fear and obedience.

Her fingers worked at the buttons of my pants, popping them open one by one. She was teasing me, taking her time and relishing each moment beneath my command. I had half a mind to make her take me between her lips here and now, just to wipe that smug look off her face. The corner of my lips tipped up, picturing it.

I raised myself slightly from the chair so she'd be able to discard the pants easily. Her eyes went wide as she turned her attention back to my naked form, ready and waiting for her. To my surprise, she didn't wait for another command before trailing slow, steady kisses up my thigh and settling herself fully between my legs. She let loose a single tantalizing breath down my length.

Fucking Depths.

She'd barely even touched me and she already had me right on the edge.

I was meant to be the one in control, the one scaring her away. And yet here I was, spiraling head first into a territory I wasn't sure I was ready to occupy. It was a dangerous game, one I feared I was hastily losing.

She gave me one last doe-eyed glance before lowering herself fully and running her tongue over the length of me. I tightened my grip on the armrest. Shadows warped around her, twining with the strands of her hair and holding her in place. I hadn't called them myself, couldn't feel them stemming from my own intention. My mind flickered with the meaning, to what extent the Mark was taking over, but my concern fell beneath the waves of pleasure.

Again she ran herself over me, the warmth of her mouth radiating up my spine. I growled, knowing I'd never live another moment of my life content unless she was taking me. My hips twitched involuntarily, pushing forward and driving towards her with impatience, forcing her to open her mouth for me.

Her lips wrapped around my cock fully, her tongue tasting its fill as she ventured deeper. My head lobbed backwards, falling against the back of the armchair. My mind flooded with warning bells. The Mark roared within me to take her blood, her body, her soul—thrashing with a vengeance I could barely concentrate on containing as she swirled her tongue over the tip of me.

We were treading a line we'd never come back from if I didn't put an end to it here and now. But the feel of her on me drowned out any other thoughts, chasing away logic and reason. Her existence would be my grave, and in this moment I would go willingly, so long as I had her till the end.

Her hair draped around her as she moved, revealing the curve of her shoulder. My eyes trailed down to the still hidden curves of her body, snapping me out of my mind. Suddenly, this wasn't enough. It would never be enough. She squeaked as I grabbed her arms and turned her, heaving her onto my lap in one swift motion. I pinned her back against my chest as I wrapped my arms around her middle.

"As much as I would love to continue seeing how well you take my cock in that pretty little mouth." She shivered beneath my touch but leaned into me as my words washed over her. "I don't think I can last another second without being inside you."

"I'm yours," she breathed, as I swept her hair away from her cheek and turned her chin to me. I rewarded her with a long, slow kiss. I could feel her melting at the contact, could sense how desperate her need was as I reached out subtly through the tether.

I slid my knees between her legs, pushing her open for me as I moved a hand down her soft skin and towards her center. At my touch she ground back, pushing my length against her ass in several punishing movements as she released a heady groan. I let the noise spur me further, ripping her undergarments to the side and finding the sensitive bundle of nerves at her core.

"So wet for me, already. Aren't you, goddess?" I croaked, teasing my fingers at her entrance. She hummed her agreement, tilting her head back in pure bliss as I moved back up to her clit, stroking small, calculated circles. I pushed my hips against her, letting her feel the hard length that was desperate for her heat. I could feel her desire dripping onto me, urging me to take her hard and fast, my cock leaking in answer.

She whimpered as I removed my fingers from her center, but I didn't give her time to process their absence as I lifted her hips and brought her back down slowly—lining myself up at her entrance. She braced a hand on each side of the armchair, waiting to feel me fully. I paused for only a moment, shoving my deception into the recesses of my mind and safeguarding it from her carefully. I lowered her onto me in one motion, bringing down the wall I'd so carefully built between us with it.

She stifled a gasp at feeling me so wholly, so abruptly, and it had me lifting my hips to dive even deeper into her. To push her further, to let go as much as I safely could so she could see and feel and sense that darkness within me.

"Fuck, goddess." My words were rough, almost unrecognizable with the presence of the Mark taking over.

You take me so well.

She sank against me, recognizing all that hearing those words through the tether meant in this moment.

Never stop, Vander, she responded, speaking back into my mind. It was the opposite reaction I'd expected. I thought she'd shrink away, beg me to stop, be flooded with terror at feeling the presence of the Mark through the tether. But it was me who was now terrified. Feeling her like this—both in my mind and on my body—I stood no chance against that power. And I could feel what small semblance of control I'd managed to maintain slipping fast.

I reached around, finding that little bundle of nerves once more as she pressed against me. I leaned forward, sinking my teeth into the hollow of her neck as she moaned her pleasure into the open air. She purred, the vibration radiating against my chest as I held her to me. But the Mark was greedy, screaming and writhing for me to claim her—and fuck did I want that too.

"Are you ready?" A smile grew on my lips, my body somehow possessed as it barreled towards release. Her head perked up, suddenly on guard for whatever I had planned for her.

"Always," she whispered. Her words alone could've been my undoing, her voice soft and breathy as she answered. I shuddered at her truth, refusing to let myself believe it. I pushed against her sensitive core, willing a shadow to wrap around her and take the place where my fingers had just been, before grabbing her hips firmly.

"Hold on," was the only warning I gave as I picked her up once more, bringing her down onto me in any way but gentle. She cried out at the sudden movement and I stilled immediately, panic flashing in my mind. Had I hurt her? Was it finally time to end this madness?

Don't stop.

The plea she sent down the tether had me lifting her again without a moment's hesitation, pushing my shadow to keep the steady rhythm against her center. Using her like this unraveled me. The Mark and I became one; its thoughts were my own and my thoughts belonged to it, as well. I felt it calling for her, wanting to feel the pulse beneath that alabaster skin and see the fear in her eyes.

The shadows became a storm around us, consuming the library as I climbed higher and higher. Books flew off the shelves at the touch of my power; lanterns toppled to the ground from the study tables, glass shattering. It was a hurricane of pleasure and darkness and fury. The Mark came alive around us, making its presence known.

It was different than it had ever felt before, present, all-consuming—but almost sentient, understanding. Even as the Mark made its ruthless hunger known within me, it reluctantly obeyed my calls to leave her unharmed. I watched as Hazel rode me like she was made to do so, like she was made to complete every dark desire I'd ever have—freeing me in more ways than one.

"There is nothing like your warmth, Hazel," I breathed against her, tightening my hold on her hips and cherishing this sacred place we'd found ourselves in. It was wrong, dangerous. And fuck if I didn't love every moment of it. Our movements grew, and with them so did her cries of pleasure.

"Vander," she pleaded, her breaths turning ragged and needy. It was utterly unholy how good my name sounded on her lips—the lips of a goddess, reduced to begging for my mercy.

I could sense through the tether just how close she was, how only a few more strokes would send her over the edge. I brought her down one, two, three more times before my own release crashed over me in waves of unrelenting pleasure. I pulled her close, pinning her against me and taking over where the shadow had once been, making sure to continue its frantic rhythm at her clit. I wrapped a hand around her exposed throat, savoring the raging thrum of her blood beneath the surface as I emptied every last drop of myself into her.

She cried out at the torrent rolling through her, through us, as I felt her release in my own mind. It was like fire and honey, frantic pleasure chased only by her pure light. The muscles in her neck restricted beneath my grasp and I tightened my hold, needing to feel more of her. I didn't let up my strokes, pushing her further with punishing circles to elongate her pleasure. She bucked against me, feeling the tremors of her orgasm ravage her body.

After I was sure she'd felt every last drop of those waves, I released my hold, falling back against the armchair. The shadows around us finally relented, ebbing to reveal the destruction they'd caused. I let out a deep breath, the feeling that was snaking through my body something so utterly foreign. I briefly wondered if this was what contentment felt like, feeling so completely at peace with this darkness inside me.

"Fucking Fates, Vander," Hazel breathed as she leaned back into me. I let her head fall against my shoulder before I turned her chin and claimed her mouth as my own.

Now that I'd had her fully, I understood the burden of the half life I'd been living in a way I never had before, the torment of such an existence. It was one thing to know an option existed and to just choose to live without it. It was another thing entirely to experience it first hand, only to deprive myself of such a thing after the fact. I would long for this every moment of my life.

My intention had been to scare her, to push her past the boundaries we'd found comfort in and show her the dark reality of what she was asking of me. But she hadn't backed down, hadn't walked away. Witnessing this unbound and unabashed version of her—knowing that it was my darkness that had brought that beauty forth—I couldn't imagine ever returning to whatever the fuck we were before.

CHAPTER 19
HAZEL

A searing pain blooming in the center of my chest pulled me from sleep. I opened my mouth to scream, unable to contain the scorching fire consuming me—but no sound came forth.

My breath was heavy as I fought through the storm, forcing my eyes open to understand what evil was attacking. To my surprise, it was not the library or my bedchamber I found myself in, but rather the shadows of the Dark Woods—in the midst of a clearing with a small, humble cottage nestled off in the distance.

Within Vander's dream.

Again.

A fierce chill chased out the fire still burning within me, ice creeping through my veins. I knew what I would find here. I looked over my shoulder, Vander falling to his knees just a few paces away.

"Vander," I whispered. But it sounded more like the billowing wind than it did my own voice.

I clambered to my feet, my body feeling as if it was not entirely my own to control. Still, I forced my limbs forward, closing the distance between us. Vander remained on the forest floor, eyes peeled to the distant sky. His arms were outstretched, his muscles straining with the power coursing through his veins.

"Vander, I'm here," I tried again. But he couldn't hear me. He was in a trance, making his deal with whatever unholy entity would hear him—and my words were lost the second they rolled off my tongue. I tried again and again. I screamed his name until my throat was raw, fighting to get closer and closer to him as he just knelt there, watching the sky.

But no matter how hard I tried to sift through the heavy fog of this nightmare, I couldn't reach him. I had no choice but to watch as the Mark overtook him and he watched my past self disappear beyond the tree line.

His pain was palpable; I could feel it through every part of my soul. It overtook the tether, piercing my mind with the force of its volume. It was an endless, bottomless black, a starved monster devouring me with each minute that passed.

I'd always thought the pain had come from the deal he'd made, taking on the darkness the Mark offered as it began to split his soul in two. But crawling to him now, feeling it radiate through my own being and consuming me—mind, body, and soul—I understood it was a pain that only came from losing something so precious, so rare. The pain of losing a mate.

A tear rolled down my cheek, the feel of its trail like venom seeping into my skin as I lay helpless in the muck of the Dark Woods. I was so close to reaching him. To helping him. And yet in this half world I'd invaded within his dreams, it wasn't enough. I wasn't enough.

I buried my face in the dirt and leaves and rocks—and I sobbed.

"I promise, I'm here, Vander. Why can't you hear me?"

No response.

"Please," I begged, lifting my head to watch him once more. "Let me in."

I woke with a start, surprised at the feel of warm flesh beneath my cheek. I ran my hand over the form beneath me, just to make sure he was real.

I lifted my head carefully, shocked to find Vander awake beside me. In his mortal form. My body was tucked carefully into the crook of his arm. I stifled the surge of hopefulness building within my body.

"Are you okay?" I whispered as I set my head back down on his chest. He grunted, the motion jarring my head.

He had never spent the night with me without remaining in his wolven form. He'd stayed with me, watched over me as I recovered from Kahlis' visits—had slept in my bed countless times over the past couple weeks. But he'd always made sure to shift to his wolven form before letting himself fall asleep.

I hadn't understood why, though I'd been suspicious of it being some method to continue distancing himself from me while we explored exactly what we wanted this relationship to be. Having him here now, in my bed as a *male* and not a wolf, I couldn't deny the spark of excitement coursing through my veins. What it confirmed in my mind after last night.

It had been surreal, the boundaries we'd crossed. The things I did to him and let him do to me. Things I never thought myself capable of. My cheeks reddened, unsure if it was pleasure at the memories or shame at examining them in the light of day.

"Do you want to talk about it?" I asked, hating how soft my voice sounded as I tried to busy my mind with the remnants of his nightmare.

"Do you?" he responded, a certain edge to his tone. I sat up at his words, turning and throwing him a confused look.

"Don't act like that," he scoffed, raising an arm to run his hand through his hair. "I can feel those emotions rising in you. You're second-guessing what you asked of me last night."

"Vander, no," I urged, resting a hand on his chest as I moved closer to him. He pushed me away, shaking his head.

"It's okay to regret it, Hazel. I'm still not convinced it was the right thing to do. Taking on the darkness of the Mark is a lot to ask of anyone, but especially you."

"Why do you say 'especially me'?" I crossed my arms over my chest, my tone turning defensive.

He sighed, reluctantly meeting my gaze. "You know as well as I do how deeply you feel things. Even now, your emotions are obvious to me—the sheer depth of them is intimidating. I feared that the full weight of the Mark would be too much for you to process, too much for you to bear."

Irritation rose within me as he trailed off. I was tired of having the same argument. It made no sense to me how he could assure me of my strength in the same breath that he doubted my ability to be with someone as powerful as him. He swallowed hard, breaking eye contact and turning his head to stare off to the other side of the room. "There is nothing I care more about than protecting you, Hazel. Even if it's from myself—especially then."

I let loose a slow breath, trying to calm the tide of anger swelling in my chest. I knew how in tune he was with the weight of my own emotions wrestling within me. But it was my curse to live with—my battle to fight.

"I feel no regret," I urged, repressing my anger as I leaned in to place a kiss on his stern cheek. No matter the frustrations I felt towards him, I knew I had to be vigilant in my argument to convince him I wanted this. Letting those feelings of anger and irritation run wild would only convince him further that this was something I was not ready for. Instead, I flooded the tether with nothing but need, desire, and certainty.

His hand was at my neck in a heartbeat, holding me in place and challenging me with the very darkness he spoke of. When he turned his eyes back to mine, they were obsidian stones once more.

"Are you sure about that, little spitfire?"

His shadows surrounded me, pulling and nipping and reminding me of their power—the power I'd experienced last night. I swallowed hard. The heat that had previously stained my cheeks dipped lower now, swirling in my belly. Definitely not shame, then.

I nodded carefully, testing the restriction of his hand around me.

"I told you last night, Vander. I want this. Whatever your darkness entails, I'm not turning away."

His eyes watched mine for a moment longer, hesitating as he searched for something there. When he didn't find whatever he was looking for, his grip tightened slightly and he pulled me in slowly. His lips found mind, his tongue parting them as he kissed me deeply. I let him, lost in the sheer force of his control, and loving every moment of it.

When he pulled back, I rested my forehead against his cheek, a grin pulling at the corners of my mouth. He wrapped me in his embrace once more, tightening his hold as his arm wrapped around my body.

"I wasn't talking about last night, by the way." I nudged him slightly, silently chiding him for jumping to such hasty conclusions.

He grunted in response, still refusing to acknowledge what both of us knew I was referring to.

"It's not the first time I've witnessed it, Vander." My voice lowered, any hint of amusement gone.

"I know," he finally answered, his voice just as quiet as mine.

"But we've never talked about it," I responded.

"I know," he said again, not giving me much room to continue this discussion.

I let out a small sigh, frustrated but trying hard to respect the boundary he was putting up. "I won't ask you to discuss it, if you aren't ready. But..." A beat of silence passed, swallowing the room in its weight. "Just know I'm here, okay? I want to be a part of your life. All of it. Even what you consider the bad."

He didn't respond, the only noise in the overly quiet room the soft sound of his hand trailing patterns over my arm. I took solace in the fact that he was here, letting me stay in his arms. But his silence was deafening, confirming no more progress would be made today.

Eventually, I slid out from his hold, making my way towards the wardrobe.

"Aerie's waiting for me," I called over my shoulder as I dug for a fresh change of clothes. "We have much to discuss after our time with the moon tribe. I, uh... I'll just be a minute." I tilted my head towards the bathing room, waiting for him to say something.

When he didn't respond, I took my leave. The sound of the door clicking shut might as well have been a thunderclap with the way it invaded the space between us. I leaned against the closed door, grimacing.

I thought about the humiliation I'd felt when Kahlis had dreamwalked to me, how exposed I felt. How helpless. I knew feeling those same things today, after all of the progress we'd made last night, would only serve to convince him he'd made a mistake.

I made quick work of slipping on the leggings and linen tunic I'd pulled from the wardrobe. I took a moment to look in the mirror, sliding my hands over my hair to smooth out the dark red strands and splashing some water on my face before returning to the tension waiting for me on the other side of the door.

But to my surprise, when I reentered the bedroom, Vander was gone.

I let out a long sigh, my head dipping low as I ran my thumb and forefinger over my forehead. I crossed the space to the vanity, popping the drawer open and pulling the Match card from where I'd hidden it away.

The early morning sun streamed in through the window beside me, hitting the card and illuminating the image. I inspected it carefully for a moment before looking out the window and flipping it absent-mindedly between my fingers.

Movement caught my eye as I watched the tree line of the Dark Woods, Vander's wolven form slipping easily between their shadows. I sighed at last, tucking the card within the folds of my tunic and turning away from the window.

The priestess' words haunted me as I took my leave, making my way through the rest of the Estate. Perhaps she was right, finding balance as Aerie and Bastian had… it was proving to be damn near impossible.

I found Aerie out in the gardens, harvesting herbs. I joined her without missing a beat, kneeling beside her and trimming the rosemary, just like she'd taught me to do.

Aerie offered me a kind smile but didn't say anything. We knelt in the quiet of the garden, working side by side and listening to the distant melody of songbirds. These moments with her calmed the rumble in my mind. Just her sheer presence beside me was somehow enough of a support to put those vicious thoughts to bed.

"Where's Bastian?" I finally asked, surprised to have felt his absence through the Estate and now out in the gardens.

"He insisted on checking the borders himself after our return from Sgàil." Aerie sighed. "I don't blame him, of course. It sounds like whatever they encountered invading the moon tribe was rather aggressive."

I tilted my head, finally forcing my eyes to meet hers. "What did they encounter?"

Aerie huffed out a breath of air. "Did Vander not tell you? Honestly, that boy is as helpless as they get when it comes to communication."

My cheeks reddened, turning my face from hers in hope she hadn't noticed.

"We were a little preoccupied after his return last night," I murmured. Aerie's mouth shut tight, trying to hide her smile. "It didn't leave much time for updates on their fight."

Aerie stifled a giggle. "So I take it the tides have turned a bit between the two of you?"

I threw my hands up, frustration threatening to take over. "I honestly couldn't tell you. I thought they were. Last night felt like a huge step forward. But this morning was... odd. He left while I was getting ready. We haven't really had a moment to talk about it."

Aerie hummed in understanding, nodding her head. "That sounds like Vander, always taking off. Sights set on his own plans rather than considering the ones around him."

I dipped my head low, trying to hide the tears threatening to spill.

"Hey," Aerie reached out, offering an apologetic look. "Like I've told you before. Just be patient with him. Remember, you're just now understanding the connection between you. He's had to live with that knowledge for over a decade." She rubbed her fingers slowly over the back of my hand. "And he didn't have you here to work out those emotions together."

I nodded, realizing everything she was saying wasn't anything I hadn't thought to myself. I knew Vander had gone through so much pain, more than I could have possibly imagined. While I was gone, hiding away in whatever pocket realm I'd created subconsciously to hide myself from Kahlis, he'd been here. Alone. Hurting. And trying to cope with whatever dark magic now flowed through his veins.

I'd had Arlo, that other half of his soul that he'd sacrificed to protect me. Even if it wasn't truly him, it was a piece of him. It was enough to spare me from whatever torment he'd gone through for losing the one he was fated to. I'd had my own trials, but I knew simply from dreamwalking to him that the well of pain he'd endured was much deeper than he ever let on.

"Even when it seems like you're on the right path, it's going to take time," she continued, pulling me out of my own thoughts.

I nodded, going quiet together as we focused back on the garden. I relished the feel of the greenery in my hands, noticing the magic pulsing through them. I sunk my fingers into the dirt, testing to see if I felt anything different as well. A hum of energy greeted me, making my magic spark to life beneath my skin.

Just like the Cosmos had called to me, affected me within the moon tribe, it appeared that the earth was doing the same here, within Talamh's borders. But as excited as the discovery should have made me, I couldn't help but feel like it was a null point. What good was harnessing this magic if it did nothing to help my more willful power, dreamwalking.

Aerie paused her work, looking over to me carefully. "Everything okay?" she asked, looking between me and the spot where I'd just been working.

I looked down at the earth, holding my hand to my chest and rubbing my fingers to release the energy that had built up there.

"If it's okay," I answered at last. "I think I'd like to focus our lesson on the power inherited from my father today, rather than that of the Divine."

Aerie's eyes went wide as I forced my gaze to meet hers. "Alright," she answered simply, turning back to the mess before her. She collected her things, bundling the fresh-picked herbs in her basket and brushing her hands off on her linen apron.

I swallowed hard, dusting my own hands on my leggings and taking her hand. She pulled me to my feet, then picked up her basket of herbs and tools, and led me back to her greenhouse.

She pushed through the closed door, setting her basket down on the worktable and motioning for me to take a seat. I did as she instructed, watching her bustle through the cluttered space as she cleared away the new harvest.

"Where to start, where to start," she mumbled as she brought forth tome after tome from her shelves. I recognized the one Vesper had given her from the archives. I reached out for it, an excited hum of energy vibrating through me.

Aerie laid her hand atop mine, stopping me.

"Not yet," she warned. She set down a small bowl of crystals she'd been cradling in her hand.

I pursed my lips, my eyes locked on the tome as my hands itched to reach out and dive into whatever knowledge it contained within its pages. But I nodded anyway, forcing my eyes closed to break the connection with it.

"Besides, you wanted to focus on your other abilities, yes?" Aerie's voice nearly sang as she went back to sorting things on the worktable. "Those less Divinely gifted?"

I nodded, taking a deep breath as she took her seat in front of me.

"Your magic is a part of you," Aerie began to explain. "It should feel almost second nature to call to it, as you've well learned. But learning its depths, how to control it... that can be tricky. And learning the magic of a fae king, let alone a *goddess*. Well, I only have experience in one of those areas, but I can assure you neither feat is going to come easy."

I let out a small groan. It seemed like everything these days was centered around waiting. The inevitability of it all was driving me mad.

"So what can I do now?" I asked on an exhale.

"You can read." She handed me a book, its rough edges scraping against my hand. "I've pulled every book I have on the fae, how to train abilities such as dreamwalking and realm walking. But honestly, the best thing to do is just start using that magic. Get familiar with its call, let it get familiar with you. Don't shy away from it when it comes to you."

I cringed at the idea, the suggestion of using my father's magic feeling so opposite of what I was wanting to accomplish.

"I want to control it," I argued. "Not use more of it."

Aerie's jaw tightened. "Hazel, I know this has all been such a huge change for you. But the only way you can learn how to control it *is* to use it. It's like a muscle. The more you learn to flex it, the more control you'll gain over it."

I rolled my eyes, folding my arms over my chest and resting my elbows on the rough wooden table in front of me.

"May I ask, why the sudden urgency to control your fae side?"

"I've been dreamwalking," I responded slowly. "Ever since closing the Rift. Not every night, but often enough."

"And what are you seeing when you dreamwalk? You're not still sensing Kahlis, are you?" Her tone felt rushed, urgent, but her face didn't betray her worry.

"No." I shook my head. "It's Vander. His... nightmares. I fear they're the reason he continues to put distance between us."

"I see." The words rolled off Aerie's tongue like thick honey, kind and empathetic and considering. "Well—" She bobbed her head back and forth, looking at me out of the corner of her eye. "If that is true, it says more about Vander than it does you. He should not be punishing you for an ability you've yet to learn to control."

I gritted my teeth, unable to agree with her sentiment. I was the one invading his privacy; it was my power taking over his dreams without permission. "I need to learn how to suppress it," I answered, too quickly. "No matter what that means."

"I will urge you," Aerie pressed carefully, "to not suppress your power. Any power, no matter from whom it came. All of it is a part of who you are now. What makes you, you."

I hated the idea that any part of Kahlis went into making me who I was today. He was detestable, vile—a monster unmatched. And it terrified me to think that some piece of that darkness may well reside within me.

"You deserve to shine bright, Hazel." Aerie's eyes met mine, her lips tilting up in a soft, reassuring smile.

Everyone kept telling me how strong this power was, how good my namesake was. Full of goodness and light. Vander had said as much just last night. But I still felt nothing but the weight of darkness within me, the spirit of my father haunting me. Separating myself from that power. *Her* power. I couldn't imagine a day where I'd feel like that magic and I were one.

Aerie flipped through a book, turning it towards me at last and pushing it forward.

"I know it feels impossible now, but it won't forever. Just promise me something."

I lifted my head from the tome she'd placed in front of me, a detailed explanation of how one could focus their magic while dreamwalking to control where their abilities took them.

"Promise me that if I teach you how to control this power, you won't use that knowledge to suppress it."

I tensed, knowing in my heart I couldn't make that promise. My mind flashed to Vander this morning, the way he shut down after I dreamwalked to him. The distance I felt him putting between us after feeling so exposed.

When I didn't answer, she let out a small sigh. "I will, of course, do as you wish. It's your choice to use your power as you see fit. I just don't want to see you get hurt. Nothing good can come from that power being repressed for so long."

She let her head fall, turning her attention back to another tome before her. I watched a moment longer, almost disappointed in myself for making her worried. But I needed this—needed the control. I didn't know how else to fix things with Vander, to ensure my power didn't continue seeping into his mind and invading his privacy. Still, I knew there was wisdom in Aerie's words, a warning I probably needed to heed—but couldn't. My eyes grazed over the pages in front of me without fully comprehending, worrying about the next dream to come, and what the fallout would be if I couldn't learn to control it.

CHAPTER 20
HAZEL

Aerie and I worked through the morning, digging through tomes and discussing methods for controlling my dreamwalking in those moments when it decides to show itself. She gave me a new herbal bundle to place under my pillow and promised to renew the warding over my bedchamber in an effort, not to dull that magic, but to strengthen my ability to navigate it.

When we'd discussed a handful of options to try, and she'd assured my confidence in our efforts, she shifted my attention to some tomes Vesper had advised may be helpful to me. She read passage after passage about how magic worked within the body, with descriptions of the different rituals chieftains would often partake in over the six tribes—each painstakingly different from the last.

She asked me to try different methods for calling my power forth, and took note of the ones that worked and the ones that didn't. She had me explain to her which tribes or rituals called to me, how my power reacted to them. While all the tribes seemed to be connected to me, the sun and moon tribes seemed to hold the most power over me, followed by the earth tribe.

By the time someone rapped at the door, my body was exhausted, and I was grateful for the distraction. Kirwan entered a moment later, carrying a tray of food.

"I was asked to bring this in to you," he offered quietly, setting the tray down on the far side of the table.

"Thank you, Kirwan." Aerie bowed her head in gratitude. The smell of the leftover vegetable soup and fresh-baked bread wafting through the room had my mouth salivating. I hadn't eaten anything this morning before visiting Aerie in the gardens. And she'd whisked me into her greenhouse so fast, I hadn't even realized how hungry I'd become over our hours of work.

Aerie passed me a bowl and I dove in immediately, not even waiting for Kirwan to leave.

"Where's your brother?" Aerie asked, looking past him through the open doorway. "I don't think I've seen him since he took up guard outside the Estate last night."

"It appears that he's ventured into the Dark Woods." Kirwan cut a quick glance at me, before bowing his head and staring down at the floor. "With Vander."

"Ah," Aerie sighed. "Any particular reason?"

"None that they cared to share with me. However, it would appear they are on the hunt for any extra Daeomi that may have escaped after the attack on the moon tribe."

Aerie nodded carefully, stirring the bowl of soup she now held in her hand. "Well, let's hope there's nothing to worry about. Kirwan, would you mind helping us with something?"

Both mine and Kirwan's eyes shot up to Aerie.

"Me?" Kirwan asked, looking around the otherwise empty room, as if looking for someone else to suggest. I didn't have any issues with Kirwan. He seemed rather nice, actually. And my heart hurt for the pain I saw in his eyes every time we crossed paths since losing Mirren. But I didn't know him well enough to ask for his assistance in something so personal as learning how to control my magic. From the Divine or the Dark One.

"Yes, you," Aerie answered, a kind smile playing on her lips. She ate a spoonful of soup before setting the bowl down and crossing to the other side of the worktable where he stood beside me. "I had hoped to have Lennox's help, given how close the two of you have become."

She glanced down to where I was sitting, a twinkle in her eye. "But with Bastian out checking the borders and your brother taking off without informing anyone, it looks like you're the one left to fill the role."

"And what role would that be?" he asked, taking a step backwards.

"Helping with Hazel's training, of course."

"Training?" The look of hesitation on his face mirrored my own.

"Aerie," I chimed in, unsure what my argument was going to be.

"Both of you hush. Vesper himself shared with me how successful the boys' collaborative efforts were to repair the moon tribe's warding while we were visiting. It seems the Cosmos' insight was helpful in more ways than one."

When neither Kirwan nor I understood her meaning, she rolled her eyes and set her hands on her hips. "Hazel, you yourself just shared with me that you react most to the sun and moon tribes' traditions and rituals, did you not?"

I nodded hesitantly.

"And Kirwan, are you not a product of both the sun and moon tribes? Does not both their forms of magic run through your veins?"

He watched her for a moment, dipping his head at last as he rubbed his forehead. "Yes," he said on an exhale.

"Perfect! Then according to Vesper's theory, such a collaboration should help with our training!" Aerie exclaimed, clapping her hands together. "I need to gather a few things and then we can go." She swept through the greenhouse, making her way towards the side entrance for the Estate.

"Go where?" I called out after her. She didn't answer as she marched into the kitchen, disappearing past the doorway.

I sighed, suddenly feeling the awkward tension as Kirwan and I were left in the greenhouse alone. I turned slowly to him, my movements feeling too stiff.

"So," I ventured, unsure what to say. "Are you okay with this?"

He scrubbed a hand over his jaw, chuckling. "I don't think I have much of a choice, do I?"

"I can talk to her," I reassured. "Make up some excuse to get you out of this. I'm sure you have other things to worry about—"

"It's okay." He cut me off, raising his hands. "I don't mind, honestly." His breathy laugh returned as he offered me a hand to stand. "Truth be told, I haven't had much to fill my days with lately. This will be a welcome distraction."

I watched his contrasting eyes as he met my gaze. I knew he was trying to make light of the situation, but I couldn't help but notice the grief still burning hot within those silver and black orbs.

"Alright." I took his hand as I rose to my feet, grabbing a piece of bread to take with me. "But we're bringing snacks."

"I think we'll work together just fine." He laughed, the sound lifting my spirits as he grabbed the rest of the loaf from the tray and ushered me through the greenhouse door and into the kitchen.

I recognized the path to the crystal spring easily, having taken it myself several times since Mirren's funeral. My stomach clenched as we broke past the tree line and entered the meadow.

The wind bellowed softly around us, wisps of Aerie's hair dancing around her as she led the way. I cut a nervous glance over to Kirwan, wondering how being here would affect him. I knew he was often coming and going from the Estate, as Nox and Vander had, but I wasn't entirely sure what the three of them did with that time. Or exactly where they were venturing off to.

Judging by the way Kirwan tensed as he crossed into the meadow, I wondered if this was his first time returning since the funeral.

I let out a small breath, reaching out beside me and taking his hand in mine. The gesture shocked him, his eyes cutting hard to our joined hands. He watched them for a moment, before slowly raising his face to mine and offering me a grief-stricken smile. I squeezed his hand once before pulling him softly, leading him into the meadow.

We caught up to Aerie easily, her movements stalling as she surveyed the land around her.

"This the spot?" Kirwan's hand slipped from mine as he stepped up to Aerie and set the basket of food down. I smiled to myself, amused that he did in fact bring snacks, as I had requested.

"Feels right," Aerie answered, turning to face us. "Are you ready?"

I chewed on my bottom lip, eyes shifting from Kirwan to Aerie. I knew I'd asked for this, but trepidation still had a strong hold on me. I doubted my ability to control whatever ancient power lay silently within me.

The more I learned about the Divine, the more others spoke to me of her legacy and the power I now claimed, it did nothing but spark apprehension. It wasn't just nerves. It was bone deep, a true belief that I could never live up to what she was, never truly fulfill those expectations. But even as I stood here, debating walking away and telling Aerie I'd changed my mind, I saw Vander's face when he'd returned from their battle at the moon tribe's borders—saw the exhausted, worn down look Bastian often carried after ensuring our own borders remained protected.

I straightened my shoulders and lifted my head to Aerie, nodding tightly.

"I'm ready." I wouldn't continue to subject them to that torment, wouldn't be the reason Kahlis' attention continued to plague our borders. And if tapping into whatever divine power lay within me—using its goodness and light to chase away the darkness my own father harbored for Tir Nadaar—then so be it.

Aerie watched me carefully for a moment, nodding at last as she turned her attention to Kirwan. She took his hands and laid his palms face up between us, motioning for me to lay mine upon his.

"Hazel's power appears to have a special connection to both the sun and the moon tribes. Which isn't shocking, considering the marks of the Divine." Aerie trailed her fingers over the mark of the sun on my palm before placing my hand carefully upon Kirwan's outstretched palm.

"I am excited to see what progress we can make moving forward with Vesper's guidance." She pursed her lips a moment, attempting to stifle a small grin. "Especially seeing how well your magic responded to his already."

I cut her a narrowed glare, rolling my eyes at the way her own twinkled with mischief. Kirwan looked awkwardly between the two of us.

"Am I missing something?"

"No," I called out, just at the same time Aerie hummed, "Yes."

Kirwan's lips twitched as he averted his gaze, clearing his throat in what I was sure was meant to be a chuckle.

I sighed. "The Sgàil chieftain may or may not have had a certain affinity for my... magic. Which he made somewhat clear during our stay."

Kirwan raised an eyebrow, the twitch on his lips turning to a full-blown smile.

"Is that so?" His eyes darted to Aerie. "And he's still standing?"

Aerie nodded.

Kirwan chuckled deeply, shaking his head. "I would have paid good money to see Vander trying to control that rage."

I huffed out a frustrated breath as both Kirwan and Aerie broke out in laughter, pulling my hands back and crossing them over my chest to show just how unamused I was.

"I'm sorry, Hazel," Kirwan said through breathy laughs. "But a tribal chieftain challenging a fated bond is no small thing, even for the moon tribe. I can only imagine how outraged Vander was. And as much as I hate to admit it, watching the broody bastard twitch happens to be a favorite pastime of mine."

I grunted, pushing hair out of my face from where the wind was jostling it. "Yes, I'm all too aware. Now, are we going to do what we came here to do or shall we keep talking about all the things that make Vander twitch?"

I regretted my word choice as soon as it rolled off my tongue. Kirwan's eyes went wide, the temptation to push further surely overwhelming him. He opened his mouth, a question all prepared, but Aerie cut him off with a warning look.

"You're right, Hazel. Let us refocus." She motioned for us to raise our hands again. We obeyed and I closed my eyes, preparing myself to tap into whatever that foreign power within me had to offer.

"Kirwan, stay patient. Allow her the time and space to discover her magic. Let your own come forth, will it to call to hers." I felt his magic spark to life in an instant, no hesitation or delay. It was warm beneath my palms, igniting the ink on my skin and caressing it.

"Hazel, recall whatever it was about Vesper's magic that called forth your own. Tap into that feeling with Kirwan."

My own magic came forth, but I knew instantly it wasn't that of the Divine. This had been my biggest frustration so far, trying to handle two different kinds of magic flowing through me. There was the tribal magic I was born with, still unsure which tribe it belonged to, or perhaps that of my father's. The thought made me shiver. And then there was the power of the Divine. It dwelled deeper, ran hotter.

The former I'd learn to call forth, not that I used it often. Aerie had trained me in such ways for the ritual she performed on Sol Litha. She'd wanted to make sure I felt confident using it before the ceremony, knowing how many eyes would be on me. I appreciated the help, but such a show of power had been so simple compared to what we were attempting now.

The latter, I'd barely dwelled on. It appeared at random, revealing itself without my say so. I couldn't figure out how to make it bend to my will. Much like the dreamwalking, it seemed to be a magic that happened to me, rather than a power I could control.

"That's not it," Kirwan suggested softly. Despite the kindness in his words, I gritted my teeth at the acknowledgement of my failure. I opened my eyes a moment to look at him, but Aerie tapped my arm, reminding me to focus. I sighed, closing my eyes once more and rolling my shoulders as I tried again.

And again.

And again.

We spent hours in that meadow, training and trying and exhausting our efforts to no avail. By the time the sun started sinking on the horizon, we were making the trek back to the Estate. Defeat ran strong through me, my body shutting down as I made up an excuse to skip dinner and retreated to my bedroom. Neither of them argued, most likely understanding today's strain on my body and my mind.

I sighed as I closed my bedroom door behind me and leaned against the solid wood. My empty bedchamber greeted me, and my heart sunk. I hadn't realized some part of me had hoped to find Vander waiting for me. I scrubbed a hand over my face, rubbing at my tight jaw as I made my way across the room.

I readied myself for bed, stopping only when something on the vanity caught my eye. A warm cup of tea was waiting for me, along with a note. I padded over on bare feet, sinking onto the vanity's stool and picking up the parchment.

Lennox and I picked up a Daeomi trail heading north. We need to stop them before they attack another tribal border. I'm sorry. But you're in safe hands. Drink. Sleep. I'll be back when I can.

Vander

If it was possible for my mood to sour more, it would have. I crumpled up the note, chucking it at the mirror. My reflection stared back at me, anger radiating off my features. I didn't doubt the truth in his words. But yet again, it felt as if he was choosing that life over me. Retreating where he felt safest instead of staying to face this tension between us.

The words started circling once more, that not-so-subtle whisper in my mind that I wasn't good enough, wasn't worth enough to him. I reached into my tunic, producing the card the priestess had given me. I studied it for a moment, memorizing the patterns scripted across its planes.

I set the card down beside the cup of tea, tapping a finger on the vanity as I lost myself in thought. Finally, I eyed the cup. I pursed my lips, sucking the inner hollow of my cheek between my teeth. After another moment I picked it up and let its steam invade my nostrils—a familiar rich, earthy scent.

It was familiar because I'd had it before—the same tea Aerie had given me after Kahlis' first attack against me. The one meant to dull my senses and keep his attacks at bay. Something I hadn't needed to consume since I'd closed the Rift.

I rose to my feet, carrying the tea over to the bathing chamber, not hesitating even a moment as I dumped it down the sink. If he wanted to keep my powers at bay, he'd have to have an actual conversation with me first. After a fruitless day of wrestling with my abilities, I was done trying.

I set the now empty cup back on the vanity as I strode over to my bed. I collapsed into it, tucking myself into the soft sheets and wrapping them around me in an effort to feel less alone. My eyes narrowed on the bedside candle flickering before me.

I lay there for the Fates knew how long, watching the flame dance and the wax drip. It was only when the wick burned down to its final moments of light that I closed my eyes and turned over, hoping foolishly for a better tomorrow.

CHAPTER 21
VANDER

"So are we going to talk about it?"

I clenched my jaw, suddenly regretting the foolish decision to bring the annoying nuisance with me on this journey.

"Talk about what?" I ground out, keeping my eyes peeled on the thicket of the Dark Woods ahead as we stalked forward. As much as I hated to admit it, Nox's hunting skills were impressive. Not quite a match for my own, but I didn't have to lecture him nearly as often as I assumed I'd need to when we first ventured out.

We'd been hunting Daeomi together on and off for a few weeks now, and it had been the first time in years that I'd been able to observe his skills first hand. It was a stark reminder of why Bastian had made him tribal spy in the first place.

"You? This? The girl? Take your pick." Nox took a few silent strides to the side, splitting our path as we came across a patch of underbrush. We cleared the possible hideaway, coming back together on the other side.

"How about," I answered smoothly, "your issues with Kirwan."

Nox straightened, stopping his steps and clicking his jaw. "I'm sure I have no idea what you mean, brother."

I rolled my eyes as I kept my pace, leaving him behind. "That's what I thought. *Brother.*"

Nox caught up easily, resuming his crouched approach as we made our way further north.

The Daeomi had always stayed south, attacking both our tribal borders and those of the moon tribe somewhat regularly. They didn't dare venture too far from Kahlis' protection, knowing even they had limits on what they'd be allowed to get away with. The tribes were united under the name of Tir Nadaar. Attacking one or two of them may not gain too much attention, but adding more to that roster would land them the full attention of the continent.

And while Kahlis was powerful, he still couldn't overcome the full weight of all six chieftains. It was the one thing ensuring he remained outside Tir Nadaar's borders, no matter how hard he fought to regain access.

So when we'd received word of a group of Daeomi pushing further north, I hadn't hesitated to take off after them. There were others out here too; Sgàil had insisted on their own hunt, but they were hours behind us. Days, even.

Nox had been on me in an instant, demanding to join me. And insisting as vigorously that we leave Kirwan behind. I wasn't sure I agreed with the sentiment, but Nox was my closest friend. And if he had his own shit to work out on a hunt, who was I to stop him?

I'd left word with Bastian, and a note in Hazel's room, before we'd taken off. I'd felt her anger through the tether, surprised the bond was strong enough for me to feel her despite the distance between us. But when I tried to reach out, tried to comfort her and offer my explanations, I was met only with a stone wall.

I knew my leaving was terrible timing. I'd been so sure the night before that this was it, the moment we turned the tide and accepted our fate. But after that lust-filled fog had cleared, I'd realized just how much I was still holding back, how foolish I'd been for indulging her to the extent I had. My nightmare reinforced that fear, reminding me of the true level of darkness I'd taken on. It whispered to me, warning me. And having her there with me only served as a further reminder of all I was risking by keeping her involved with this power.

I sighed, slowing my stride. Nox mirrored me, stopping completely to face me head on.

"You know, you are allowed to share things. Being your best friend does entitle me to a certain side of you others might not have the privilege of seeing."

I rubbed my forehead, pausing to sneer at him between my fingers. "I hate to break it to you, Lennox. But you are not my best friend."

Nox scoffed, raising a hand to his chest. "I'll look past your offensive accusation, because I know the fragile state you're in right now. Repeat after me, Nox is friend. Not enemy."

I shoved a wall of shadow at him, knocking him back as I turned back to the path we were on. His chuckle slipped through the trees around us as he jogged to catch up with me.

"Come on, brother. I'm serious. You're clearly going through some shit. What good am I if you can't talk to me about it?"

"I'll start talking about my issues with Hazel when you start talking about your issues with Kirwan," I bit back, picking up my pace in order to force some distance between us. Nox gave me a wide berth of room, keeping his slow stride for a minute before coming up beside me once more.

"I'm concerned for him," he called out after several moments of blissful silence. His demeanor had shifted, that sarcastic facade slipping away for a moment to let through the grief within. I slowed, turning my attention fully to him and motioning for him to go on.

"Something's not right with him lately." Nox sighed. He started pacing before me, rubbing a hand through his bright copper hair. It was his one giveaway in the otherwise dark forest.

"Nox, you both just lost—"

"I'm well aware." Nox spun, his features tightening as a wave of pain washed over him. "But this isn't that. This is something else. And the bastard refuses to speak on it which leaves me little choice other than to just make decisions for him. Protect him before he gets himself killed."

I nodded, thoughtful. I'd noticed the shift in Kirwan as well, but I wasn't sure it was anything more than residual guilt after everything that had happened to Mirren. That kind of loss could do things to a male.

The Mark burned against my skin in silent agreement.

Nox narrowed his eyes on me, stalling his pacing. "Sounds an awful lot like someone else I know," he jeered.

I rolled my eyes, throwing him a crude gesture. "I'm sure Kirwan is fine. He's just dealing with a lot. As are you. Things aren't going to be the same as they once were. Loss changes people, Nox. Best to just give him space to work out that grief, just as you are by being here with me."

Nox raised a brow, folding his arms over his chest. "Brother, my insistence on coming with you was more for your benefit than mine. I don't find relief in taking my frustrations out by murdering other creatures."

I scoffed, incapable of finding that even remotely true. Nox rolled his eyes, bobbing his head from side to side.

"Okay, maybe I do." He raised his hand, squeezing his thumb and forefinger together. "Just a little bit. But not in the same way you do. Nor in the way Kirwan has apparently grown fond of."

"So why come then?" I pushed, voice louder than I'd meant for it to be. This incessant conversation was grating and I wanted nothing more than to get back to the hunt.

Nox furrowed his brow, tilting his head and looking at me as if I was an idiot. "Are you honestly that clueless, Vander?"

I gritted my teeth, shadows reaching out from my clenched fists.

"Just as I'm worried about Kirwan, I am equally worried about you, brother."

I threw up my hands, frustrated that we'd made it full circle back to me. I turned back to the path, storming off and effectively ending the discussion.

"I'm serious," Nox called after me, catching up with frustrating ease. "Bastian agrees, as does Aerie."

"Of fucking course," I grumbled, keeping my eyes trained on the trees before us and assessing for any threats. "What, are you all just having nightly meetings about me?"

"Well, I wouldn't say nightly. But biweekly for sure."

I growled, shoulders tensing as I kept walking. Nox cut in front of me, putting his hands up in an effort to get me to stop.

"I'm only joking! Damn, you really are on one lately."

"And am I not allowed to be?!" I exploded on him. I tried to reel in the anger, to shove it back down. But the control slipped as my words poured out: "After losing my mate, after thinking for a decade that she was dead, or *worse* at the mercy of Kahlis? After spending all of that time looking for her and learning how to live with the Mark and losing all hope? Only to find she'd been hiding in some pocket reality the entire time? With the better half of my soul that I made a deal to create in order to protect her? And what, now that I have her back and he's gone and we've acknowledged the bond between us, everything is just supposed to be all sunshine and rainbows?"

"Vander, I—"

"No, you wanted me to talk, so I'm talking." I advanced on him, all too aware of the darkness unfurling within me. Nox could sense it too, his features tightening as he stood his ground and prepared to go head to head with me.

"It's not that simple, Lennox. It's *never* that simple. I may have her back, but she's wholly different than the female I fell in love with. Fuck, she's different than the female I found upon her return. She is an ever-changing, Cosmic force of light and power. And I don't know how to be there for her like she deserves.

"Not after everything she's been through. What she had with Arlo. What she could have with another male. Vesper? *You?* How am I supposed to damn her to an eternity with this darkness?"

"Vander, you have to know there was never anything between us. We were just fucking with you—"

"I know!" I yelled. "Don't you think I know that? That I trust you? That I trust her? It was never a real concern in my mind. But it is a haunting reminder of the options she *could* have, if she weren't bound to a fucking monster like me. That she could have, if I was just strong enough to walk away."

Nox took a step back, concern wracking his face. "You can't possibly be saying what I think you're saying."

I didn't answer, guilt taking over.

Nox lowered his voice, leaning in. "You'd really consider it? Breaking the bond?"

It was something I'd more than considered. It was a desperate effort, a hopeless piece of information I'd tucked away long ago, for fear I'd never find a way back to her. And when Arlo had made his way into Tir Nadaar and everyone finally understood the true extent of the deal I'd made, I'd begun researching the subject again—preparing myself to make such a sacrifice.

And I hated to admit how many times I'd thought of it since then.

Breaking a bond set in place by the Fates themselves, it was near impossible. But there was a way—for the most dire of circumstances. And given the darkness of the Mark on my arm, the entity to which it tied me, I assumed such a ritual would work—if it came to that.

I would always be bound to her, our life threads crossing for the entirety of our existence. But if I chose to break the bond, to go against the Fates themselves, it would free her to live a life she wanted. A life without being tied to a monster like me.

"You can't." Nox pushed forward when I refused to respond. "Fuck that, brother. You're not thinking right!"

"Maybe I'm thinking clearly for the first time in a long time," I lamented.

"And I suppose you haven't even asked Hazel what *she* wants?"

I remained silent, hardening my eyes as I watched his judgment pour over me.

"Fucking Fates, Vander. What is wrong with you?" Nox turned, resuming his pacing, hands in his hair as he tried to process what I was sharing.

"It's easy for you to cast your stones when you don't understand the things I'm wrestling with," I bit out.

He spun on me, finger to my chest, blade pulled in his other hand. "No. You don't get to claim that shit. We're *all* dealing with pain, Vander. We all have darkness we have to manage. So don't stand there and tell me how you're thinking about ruining something so good, so pure, and hurting not only *yourself* but her as well. All of us. For some selfish idea that someone else, anyone else, deserves her more."

He raised his blade to my chest, replacing the finger digging into me. The metal pierced skin, blood trickling down my body.

"Don't throw that shit at me after I had to watch *my* one good thing get ripped from my fingers." Tears shone in his eyes. "After I had to carry what was left of her body home and prepare her for the funeral pyre."

I swallowed hard, trying to suppress my own grief. I reached forward, swatting away the knife and pulling Nox in.

He wrapped his arms around me, choked sobs muffled by the fabric of my tunic.

"She was too young, Vander. Why—"

His voice cracked as he spoke, the words barely understandable through the grief that had overtaken him.

"I don't know, brother." I tightened my grip, fisting my fingers into my palm as I tried to offer what little comfort I could. He pulled back, clearing his throat and swatting away the tears running down his reddened cheeks.

I watched him carefully as he pulled himself back together, hands still gripping his shoulders to keep him facing me.

"If I had listened to her, if we had... She would have been with us, inside Aerie's wards. Not out roaming to be found by that sadistic fuck."

The guilt was palpable, the anger at not only Kirwan for insisting she'd stayed home that day but also at himself for not arguing harder to let her have her way. My shadows could taste it on him, wrapping around him and lapping at the emotion.

"So no." Nox finally straightened, regaining his composure. "I'm done watching the females in my life get ripped to shreds because someone thought they knew what was best for them. That decision affects so much more than just you. And you *cannot* make it for her."

Nox shrugged out from my hold, taking a step back and hardening his expression. "Besides, Hazel has nowhere else to go, and we both know Aerie and Bastian wouldn't let her leave, even if she tried. Which means if you break that bond, it's going to be you that has to go. And after everything we've lost, you cannot do that to us. To Bastian. To me. But especially to Hazel."

I nodded slowly, already having told myself everything he was voicing out loud now. It was what had kept me from breaking it thus far. I'd figure out a way to deal with the pain of losing her, of spending a lifetime chasing away a need that would never be satisfied. But the ramifications of directly defying the Fates had a way of coming back to bite one in the ass. And I didn't want to endanger her, or the rest of my family, further. It was what kept me here, searching for a loophole—some way to tiptoe around the bond and coexist with Hazel without accepting it fully.

But after our last night together, there was no more denying it. The pull to her was too strong and the longer I spent by her side, the less control I had over both that bond and the Mark. Fear was creeping in at what that meant—what being fated and fully accepting a bond to a darkness such as mine would mean for her goodness and light. It was one thing when she was Hazlenn. An ordinary female who had stolen my heart and soul.

But she was so different now, with so many responsibilities and powers that were bigger than us, than what we wanted. And the more time that passed with this Mark on my arm, the more I was starting to understand that perhaps the same was true of me. And that scared the fuck out of me.

"I know, Nox," I responded, at a loss for how to explain all of that to him. "I vow I will not break it."

Nox nodded, relief flushing through him.

"At least, not without discussing it with her first."

He froze mid-nod, narrowing his eyes in disappointment. But he didn't fight me further.

"That sounds like a fun conversation," he jested, burying the grief and pain once more within him. I forced out a laugh, shaking my head.

"I hope it is one I never have to have. If I could just figure out how to control this fucking mark on my arm, it wouldn't be necessary."

Nox's contrasting eyes cut down to the Mark, noticing how it had come to life against my skin.

"Well, I may not have all the answers." He pointed down at my arm. "But I know what that means when I see it."

The ink danced in silent need, calling for me to spill blood.

"You've spent years trying to learn how to control it. It seems as if it's time to try a new angle."

I cocked my head, my brow furrowed. "What is that supposed to mean?"

Nox reached out, causing me to retreat a step. He put his hands up, sheathing his blade once more as he gently reached forward towards the Mark.

"I mean," he said, taking my arm and running his fingers over the jagged skin. "That not much good has come from you trying to tame the monster, right? So perhaps we try letting the monster free. Seeing what all the fuss is about."

I sneered, pulling my arm back and rubbing my hand over the Mark.

"Cut the sarcasm, Nox. It's not fucking funny."

"I'm not joking, brother. What do you think would happen if you let us see that side of you *all* the time? If you didn't feel the need to repress all that power?"

I clenched my jaw, averting my gaze.

"Because I'm here to tell you, I'm not going anywhere. Kirwan? Bastian?"

He reached out, clutching my shoulder and pulling my gaze back to him.

"Hazel? Not going anywhere."

I swallowed hard. Images of Vesper and his priestesses kneeling before me, his gratitude and respect for saving his village, flashed before my eyes. Hazel's words echoed around me, her consistent insistence to experience my darkness. I couldn't imagine a world where I let the Mark reign free, not keeping its power in check. But if my options were this, or walking away from not only Hazel but the only family I'd ever know, I wasn't sure what else to do.

Nox patted me on the back, ushering me forward as confidence in his argument filled him. "Let's go find us some Daeomi to feast on, brother. Until your little dark heart is content. And then let's go home and you can have that talk with Hazel."

I grimaced at the idea, but perhaps it wasn't the worst thought he'd ever had. Perhaps the loophole wasn't a loophole at all. Perhaps letting that darkness free would be the very thing that allowed me to accept the bond fully. If I could keep the Mark fed, content by not trying to constantly suppress it, perhaps it would feel more stable in Hazel's presence.

Even as my body revolted at the thought, the power in my veins hummed—as if in agreement. I let a slow, hungry growl slip from my throat as I turned my attention back to the depths of the Dark Woods. A silent pact was made between me and whatever darkness resided inside me—a promise to consume, to let the full extent of that bloodlust reign, so long as it let me have my goddess.

CHAPTER 22
HAZEL

Kirwan, Aerie, and I spent the next several days venturing back and forth from the Estate to the meadow in an attempt to keep training with Vesper's technique. Much to my relief, Aerie worked on different things each day, venturing into the realm of dreamwalking and testing other possible manifestations of my magic.

We hadn't found anything else noteworthy with my power, no lingering dark magic left behind by my father either. But I couldn't rest, despite the information. When my body became exhausted from trying to call forth the Divine power within me, Aerie focused instead on my mind, trying to teach me how to focus my subconscious and control my movements, even in sleep, in an effort to help with my dreamwalking. It wasn't all that different from the exercises we did to strengthen my mental wards, and I found more success in those endeavors than I did in exploring the Divine's magic.

Both my body and my mind felt like soup as I walked through the Estate and tried to rally my efforts for the trek back out to the meadow this morning. Kirwan was waiting for me just outside, another basket of snacks tucked carefully in the crook of his arm. I looked around, rubbing sleep from my eyes.

"Where's Aerie?"

"She's not feeling well today. She asked that I continue your training without her."

"Oh." My face fell, concern chasing away any remnant of sleepiness. I turned back to the Estate behind me. "Is she okay? Maybe I should go check on her."

"Bastian's with her," Kirwan assured me. "He knew you'd be worried, but promised to take good care of her while we worked."

"Did he say what's wrong?" I asked. I'd never seen Aerie sick before. It was so unlike her to be unwell and, despite Kirwan's reassurances, I couldn't help but feel like I should stay and help in whatever way I could.

Kirwan shook his head. "Bastian didn't offer and I didn't ask. But it seemed as if it's nothing out of the ordinary for them, based on how Bastian was behaving. I'm sure everything is fine."

I nodded absent-mindedly, still looking back at the Estate.

"We, however, will not be fine if Aerie finds out we missed a day of training to sit around the Estate and worry about her." Kirwan stepped forward, offering a hand.

A small grin slipped over my lips, looking down at his hand and placing my own in his hold. "You're right," I said at last, letting him turn me away.

"I figured we could remain closer to home, just in case something arises and Bastian needs us?" Kirwan led the way over to a grassy knoll just past the gardens of the greenhouse.

I appreciated the sentiment, not sure I had it in me to venture all the way back to the meadow today. My mind was now preoccupied with concerns about Aerie. But even if it hadn't been, Vander and Lennox had still yet to return. My spirits had fallen once again when I woke up this morning to find they were still gone.

I knew by the way Kirwan watched the horizon that his mind was there too.

"Have you heard anything from him?" I asked.

Kirwan's gaze fell from the distance, finding mine beside him and holding it for a brief moment before shaking his head. "I fear I may have overstepped some things with Lennox. And unfortunately that means he's not keeping me privy to his whereabouts."

I nodded, stealing a glance at the twin's contrasting eyes.

"You?" he asked, setting the basket down and circling the knoll for the best spot to set up for training. I cleared my throat, embarrassed to admit the emotion that was coming over me at the question.

"Nothing yet. I fear I may be in the same predicament with Vander as you are with Nox."

"Ahh," Kirwan called out, finding his spot and turning to face me. "It appears we are being iced out, then."

The confession had a weight to it, but the twinkle in his eye pulled a small laugh from me. At least if I had to endure this punishment, I wouldn't have to endure it alone.

I decided not to share how I'd been doing some icing out of my own, making sure to keep my barriers up while Vander was gone. I knew they were no real threat to him, that he could easily break them if he wanted to, or needed to, reach me. The tether was no match for the sorry excuse of restraint I feigned through our bond. But it made me feel a modicum more in control by keeping them there, letting Vander know any time he tested the connection that I wasn't interested in what he had to say, unless he was ready to say it to my face.

Kirwan clapped, breaking me from my thoughts. "Ready to begin?"

I nodded, stepping up to him and offering him my palms.

"I figured we'd focus on the Divine magic again, as I'm not as skilled in the other areas as Aerie is." He took my hands, turning them over and cradling them gently so I could see the ink staring up at us. "Remember what she said, focus specifically on that deeper power. Think of the things that connect you to it. The soft grass, the sunlight on your skin. Whatever it is, hold onto that and only that."

I nodded, closing my eyes as he turned my hands back over. I relished in the warm feeling of his magic against my palms. I thought of the way Vesper played with the Cosmos, the stars answering to his call. I thought of the way it felt to harvest herbs in the garden with Aerie, the feel of my fingers in the dirt and the sun beating down on my neck.

Still, nothing happened.

"It's okay, keep trying." The words should have been an encouragement, but after hearing nothing but those four words for the last several days, they did nothing but irritate me. I dropped my hands, groaning as I retreated several steps.

"Perhaps this is pointless." I threw my hands up, gesturing between us. "Aerie thought your magic would help call my own forward, but all I've been able to summon in the past few days is what little bit of lesser magic I've been capable of controlling for weeks now. Perhaps that is all I'll ever be able to summon."

Kirwan plopped down on the ground, patting the spot beside him. Reluctantly, I joined. He pulled the basket towards us, rummaging around until he produced a jar of chocolate morsels. He popped one in his mouth, then offered one to me. I took it, biting hesitantly into the candy and stifling a moan at the way the chocolate melted in my mouth.

Kirwan watched me carefully, a smile playing at his lips.

"You know, you remind me a lot of my mother," he said abruptly. I straightened, cocking my head towards him.

"Really?" I asked.

He nodded, taking another piece of chocolate and popping it in his mouth. "You would have loved her. She loved to be outdoors, too. Many in the Auris tribe do, it's not surprising. But there was something different about the way she revered the world around her."

He turned his head, staring up at the sky above. "Being her child, seeing her love and passion for all of this, it was like witnessing some sacred connection."

I hummed, understanding the pull. I turned my face skyward as well, closing my eyes and feeling the warmth of the sun's rays on my face.

"But it wasn't nature that made it special," Kirwan continued. I opened one eye, peeking out at him. "She could have loved anything to that same extent and it would have been just as inspiring to witness.

"It was the care she took when experiencing the thing she loved. The passion she refused to hide, because she knew she had me and Nox in tow, taking after her and mimicking everything we could. She wanted to make sure, more than anything, she raised us to have a passion for, well, *passion*. A desire to love and to understand the importance in pouring energy into ourselves, feeding our souls with the things that brought us joy."

He turned his attention to me, throwing me a wink. "Being unapologetically us."

I returned his smile, slightly embarrassed at how awkward his story made me feel. I could see that part of their mother in both Kirwan and Nox, could even see her light in them. The twins were both the definition of 'unapologetically' them. But it was a sentiment I didn't think I could relate to. Something I'd so rarely felt.

"Hazel, do you mind if I ask you a question?" He continued on, looking back at the tree line.

I sat for a moment, considering, before bowing my head as permission.

"What do you think about? When you retreat within yourself in an effort to differentiate between those two forms of magic within you?"

I hummed, turning to look out at the land before me. "This," I offered, gesturing to our surroundings. "Just like you said, the feel of the sunlight, the soil, things that connect me to nature."

He nodded, following my gaze. "I know as well as anyone how hard it can be to differentiate dueling powers. There was a time where my tribal magic from the moon tribe and the sun tribe existed as separate entities within me. I could call upon each as I wished, but never both at the same time."

He lifted a palm, letting tendrils of the golden light of the Auris tribe forward, mimicking the motion as his other palm released an orb of silvery moonlight.

"But it took me years, decades even, to realize that keeping those powers separate was only weakening them. Weakening myself." He brought his hands together, the lights twining to pulse brighter and grow into something different. Something grander.

I reached a hand out, fingers tracing the show of magic hanging in the air between us. It recognized me, sought after me, and before I knew it I was giggling as the power played and danced around me before dispersing as Kirwan lowered his hands.

"Perhaps that's the key for you as well. You have all of this contradicting power inside you. That passed down from the tribes though your mother, some sort of fae abilities from—" He paused on the name, as if it pained him to say it out loud.

"Kahlis," I offered, hating the sound of it just as much as he did. He grimaced, but nodded.

"And somehow, the Divine has returned, manifesting her power inside of you. For whatever reason, she chose you. She believed in you. Or else it would have not been so."

I pulled my knees up to my chest, leaning against the tops of them. "I think on some level I must know that. It's the logical answer to all of this. But it's hard to believe she would have chosen me. What makes me so special?"

Kirwan hummed, picking out another chocolate from the jar between us and offering it to me. "Perhaps that's exactly what you're meant to discover. Why we must persist. Learning to embrace that power, *all* of that power within you, it will give you the best understanding of why."

I huffed out a sigh, laying my head down against my legs. "I suppose."

"Have you gained any insight from the reading Aerie has given you on the Divine?" Kirwan popped the chocolate into his mouth.

I sighed. "Nothing groundbreaking. Despite the copious amounts of reading both Aerie and I have been doing, nothing has specifically pertained to my powers yet. Just a lot of adjacent insight that hasn't helped much."

"Ah," Kirwan nodded. "And what of your mother's journal? Have you been reading that as well?"

I nodded, unenthusiastically. "It's been less than helpful I'm afraid. A lot of lamenting about the choices that led her to my birth. A lot of guilt-ridden explanations about the love she harbored for my father, despite his darkness." I scrunched my face up in disgust, picking at the grass beside me.

Kirwan hummed.

"What?" I asked.

"It's just interesting to me," Kirwan mused. "The way your mother's relationship with Kahlis kind of mirrors yours with Vander."

I scoffed, my body jerking in protest at the wild accusation. "It does not."

"Doesn't it?" I could see the corner of Kirwan's mouth tilt up at my irritation, that playful side he shared with his brother coming through.

"Vander is nothing like Kahlis," I argued.

"I'm not saying they're the same," Kirwan agreed. "But you have to admit, both males have a darkness in them. Both have blood on their hands, lives lost by their tempers."

I grunted under my breath, refusing to admit the logic in his reasoning.

"All I'm saying is I find it interesting that your stories hold so many similarities. It's an odd twist of Fate."

I fell silent for a long time, uncomfortable with the similarities Kirwan was pointing out. But the longer I sat with it, the more it did feel odd. Why would the Fates weave our life threads together, knowing the darkness and heartache that I was born out of?

"We're different," I said at last, speaking the truth into existence, even if doubt was making its way into my heart. "We won't end up like them."

"Of course not." His voice had softened, sympathy and something akin to pity leaking into his words. "I didn't mean to upset you. I was just making a poorly timed observation."

I sighed, digging my hands into the dirt beneath them.

"Forgive me for speaking out of turn?" Kirwan asked when I didn't respond.

I nodded, but something else had come to mind. Kirwan's observation reminded me of another prediction given to me not too long ago.

"Have you ever heard of the card Discord?"

"Ah." Kirwan chuckled softly. "So you've been getting readings from the priestesses then? Did Lennox not warn you against them during your trip?"

I pursed my lips, shaking my head.

Kirwan hummed, toying with whatever words were on the edge of his tongue. "Hazel, the priestesses' readings are always elusive, confusing. And while the members of the moon tribe may enjoy dabbling in the magic of the Cosmos, it's not often perceived as reliable."

"But you're not saying they're wrong or untrustworthy," I pushed. "Just that they're misunderstood, essentially."

Kirwan raised an eyebrow at me. He chewed on the inside of his cheek, making his face appear hollow. "I suppose," he answered at last. "While not everyone agrees with their methods, I do believe their predictions and prophecies are genuine... if not inherently convoluted.”

“So do you know the card?” I pressed again.

“I’ve heard of it.” He nodded, fidgeting against the grass as he repositioned himself.

“Perhaps it has something to do with the similarities between me and Vander and my mother and father’s relationship?” My voice sounded hopeful even as my heart sank. As much as I wanted to avoid facing the uncomfortable truth of the comparison, I craved understanding—clarity. “Perhaps you’re picking up on the same thing the priestess did when she offered me my reading, when she pulled that card.”

I thought he was going to dismiss me, to tell me to forget he ever said anything and tell me that everything would be fine. Instead he closed his eyes, retreating to some inward part of himself—as if tapping into his tribal magic.

“The card of Discord can be interpreted many different ways, too many to make any real kind of prediction. It is true that there are ties between your relationship with Vander and your mother and Kahlis’ own relationship; however there are many differences as well. Not to mention you have a Cosmic magic within you.”

I felt its warmth bubble within me in response.

“I suppose you could say Vander does as well,” Kirwan added. My eyes snapped back to him.

“What do you mean?” I asked on an exhale.

Kirwan’s eyes opened, brow furrowed. “His deal with Death, the Mark on his arm? Whose magic do you think stains his soul?”

I shook my head. I'd known of Death, of the deal Vander had made, but I supposed we'd never talked about the source of his magic in that way, nor had I ever correlated my connection with the Divine to Vander's connection with Death. The tome Aerie had found in the Sgàil's archives flashed through my mind. She'd called it the story of Death and the Divine, yet she'd insisted I wait to read it. She must have understood the juxtaposition of our relationships as well, which made me wonder if I was the only one who'd yet to connect those dots.

"So what are you saying?" I asked, shaking my head again as I tried to make sense of the tangled web inside my mind.

"That I can't say anything for sure. As I told you, dabbling with the magic of the Cosmos is not always exact. But I can say that regardless of these similarities with Kahlis and your mother, regardless of the cards pulled by the priestess, you can rest easily in the comfort of your bond with Vander. It doesn't take a seer to know that the bond you share is a strong one. Regardless of whatever possibilities lie in your future, there will always be that."

I fell back in the grass, sighing audibly as I covered my face with my hands. "I'm so tired of feeling so confused," I admitted behind my palms. " Kahlis, the Divine, everything going on with Vander—it just all feels so impossible."

Kirwan laughed, laying a hand against my knee and tapping. "Come on, a bit of chocolate always helps. Let's try again." He helped me to my feet, taking my hands once more. "This time, rather than focusing on the things that connect you to that power within you, focus more on what makes you feel like yourself. That uncensored, fully accepted version of you."

I cleared my throat, nerves ravaging my body. I tried to steady the shakiness in my hands. Kirwan must have noticed, because he wrapped his own hands tenderly around mine. Somehow, this prompt felt far more intimidating than the one Aerie had been using to coax that Divine power from me.

I closed my eyes and let the world around me fall away. The wind caressed my body in soft encouragement, the song of the birds and bugs surrounding me and transporting me to a new place entirely.

I didn't need to think about Kirwan's words, didn't need to debate where that unabashed version of myself existed. Instead, I pictured standing amongst Vander's shadows. Watching them part for me as he finally let me in, breaking down each and every barrier he'd once built to keep me out.

Suddenly, I was no longer on the knoll with Kirwan, I was kneeling before Vander. I was collapsing in the hold of his shadows, staring up into his obsidian eyes. Letting him see the most stripped down, raw version of me. He was everywhere, all around me, invading all of my senses claiming every part of my soul. I existed within a different world, a sacred space that allowed me to be me, and didn't require anything more.

A new sensation burst forth, an energy buzzing through my body that I couldn't tame. My eyes shot open, warmth pooling there. Kirwan's gasp confirmed what I suspected, the power of the Divine flowing freely through me. The grass stretched up to reach me, the wind shifted course to circle me, the earth itself turned its attention to where we stood.

I pulled my hands back, an excited noise bubbling up inside me and bursting past my lips as I looked down at my hands then back up to Kirwan. He was equally as shocked, pride beaming from him.

I threw my arms around him, his own wrapping around my waist as he lifted me into the air and twirled me, both of us hysterical with the sign of progress. After several spins, he set me back down, backing away and running a hand over his jaw.

"That was brilliant, Hazel. Truly, well done."

"I can't believe that worked!" I squealed, unable to pull my eyes away from the ink still glowing on my palms.

"Neither can I," Kirwan admitted. I shot him an offended look, swatting at his arm. He held up his hands as he feigned defense. "I'm sorry, but it's not like I've had any experience in training a goddess before, love. How was I supposed to know if that advice would actually work?"

I smirked at him, incapable of keeping the laughter at bay. "You called me love," I teased after our amusement settled some. Kirwan's jaw tightened briefly.

"I, uh—" He cleared his throat, any hint of laughter dying away, something like dread or regret taking its place. "I did. I'm sorry. I know Lennox uses the nickname for you. I suppose it's influenced me. I will refrain from using it again if it doesn't suit you."

I hummed, watching him squirm for a moment longer before answering: "I think it fits well." I reached down, grabbing the jar of chocolates and tossing one in my mouth before throwing one his way. "I think we've earned it, don't you?"

He chuckled, savoring the taste as his mouth closed around the sweet treat.

"Thank you, Kirwan. Truly. I don't think I could have done this without you." I pulled him into a hug once more. "I'm lucky to have you as a friend."

He tensed around me, so at odds with his behavior from just moments before. I pulled away, wondering if I'd suddenly overstepped.

"HazeI—" He raised his hand to the back of his neck, rubbing and avoiding my eyes. My brow furrowed, not understanding the sudden shift in his mood. "I have something I need to tell you."

I opened my mouth to speak, but a whooping sound cut me off. We both turned our attention to the tree line, finding Vander and Lennox emerging from the Dark Woods. Nox waved excitedly, emitting another obnoxious whoop as he took off in a run to greet us.

I was running in an instant, meeting Nox halfway and throwing my arms around him in greeting.

"I was so worried about you," I chided, shoving him backwards when he finally let me go.

"Worried about me? What, like a couple of Daeomi were any true threat to my power?" He chuckled as Vander came up beside him. "And you know, having the Shadow of the Grimm with me may have helped a little."

I shook my head, rolling my eyes as I turned to greet Vander. I hesitated, unsure what exactly to do. Vander looked down, hiding a hint of a smile as he stepped forward and pulled me into a hug. I melted against him, a wave of relief flooding my senses at finally seeing him, safe and home and in my arms once more.

"So you tracked them down?" I asked, attempting to turn back to Nox. Vander let me turn but kept his arm around me, barely a breath of space between us. Kirwan joined us as well, exchanging awkwardly formal nods with Nox and crossing his arms over his chest.

"Of course, love. Was there ever any doubt in your mind?" Nox threw me a wink, turning back to the Estate ahead. "Now where's the food? I'm famished."

We followed his path, making our way back up to the Estate. Kirwan lingered behind to grab the basket and other items we'd brought out. I slipped out of Vander's arm, motioning for him to give me a moment as I made my way back to Kirwan.

"It's alright, Hazel. I can get it," he called out as I trotted up beside him.

"Now what kind of friend would I be if I didn't help you? After all, you've already done so much for me today." The buzz of my power was still warming my skin, just within reach. I was giddy at the sensation, antsy to start learning how to use it, control it. He offered me a kind smile, but it didn't quite reach his eyes.

"Oh, what were you wanting to tell me?" I asked. Kirwan looked at me a moment, glancing over my shoulder to where Vander waited for us. I followed his gaze and wiggled my fingers at Vander in a sarcastic wave.

"Don't mind him," I turned back to Kirwan. "He's just marking his territory." I rolled my eyes, making a gagging sound that made Kirwan laugh.

"It wasn't anything important. We can discuss it later."

He bent down to grab the basket, taking the jar of chocolates from my hand and tucking them inside.

"Are you sure? I don't mind making him wait," I offered.

"I insist," he pushed, stepping forward and lacing his arm through mine. "Let's get them inside and fed before Lennox starts rioting."

I laughed, following his lead and turning back towards Vander.

I knew how much work we had to do from here—the sheer size of it had me grimacing. But I'd finally tapped into that Divine power within me. Had figured out how to call it forward, the first semblance of control I'd been able to muster over it. And now with my boys home, and everyone I love tucked safely under one roof, I couldn't help the smile beaming on my face as we made our way back into the Estate.

CHAPTER 23
HAZEL

The four of us moved around the kitchen, filling the small space with chatter and laughter as we prepared some simple foods and set them out on the center counter for a late lunch. Nox filled us in on the more gruesome details of their journey, my stomach souring at the constant reference to the amount of bloodshed that took place.

Vander nodded quietly, agreed with Nox when he turned to him for confirmation and rolling his eyes when Nox exaggerated details. Kirwan and I listened intently, his eyes occasionally finding mine as if to ask when I'd share my own victories.

I pretended to ignore it, not wanting to take away from Vander's moment.

"You should have seen him, Hazel." Nox's words boomed through the small space. I longed for the sound after spending so many days in the half empty home. "I've never seen him fight like that. Here one moment, there another. Ripping those Daeomi trash apart, limb from limb. There must have been at least a dozen of them traveling in the horde."

I suppressed a shudder at the idea of that many all in one place. It was a nightmarish image, one I hoped to quickly forget.

"Of course," Nox added, placing a hand to his chest and batting his eyelashes. "I did take out my fair share."

"Bullshit," Vander scoffed. "You think I would have been fighting that hard to keep up with them if I could have relied on you to take care of your half?"

"Hey, hey," Nox argued, throwing his hands up. "Not all of us can cheat our way through battle, alright? I handled my share and left the rest up to you, because I knew you couldn't help yourself."

Vander growled in response, his shadows snaking their way around the kitchen. My stomach tensed at the sensation, hating to admit how the feel of their presence heated my core. Vander must have sensed it, too. His gaze cut over to me briefly, his forearms flexing as he folded his arms across his chest.

"Come on, brother," Kirwan cut in, snapping us both back to the conversation at hand. "We've both seen you in battle, there's no point in trying to fool me. And I'm not going to stand by and let you convince Hazel of your valiance when we all know you're more akin to a snake than you are a beast."

I shifted my weight, clearing my throat at the sudden mention of my name. Nox cut Kirwan a look that could kill, giving him only a moment to retreat before he pounced on him, wrestling his twin and knocking dishes over on the counter.

"What in the Depths is happening in here?" Everyone froze as Bastian strode in, looking exhausted. A small grin teased his lips though, as he looked down on the twins finally returning to some semblance of normalcy.

"Lennox is attempting to convince them he took down an entire horde of Daeomi without a lick of help from me," Vander drawled, leveling Nox with a wicked grin. "And I was about to explain how using my shadows does not, in fact, count as cheating when it comes to battle."

Bastian's eyebrows raised, turning first to face Nox. He lifted a finger, pointing at where Kirwan still had Nox pinned in a head-lock, refusing to let go. "No one is going to believe that your weasel ass took on more than one Daeomi and walked away alive."

"Hey!" Nox objected, shoving Kirwan off of him and righting himself. Bastian paused mid-turn, looking back over his shoulder at Nox and bobbing his head.

"Okay, two tops."

Nox opened his mouth to argue, but Bastian turned to Vander and continued before he had the chance to fight back:

"And you using the power of the Mark *definitely* counts as cheating."

"Thank you!" Nox shouted, throwing his arms up in the air.

Bastian dipped his head in regards to Nox, before turning back to Vander and winking at him. Vander watched for a second, debating taking the bait. But to my surprise, he dropped it, letting a deep chuckle slip past his lips before coming up to pat Bastian on the back.

"Whatever you say, Chieftain."

This started a new influx of arguments between Nox and Kirwan, Bastian chiming in with jests and jabs when he saw fit. It was food for my soul, seeing them all get along so well, filling the Estate with laughter and joy for the first time in weeks.

Vander caught my gaze as I sat back and watched their bickering, motioning to the side entrance and slipping through the doorway in graceful silence. I looked back to the other males, so lost in their arguments that they didn't even notice, and slunk out after him.

Vander was just outside the kitchen, leaning on the wall of the greenhouse and waiting for me. I slowly clicked the door shut as I turned to face him. The way the setting sun hit his skin should have been a violation of tribal law. It was too golden, too beautiful. I let my eyes wander over the ribboned muscles of his arms and exposed chest.

Vander whistled, bringing my attention back to his face.

"Eyes up here, little spitfire," he teased, an annoying smirk waiting for me when I finally processed what he'd said.

"You sure are rather full of yourself," I scoffed, pushing forward and walking past him towards the grassy knolls Kirwan and I had occupied earlier that day. I wasn't sure where I was going, but I knew I needed to keep walking or I'd never be able to keep my eyes off him. And I wasn't ready to let him think we were okay.

"So you're not going to act like you weren't just imagining the sight of me naked and basking in the sunlight?"

He cut in front of me, throwing off my stride. I stumbled into him, but he caught me easily—his hands lingering as he righted me. His touch was electric, going straight to the apex of my thighs. I pulled my arm from his grasp.

"You can't do this, Vander."

"Do what." It wasn't a question. It was an invitation to state my accusations. As if he already knew my anger and was merely antagonizing me further. I ground my teeth, taking a step backwards and planting my feet.

"You cannot continue with this back and forth. Wanting me one minute and running away the next. You cannot let me in one night and take off the next day, because you're too scared to admit you want this as badly as I do."

Vander scoffed, rolling his eyes. "I am not scared."

"Yes, Vander, you are. Or maybe my worst fears are real and it's not that you're scared..." His eyes snapped to mine, his jaw clenching as he waited for me to continue. I licked my lips, my mouth suddenly going dry. "It's that I'm not enough for you."

He wasted no time closing the distance between us. He invaded my space, everything about him filling my senses. His shadows wrapped around us in hungry desperation as he gripped my chin and forced my downcast face to meet his gaze.

"How the *fuck* could you ever think you aren't enough for me?"

"What else am I supposed to think?" My words came out too quiet, pain laced through every one. "When you continue to toy with me? When I'm getting whiplash from your indecisiveness? I know this isn't what you chose, Vander. The Fates wove our life threads together, not you. But when you act the way you have, of course I'm going to have my doubts. I've stripped myself bare for you, countless times now. And yet you still continue to run away."

His fingers stroked down the side of my cheek, the pad of his thumb whisking away a tear I hadn't realized had escaped. His throat bobbed, his eyes full of pain as he looked down on me.

"I never meant to make you feel that way, Hazel. Of course I fucking want you."

I squeezed my eyes closed, pursing my lips at the words I couldn't believe.

"That's the issue, little spitfire. I want you so bad that it's consumed my entire being. Any semblance of control I once had over my darkness has evaporated in your presence. I've told you this already, but you just don't fucking get it." He closed his eyes, breathing deeply for a moment. I peeked up, watching the way his nostrils flared as he tried to keep his composure.

"I get it, Vander. I do, but—"

"You're too stubborn to listen to me." His voice rose, cutting me off. "To accept it. You said I'm scared—you're right, I am. But not to be with you. I'm scared of what I may do to you when I can no longer hold back the Mark. When this facade of control I've put forth crumbles and you see me for the monster I am."

"You've shown me your darkness, Vander. I accepted it. I *want* it. We've been over this."

"I know," he sighed. He pinched the bridge of his nose with his thumb and forefinger. "But what I showed you was still only a fraction of the Mark's influence. Even in those darkest moments..." He paused, his jaw flexing as he averted his gaze. "I was still holding back. Still testing you to see if you were truly ready."

His voice was soft, regretful. It did nothing to help lighten the blow. Even in our most vulnerable moments, it had still been a facade. Even when he said he wasn't holding back, he had been. What I thought was a turning point for us had been nothing more than another game to him. I felt gutted, raw, hopeless even as he pulled me in.

His touch felt suddenly foreign, so at odds with the male I was used to. If he had decided to stay at an arm's length, to deny me what I'd been begging for, then why was he here now, revealing all of these truths to me?

"Take a walk with me," he said at last. I pulled back, cocking my head to the side at the abrupt request.

He offered me a small grin, dropping his arms to grasp my hand and pull me towards the tree line in the distance. My stomach tightened at the thought of walking with him through the Dark Woods, but his shadows swirled at my feet in silent reassurance of my safety.

So I followed him, willingly, into the darkness beyond.

He didn't speak again until we were deep within the clutches of the Dark Woods. It always shocked me how dark this place was, even when the sun was burning bright on the horizon, just beyond its borders. Every stray leaf and distant shadow had my teeth on edge. Fear flooded my veins, but any time it rose too high, a familiar tug of the shadows around my legs brought me back down.

With his protection, there was nothing for me to fear here.

His stride slowed as he brought me to a small cluster of gnarled roots. They broke from the ground, wrestling with each other in massive waves of bark and knots until they burst forth into a wooden fortress of tangled limbs that reached out around and above us.

"Sit," he ordered. I obeyed without question, recognizing this as his territory.

I sat on one of the raised roots, tracking his movements as he began pacing before me. His hands were clasped behind his back, his posture more formal than I was used to. It struck something in me, making my hands fidget in my lap as I waited for him to get on with it.

"I brought you here to make you a proposition," he said at last. My stomach tightened. "Our bond, this connection we have—you're right, we cannot go on as we have been. I've been trying for some time now to find a loophole. A way to be with you without fully accepting the bond. Or without fully releasing my hold on the Mark. I'd thought I'd come close the other night, but it wasn't enough."

Pain blossomed in my chest as I tried to suppress the relentless echo of vicious thoughts ringing out to be heard. He turned his full attention to me, shadows growing as he narrowed his gaze and silenced the voices.

"But not because you are unworthy of me, little spitfire. Quite contrary to that, actually." He stepped forward, kneeling before me. "It is I who feels unworthy of you. Your goodness, your heart." He reached a hand out, resting it against my chest. His shadows pulsed to the rhythm of my heart, growing larger with each passing beat. He forced himself back after a moment, his shadows shrinking. "And the closer to you I get, the closer I get to accepting our bond, the more I lose control of the Mark. It frightens me, so much so that I was convinced I needed a way out."

"A way out?" I echoed, eyes squinting and head shaking as I tried to understand his meaning.

He took a deep breath, averting his gaze as he stared down at the forest floor.

"A bond made by the Fates may be broken, in the most dire of circumstances. It has its repercussions, obviously, but it's nothing I'm not prepared to take on. And you should be free and clear of any such consequences, so long as I was the one to break the bond."

I stood, the world around me caving in. "Breaking the bond? That's your solution?!" He didn't respond, just pursed his lips together and stared at the ground. "I thought this wasn't something that could be broken? That the connection between fated mates was woven by the Fates themselves, an impenetrable force?"

"It is." Vander raised his hand in a suggestive manner, as if I needed to calm down. It frustrated me further, my teeth grinding against each other as I waited for him to explain. "The Fates have woven our life threads together, and what they set in place, no creature is to disrupt. That is true. But if I break the bond—"

I rose to my feet, shouting back at his ridiculous notion as I charged towards him. He stepped back, pressing on and speaking over my objections.

"If I *choose* to defy the Fates, if I choose to deny the bond... it would sever our connection. At least for you."

"For me?" I repeated, nearly yelling as my frustration reached a fever pitch.

He nodded, swallowing hard. "The punishment for defying the Fates would mean that the bond would never be fully deconstructed for me. I would live a life chasing the need to claim you. But you'd be free to move on, to fall in love." His voice broke, the first sign of emotion he'd shown since he started talking.

"It's your one opportunity to find something better, Hazel. To be free of this darkness and live a life you deserve."

"Don't you dare stand there and tell me what I deserve." I shoved against his chest hard, my voice shaking. I followed him as he stumbled backwards, closing the distance between us even as I raised my hands to push him again. "When all I've ever done is tell you how much I wanted you. I've done nothing but accept your darkness, welcome *every* side of you. Even when you've lied to me and refused to let me see you fully. And this is how you respond? By pushing me away and sacrificing yourself to some half life of pain and anguish?"

"I'm already living a half life," he whispered, a sad grin stretching across his lips. "My soul is fractured. This darkness has consumed what small piece of it I still cling to." He gestured down to his arm at the Mark. "And without embracing the bond fully, there's not much difference between the life I'm living now and the one I'd be subjected to—after. But it would be different for you. Better."

"I cannot believe you would actually consider this." Tears pricked my eyes, realizing just how thought-out his plan was. It wasn't a whim, some half assed idea he'd decided to voice. It was methodical, intentional. And that broke my heart even further.

"I need you to understand how desperate I am, Hazel. The closer I get to you, the more unstable my magic becomes. I cannot allow myself to hurt you—"

"Hurt me?! You wont even fucking *look* at me, Vander!" He flinched at the accusation, his eyes dutifully trained on the ground before him. "You want me to believe you're this strong, monstrous creature? Someone I should fear? All I see standing before me is a *coward*. And while you've come up with this grand plan to keep yourself from hurting me, all you've done is tear me down. Your sacrifice is *meaningless*, nothing more than self-deprevation because you're incapable of knowing how to love."

"I know." His voice was a whisper, a plea for forgiveness. I shook my head, running my hands through my hair. "But I've made a decision, little spitfire."

"Well thank the Fates for that." I turned to face the trees, throwing my hands into the air. "Vander Darroch has finally made a decision. Fuck the rest of us, but at least he has made a decision!"

A smirk peeked out from his still bowed head, making me want to scream at him. I rushed forward, shoving him again at the sight.

"What exactly about this is funny, Vander?" He didn't even budge this time, my strength no match for his, even on my fiercest day.

"I quite enjoy the look of wrath on you." Gone was any hint of remorse, any morsel of pain or regret. That familiar darkness was taking over, snuffing out what little light was left within his being.

"You want me to fight you, Vander?" I asked, fury diving deep within my veins and grabbing for that foreign fire.

He remained silent, waiting. Testing. Playing his little games, even now.

I sneered, lifting my hands and calling forth the power I'd felt earlier today. It flowed from me without a second thought, bursting to life in fierce determination. The Dark Woods came to life around me, my light chasing away the shadows as the foliage exploded in shades of green and brown.

Vander raised his gaze to meet mine. Nothing but pure onyx greeted me there, matched in darkness only by the twisted smile that snaked its way across his face. He stood stock still in the crest of our dueling power, completely unmoved and unbothered.

"I see you've been practicing, goddess."

"What other option did you leave me, than to learn to control this power that fills my veins, in order to protect you? To protect myself?" My chest heaved with the effort I put forth, my hands still outstretched before me. "Yes, I've been practicing, you bastard. For *you*." Roots broke forth to kneel at my feet as I spoke. The trees bowed to me. Even Vander's shadows paused their battle with my light and turned their attention to me.

"Because what else was I supposed to do while you ran off galavanting through the Dark Woods, leaving me alone to feel inferior? Worthless? What else was I to do to get your attention, you jackass?!" I pulled my hands back only long enough to throw them forward once again, doubling down on the fire burning inside me. In a flurry of rage, the Dark Woods descended upon Vander.

The trees bent towards him, the roots snaking across the forest floor reaching up to him. Even the wind shifted, swirling around his form. My mind cleared the moment I saw it consume him, fear and regret smothering any fight I had left to give. I grasped for control, pleading for my power to rein in, to fix this mistake before I hurt him.

But to my surprise, Vander's shadows rose, swallowing the foliage descending upon him. Merging with it in an intimidating, all-consuming, sea of black.

Another shadow shot out, binding my wrists before me. I attempted to break their hold, but the power still buzzing through my body was still so unfamiliar, too difficult to control. Instead of coming forth again, it sank deep into my bones, accepting the fate I'd been dealt.

Vander stepped out of the chasm of black before me, stalking forward with a determination that had me shrinking back. His body was too calm, his eyes too intent, as he raked his gaze over my bound form before him.

"You made a great show of power, Hazel. Rather impressive. But you've made one mistake in all of this."

"And what's that," I spat at him with feigned confidence, squirming beneath his shadows even as I retreated further back.

"You didn't let me share what decision I made."

"I'm well aware of what you're attempting to tell me, Vander. I didn't need to hear you say it. Or are you set on twisting the blade you've stabbed in my back?"

He stopped in front of me, lips pressed tightly together as if he was trying to contain a laugh even still. I furrowed my brow, thrown off by his demeanor and wondering how he could be so cavalier.

"It is true, I had seriously thought about breaking the bond. But then..."

My heartbeat picked up speed, but I refused to let this bastard toy with my emotions again.

"I decided instead to see what it felt like to embrace that darkness. To let it take hold. Consume. Fully. For possibly the first time since it claimed me."

"And how am I supposed to trust you're telling me the truth this time?" I whipped my head around, trying to follow his movements as he began to circle me. Like a wolf on the hunt.

"Because, little spitfire." His lips teased at my ear from behind, making me jump. "If I can't control the darkness, then I must let it control me." His fingers brushed the curve of my shoulder. "And the darkness wants you. Possibly more than any other being in the Cosmos."

He chuckled deeply as he came back into my field of view, rubbing a hand along his jaw. "Something the Mark and I seem to have in common."

My core tightened, a swirl of desire snaking its way into my system.

"So then, you're... not breaking the bond?" I asked hesitantly.

He made his way back in front of me, his tall form overbearing in the way he closed in on me. He looked down, letting out a breathy laugh.

"No, goddess. I'm not. I'm choosing you."

I looked up at him, tears stinging my eyes. My mind couldn't handle the flood of emotion he was pulling from me. My body felt exhausted, my limbs shaky as I searched his face for any hint of deceit or trickery.

"Really?" I whispered, my voice rough and raw.

"Really." He lifted a hand, tucking my hair behind my ear. He tipped my face up to him, kissing away the tears now freely falling down my cheeks.

"I've made a deal with my darkness," he whispered against my skin. "You see, as long as I give my darkness what it wants, feed its desires and stop fighting its influence, you'll remain safe."

"And what exactly is it that your darkness desires?" I asked, breath heavy, nerves crippling.

"Right now?" Vander asked, dipping his head to the last tear lingering on my cheek. My core went molten as his tongue darted out, licking up the moisture. He hummed, pressing his forehead against my skin as he thought for a moment.

I gasped as the shadows broke away from my wrists, freeing me from their hold.

"Right now, my darkness wants you to run."

Vander stepped back, eyes black as night as he waited for me to make my decision.

"What?" I gaped. I didn't understand his words, sure I'd misheard or misunderstood them.

He clasped his hands behind his back once more in that unsettling way that set me on edge. He didn't speak aloud again, just lowered his chin to watch me through hooded eyes as he let a singular word radiate down the tether.

Run.

CHAPTER 24
HAZEL

I turned and ran, not waiting for him to repeat the command again. He didn't move, not at first, giving me a head start as my footsteps pounded against the solid forest floor. My mind raced faster than my feet as my vision tried to adjust to the blur of trees passing by. My stomach fluttered, a mix of excitement and fear and confusion fighting to take over.

My legs threatened to give out, the muscles in my thighs shaking with each stride. I pushed myself harder, refusing to give him the satisfaction of such an easy chase. I didn't fully understand what he was wanting, the overwhelming confusion of the journey he'd just taken me on still untangling itself in my mind. I wasn't sure if I obeyed to appease him or if I was genuinely terrified of what would happen if he caught me.

But if there was one thing I did understand, it was that the Mark was in control at the moment, and it wanted me. More importantly, it wanted me to run.

So I ran.

I felt his shadows nipping at my heels, a deep chuckle reverberating down the tether. I blew hot air through clenched teeth as I tried to muster as much strength as I could. I cut left, darting into a thicker part of the forest in hopes that the foliage would provide some coverage as I tried to force more distance between us.

A wall of shadow stopped me hard. I recoiled, hissing at the sharp pain that radiated through my body as I rebounded off the solid barrier.

Not that way, little spitfire.

Not fair, I shouted back through the tether.

I took a quick look at the other options around me, spinning desperately before deciding a moment later to cut back to the right. It wasn't the path I wanted to take, but if he wanted me to go this way, then I would.

At this point, sprinting through the Dark Woods, sweat dripping down my face and legs burning like fire from the Depths, I wasn't sure there was anything he couldn't make me do.

I didn't know what it was, but there was an inherent need within me, a primal desire to obey his every command. Even if I'd wanted to walk away, I didn't think I could.

I ducked behind one of the broad hemlocks, stilling my motions and covering my mouth to listen for him. The rough bark cut into my back, but I pressed further into its shadows, flattening myself against it. The forest had gone utterly silent, as it often did in his presence. But I couldn't track his movements anywhere. I peered out into the darkness, trying to decide which direction was the safest bet.

What he'd said about letting the darkness control him had frightened me in a way nothing else had before. My instincts were kicking in, telling me this was foolish. Dangerous. After all, he'd admitted he was no longer in control. Whatever we were doing, it was like playing with fire. But what I was feeling now wasn't true fear, the kind I'd felt when I'd been chased by the Daeomi or when Kahlis had invaded my dreams. This was different, stronger. Visceral.

It was a sensation I craved, this game we were playing. Just as I had loved it when he'd made me kneel before him the other night. It had always been there, this deep desire to experience his darkness. To obey his command. And now it was happening; he was setting it free and showing me all sides of himself.

That singular thing would keep me going. Running. Hiding. Doing whatever he demanded of me. So long as he kept himself open, continued showing me who he truly was, I'd keep playing his games.

I crept out from behind the tree, head on a swivel as I tried to determine my next steps.

"I thought I said *run*, goddess." The sheer closeness of his voice shocked me, a clipped cry breaking through my lips. I slammed my hands over my mouth, whipping around to see where he was. But I found nothing.

"Looking for someone?" he whispered again, this time from the other direction. I spun again, confused how he was close enough for me to hear him so clearly while hiding himself so well. A tendril of shadow eased through the Dark Woods, teasing at my skin as it reached out and twined around my body, caressing my ear.

"The scent of your fear is so strong. So tempting." The shadow dissipated as it released the carnal warning into my ear. I grimaced at my stupidity, suddenly realizing how difficult hiding from the Shadow of the Grimm would be. Especially in a place like the Dark Woods, where the shadows answered to his call and the trees kept watch for him.

Another tendril of shadow snaked its way towards me, but I turned and started running once more. The world around me blurred as I lost myself in the chase. The air stung my cheeks. My lungs burned as hot as my legs and I propelled myself deeper into the trees until I recognized nothing around me.

I spun as I ran, searching for Vander—and seeing him everywhere. I could feel his presence as I stumbled through the trees, could sense the amusement he felt at my fear. My labored breath turned frantic, my grip on reality slipping as that fear barreled through me, daring to consume.

Suddenly everything felt as if it was closing in on me. The trees betraying me, the roots reaching up to drag me down. Panic was surging fast and hard as I stumbled, slipping for only a moment before finding my footing and pushing myself forward.

"That's right, goddess. Keep running. Because once I catch you, I will fucking *consume* you."

Another wave of shadow evaporated around me, coming from seemingly nowhere. I looked back as I pumped my legs to move faster, seeing tendrils creeping from every direction, closing in on me. I grunted, frustrated at my own body's limitations. Bitter tears burned in the corner of my eyes as I tried to determine a direction to my aimless running, some sort of plan to outsmart him.

Because I knew I couldn't outrun him. And he knew it, too.

My foot caught on a gnarled root, causing me to tumble forward. I met the ground with a sickening thud—body rolling, limbs flailing, as my momentum threw me forward. An angry shout escaped my lungs, knowing I'd made a fatal error.

I scrambled to flip myself over, inching myself backwards and tucking my form into the shadows of a hollowed trunk. My legs were too tired to keep pushing, my body now sore with bruises from my fall.

My breath picked up, my eyes narrowing on every snapping twig and skittering animal. Fear had long since overpowered the desire that had once been building within me. I became all too aware of the reputation of the woods around me, the reputation of the monster hunting me. And I was at both of their mercies.

No longer was I looking for Vander, no longer was I playing a game. I was trapped, lost to whatever sinister creatures inhabited the Dark Woods, at the mercy of a bloodthirsty omen of death. He'd warned me. Time and time again he'd tried to save me from this. But I didn't listen. I continued to push him to let me in. And now he had, and I didn't know what waited for me on the other side.

My chest tightened, my breathing erratic as everything around me began to blur together in a nightmarish cascade. The Mark wanted me terrified, panicked, helpless. And that's exactly what I was.

Breathe, Hazel.

Vander's presence in my mind was like ice water, shocking my system and snapping me out of my hysteria. I squeezed my eyes shut, pressing my back into the hollow of the hemlock. I nodded, unsure if he was even close enough to see the motion.

I forced slow, steady breaths into my lungs.

Tell me to stop. Or I won't be able to turn back.

Slowly, I shook my head. I wouldn't tell him no. No matter the fear consuming me, I knew I trusted him. I wanted this. I wouldn't let the fear consume me. Instead, I used it, let it fuel me, my desire. I honed in on that feeling, chasing the pleasure it promised until the panic passed and the fear receded, just enough.

When I opened my eyes again, two golden ones stared back at me just beyond the next cropping of trees.

My breath hitched, my jaw tightening as I sat up straighter. A great wolf stalked forward, his midnight fur melting into the shadows surrounding it till I couldn't tell where the darkness ended and the fur began. He prowled the Dark Woods, a deep, thunderous growl slipping from his throat. A force to be reckoned with—as if he commanded the very ground he walked on, ruled the trees he slipped between. He was a king, a god, owning the earth and the sky and the shadows. And he was coming straight for me.

Vander shifted to his mortal form as he closed the distance between us. My fingers fisted into the hard soil beneath them at the sight. He stopped just in front of me, naked and glorious in the shadows of the Dark Woods.

My core tightened, heat creeping into my cheeks. He looked so powerful, so beautiful. An entity ready to be worshiped. And here I was, once again sitting at his feet, desperate to show just how dutiful an acolyte I could be.

He dropped to one knee as he looked over my body, brushing away the dirt and grime that now coated my face.

"Not fast enough." His voice was thick, heady. My body reacted immediately.

His eyes shifted, dipping low to my core as if he could sense my arousal. He sucked his bottom lip between his teeth, scraping the skin and making it glisten. Gone was the sensitive side he rarely showed for anyone but me; instead I saw a ruthless monster ruled by primal need.

His hand fell from my face, landing firmly on my ankles. He yanked, hard.

I yelped at the movement, my body sliding through the moss and dirt till I was staring up at the canopy above. Vander filled my view as he centered himself over me. His weight pinned me beneath him, the wicked look on his face reminding me once again of the power he held over me.

"No more games," he ground out. His restraint was palpable. The veins in his forearms and neck pulsed with carnal need. "You wanted me to make a decision? I have."

He leaned in, his solid length pressing against my pelvis, spurring my hips to meet his. He lowered his mouth to the shell of my ear, his smoky scent invading my senses as his words warmed my skin:

"I've decided that I won't spend another day denying our fate. That even if I did something as foolish as trying to break that bond, I'd never stop chasing you. Because I cannot control this *need* to claim you. Bond or no bond."

His teeth grazed the lobe of my ear, forcing me to suck in a sharp breath.

"And maybe it's fucked up, but I can't risk going after you in the future, when my restraint inevitably wears out, and find I gave you the opportunity to fall for someone else. Only because I know I won't be able to stop myself from ripping them apart. And I refuse to subject you to a lifetime of grief like that."

I shook my head, ready to argue that I would never, *could* never, want anyone other than him. He raised a finger to my lips, refusing to let me speak. He leaned back just far enough to look me in the eyes.

"I lost you once, little spitfire. And I vowed a long time ago I would never lose you again."

He forced his finger between my lips, coating it with my own spit before trailing it down my chin and over my tunic, marking a path to my center. Slipping his hand inside my leggings, he dipped that same finger between my thighs. I gasped, my eyes rolling at the sensation I'd been craving since he'd first ordered me to run.

"But I needed you to know it was there. That option to let you go. If you asked me to, even now, I'd release you. I needed you to understand, because once we accept this bond, accept our fate *fully*, there's no going back."

As he spoke, his finger pumped into me. It was a true effort to keep my gaze on him, and not let my eyes roll back as waves of pleasure overtook me.

He retreated, grabbing onto the waist of my leggings and shoving them down.

"So tell me." His voice was raw with need as he let his gaze dip down my body. "What is it you want?"

"There was never anyone but you, Vander." My voice was a pathetic whimper in the darkness, a desperate cry of need. "Even when it wasn't you, it was still you."

Images of Arlo flooded my mind, their likeness, their similarities. How I hadn't noticed it when I'd first returned to Tir Nadaar, I would never understand. I'd been in love with two halves of the same soul. And that instinctual love had only grown when I'd let Arlo go, when the Divine's magic had consumed me and turned me into whatever I was now. He was my everything.

I hadn't thought it possible for it to grow stronger still, but seeing Vander now, embracing all of that darkness that filled his veins and stained his soul, it had taken over my body and mind. My very soul cried out for him, a blinding, deafening demand to accept him once and for all.

I reached out, brushing away a single tear that had escaped his obsidian eyes. "You are my only future, my perfect match. My love for you burns brighter than the Cosmos."

His eyes fluttered closed for the briefest of moments, the tension racking his body washing away on a wave of acceptance.

"Claim me, Vander. Don't force me to spend another moment of this agony separate from you."

His eyes snapped open, his face hardening with primal desire. And then he did.

His length filled me not even a second later, the sheer size stretching me till I was sure I'd break in two. I cried out, letting the pain ravage me as the pleasure chased it away. He loomed over me, grabbing my hips and pulling me to meet him stride for stride.

"Mine," he breathed out. "You. Are. Mine."

I nodded frantically, trying to keep up with his pace.

"Say it, goddess. Let the whole forest hear how you belong to the Shadow of the Grimm."

"I am yours," I breathed out, trying to strengthen my voice. But the orgasm building within me was too strong, barreling too fast to release. "And you," I panted, my hands scrambling to find purchase. They sunk into the moss at my sides, incapable of finding anything else as he lifted my hips to slam into over and over. "Are mine."

He released his hold, slipping an arm behind my waist as his free hand dove towards my center. He found that sensitive spot with ease, flicking hard as he called out, "Louder."

I cried out at the pain lacing through my body, dancing dangerously with the pleasure consuming me until I couldn't tell where one ended and the other began.

"You—," I yelled, no longer capable of controlling anything within myself. "Are mine!" My voice echoed through the trees, carried on the shadows lurking in their midst to let all of the Dark Woods know to whom he belonged.

My body was lost to whatever this was, some new dimension we'd created solely for this moment. I exploded around him, my very soul altering. The space around us burned with the light of a hundred suns, my magic somehow coming to life as I came undone around him.

A roar ripped from Vander's lungs as he accepted my truth, shaking the ground and rattling the trees as it echoed through the forest. His muscles went taught with the power coursing through his veins, radiating around him. The ground quaked in reverence; the trees bowed as they recognized the Cosmic shift taking place.

Vander's shadows erupted to swallow my light.

No, not swallow. Embrace.

The melding of our magic in the air around us echoed only by the markings left on each other's soul.

PART 2:
DISCORD

CHAPTER 25
HAZEL

Vander led me back to the Estate. Night had fallen by the time we returned, and I was grateful for the darkness to hide my disheveled state. Vander wasn't much better, having lost his tunic somewhere in the Dark Woods. However, missing clothing wasn't all that unusual for him, and he walked with frustrating ease as the moonlight reflected off his muscled chest.

I clung to the fragments of clothes loosely hanging off of me from where he had ripped them, too conscious of the skin that was visible through the torn fabric. My hair was a mess, and despite my best efforts to hastily clean myself up on our walk home, I could still feel the layers of dirt clinging to my skin.

But I couldn't keep the smile from my face as he pulled me into the kitchen, wrapping me in his arms as he closed the door behind us and pushed me up against it.

His lips were warm, hungry still but less frantic than they had been in the Dark Woods. As if he still needed more of me, but no longer feared the slowness of the moment. Comforted by the thought, I wrapped my arms around his waist, encouraging him to kiss me deeper.

"For fuck's sake," a voice muttered somewhere deeper within the Estate. I jumped in surprise, pushing Vander off of me as I wiggled out from his grasp. Vander growled, unapproving of my quick retreat.

Bastian was entering the kitchen from the sitting room, shaking his head. "There's multiple empty bedchambers in this Estate, and you have to choose the kitchen for your midnight antics? This is where we eat."

Vander turned around, reluctantly, to face Bastian. "My apologies, brother. But I hadn't expected anyone to be awake." He wrapped his fingers around my elbow, pulling me abruptly in front of him and enveloping me in his hold. My cheeks went crimson as he leaned down, placing a lingering kiss to the side of my neck.

"We really are so sorry," I reiterated, feeling as though Vander's words were not sincere enough. "We were just coming to get a small snack, since we missed dinner."

"Speak for yourself. I only have an appetite for one thing at the moment." Vander's voice was low beside me, his chest rumbling against my back. I stifled a squeal when Vander nipped at my ear, elbowing him softly as a not-so-subtle warning to knock it off. Heat was flooding my core and I couldn't be letting my thoughts drift like they were with Bastian standing here staring at us like he was.

Bastian rolled his eyes, making his way through the kitchen after a moment. An orb of fae light followed behind him, settling against the logs in the hearth and coating the room in a soft orange glow as a fire bloomed. "I'll be out of your hair in a moment. Just came to make Aerie some tea." He stopped at the cupboard, glancing back at us for a brief moment before adding, "And then you can get back to, uh—getting a snack."

His lips quipped up, eyes glinting with sarcasm. I grinned, averting my gaze in embarrassment. Vander stepped out from behind me, joining his brother in the kitchen. His sudden absence felt too cold, the lack of his warmth surrounding me sending a shiver down my spine. I wrapped my arms around myself, sinking slowly onto one of the open stools as the brothers worked around each other in unison. After setting up a tray with a couple leftover pastries, Vander disappeared into the root cellar in search of more items to add to our spread.

Bastian brought two cups of tea over to where I sat, setting them on the middle counter and letting his eyes roam momentarily over my ragged state. Wordlessly he retreated to the sitting room, returning with a blanket and wrapping it around my shoulders. I folded in on myself, thankful for the cover.

"Again, I'm so sorry about this." I lamented. "If we had known anyone was awake—"

"It's alright," Bastian chuckled, raising a hand to cut me off. "You aren't the first couple to fuck within the Dark Woods. And I'm certain you won't be the last."

My eyes went wide at his bluntness. Curiosity was fighting to take over, a question on the tip of my tongue. But by the way he was smirking at me, drawing his cup of tea up to his mouth and winking at me over the rim, I knew I already had the answer. I matched his smirk with my own, dropping my gaze to my lap as I picked at my dirtied nails.

"You doing okay with that?" Bastian asked after a moment of silence. He cocked his head towards where Vander had been a moment ago. I hummed in amusement, watching the dark cellar's entryway briefly before letting out a breathy laugh.

"Yes, actually. *That* seems to have figured things out." I smirked at Bastian, his own amusement playing on his lips as he watched me for a moment longer before nodding.

"Good. You let me know if he fucks up again. I wouldn't mind delivering another beating."

"Another?" My mouth popped open, just as Vander made his way back into the kitchen with an arm full of food.

"If I remember correctly, I beat *you*. Not the other way around." Vander dropped his findings on the middle counter, arranging the food on the tray he'd left there.

Bastian scoffed. "Whatever you need to tell yourself to sleep at night, brother. But I'll only indulge your delusions for so long. Especially if you hurt her again."

I couldn't contain the laughter that bubbled up inside me. Vander stopped short, growling as his eyes found mine. He shifted his gaze from me to Bastian and back.

"Oh, I am *definitely* planning on hurting her again," he promised. Before I could even roll my eyes, he came around the counter, pulling me into his hold as he bent down and wrapped his arm around me just below my waist. He hoisted me over his shoulder while swiping the tray of food off the counter and balancing it in his other hand. I squealed in shock, quickly stifling the sound of my own voice in an effort to not wake the rest of the Estate.

Vander sauntered through the sitting room, towards the hallway that would lead us to my bedchambers. I could see Bastian shaking his head through my distorted view of the kitchen, the image bobbing with each of Vander's steps.

"Say goodnight, little spitfire." Vander's tone was low, hungry. I bit down on my lower lip, my core tightening at his orders.

"Goodnight, Bastian," I called out timidly, mortified. Vander's arm flexed around my ass, a sign of his approval at my obedience.

"Goodnight, lovebirds," Bastian called out, the amused disgust in his tone impossible to miss.

I wiggled in Vander's grasp the whole way to my room, squirming and squealing as he carried me over his shoulder.

"Cut it out or you're going to spill our dinner," he chided.

"Believe it or not, dinner isn't exactly what's on my mind at the moment," I huffed, giving up at last as he slowed before my door.

"Trust me, Hazel. I know exactly what's on your mind at the moment."

I scoffed, beating my fists against his back once more. "That is not what I meant!"

He sniggered, kicking the door open and dipping inside my room. I watched the door shut softly behind him as he sent a shadow out to lock it. He moved over to the fireplace, squatting briefly to slide the tray of food onto the low table in front of the hearth. He rose to his feet, still refusing to put me down.

"Vander Darroch." My voice was a cross between desire and rage. "Set me down right now or I—"

"Or you'll what?" he asked, righting my body and wrapping my legs around his waist so that he was still holding me, but could see my face. His eyes were dark again, hungry. And it had me sucking my bottom lip between my teeth and gnawing at it nervously.

He raised a hand to my chin, popping my lip out from between my teeth.

"I believe that's mine to bite," he taunted, leaning in and nipping at the tender flesh. I moaned in response, incapable of stopping the sound.

"See? Mine." He smirked as his lips trailed over my jawline. I nuzzled my face against his, returning his kisses and doing my best to urge us towards the bed behind him.

"Ah, ah, ah," he scolded, sauntering forward and dropping me in the chair nearest the hearth. I landed with a resounding grunt, crossing my arms over my chest in protest as he backed away. He chuckled watching me, gesturing to the tray of food he'd brought in.

"First you eat," he stated. As if I had no say in the matter. "Then you'll get dessert."

"Dessert?" I sneered, rolling my eyes at his ego. He didn't answer, didn't even look at me as he dished food out on my plate. When he was done, he rose to his feet and strode forward. It was hard not to watch him, his movements so fluid, so hypnotizing. It did nothing to swallow the heat growing inside of me.

"Eat." He handed me the plate, a frustratingly arousing smirk on his lips.

I took it begrudgingly, cradling the dish in my lap and watching him make his way over to the hearth. He grabbed a handful of logs off the stack beside it and laid them meticulously within the firebox. Within moments he had a fire going, standing once again and dusting off his hands. He turned back towards me, leaning against the stone hearth and crossing his arms over his chest. His gaze cut down to my untouched plate, then back up to me.

"I'm not hungry," I scowled, pursing my lips and refusing to touch the food. We stared each other down, neither one of us budging.

If you want me to touch you again tonight, little spitfire. His voice slid through my mind like velvet. *Then I suggest you obey.*

I tried to keep up the facade, tried not to reveal how molten my body was becoming for him. But he knew as well as I did that I would do anything he requested of me. That this rebellion was just a way of testing his limits, pushing him to become more forceful because, damn, did I love it when he became that other being.

I let out a breath, letting my eyes fall to the tray of untouched food. A leftover pastry from this morning, an assortment of berries, some dried meat, and my favorite, of course. Cheese.

I picked up the pastry, tearing apart the bread and popping a bite into my mouth. I watched him the whole time I chewed, making sure to swallow it slowly. His eyes dipped to the bob of my throat, his teeth digging into his lip in response.

My smile grew as I took my time, realizing quickly that while he might be the one giving orders, it was my decisions that were currently controlling the situation. I picked through the food, letting the minutes pass as I grazed on the selection he'd grabbed for me. His fingers tapped impatiently against his skin, his arms folded across his chest. The noise only worked to make me eat slower, enjoying the view of his control backfiring. When most of the plate was gone, I dusted my hands and tipped the scraps left on the surface towards him.

"Satisfied?" I asked, raising an eyebrow.

"Not even remotely," he ground out. He stalked forward, taking the plate from me and setting it on the table.

"What was it now? First eat, then..." I mused, taunting him to keep pushing deeper. Darker.

His eyes narrowed in answer. "You seem to be rather confident for someone who's about to be at the receiving end of my shadows."

"Maybe that's because—" I stood from my chair, bunching up the fabric of my torn tunic in my hand as I stepped forward, lifting it over my head. The light of the fire reflected off my bare skin, Vander's eyes tracking the movement. "Your shadows don't scare me anymore."

He chuckled, the dark sound filling the room with its power. His shadows emerged in response to my challenge—not only coming from him but breaking forth from the corners of the room, the walls, and the floorboards. They all converged in a sea of black as they turned their attention to me.

My chest dipped at the sudden attention. Nerves crept in. But not fear.

Never fear, anymore.

I laid a hand against his bare chest, breathing in the presence of the Mark. It surprised me how much I was growing to crave it, that dark presence between us. I could feel it, always.

My magic burned just beneath my skin, responding to his. I closed my eyes, relishing in the feel and letting it give me the confidence to keep going.

"When will you accept that I want you. All parts of you? The Mark is not just something I put up with because I know there's no other way. I want it, Vander." I leaned into him, letting my skin brush against his. "I *ache* for it."

He shuddered, his eyes fluttering closed for a moment as the shadows danced around us. I removed my hand from his chest, turning to the nearest one and running my fingers gently over its smoky tendrils—playing with the magic. Vander's muscles tensed, his arousal unmistakable through the tether.

"Do I need to keep going? Or have I proven my point?" I teased, giggling at his obvious reaction to my torment. I moved to another shadow close by, running my finger up its outline. His hand darted out, catching my wrist fast and hard.

"Keep going and you'll only be adding to your punishment, *goddess*. I don't appreciate you toying with me."

I paused a moment, surprised by his reaction.

Punishment? I asked through the tether, raising an eyebrow. I tried to stifle my smirk, tried to hide my excitement, as I bowed my head. Obedient as ever, I stepped back from his shadows. "If that's what you want, *Grimm*."

His eyes snapped to mine at the title, the look in them going feral. Before I knew what was happening, he was on me, pushing me down in front of the fire and seating himself over me. His hand clamped around my throat, his fingers flexing to feel my blood pulsing just below my skin.

"Say it again," he ordered. I swallowed, testing the restriction. He cocked his head to the side, baring his teeth as he tightened the grip. A challenge for me to defy him.

My tongue darted past my lips, licking them slowly as I cleared my throat around the feel of his grip. "My," I whispered, wrapping my hand around the flexed muscles of his forearm. "Merciless." I tightened my hold, feeling the strength radiating there. "Grimm." I let my own magic rise, fortifying his hold around my throat.

My eyes rolled back, black spots filling my vision. His mouth was on my collarbone instantly, his grip steady against me as he kissed my skin. He ventured further down, lowering his mouth to the peak of my breast and biting down hard.

I cried out, the pain electrifying the power in my veins. He wasted no time to nurture the wound, caressing the peak with his tongue before moving on to the other side and doing the same. I rolled beneath him, desperate for some sort of friction against my center.

A deep laugh rumbled against my chest, doing nothing but intensifying that heat within me as he finally released my throat. His palm flattened against my hip, pinning me in place. When he clamped down on my peak again, my hands grabbed at his hair. I pulled hard, letting the spark of pain radiate through my fingers as they returned the gesture.

He brought his free hand down to my thigh, slapping his palm hard against the bare skin. I gasped, eyes snapping wide open as I looked up at him.

"Are you ready to receive your punishment?" He ran his nose up the length of my jaw till his breath was skittering against the shell of my ear.

I bit down on my lip, anticipation building in my core.

He released a breathy laugh, the sensation against my ear eliciting a gasp from my lips. "Perhaps I'll have to come up with another method for punishing you. I have to find something to correct that little attitude you've seemed to develop tonight. It appears you need a reminder of the natural order of things."

"Is that so?" I asked, incapable of keeping my mouth shut.

He hummed, the sound never fully leaving his throat. "I think all of that Divine magic is going to your head."

I nodded as he pulled back, his eyes raking over me. "I agree," I teased. "Best if you put me in my place before I start thinking too highly of myself."

He sat back on his heels, still pinning me beneath his hips. I writhed, desperate to feel his touch.

"That right there." He clicked his tongue, shaking his head. "That's the fucking attitude I'm referring to. Too Fates-damned brazen for your own good." His shadows snaked across the wooden floor, over the woven rug, until they reached my body. Their descent was slow, threatening, and desire pooled in my core.

"So now I have to figure out what to do to instill that fear within you that you once held for me. The reverence I deserve." He folded his arms across his chest, watching closely as his shadows licked at my bare skin.

"Perhaps I'll release you to the Dark Woods again. Let some truly vile beast come after you and wait till you're utterly convinced that I've abandoned you before I come to save your life." His eyes darkened as he spoke. "I'd rip apart the creature in front of you." He ran his fingers over the curve of my exposed body. "Bathing you in its blood."

I shouldn't love this. My body shouldn't be having the visceral reaction it was having while listening to him speak like this to me.

But I couldn't deny the hold he had over me. My back arched, my chest calling out to take more of his torturous touch.

His shadows shoved me back down, taking special care to avoid the peaks of my breasts. "See, goddess? That shouldn't excite you. That should *terrify* you. *I* should terrify you. And yet the darker I go, the more you chase me. So what am I to do with you?"

"Give in?" I offered, my words frantic as his shadows still toyed with my body. Their chilling presence chased away any warmth the fire once provided.

His jaw tensed, the ink of the Mark dancing in wicked agreement. "Maybe I should just deny you again. Shut you out completely and walk away. That would be a true punishment."

My stomach dropped, an icy fear taking root in my chest.

His hardened look shifted slightly, nostrils flaring as he breathed in my scent. He lowered himself to me once more, inhaling deeply as he pinned my wrists beneath his hold on either side of my head. "But I suppose," he said after a moment of tense silence, "I already tried that."

I ground my teeth together, jaw set in a firm line as I lay still beneath him. He pulled back just enough to show me his amusement at my reaction.

"Didn't seem to stick." He threw me a wink, drawing an irritated scoff from me. I was growing tired of his games, his jesting. He'd barely touched me, and yet I was so desperate with need that my body was shaking from his intentional lack of pleasure. He was toying with me and I'd had enough. I opened my mouth to voice as much.

But the moment was lost, chased away by the suddenness of his movements as he grabbed my hips and flipped me over. Shadows rushed to my wrists, pulling them out in front of me and binding them tight. My cheek pressed into the woven rug, my eyes staring directly into the flames dancing before me.

He gripped my hips, raising my ass in the air and kicking my knees apart so that I was fully exposed to him.

"I think the best course of action," he said, leaning over me and trailing a finger down the length of my spine, "is to remind you—tonight and every night—how my darkness is in control."

I smirked, ready to make a comment about how that was exactly what I wanted him to do. But another shadow snaked over my shoulder, wrapping around my mouth and efficiently silencing me. I grunted in irritation, pulling a sultry laugh from Vander.

"I told you, goddess. You are not in control." He tapped his fingers against my lower back before letting them dip lower, caressing the curve of my ass and playing with the edges of my undergarments before sliding further down. He growled when he discovered the slickness already gathering at my center. He circled my clit delicately, tentatively, before plunging two fingers inside me and pumping slowly as he sucked a sharp breath in between his teeth.

"I am not even in control," he continued, pulling his fingers out. I furrowed my brow, trying to focus on his words but becoming entirely lost to the heady need building within me.

"The Mark, however." He paused a moment, not touching me, not speaking. I tried to crank my head back to see what he was doing. I shrieked through the shadow still biding my mouth as he brought his palm down against my center. Hard. His fingers were inside me again, giving no time for the sting between my legs to subside. I whimpered, my mind reeling to try and keep up with the varying sensations.

"*That's* fully in control. And it's hungry for your blood. Ravenous for your fear."

He didn't stop, pumping his fingers meticulously and adding his thumb to stroke punishing circles around the sensitive spot just above my center. I moaned against the restraining shadow, sinking against his steady rhythm and letting myself come apart beneath his touch.

Just as that need wound tight within me, threatening to burst over the edge, he retreated. His absence left me feeling hollow, empty. I was nothing more than a vessel for his power. And without it, I became nothing.

Vander, please. My words sounded distant, as if they didn't even belong to me. I'd retreated so far within myself—no, so far within the tether, that I couldn't find my way back. Not without him.

When his touch returned, it was no longer his fingers teasing my entrance. I let out a shuddering breath as he sank himself into me. His fingers dug into my hips, his shadows tightening at my hands and mouth.

If I need to stop, tell me here. His words washed over my mind, reminding me that I would always have a say in this. That while his darkness was in control and it beckoned for my fear, there was always a limit, a way out, if I needed it.

I nodded, my cheek rubbing against the rough texture of the rug. I squeezed my eyes shut, bracing myself. To my surprise, his thumb trailed over our connection, sliding through my arousal before retreating back. I stiffened as a new sensation flowed through me. A vicious pressure overtook me as he sunk his thumb against my back entrance.

"Relax," he purred, gently splaying his free hand over my lower back. He rocked his hips against me, pulling more pleasure from me. I obeyed on instinct, the need for his touch taking over any apprehension lingering within me. He picked up his rhythm, following my lead as he filled me more and more.

"Fuck, Hazel. The feel of you around me is too damn good." His encouragement had me sinking back further, ready for more. He groaned, fully seating himself within me. "You're taking me so fucking well."

I tightened my core in response, practically the only thing I was capable of in this position. He hissed, pushing against my ass in an effort to stop the movement.

"Do that again and I won't be keeping up this gentle pretense," he ground out.

Who said I wanted you to? I spoke into his mind, caressing his thoughts as he battled to contain his composure. *Let go, Vander.*

I could feel the torment weighing on his soul. How, even now, he was still tempted to contain that part of himself. Perhaps I could feel it even more now, as if a veil had been lifted between us.

I pushed against him, enticing him. He groaned, the sound vibrating through the floorboards beneath us.

Show me how dark you can be. Show me the merciless Grimm.

His groan grew into a roar, his composure exploding around me in a dark abyss of power. His restraint had snapped, his free hand gripping hard at my hip as he slammed into me again and again.

I cried out through the shadow still stifling my mouth, the sound muffled and reverberating back through me. I tried to hold on to something, desperate to push against him and meet him stride for stride. But with the position he had me in, there was nothing I could do but be completely at his mercy.

The desire within me began to build again, intensifying far past the point it had before. His thumb sank fully within my back entrance, the mixture of sensations filling me with new-found pleasure. It was heavy, full, and wickedly delicious.

My whole body tightened, waves of pleasure crescendoing through my entire being as I burst over that edge, plummeting headfirst into his darkness. I felt it between my legs, at my center, in my soul.

His movements were frantic, selfish, as he chased my release with his own. It only served to draw out my orgasm, sure I'd never known such a soul-penetrating pleasure. My core tightened once more as he spilled into me, his rough grunts melding with a breathy laugh as he finally released his shadows and held himself against me, catching his breath.

He retreated from me only long enough to switch positions and lay me in the crook of his arm. He watched me in the light of the fire, brushing a stray strand of hair off my face.

"How do you feel?" he asked after we'd both come down from the ecstasy.

I closed my eyes, soaking in the smooth cadence of his voice. My chest rose and fell as my lungs tried to recover from the abuse they just took. My body was sore, thoroughly used and aching for tender attention. But I didn't think I'd ever been more at peace, more content with life, as I had in that moment.

"I feel as if..." My voice was low, exhausted as I tried to put thoughts to words. "I am becoming exactly who I was meant to be."

He huffed out a laugh, taking one of my wrists in his free hand and massaging where his shadows had bound me. I closed my eyes, my mind a blank slate as I concentrated on nothing else besides the feel of his tender touch. He moved on to my other wrist, leaning in and planting a slow kiss against my temple.

"Come on, Hazel. Let's get you cleaned up."

I barely heard his words through my lust-filled haze, barely registered his movements as he scooped me off the floor and cradled me across his body, carrying me into the bathing room.

He set me down in the bathtub, turning on the tap and climbing in after me. He cradled my palm, splaying it over the water. His magic called my own to life, warming the water instantly. Had I any energy left within my body, I would have been surprised by my own show of magic, ecstatic at being able to accomplish what was surely a simple task to others. Instead, I sighed into his embrace, comforted by the feel of his solid form behind me in the tub. My eyes fluttered closed as I drifted in and out of consciousness, only the silhouette of his hand passing with the soap over my dirtied skin dancing behind my eyelids.

This was it, the moment I'd been chasing.

This was pure bliss, in the arms of my mate with a bond fully accepted. And nothing could take that away from us.

CHAPTER 26
VANDER

I awoke from a restful slumber for what felt like the first time in a long time. No nightmares plagued me, no violent call pulled me from my bed into the Dark Woods. But there was no denying the gentle vibration of the Mark's magic within my veins, somehow satiated at last.

Mine. She was wholly and undeniably mine. And now, I was hers.

The moments between us last night played back in my mind, reminding me of the pure magic we'd created together under the trees and beside the fire. She'd told me—fuck, she'd told me so many times that she could handle my darkness, could handle the Mark. She wanted it all. And I'd been so hesitant to give it to her, for fear she wouldn't be able to handle it. Because I could barely handle it most days. But Nox's advice rang true. After so many years of barely surviving through these methods, it was time to try a different approach. Time to not deny who I was any longer.

The Mark was a part of me now. It wasn't going anywhere, no matter how much I wished it away. But perhaps this was the path to coexisting, the bond between me and Hazel seemingly a focal point for my darkness, my shadows. Accepting it fully—hopefully that would serve to be the answer for the Mark's erratic behavior. Either way, I'd made my decision. All that was left to do was to see how the Mark responded.

Hazel stirred beside me, sinking further against me and leaning into my touch. I bristled briefly before relaxing into her and letting her bare skin warm mine. It still felt so odd to me, occupying her bed in my mortal form. I supposed there would be a myriad of new sensations to become familiar with.

She hummed, drifting into consciousness with a smile on her face.

"Good morning, goddess." I leaned in, my lips finding that sensitive spot just below her ear.

Her voice sounded as smooth as sunbeam whiskey as she moaned softly. "Are you ever going to stop with that ridiculous nickname you've grown so fond of?"

"And risk the wrath of the Divine?" I jeered, closing in quickly to nip at her lower lip. She squealed at the sudden pain but didn't pull back. I could feel her pain through the tether—stronger than ever—and the way that it melted into something needier, hungrier.

My eyes honed in on her as my lips turned up in a wicked smirk—the one I knew always captivated her. I wrapped my hand around her hip, turning her towards me and grabbing her chin. I pulled her in until my lips were on hers, my tongue chasing after the taste of her.

My hands travelled over the planes of her body, ready to demand more. But she broke away from my kiss, stifling a cry. I looked down to her thigh where my fingers had dug into her skin in eager hunger. I cursed under my breath, pulling my hand back fast as I noticed the early stages of purple hues forming to reveal a large bruise beneath my fingers. She winced, pulling the bedding back over her legs quickly in an effort to cover the injury.

I pushed her flitting hands aside, shoving back the bedding and pulling her leg over to assess the bruising.

"It's fine," she lied, still fighting past the wave of pain. I didn't know why she insisted on trying to cover up the truth when the tether existed. I could read her like a book. Could *feel* her completely. There was no amount of magic or barriers that could block me from our connection.

Not now.

"It's most definitely *not* fine," I shot back. My voice had dipped low again, as it often did when the Mark was creeping forth to take over. So much for being satiated.

I let her leg go, sitting up and releasing a heavy sigh as I rubbed my fingers over my forehead. She eased herself up to sit beside me, the stiffness that wracked her body too obvious to miss.

"This was my fault, Vander. I'm the clumsy one that tripped over a root in the Dark Woods. You had nothing to do with that."

"As if a simple tree root could cause an injury like that." I scoffed, gesturing to her now covered leg. "You and I both know who gave you that injury. I should have been more careful, more mindful."

I shouldn't have taken her out there at all.

She shook her head, and I could tell by the way her eyes glazed over that she was disappearing into the memories of last night, replaying them over in her mind. The thought had tension tightening in my core, embarrassed at the extent of my power.

"It won't happen again." I'd meant it as a promise, but it came out as a threat, full of rage and regret.

"You cannot tell me what I'm allowed to want." Her voice was soft, low. But there was a power there, a fire to fight back that was all so new for her. She reached out slowly, taking my hands in hers. My body tensed at the contact, heat radiating off my skin. Shadows darkened the room, drowning out the sunlight streaming in.

"This will not work unless we have trust, Vander. I trust you."

My eyes didn't look to hers, but rather cut decidedly to the Mark on my arm.

"Even with that," she added, nodding her head towards where my gaze had shifted. "I trust you. If I didn't, I would have never let you touch me."

I made to roll my eyes, but she squeezed my hands harder, pulling them towards her so I wouldn't retreat.

"I'm serious. I *chose* this. I chose you. You didn't force me into anything I did not ask for last night."

She lowered her head to peer up at me, the deep green of her eyes swirling with anything but judgment and fear. I watched her for a moment, jaw set firm—nodding at last.

"But that trust needs to go both ways," she pressed on, scooting forward on the bed so the covers fell away and her naked body invaded my own. She straddled my thighs, settling herself against me and wrapping her arms around my neck. My own arms fell to her hips, tracing circles on instinct as I listened to her words.

I pressed my forehead against hers, eyes trained again on her bruised thigh.

"I know, I'm sorry. I just—" I sighed, closing my eyes. "This power within me... It runs deeper than even I know. And I've spent a long time learning to control it. It goes against everything I've taught myself to let it flow freely now. It's just going to take some time to adjust."

"I know." She laid a hand against my cheek. "But I promise, you won't hurt me." She pulled my lips to hers, kissing deeply before moving to my ear and lowering her voice. "At least, no more than I allow you to."

A breathy laugh escaped me, my hands gaining confidence as they started exploring once more. "The goddess seems rather sure of herself, especially for someone who still hasn't learned to even control that power."

She pulled back fast, grinning hard as she settled on her knees in front of me. I cocked my head to the side, watching with curiosity as her giddiness grew.

"You seem to be forgetting yourself." She held her hands out between us, palms up, as she took a deep breath and closed her eyes. Within mere moments, an energy overtook the space between us. A new energy. One I'd felt last night when she'd surprised me with her power in the Dark Woods. One that echoed in my very soul, now. A gilded light gleamed from the markings on her skin, answered only by the overwhelming presence of my own shadows circling us.

A slow grin crept across my lips, pride beaming within me as I recognized the source of this magic, the progress it meant she was making in her training to be able to call it forward unassisted, freely. She dropped her hands, giggling. The sound was a blessing from the Cosmos, a salve to my tattered soul.

"You were right, I've been practicing. Kirwan and I had a bit of a breakthrough with my training just before you and Nox returned yesterday—"

I lunged forward, scooping her up and consuming her wholly. My tongue was greedy as it claimed her mouth, my lips hungry as they devoured her. I was so fucking proud of her, and I couldn't wait another second to show her just how deeply that pride emanated.

I pulled back, cupping her face in my hands and trailing more kisses over her cheeks, her nose, her eyes. She rewarded me with more of that silky laughter.

"You are incredible," I breathed out between kisses. My tongue trailed down her jawline until my teeth found the spot they were searching for, clamping down and sucking on her velvet skin in the hollow behind her ear as if it were my last meal. "Your being, your power, it's all fucking incredible, Hazel." Her fingers wove their way into my hair. I could feel her smile against my cheek as I inhaled the intoxicating scent of her.

This bliss, this connection—it was otherworldly. It wasn't enough to have her, to hold her. I craved more, my soul crying out in recognition of hers. The tether sparked to life at the call, my thoughts echoing down as she stilled in my arms.

She pulled back, eyes searching mine as she felt the depth of my need for her through our bond. A bond that had somehow been fortified tenfold overnight. A bond that, for the first time, felt solid.

Complete.

"I fear you're going to wreck me, little spitfire." I breathed out, laughing as I watched the apples of her cheeks crinkle with the hint of a smile.

"Stay right here," she whispered, leaning in slightly before jumping up and wrapping the discarded quilt at the foot of the bed around herself. She padded on bare feet over to the vanity across the bedroom. I leaned back on my palms, enjoying the view of her struggling to keep the quilt clutched around her as she dug through one of the vanity drawers. I sent a shadow her way, pulling gently on the quilt and making it slip as she turned back to face me.

Her eyes narrowed, a heated smirk settling across her lips as she shoved the shadow away with a wave of her hand. It obeyed, though reluctantly.

"Stop that," she chided, making her way back over to me. Something was clutched in her hand, but my eyes were too distracted as she climbed back up on the bed to care.

"Vander," she hummed, breaking the spell her body held over my gaze. I smiled lazily, licking my lips as she rolled her eyes. "I have something to tell you, so I need you to stop looking at me like that."

"Like what?" I asked innocently.

She leveled her gaze, folding her arms over her chest—which proved to be rather difficult given the way she was still clutching the quilt around her.

"Like you're one wrong move away from devouring me."

I raised an eyebrow at her.

"Again," she added, her mouth quirking up.

Before I could prove just how right she was, she pulled out a card and laid it on the bed between us. Against my better judgment, I dragged my gaze off her and down to the card. An image of a carefully painted rendering of the same marks that claimed her palms looked up at me.

I took a moment to study the card before looking back up at her, shifting my weight to lean on one arm as I waited for her to explain.

"When we were visiting the moon tribe" she started. My muscles tightened instinctively, remembering the way Vesper had paid too much attention to *my* mate. She paused, cutting me a warning glance as she sensed where my thoughts had turned, before continuing:

"I had a run-in with one of the priestesses—actually, the very one who crafted this." Her fingers trailed over the jewelry still hanging around her neck, tracing the outline of the crescent moon. I tried to recall the day I'd purchased it, imagining the vendor who'd sold it to me. No details came to mind, but I still found it rather surprising to learn it had been a priestess of Sgàil.

"Anyways." She shook her head, as if to clear a fog from her mind. "She offered to do a reading for me. And for whatever Fates' forsaken reason, I agreed."

I huffed out a laugh, shaking my head. "Never accept a reading from a priestess, Hazel. That's rule number one of traveling in Tir Nadaar."

Her brow furrowed, her canines gnawing on the corner of her bottom lip as she looked from me, to the card, and back. "Yes, Kirwan mentioned that. But I didn't know then why it was ill advised."

I sucked in a breath, stretching my arms over my head as I sat up. "Because they're too elusive for their own good? Because only the Fates know the true path for our life threads? Because no good can come from someone attempting to peer into a future that wasn't meant for their prying eyes? Because—"

She held up a hand, stopping me. "Okay, okay. Yes, I get it now."

I bowed my head in apologies, fighting the urge to smile at her naivety.

"I allowed her to do one, regardless." She gestured down to the card between us. "Seems like a rule someone should have shared with me before visiting the tribe, though," she grumbled under her breath.

I winced, cursing myself for how foolish I'd been at the time. I regretted my behavior towards her over the past couple weeks, probably more than she understood. But before I could even open my mouth to apologize, she ventured on.

"The reading overall, as you shared, was rather elusive. But this one card was drawn." She picked it up, holding it up for me to inspect further. I took it from her, turning it over in my hand. "The priestess offered it to me. To keep. Due to its similarities with the markings on my palms."

She held out her hands, unfurling her fingers to reveal their similarities.

"Alright," I said on an exhale. "Did she happen to share *why* they were so similar?"

She closed her palms again, pursing her lips. I rolled my eyes, her lack of response answer enough.

"All she said was that this card is something called the Match." She paused, a rosy hue staining her cheeks. "Also known sometimes as the Lovers."

I hummed, sending a tendril of shadow out to caress her bare shoulder, thanks to the slipping quilt. "Then I'd say thank fuck for her reading, if it helped push us to this."

She smiled, but it didn't quite reach her eyes. She brushed away the shadow and I reeled it back in, trying to understand what her hesitation meant.

"That's not what I'm trying to say." She paused again, battling with her words for a moment. I gave her space to figure it out, not wanting to push her before she was ready to share. "I didn't want to bring it up before," she said at last, "because I didn't want it to sway your decision."

"Hazel, no vision from a seer or a priestess would ever—"

"I know," she cut me off. "But for my own peace of mind. I had to know this was something you chose. Something you pursued. Not something influenced by other forces."

I reached out, pulling her against my chest as I moved back against the headboard. I cradled her against me so that my eyes were still on her. She clutched the card against her chest, as if scared to let it go.

"What else is on your mind?" I knew there was more she wasn't sharing. And as tempted as I was to reach out through the tether, I wanted her to tell me in her own words, with her own voice. In her own time.

Her free hand twirled a strand of hair between her fingers as her eyes studied a spot on the wall beside the bed. "I just—she said the Match was all about finding an equal. Someone matched not only in your desires but also your power."

I nodded, trying to conceal my surprise at such a claim. I couldn't fathom anything that would be able to match the darkness of the Shadow of the Grimm, even the magic of the Divine.

"But she warned of the difficulty in maintaining a balance between our powers," she went on. "She warned—" A shudder ran through her body, raising gooseflesh on her skin. I pulled her in closer, instinctually. "That if we couldn't maintain that balance, our story would only end in tragedy."

"Well," I hummed, a hint of irritation slipping through. "Did she have any sound advice on how to *avoid* that?" My jaw tensed on the words, the Mark purring with threatening intent for the fear I could sense coming from Hazel.

She huffed out a laugh. "Actually," she said, raising up on an elbow to meet my gaze. "She seemed to think your brother and Aerie were a rather perfect example of maintaining that balance."

"Perfect," I said, gritting my teeth and rolling my eyes. The last thing I needed was more relationship advice from my younger brother.

Hazel laughed, sitting up fully now. "Perhaps it's not the worst idea, Vander. They've kept up a rather successful relationship for the past ten years. Not to mention while running an entire tribe and retaining the love and adoration of its members."

I grunted in answer. Which only seemed to amuse her further.

"That reminds me actually," Hazel said, pushing once again from the bed. My irritation grew as I sensed where this was going. "Aerie seemed to be unwell yesterday. I wanted to go check on her this morning and see if she was feeling any better."

Hazel strode over to the wardrobe, digging for a fresh change of clothes. When she found what she'd been looking for, she draped the quilt over the chair at her vanity and changed into the new outfit.

My eyes found the discolored patch on her thigh instantly, my jaw locking up at the evidence of the Mark's strength. My strength.

I knew she said she'd wanted it. That she could handle it. But the sight of her perfect skin marred by my darkness was a burden.

I closed my eyes, letting her call for trust echo through my mind. She was right. I knew she was right. And I hoped there'd be a day where I delighted in any markings I'd left on her body, as a sign of her love and acceptance for me—a sign of my claim on her soul. But seeing it now, so soon after the boundaries we'd moved past, so close to the transformation we'd made—it had my skin crawling with that all-too-familiar hatred that stained my soul.

"Perfect," I answered at last, opening my eyes and reaching down to grab the pants that lay discarded beside the bed from the previous night. "We need to see her about that lesion anyways."

My voice was too rough, too laced with my internal battles to fool her. She turned to face me, dressed in a cotton gown with an embroidered bodice. I came up to her, turning her around and gathering her hair to the side so I could help her lace up the back.

"I told you it's fine." Her voice was quiet, concerned. I secured the strings, dropping her hair back in place and turning her back to face me.

"I know." I offered a small smile, lips pressed together. "But I need you to let me fix it."

Her eyes watched mine for a moment, searching for something.

"Okay," she conceded. "So long as you keep doing... the other thing, too."

My eyes darkened as I caught her meaning, my body leaning down towards hers without a second thought. The Mark sparked to life in an instant, its power slipping into my voice as I whispered in her ear.

"Trust me, goddess. I couldn't stop chasing you, even if I wanted to."

CHAPTER 27
HAZEL

Aerie laced her arm through mine as we trailed behind our males. It appeared she was feeling much better today, enough so that she'd recommended an afternoon stroll when Vander and I had finally emerged from my bedchamber.

She threw me a sidelong glance, cutting her gaze back and forth between Vander up ahead and me beside her.

"What?" I asked, a breathy laugh on my lips after the fourth look from her.

"Nothing," she hummed, bobbing slightly in her step as she perked up to pretend she hadn't just been watching us.

"You are insufferable," I jested, rolling my eyes.

"No, if I was insufferable," she argued, a devious twinkle in her eye, "I'd be pestering you with questions like why there's such a sudden yet obvious shift between the two of you, or perhaps what exactly happened to incur such an injury as what Vander insisted I tend to this morning before our walk. Or maybe even why Bastian came to bed last night recounting quite the run in with the two of you in our kitchen."

I scoffed, the noise sounding too forced. Frankly, they were fair questions to be asking.

"But instead I've decided to let you tell me in your own time. When you're ready," she quipped, turning her eyes upward as she assessed the trees above us.

"Thank you," I hummed, following her gaze and seeing just how long it took for her to break. We walked in pained silence for a minute, the curious energy radiating off Aerie almost too much to bear.

"However, if I *did* feel like being insufferable, perhaps I'd start with a simple question."

"Aerie." I laughed, shaking my head. "Alright, what is it?"

She slowed her movement, letting the males get ahead of us several strides before she leaned in and lowered her voice.

"How are you feeling?"

"You said a simple question. That feels rather complicated to answer." I raised an eyebrow to her, a small smile playing on my lips.

She laughed, patting my arm. "I think you're confusing simple with easy. They are often not the same thing."

I let out a sigh, turning my attention back to our path as I continued forward. For several moments the only sound was the crunching of leaves beneath our feet.

"I feel... different," I answered at last. I turned the word over on my tongue, debating if it explained all that was currently coursing through my mind. Aerie nodded, staying silent to give me space to explain. "I have known for some time now that Vander and I were fated, that this bond existed between us. But it seems that after last night something has—"

"Shifted?" she suggested, inclining her head towards me.

I pursed my lips together, watching Vander up ahead in careful consideration. His mood seemed softer than usual, his demeanor light as he joked with Bastian. I reached out through the tether, quietly testing the connection and feeling for whatever emotion revealed itself. To my surprise, the usual presence of the Mark felt significantly less pronounced. I could still sense it, but the malice within its darkness had lifted, leaving behind a subtle purr of approval.

"*Shifted* would be a good way to put it," I finally answered, pulling back and shaking the jarring presence from my mind. "I feel connected to him in a way I haven't before. Stronger, perhaps. But more than strength, I feel stability." I chewed on the inside of my cheek, unsatisfied with the word.

"Safety," I added, almost laughing at the concept. After the things Vander had requested of me, the things he'd done to me, *safe* shouldn't have even remotely been the word that came to mind. And yet, it felt too perfect not to state. As if my entire world, my entire being, now rested within the fold of his power.

I cut a quick glance to Aerie, realizing her silence. An unbearable grin stretched from ear to ear as she watched me. She pursed her lips together, her teeth hidden behind a clenched jaw as she tried to subdue the obvious joy, but it was near impossible to miss.

A sound understanding shone in her soft blue eyes, the kind of empathy that could only come from someone who'd been where you'd stood.

"What is it?" I asked, pushing into her, lowering my voice.

"Your bond," she answered, finally abandoning the effort to rein in her happiness. "Albeit a rather strong and powerful one. But Hazel, that's the feel of a bond—fully accepted."

I wasn't sure how to describe the emotions rolling through me. I supposed a part of me already knew the answer. But it had been a hard journey to this moment, so much so that I'd somehow begun to assume we would never get here, had refused to accept it would ever be our reality.

Aerie tightened her hold on my arm, the bounce in her step growing tenfold as my gaze turned slowly back to Vander up ahead.

His body stiffened, sensing my presence as I reached out through the tether once more. I didn't say anything, just remained in his mind for a moment. Even though only a few paces separated us, it felt like too much. I needed to be near him, to remember that this was real and he was here. And he let me, surrounding my mind with a sense of warmth and calm matched only by the rays of sunlight streaming through the canopy above as we walked through the woods.

"Now, back to that bruise on your thigh," Aerie teased, cutting a glance down to my now healed leg and pulling my thoughts back from the tether. I huffed out an amused breath, rolling my eyes.

"I promise, Aerie. It was nothing."

She watched me through a sidelong glare, evaluating with precise scrutiny. "If you say so," she hummed at last, the tone of her voice sounding more like a song than a sentence. "Just promise me you both are being safe?"

"We are," I assured her. There was no place I felt safer than with Vander. Even when the Mark took hold. Perhaps even more so in those moments.

"I know you don't need me mothering over you. You are both grown beings capable of making your own decisions." Her tone was hesitant, as if she wasn't sure she should keep going. "I just know how intense a bond can feel when initially accepted. And given Vander's strength and the depth of your connection—"

I suppressed the urge to laugh, the look of Aerie feeling uncomfortable being a sight I wasn't sure I'd ever experienced before.

"All I'm trying to say," she added at last, tossing her hair over her shoulder with her free hand and pretending she didn't notice my giggling, "is know your limits. Both yours and Vander's. And for the love of the Fates, please communicate them and honor them. No matter what."

I straightened slightly, turning my head to look over at her.

"Sounds like someone may be speaking from experience," I mused, cutting a quick glance to Bastian up ahead. He was a gentle giant, the sweetest male I think I'd ever met. But seeing Vander in this new light—and Bastian by his side—perhaps the brothers were more alike than I'd initially thought.

I turned back towards Aerie, a vicious smirk teasing my lips. "Are you trying to tell me—" But her gaze was suddenly elsewhere, peering into the distance. Her movement slowed, then stopped altogether. The sudden motion, or lack thereof, jarred me. I stumbled a few steps before turning back to tug her along. She refused to move, eyes tracking something in the trees beyond.

"What is it?" I closed the few steps between us, grabbing hard onto her arm as a swift panic crept in.

"I thought I saw—" Her voice cut off abruptly, head spinning to a new spot, as if she'd once again found whatever it was she was looking for.

"Aerie?" I pulled on her, trying to remain calm but incapable of keeping the fear at bay. Vander must have sensed it, because the boys had halted their walk as well, turning back to see what was the matter.

"Aerie," Bastian called out. I looked over my shoulder at them, both as confused as I was.

Without another word, Aerie took off running. She kicked her slippers to the side, hiking up her linen skirts as she picked up speed. I stumbled forward, so shocked by the series of events and thrown off balance by her sudden absence.

"Fucking Fates." Bastian breathed out, taking the smallest moment to jump into action. "Aermidh!" he shouted as he blew past me, sending me reeling once more. I threw a hand out, trying to find something to brace myself with. Vander was beside me in an instant, catching me and setting me back on my feet.

"What in the Depths is going on?" I asked. My voice was shaky, and I hated to admit how crippling the sudden panic was becoming.

"I'm not sure," Vander growled. The Mark was alive against his skin, shadows growing as he ushered me forward to follow Bastian's path. We rushed through the trees, trying to keep up with them. Minutes passed that felt like years as we picked our way through the thick foliage, gaining speed.

My feet slammed against the forest floor, my heart pounding as I pushed my legs to carry me further, faster, in an effort to keep up with Vander. With each passing moment, that grip on my chest tightened, fear whispering all sorts of vicious lies to me about what must have gone wrong.

Aerie had been so focused, so concerned. I didn't know what she saw that would make her take off like that, but the feeling in my gut told me that we needed to find her fast. I couldn't lose another life. I didn't know what I could do to protect her, but I knew I would do everything in my power to help keep her safe.

We burst through the tree line, my body flailing as the thicket of the forest transitioned to sweetgrass brushing against my legs. I stopped, body doubling over as I tried to catch my breath. My eyes searched crazily, wide and wandering as I surveyed the clearing before me.

Vander held my hand gently, Bastian frozen just steps away.

My breath was ragged, my lungs hungry as I tried to force my body to recover. Despite the exhaustion rattling me, my breath hitched as I caught sight of the charred remnants of a small cottage nestled into the clearing, taken over by the wilderness surrounding its remains. Aerie was just before it, her steps light as air as she made her way into its grasp. I couldn't tell what she was looking for, though. I straightened, peering past Bastian's large form and tiptoeing forward on near silent feet as I squinted into the bright space ahead.

Aerie veered slightly to the left, moving just enough to give me a glimpse of something else in front of her.

A small fawn lifted its head, shifting nervously within the hollowed out husk of the cottage. Her form was practically swallowed by the overgrown sweet grass and tangled vines that surrounded her, making me second-guess what I was seeing.

But she was there.

I took a step forward, mere moments away from rushing ahead and joining Aerie. A hand wrapped around my arm, stopping me. Vander raised a careful finger to his lips, motioning for me to be quiet. It was a reminder to slow down, to calm my mind and my body rather than storm forward and spook the creature.

He let his shadows wrap around our legs, swallowing the sound of our footfall as we made our way forward. When we reached Bastian, Vander's shadows covered him too. It took a second for him to move, though, eyes dutifully trained on the fawn and how close Aerie was to her now.

Vander pressed, soft but firm, urging his brother forward. Bastian cut a quick glance to Vander, tears threatening his dark brown eyes. It was all the confirmation I needed, my own mind running wild with the hope that this wasn't just simply a fawn. Just as I could tell this wasn't just simply a burnt down cottage in the woods.

The three of us moved forward slowly, taking special care to step over the charred wood that littered the ground as we entered what I assumed was once the front door. Aerie had already ventured inside, closing the gap between her and the small fawn. She knelt before the fawn, the mystical creature nudging towards Aerie as if she knew the safety she offered—finding familiarity in her touch. The creature seemed otherworldly, as if possessed by something bigger than us.

Tears stung my eyes as we stopped before her. I knelt without even thinking. This was sacred ground. The home of Aerie's lost coven. But it was more than that. I knew in this moment we were in the presence of something else. Something *more*.

The fawn lifted her head, recognizing our presence. She held our gaze for a moment, before turning back to the overgrown patches of grass around her to graze. My breath was shaky as I exhaled, grateful for her acceptance.

I scooched forward on my knees, taking special care to make my movements as small and meek as possible.

Easy, Vander's voice whispered through my mind. Even in the confines of our tether, he was making sure to stay calm, careful. He pressed his hand against my back, offering his support as I closed the short distance between us and the fawn. She didn't even so much as lift her head again. She'd done her assessing. She'd seen no threat, no cause of concern. And there was no need for her to regard our presence further.

I lifted my palm, the rays of inked sunlight catching in the edge of my vision as tendrils of my magic lifted into the air of their own accord. They reached out, inching closer and closer to the fawn, where she lingered still unconcerned as she found a new patch of wildflowers to munch on. I held my breath as my magic twisted hesitantly around her, caressing the side of her face.

She leaned into the embrace, lifting her head finally as she nuzzled against the golden glow of my magic. Everything around us stilled. The birds, the insects. Even the wind stalled as the grass swaying in the clearing froze. As if all around us knelt before the fawn, just as we had.

My gaze swept over the clearing, astounded at the utter stillness surrounding us. Aerie's movement beside me pulled my attention back towards the makeshift circle we'd created. She dug in the pocket of her skirts, producing a small teal stone. She bowed towards the fawn, reaching out softly and placing the stone on a level spot amidst the rubble.

I wasn't sure what it meant, wasn't sure what to do, but I felt led to copy her movement. I lowered my head to the soot-covered floor, letting the rough ground press into my forehead as I bowed. Judging by the soft sounds behind me, I assumed Vander and Bastian were doing the same.

I waited, taking in the serenity of those moments. I hadn't existed in such a stillness before. It was deafening, that kind of quiet. And yet, it didn't cause discomfort in me. I closed my eyes, taking a deep breath as I absorbed whatever this moment meant. It was an understanding above my capacity, but I could feel the depths of its importance in the air.

The fawn crept forward, walking softly between where Aerie and I still bowed. She leaned into Aerie, nuzzling against her for the briefest of moments. A whimper slipped from Aerie's lips, shattering my heart as tears began trailing down my cheeks and dampening the floor below.

The fawn didn't linger though, turning at last to Bastian and doing the same. I turned my head slightly to watch the interaction from my bowed position. She circled back in front of us, pausing a moment as if waiting for us. In unison, the four of us rose. She made eye contact with each of us, landing finally on Aerie and holding her gaze the longest—as if to take in one final look—before she darted out of the cottage and disappeared into the woods.

I turned fast, trying to follow her movements, but she was gone. No trace remained, not even tracks in the ground around us.

CHAPTER 28
HAZEL

Vander insisted on returning to the Estate, quickly and quietly, before discussing our encounter within the Dark Woods. We all knew well that our safety wasn't ensured until we were safely nestled back behind Talamh's tribal warding.

Vander was on high alert as the four of us silently made our way home. But despite his concern, he made sure to give Aerie and Bastian a respectful distance. I saw, even from that distance, the grief ravaging their bodies. Bastian had pulled Aerie in tight, his head on a swivel as his dark brown eyes kept watch over his mate. His other hand rested on the battle axe strapped to his side the whole way home. Aerie was trying to be strong, but I glimpsed the dampness of her cheeks every now and then—heard the stifled sobs echoing through the trees.

When we made it back to the Estate, we settled into the sofas in the sitting room. Bastian passed out glasses of sunbeam whiskey to everyone, taking his seat at last beside Aerie. She curled up into him, the adventures of the day wearing on her heavily. She looked absolutely exhausted, her eyes hooded and skin stripped of color as she leaned on Bastian and stared off into the distance.

"Would anyone like to explain what the fuck happened out there?" Vander's gruff voice broke the silence.

Nox strutted in, completely oblivious to the events that had just transpired. "Something happened?" He raised an eyebrow as he poured himself a glass of the sunbeam whiskey. He turned around, leaning against the built in bar as he sipped on his drink—observing the mood of the room.

Bastian sighed, rubbing his thumb and forefinger over his brow. I cleared my throat, an offering to take over for Bastian who was clearly having a hard time finding the words.

"We went for a walk," I started, gesturing towards the woods beyond the Estate. "Aerie caught sight of something while we were out and took off after it. When we caught up to her we saw the—" My words stalled, a pang of emotion leaking into my quiet voice as I finished: "the fawn."

Nox stood a bit straighter, cocking his head.

"What fawn?" he asked. But judging by the intensity in his eyes, he already understood.

"There's no way to know if it was truly her," Bastian cut in, eyes darting down to Aerie as if to urge our neutrality. She still hadn't stopped staring off in the distance, as if she wasn't fully here with us.

"But it was a fawn, yes?" Nox trudged forward. I understood why he insisted on answers. Mirren may have been like a daughter to Aerie, but she was his sister.

Vander nodded. "Perhaps something in the Cosmos is trying to get a message to you." He gestured towards Bastian and Aerie with his glass. "Maybe to all of us. And they knew exactly what to do to get our attention."

"But what message?" I quipped after several moments of tense silence. Gazes rose slowly to me. All but Aerie's. "What does it mean?"

"A warning perhaps?" Vander offered, albeit somewhat half-heartedly.

I sucked in a short breath, mumbling words to myself as I recalled them from my memories.

"What did you say?" Bastian lifted his head, cocking his head towards me. I swallowed, closing my eyes for a moment.

"Be careful, my goddess. For the Cosmos are warning you... It's what one of the priestesses told me during her reading, when we were visiting Sgàil. I didn't think it was a real warning. Until now."

"New rule." Bastian's gaze jumped from mine to Vander's before shaking his head in frustration. "From now on, if anyone gets cryptic messages from the Cosmos, no matter how ridiculous they feel, you share them with the group. Deal?"

No one responded, a silent agreement passing between us as we let the reality of what just happened sink in.

"Whatever it was," Bastian said at last. "We need to be mindful moving forward. I can't shake the feeling that something is coming. Something we are missing. Between Aerie finding that book in Sgàil's archives and this omen leading her back to that cottage—" His words cut off, a swell of emotion making him clear his throat. "I don't like what it's insinuating. And we all need to be on guard."

"But what do you think it's insinuating?" Nox's voice rose, desperation laced through his tone.

Aerie sat up straight, eyes going wide. What little color was left in her cheeks drained as she turned her attention to Bastian. "You think this involves my father."

My mouth dropped open. The room went utterly quiet as Bastian sat with Aerie's accusation for several painful moments before responding.

"How could it be anything else, sunshine?" He looked over to her, offering a half smile that was only laced with pain. "It guided you back to that wretched place, back into the destruction and pain he caused you. Forcing you to step foot in that cottage for the first time since I found you all those years ago."

He brushed a hand over her face, tucking her hair behind the pointed shell of her ear. "I don't want to worry you unnecessarily, but this was divinely timed. After yesterday, going back there—"

"Wait, what happened yesterday?" Vander leaned forward as he sensed a piece of the puzzle he was missing.

"Aerie felt sick yesterday," I answered slowly, turning my gaze from a worried looking Vander, back to search Aerie's features. "So she didn't join us for training. But Bastian never said what you were sick with."

Aerie bowed her head. "I believe I've mentioned before. Because of the magic my father infected me with, I am incapable of having children. But at times that magic... falters." Bastian laid his hand on hers, his knuckles going white with the pressure squeezing her fingers, some sort of desperation to remind her she wasn't alone. "My body is not always incapable of being with child," she went on as all of us listened, leaning in with various looks of confusion and concern. "But rather *staying* with child."

My fingers pressed against my lips, stifling a gasp as I understood the words she could not stay. "So yesterday..." I trailed off, finding myself incapable of speaking them aloud as well.

Silent tears stained Aerie's cheeks as she sunk into Bastian once more. He swallowed hard, nodding his head at my unspoken question.

I let out a shaky breath, my mind fighting between sorrow and panic as I processed what they'd shared. My heart hurt for my friends, for the neverending pain they seemed to be going through. There were no two souls more deserving of happiness. And yet, heartache continued to find them.

"That's why I had the chrysocolla, why I left it as an offering to the omen," Aerie explained. "A stone most soothing to the soul. It is said to bring forth divine feminine energy, encouraging harmony within the body—protection. I've made a habit of carrying it with me when I sense my courses coming. Or when I sense..."

Her voice trailed off, but I didn't need her to finish. I knew what she meant—that she carried it with her when she believed she was with child, in hopes that it would help her fight her father's magic. That's why she'd had it in the woods.

"Anyways." She cut her gaze down to her lap, hands dipping into her now empty pockets. Her eyes had returned back to that distant nothingness. "So much for that."

Bastian wrapped his fingers around her arm, letting her curl in against him.

"She wasn't far along." Bastian took over as Aerie retreated within herself. "No more than a couple of weeks. It always happens early; her father's magic acts fast. We've tried everything to loosen his hold, to expel his curse." Bastian shook his head as his own tears swelled in his eyes. "But nothing has worked. And now, just a day after his vile power was writhing through her body, taking from us once more, a spirit visits us and leads us back to the very place where he cursed her with that infection?"

Bastian shook with unspent rage, grinding his teeth together as his whole body flexed its power. "That is no coincidence."

I shook my head, unsure what to say. To find out the very possible likelihood that something from the spirit realm was trying to warn us of her father's involvement once more... We already had enough darkness to overcome without something like this weighing us down further. Aerie hadn't shared much about her father with me, but I knew from the little she had that he was just as vile and sadistic as Kahlis.

If not possibly more so.

He was evil, but more than that, he was mad. Driven insane by a lifetime of isolation. To think that we could have not one but two fae kings coming after us—my body shuddered.

"The question is, in what capacity might he be involved," Bastian said at last, his demeanor slowly shifting into chieftain mode.

"Or if it's a metaphorical involvement rather than a physical one," Vander responded. His elbows were on his knees, hands clasped between him. His sudden alertness in the woods was starting to make more sense, those instincts taking over once again as he focused on the possible threat, his mind whittling away at a plan to keep us safe.

"How do you mean?" I asked, lacing my arm through his and tucking my feet under me.

"Perhaps it's a warning of the type of magic, rather than the individual."

"He and Kahlis do have similar types of magic," Bastian agreed. He cleared his throat, shoving away the emotion that had been woven through his features moments ago. He swirled the last bit of his drink in his glass as he thought for a moment before tipping it back and swallowing the rest of the liquid. "But why risk bringing us a message to warn us about Kahlis? We are already all too aware of his continued threat to the tribes."

Bastian leaned forward, setting the now empty glass on the low table in front of him. Despite his movement, Aerie stayed tucked safely within his grasp, drifting in and out of consciousness.

"Maybe there's something else coming, something bigger than what he's done before?" I asked, trying to ignore the chill creeping down my spine.

Bastain sighed, rubbing his free hand over his face. "I don't know the answer," He pulled Aerie fully into his arms, cradling her across his body as he rose to his feet. "But my wife is exhausted and I'm going to see her to bed before we discuss this further."

"You'll let us know if she needs anything?" I pressed, sitting up.

It felt so odd for our roles to be reversed. Aerie was the one to constantly look after me. But my friend, my sister, was hurting. And it broke my heart to feel so helpless. If there was anything I could do to help, I would. Bastian nodded once, his eyes softening before turning and disappearing down the hall, Aerie sleeping soundly in his arms.

I fell back against the sofa once they were out of sight. "What are we going to do?" I asked, chewing frantically on the edge of my thumb.

"Well, for starters, I'm going to go inspect every inch of those ruins," Nox announced. "See if I can find any other of these signs from the Cosmos to make heads or tales of the situation at hand." He downed his drink, refilling it before crossing the sitting room and taking Bastian's seat.

"No," Vander warned, his voice a low rumble.

"No? You come home telling me you saw the spirit of my sister and you expect me *not* to go look for myself?"

"You didn't feel the energy out there, Nox. The Dark Woods was buzzing, heavy with power. Until we know for sure what's going on, no one goes out there alone."

"No one? Or just us commoners?" Nox inclined his head, a brittle smile plastered on his face. Vander didn't respond. Instead, he lifted his glass to his lips, drinking deeply as his eyes stayed trained on Nox.

"Do you really think Aerie's father could be involved?" I asked, desperate to break the tension. I rocked subtly on my knees, looking between Nox and Vander. "Fighting Kahlis already felt impossible enough, let alone adding another fae king into the mix. And a mad one, at that."

Vander set his free arm across the back of the sofa, leaning over me. His gaze dropped to mine—his eyes softening. "It's probably nothing, little spitfire. Don't let this worry you."

"It's worrying you," I shot back, gesturing to him.

"I just want to ensure your safety, is all. There's too many unknowns happening at the moment to drop my guard, even for a second." But even as he said it, his eyes cut momentarily to meet Nox's, something exchanging between them—too fast to catch.

He leaned down, planting a soft kiss on the top of my head. My skin warmed under his touch, my eyes drifting closed as he tightened his hold. I let out a slow sigh, feeling my panic melt away. This is what I'd meant when Aerie had asked me about our bond. I'd spent so much of my life in constant worry, sure that there was always something going wrong, something deeply troubling on the verge of imploding.

But the bond had changed things. I found rest in him. A rest unlike anything I'd known before. So much so that even in the face of trouble, I felt no need to fear. Worry, perhaps. But not fear. I hummed softly, soaking in the warmth of his arm around me.

"I know this will do no good," he whispered into my hair, lowering his voice so that Nox couldn't hear. "But please try to keep your emotions under control."

I huffed, peering up at him through narrowed eyes. He held me firmer, cutting off the retort ready to slip past my lips.

"Not because you don't have every right to feel them. But because I can't fucking control myself when I'm feeling you so fully. And it is not exactly the time or the place to be giving into the Mark's demands for your flesh."

I bit down on my lower lip, throwing up a wall of warding to try and keep him from the tether in the only way I knew how, even as my cheeks heated in response.

"I think we're a bit past shielding, Hazel." He sat up, looking down at me with annoying smugness. He threw me a wink as he blasted past my walls with ease, and spoke into my mind.

Don't you think?

Vander's eyes broke away from mine, lingering for just a moment on the corner of my mouth where my lips were tipping up, just as Bastian returned.

"Lennox, where's your brother?" His abruptness was startling, his patience clearly thin. He snagged his glass off the middle table and refilled it, pouring an extra serving for good measure.

Nox cleared his throat, trying to hide the fact that he was rolling his eyes. "No clue. He took off shortly after you lot this morning."

Bastian paused mid sip, narrowing his gaze on Nox. "To go where?"

"How the fuck am I supposed to know?" Nox exclaimed. I winced at his lack of tact.

"Excuse me for thinking you may have a better inclination as to your brother's whereabouts," Bastian grumbled.

"What about your weird twin magic, can't you just tune into that and see where he is?" I asked.

Nox bristled, the muscle in his jaw twitching. "Kirwan hasn't been exactly forthcoming with his whereabouts lately."

Vander snapped his head to Nox. "You mean, you can't see what he's doing?"

"No," Nox ground out through clenched teeth. "Not all the time, anyways. Not right now."

Bastian let out a loud sigh. "Well, if it changes, let me know. He needs to be brought up to speed on what's happened and he's been missing far more lately than he's been around. We need to start being mindful of our position. Stay within the tribe's borders when we can."

Nox nodded, briefly, before rising from the sofa and turning to leave.

"I want both you and him to do some digging on this," Bastian called after him. "See what you can find. Together. If there's another threat we're not yet aware of yet, we need to find it."

Nox paused for a moment by the entrance to the kitchen, accepting his orders, before storming through the house and out the door without another word.

"Were you aware of this?" Bastian asked, cutting a look towards Vander as he took his seat across from us.

Vander rubbed a hand against the back of his neck, sitting back at last. "Nox had voiced some concerns about Kirwan's behavior as of late, but it was nothing I considered necessarily concerning."

"Yes, because you've had such a reputable history for noticing concerning behavior," Bastian sneered. Vander huffed, rolling his eyes and raising a crude gesture towards his brother. I stifled a laugh, but not before Vander caught on to my amusement and turned a raised brow towards me.

"What?" I asked, innocently. "You really expect me to disagree with that statement?"

Vander growled, his hand darting out around my legs and pulling me towards him till I was practically in his lap, effectively silencing me.

"I'll deal with you later," he half whispered as he fixed me with a dark glare. "And you." He turned his attention back to Bastian. "Let the twins work out their shit on their own."

"They're in service to my tribe, Vander. If their spat is interfering with their ability to perform their duties, then perhaps it's time for me to step in."

Vander rose to his feet, setting his half emptied glass down on the table. "You're their friend first, brother. Don't overstep or you'll risk damaging that relationship."

"And as their friend, am I not duty-bound to help them?" Bastian argued.

Vander sighed, shaking his head. "Do what you think is best, Bastian. I'm retiring for the evening. I suggest you do the same. It's been a long day."

Vander reached for my arm, pulling me to my feet. I stumbled forward at the sudden motion, wrapping an arm around his waist to help steady myself. He didn't let go as he made his way around the sofas and down the hall towards my bedchamber.

The door clicked closed softly behind us, a fire already steadily burning and bathing the room in a warm glow. He led me to the bed and sat me down on the edge before retreating to the wardrobe in the corner to fetch some night clothes.

"I can't imagine how they're feeling," I called out, my voice feeling at odds with the otherwise silent room. "I wish there was more we could do."

"I know," Vander agreed, returning to the bed. He motioned for me to stand up and turned me around before working to release the strings of my cotton dress. "But Bastian and Aerie are some of the strongest people I know. I have no doubt they will make it through this, as they have before." His touch was soft, gentle, and when he'd finished undoing the ties, he ran his hands down the length of my arms.

I sighed into his touch, leaning back against him. He slipped his fingers beneath the collar of the dress, pushing it down my body and letting it pool on the floor. He reached around me, grabbing the nightclothes from the edge of the bed.

"Do you truly believe the fawn was a warning?" I asked, my voice dropping low. As if I was scared to voice the question out loud, for fear of summoning the omen once more.

Turning me back around, he motioned for me to lift my hands as he slipped the linen gown over my head. It fell in place against my body and he reached around to swipe a hand beneath my hair, releasing it from beneath the gown.

"It's hard to know anything for sure right now." He exhaled, cupping my face in his hands. "But we will figure it out. Let's just focus on what we can do for now."

"Which is what?" I asked, feeling utterly hopeless in the midst of everything the day had revealed.

He swiped a thumb over my cheek, the rough feeling of his skin grounding me. "We can take care of Aerie. We can rest." He reached around me, pulling back the covers on the bed and urging me back into it. "We can take advantage of this time we do have together, before whatever chaos could be coming."

He settled in beside me, tucking me firmly under his arm as he pulled the covers over us. He leaned down, softly kissing my forehead.

"I'm not sure I appreciate your mindset," I grumbled, nestling against him. "But I could get used to sleeping beside you."

Vander huffed out a breath, rubbing his hand up and down the length of my arm in soft, reassuring strokes. "You've slept beside me for many weeks now, Hazel."

I rolled my eyes, tilting my head to peer up at him. "In your mortal form, I mean."

"Ah." He smirked, knowing full well what I had meant. "Yes, I do believe I could get used to this. Makes me wonder why I didn't take advantage of the opportunity sooner."

I rolled my eyes, a million retorts running through my mind. But I could feel the amusement radiating through Vander, the smirk settling across his face, knowing he'd struck a chord.

You are so not funny, Vander Darroch.

His smile deepened, his amusement growing as I sensed it through the tether.

Sleep, little spitfire, was his only reply. And without even trying, I was settling once more against him, drifting from consciousness at the steady rhythm of his touch caressing my arm.

CHAPTER 29
VANDER

Hours had passed since Hazel drifted off to sleep. I held her in the crook of my arm, brushing my fingers through her hair as the sound of her peaceful breaths filled the room. The fire had begun to dwindle, casting deeper shadows along the walls around us. They greeted me, called out to me—keeping me awake.

My gaze was fixed on the window facing Hazel's bed, the moon hung high above the treetops of the Dark Woods. There were shadows there too, calling out for me to join them. It was an impossible pull, a force incapable of being denied.

My mind was wired as I tried to ignore it, using all of my mental stamina to focus solely on the feel of Hazel in my arms. But even hours later, I couldn't drown it out. The Mark had been silent much of the day, bestowing within me a false sense of security in the path we had chosen. But now, it was growing with a fearsome sort of intensity that I couldn't seem to hinder.

I lowered my lips to Hazel's cheek, giving her a soft kiss, then slipped my arm out from underneath her, careful not to wake her as I lifted myself off the bed. Slipping out the door, I paused, turning back to watch her a moment longer in her blissful slumber.

I couldn't help but agree with her sentiment the night before. She was looking more and more like herself, becoming that version of her that she was always destined to be. And fuck if it wasn't driving me mad. I swallowed hard, pride coursing through me as I thought of everything she'd overcome, was still battling. And yet, she'd never stopped fighting.

But it seemed as if the opposite was happening to me. With each time we came together, with each layer we peeled back to recognize the bond for what it was, I felt pieces of myself slipping away. It wasn't consistent, but I could feel it. The way the Mark's hold felt more possessive each time its power roared to life within me. It was proving to me with each passing day the depth of the claim it had on my soul. And I didn't know how to stop it.

I blew a breath of air out, casting my gaze downward as I backed away and pulled the door shut with a soft click.The Dark Woods was calling, and fuck—I couldn't fight it a moment longer. At one point it had been something I'd willingly accepted, the need for bloodshed. But now that it was taking me away from my mate, I wanted nothing more than to deny it.

My soul ached to be near her, to experience her being. Even if I still felt unworthy of her attention. But so long as the Mark commanded my soul, I'd be subjected to this other existence—a half life of hunger and bloodlust, cursed by darkness.

I cleared my throat, hating how the sound echoed down the empty hallway, and pushed forward. I would answer the call, satisfy this unrelenting itch as swiftly as possible, and I would be back in her bed come dawn. It was a promise to the Fates themselves, a vow to return to the peace she offered, because there was nothing I wanted more in this world than to have her in my arms. Even if doing so was descending me into madness.

The air was warm as I made my way outside, heavy with a sickening moisture that had me instantly pulling my tunic off and tossing it to the side. I rolled my shoulders, testing my restraint as I considered the possibility of refusing the call entirely and returning inside. The Mark protested, a twinge of pain slicing through my chest as if in warning of what would happen were I to not obey.

I growled in answer, my wolven form slipping through my mortal one as my vision shifted.

"You want me to kill? Fine." My voice rumbled through the night, not another soul around to hear my words. "But make it quick. I have a goddess in my bed that I don't intend to keep waiting." The Mark purred within me, filling my veins with a sickening vibration that had me flexing my hands as I slunk through the trees.

My head was on a swivel, looking for whatever threat had summoned me out here. The shadows wouldn't have called unless there was something lurking. But even as I made my way deeper into the Dark Woods, I found nothing.

My mind went back to the spirit that had visited us, the eerie feel of its magic. I'd had this same feeling when we'd made our way home after the encounter. As if there was something I was missing, something I could not see. But I knew the power of the Mark, the strength of the Grimm. There was not a match for my power within the tribal borders, nor the Dark Woods, making it impossible to imagine a being within these trees capable of hiding itself from me.

With each stretch of land I covered, my searching turned more frantic—the elusiveness of my prey filling me with a primal rage. My breathing was erratic as I let more of that monster slip through, tearing apart the Dark Woods for whatever the fuck dared invade my territory.

"Come on!" I yelled, the power of my voice shaking the trees. "Show yourself!" I spun, my eyes looking everywhere at once. I could sense it—the presence here with me, lurking in the shadows. It called to me, toying with me. But never revealing itself.

My vision blurred, my feet stumbling as I braced myself against a nearby trunk. A vicious fire burned beneath my skin, behind my eyes. A layer of sweat broke out across my chest. I sucked desperate breaths into my lungs, trying to calm my power within me.

It had never burned so hot. It was eating me alive, consuming me with a ferocity I'd never experienced before. The Mark danced on my arm in sadistic amusement, making my anger tip over.

"What do you want?!"

My voice echoed around me, morphing into its own entity and ringing in my ears. Visions of my nightmares flashed through my mind. A day long ago where I'd been so foolish. So desperate. A deal had been made. A bond, forged.

And the time had come to pay my dues.

I grabbed at my hair, digging my fingers in and pulling as I tried to regain control over my own mind. My body moved forward of its own accord, stumbling through the foliage of the Dark Woods.

I yelled, screamed, fought as whatever possessed me tried to claim my life. I wouldn't let it win. I couldn't. Not when I'd just accepted the goodness and light that waited for me back at the Estate. I'd finally started to let myself be happy. To accept a future with her.

To hope.

And now...

I fell to my knees, a scorching fire blazing through my veins. This was the consequence of my actions, the grave reality of accepting the Mark and letting it have total control. I knew it was there, that this reality would come to pass. And I'd ignored it for my own foolish happiness. The Mark would never be content until it consumed me—mind, body, and soul.

I'd known as such when I'd made the deal. And I'd accepted it anyway. Nothing felt like too high a price to save her. To protect her. But now that I had her back, I couldn't abandon her. I'd give up my life if it meant saving hers, but leaving her behind when we'd finally accepted each other was a torment I couldn't bear.

My cries of anguish circled the Dark Woods, gathering the shadows and summoning them to me. They covered me, a storm of obsidian smoke as I lost my mind completely. I pleaded with them, begging them to save me. But they were no longer mine to control.

I was at their mercy, at *his* mercy. And even as I clung to the world around me, I could feel my body being ripped apart as it descended into chaos.

CHAPTER 30
HAZEL

I sat up in bed, suddenly aware of Vander's absence. I peered into the darkness, patting the empty bed beside me just to make sure my eyes weren't playing tricks on me. I gnawed on my bottom lip, my gaze sweeping across the room and towards the bathing chamber.

There was not a soul to be found.

I blew a breath out through my nostrils, torn between irritation and fear. It wouldn't be at all unlike Vander to sneak off to the Dark Woods, but given the recent shift in his demeanor, I felt at least a tiny bit hopeful that the need—the hunger—wasn't so consuming. I folded my arms over my chest, tapping my fingers idly against my bare skin as I let my gaze linger on the window across from the bed, and the periwinkle sky beyond.

It must have been near sunrise, still too early to be up, but late enough that whatever hunt Vander must have snuck off to would be nearly over.

The embers in the fireplace glowed a subtle orange, the flames long gone. Despite the warm season, a chill crept into the air. It pushed me from bed, my bare feet padding across the frigid floor in haste as I pulled a fresh set of clothes from the wardrobe. I dressed quickly, thankful for the warmth of the leggings and long sleeve tunic as they wrapped around my cold skin.

I gave the bedroom one last look before I ventured into the hallway. Tiptoeing carefully so as not to wake anyone, I crept through the Estate and out the side entrance. My bare feet sunk into the dewy grass, the sensation calming the worry in my chest as I paced outside the kitchen entrance—eyes trained on the tree line.

Minutes passed, possibly an hour or more, like that. Pacing just outside the Estate like I'd lost my mind, eyes never leaving the dark shadows of the trees beyond. Still, I didn't venture closer, didn't dare enter that depraved darkness without the protection of Vander by my side.

Something didn't feel right. It wasn't a stretch to assume he was in there. It was actually the most plausible case. But too much had changed between us, too much had happened over the past two days, for him to take off like this. Again. And no matter how long I watched the forest, it gave me no signs of his presence amongst its shadows.

I froze in my steps, realizing for the first time since I'd awoken that I couldn't feel him down the tether. The bond was so strong that it was impossible to focus on anything else at times. But now, it felt eerily silent. I reached out through that connection, letting my worry and desperation lead the way as I called out to him.

Tears pricked behind my eyes as no answer greeted me.

Either Vander had shut me out, shielding me from whatever it was he was doing or—

No, I wouldn't let myself go there. I couldn't let my mind trick me into assuming the worst. This was normal Vander behavior. A call to the hunt. That was all. I shook my head, running my hands over my arms as I tried to calm the chill that still tickled my skin. I'd go back inside, maybe make myself some breakfast and wait for him to return home. When he did, we'd talk about the need to communicate these urges, how his constant need to just take off was difficult for me to handle, given our history.

I nodded once, convinced of my plan. I let my eyes linger just a moment longer on the tree line, giving him every possible chance to return and answer my call. When he still didn't show, I sighed, letting my gaze fall to the ground and turning around to head inside.

I stifled a shriek as I ran into another body, its sudden and silent presence sending me reeling. "Kirwan," I gasped, sucking down desperate breaths as I tried to calm my heartbeat. "You frightened me." My hands gripped at my chest, my panic melting away to a breathy laugh as I looked up at my friend. He watched me, his features vacant for a moment too long.

"My apologies," he answered at last, offering me a small smile. "It's so early. What are you doing out here?"

I looked back over my shoulder, gesturing to the woods. "I was hoping to find Vander." I turned back to Kirwan, running a hand through my hair. "I couldn't sleep knowing he was out there."

"Ah." Kirwan nodded, looking over my shoulder to the shadows beyond. "You sure that's where he is?"

I stood up straighter, cocking my head to the side. "I assumed he was. Why? Have you seen him?"

Kirwan paused a moment, watching the trees. "No," he finally answered, gaze cutting back to mine. When he saw the worry that was surely laced through my features, he let out a small laugh, shaking his head. "No, I'm sorry I gave you that impression. I was just curious, as I haven't seen him either."

"Are you looking for him?" I asked, my brow furrowing.

"You could say that." Something flashed through Kirwan's eyes, too fast for me to identify. "Let's get you inside, though—there's a chill. I'm sure Vander doesn't want you out here, cold and waiting for him."

Kirwan reached for my arm, wrapping his fingers around my wrist and pulling me towards the Estate. I looked back over my shoulder, reluctant to leave.

"Come along," he called back to me. "He'll be back soon."

I sighed, relenting at last and following his lead into the kitchen. He sat me down at one of the stools by the center counter, before moving over to the cast iron stove and setting a kettle on the stove eye to boil.

"Tea?" he offered as he moved around the kitchen. He produced two teacups from the hooks on the wall, setting them on the counter before me. I nodded absent-mindedly, taking the empty mug and cupping it carefully in my hands.

"It's the one on the far left," I called out to Kirwan, noticing him sifting through the cupboards aimlessly. He followed my direction, digging out one of Aerie's tea blends and bringing it back to the counter.

"Forgive me." He laughed quietly, staring down at the herbs. "It's been some time since I've used this kitchen."

I grinned at him, mirroring his laugh. "I'm sure Aerie has taken rather good care of you since your return. Both your and Nox's service to the tribe has meant so much to her and Bastian."

Kirwan nodded, clearing his throat and turning back to the stove as the kettle began to whistle. A soft silence hung in the air as he prepared our cups. I watched him work, finding the rhythm of his movements soothing. He measured out the tea leaves, adding them to the kettle and letting them steep as he began a new search for some sieves for the teacups.

"Center drawer," I called out, amusement seeping into my words. He raised his head from where he was digging around in the far drawer. His eyes softened briefly as he shook his head and altered his course.

He placed the sieves, filling the cups with the golden brew. The sweet aroma of chamomile filled the kitchen, my eyes snagging on the tendrils of steam between us. He set the kettle down, drumming his fingers on the wooden counter as his eyes darted around.

"I don't suppose you'd know where a bit of honey would be?" He raised a tentative eyebrow toward me.

I sucked in a breath through my teeth, pushing myself off the stool. "I do," I answered, leaning towards him. "But it will cost you."

He narrowed his eyes, his brow furrowed. He watched me for a moment, apparently not catching the jest.

"I'm just messing with you," I assured him, my lips ticking up in a devious smirk. The lines across his face went lax as he dropped his head, laughing again and rubbing his hand over his forehead.

"I fear I did not sleep well last night. It appears that lack of rest is more evident than I'd like."

I scoffed, watching him as I moved through the kitchen and towards the root cellar just beyond. "Perhaps you should return to your bedchamber then," I called over my shoulder. "And try getting some more rest." I found the honey quickly, sauntering haughtily back into the kitchen. I held it up between us, waggling it in front of him.

He grabbed the jar, shooting me a glare I couldn't quite interpret before turning back to the cups and adding a spoonful to each one. He took the cups in each hand, closing the distance between us and handing me one. I took it gleefully, inhaling the delicious scent. It was a blend I'd come to love, the mixture of herbs bringing me an overwhelming sense of calm.

Something in me wondered if Kirwan knew that when he'd grabbed the blend, or if it had just been a happy coincidence. I took a deep sip, the warmth seeping into my bones. I let out a content sigh. I opened my eyes, unsure when I'd even closed them, to find Kirwan staring at me over the rim of his own teacup on his lips.

"What?" I asked, laughing awkwardly at the sudden displacement of energy.

"I don't mean to stare, it's just that your appearance is so..." He trailed off, his mind lost in a haze. "I see so much of him in you."

The boldness in his words startled me. I tilted my head, trying to understand his meaning. "So much of who?" I asked tensely. I took another sip from my cup, in an attempt to let the warmth of the tea ground me.

His vacant eyes met mine, devoid of their usual care and consideration. The chill I'd felt earlier grew tenfold.

"Your father, of course," he replied at last.

My blood went cold, my body frozen as I watched him. "What do you mean by that?" I asked at last, my voice shaking.

"Hazel." Kirwan opened his arms towards me. I retreated a step. His hand shot out, grabbing my arm before I could retreat further. "Do you forget that I've spent intimate time with your father? Under my title as tribal spy? I was simply commenting on your similarities as I've come to know the both of you."

I knew Kirwan had spent time with Kahlis. But something about his words felt careless, cruel, like a mask slipping. I bristled at the juxtaposition of the male I'd come to trust as my friend, the kindhearted, warm Kirwan to the male before me now.

"Kirwan." There was an edge to my tone. "Let go of me."

He blinked back, no recognition of my plea in those cold eyes.

My heart thrummed in my chest, suddenly sick to my stomach. Perhaps Kirwan had become a friend in more recent days, but I was suddenly all too aware that he had first been a servant to my father.

"Vander will be back any moment," I warned, my voice rising. "And when he finds you here with me, he will not hesitate to claim your life if you wish me harm."

Kirwan hummed in consideration. His thumb began stroking a pattern over my skin, the trail of his touch burning me. I hissed through gritted teeth, looking down at where his hand gripped me. I tried to pull away, but he held firm, continuing that poisonous motion against my arm.

My vision blurred, even as I fought to break free. I opened my mouth to scream—to warn the others—but found myself incapable of the noise. My eyes widened as I met his gaze, the only muscle seemingly able to respond to the panic taking over my body. I was frozen, paralyzed by a magic I'd never felt before. No matter how badly I wanted to fight back, to run, to be free of his hold—I was at his mercy.

And he knew it.

I barely registered the sway of my body, a solid, intrusive form enveloping me as my vision went black.

Fire burned within me, so hot it almost felt cold. I shuddered, the motion spurring a blinding pain through my numb body. I cried out within my mind, nothing but silence surrounding me. I begged for mercy, for relief.

A muffling of voices answered me, pulling me back into consciousness. I blinked—at least, I thought I did. But only blackness surrounded me. I concentrated on the voices, letting them guide me as I waded through the crippling darkness. I couldn't make out what they were saying, couldn't place if I knew to whom they belonged, but the deeper I followed them, the clearer they became.

Slowly, the haze cleared from my eyes and the world around me took shape.

I looked around, unable to place where I was. Fine satin sheets stretched out beneath me, covering an oversized, extravagant bed. The room was large, elegant and impressive. Beautiful tapestries hung on the wall, accented by gilded ornamental decor. The furniture was just as extravagant, made of rich fabrics and finely crafted blackwood.

On the other side of the room, a fire burned in an oversized hearth. Two beings spoke softly beside it, owners to the voices I'd heard moments ago. I tried to focus my eyes, to see who they were, but whatever poison had riddled my system was still clinging to me.

I stiffened, sitting up slowly as I remembered the series of events that had led me here. I had been home, in the kitchen. With Kirwan. His touch, it had done something to me? Put me under some sort of spell, poisoning me with some kind of sedative. My body was still numb, tingling all over as it tried to shake the magic's hold.

The two voices cut off, turning their attention towards me. I blinked rapidly, feeling suddenly defenseless with my dulled senses.

The one on the left clapped his hands together. "Ah, Hazlenn! You're finally awake."

Every fiber of my being screamed within me at the voice. I didn't need him to come closer, didn't need my vision to clear, to know who it belonged to.

Kahlis.

I closed my eyes quickly, squeezing them shut with a viciousness as I tried to reach out to Vander through the tether. He'd always been able to find me before. If I wanted to wake from this nightmare, I needed him to find me again.

But no matter how much I called out, how much I screamed and begged and banged against our connection, I couldn't find him.

"That little trick isn't going to work this time." The voice chuckled as he crossed the room. My eyes shot open, my limbs scrambling quickly to get off the bed and keep the distance between us. I stumbled over dead feet, falling against a mahogany bureau. My legs felt as heavy as wet sand as I turned, keeping him in front of me.

"Release me." I raised my voice, despite how hoarse and raw it sounded. I grabbed a candelabra off the bureau, thrusting it over my head. "Whatever you're doing to trap me within this realm, end it now. Or you'll live to regret it."

The other male crossed the room, cornering me. . As he stepped closer into view, the dual black and silver eyes were unmistakable.

Kirwan. He gave away nothing, his hardened eyes steadily trained on my body, assessing my next move.

A wicked chuckle brought my attention back to the male in front of me.

"This isn't like before, Hazlenn." Kahlis' eyes narrowed, tracking my movement. "There's no realm to escape from."

My fingers shook as I fumbled with the candelabra, refusing to believe this wasn't all in my head. It had to be. Just another nightmare that he'd trapped me within.

"You're home, little one. Where you belong—beside your father."

CHAPTER 31
HAZEL

"No," I argued. My eyes darted between Kahlis and Kirwan, refusing to accept this fate. "This must be another trick. Another form of your relentless torture."

My eyes roamed over the room, over his body, looking for any sort of tell to give away the illusion. I'd forgotten how terrifying he was, how his tall, lean form loomed over his prey. Deep red filled the cracks and crevices of his skin, down to his bony, bloodstained fingers. His eyes were dark and depraved, mirroring the black hue of his hair. He was an endless sea of darkness, parted only by the streak of ghostly white hair that fanned over the top of his head. It was a sight that sent a chill down my spine.

Kahlis scoffed. "I promise you, daughter. This is real and you are truly here."

"Don't call me that," I seethed, lifting the candelabra once more.

Kahlis put his hands up, a mock of surrender as he ventured closer still.

"As you wish. But I promise you, this is all real."

"Why?" I asked, incapable of biting back the emotion in my voice. "Why can you not just leave me alone?"

"You're far too important for that, little one."

I shook my head, blinking away tears. "I'm not," I argued.

He leveled me with a pitiful gaze, shaking his head. "I've been in your mind. I've seen how deep that lack of self-worth goes, so I will not sit here and try to convince you otherwise."

Kirwan's hands shot out, snagging the candelabra from me and tossing it to the side before pinning my back to his chest and holding me in place for Kahlis to approach.

"However," continued Kahlis, "even you cannot deny the power that now courses through your veins. I can feel it just standing in this room with you. So I know you must feel it as well, even if you try to deny it."

I snarled, thrashing against Kirwan's hold. But that familiar ice crept over my body, numbing my muscles and drowning out my fight.

"His magic is quite the rarity, isn't it?" Kahlis hummed, an irritating grin settling against his lips as he stopped just in front of me. "It's why I've kept him in my employ for so long."

I tried to lunge forward, tried to thrash beneath his hold, but with each passing moment, I lost more of my strength.

"The magic is in his touch." Kahlis held his bloodstained fingers up before me. He rubbed his thumb and forefinger together, his long nails clicking in a sickening rhythm. "Just one small caress and he controls you. Nothing more than a slave to his desires. Which, as he is in my employ, means you are a slave to *my* desires."

As if in show of that power, the weakness in my body gave way to something else. My body straightened, chin upturned as I lifted my palms out for Kahlis to inspect. Against my will.

Kahlis took my palms in his hands, studying the markings there. "Tell me, Hazlenn. Have you connected with the Divine? Have you felt her power?"

I bit down on my lip, refusing to answer. Kahlis watched me for a moment before shooting a look at Kirwan over my shoulder. He tightened his grip in answer, letting more of his sickening magic seep into my skin. It was a skill I never knew he'd possessed. It had my stomach turning to think about how many times he'd possibly used it on me without my knowledge.

"Yes," I ground out through clenched teeth, hating how weak I felt.

Kahlis inhaled deeply, running his crimson fingers over the markings on my palms. His dark eyes rolled back, fluttering closed as he lingered there. The feel of his touch on me made my skin crawl. But no matter how much I urged my muscles to move, to fight, I stood still.

"Yes," he repeated to me. "I bet you have. That kind of power is too high a temptation not to dive into, I'm sure." His eyes flicked open, finding mine instantly. "The kind of power others would kill for."

He dropped my hands, breaking out in a cold laugh as he motioned for Kirwan to drop me. "Where are my manners? Let's show our guest some hospitality."

Kirwan's grip loosened and I immediately felt the rush of his magic leave my system. I scrambled away from his reach, turning and watching him carefully. Neither of them paid attention to me any longer, moving through the expansive bedchamber.

Kirwan went to the door on the far right, motioning in someone from the other side as Kahlis took a seat on one of the plush sofas.

"Come, Hazlenn." He motioned for me to join them. Kirwan took a seat opposite Kahlis, leaving no safe spot for me. A female brought in a tray of food, setting it out carefully on the low table between the two sofas.

Her appearance was haunting, her face hollow and lacking color. Milky eyes stared out at me, her movements restricted by shackles around her throat and wrists. I followed the chains with my eyes, observing how they wrapped around her chest like a corset, down to her waist—turning her own body into a metal cage. The chains were covered in markings etched in a different language.

I'd seen similar markings on Bastian's axes. Knowing what I did about their meaning, I assumed they must have held some sort of warding against the prisoner. Little else covered her thin frame save some thin strips of iridescent material held in place by the chains. My heart broke for her as I watched her complete her duties mindlessly, my stomach turning as I noticed the way Kahlis delighted in watching her obedience.

"Sit," Kahlis called out again. He leaned back, sipping on the cup of tea the prisoner had made him.

I eyed the still open door, debating taking my chances and running. But Nox had shared with me before the horrors that he'd witnessed within Kahlis' kingdom. And if I was to believe that I was truly within the exiled fae king's borders, it would take a lot more than making it out of this room to escape Kahlis' clutch.

No, I'd need to be smart about this. I knew nothing about his kingdom, no inkling of which way to go or how to get out safely. And only a small understanding of the creatures I'd meet beyond those doors. Which meant for the time being I'd need to stay put, form a plan. And get as much information from them as I could.

I took a seat beside Kirwan, choosing his familiarity over the fearsome presence of Kahlis. His betrayal stung deeper than I could manage to assess. My mind was clinging to any explanation it could muster, rationalizing why my friend would betray me like this. Regardless, I hated to admit that I still felt safer with him, the history between us tricking me into a false sense of security.

Kahlis gestured to the spread of food on the table before us. "Please, help yourself."

I shook my head, folding my hands firmly in my lap. My knuckles went white with the effort of my grip.

"You're not hungry?" He raised an eyebrow at me. When I refused to answer, he shrugged, lifting his tea once more. "Suit yourself."

"Sir, should we not begin?" Kirwan asked beside me, clearing his throat.

"Yes! Thank you for reminding me. Hazlenn, I've brought you here for one very important reason."

"To torment me?" I shot back. Kahlis' eyes twitched, just slightly, as he paused. His teacup hung in the air, poised just before his lips. His mouth twisted into a crude smile.

"Not in the least, little one. I've brought you here to make amends."

I scoffed, the rage building within me chasing away the fear that had paralyzed me thus far.

"Now I know we've gotten off on the wrong foot," Kahlis continued, refusing to acknowledge my reaction. "But I truly believe it was nothing more than miscommunications—"

"Was Mirren a miscommunication?" I glowered at him.

He cocked his head. "Who?"

"The fawn," Kirwan answered, an utter lack of emotion in his voice. I gaped at him, shocked that he could address the loss of his sister with such indifference. The stillness of his features was unsettling—as if he was trapped in a daze, caught in a spell.

His familiarity faded away, small details seeping through as I took him in once more. His hair was not quite the right shade of red, the cut of his jaw too sharp; his humor and charm had not been quite as refined as it usually was. They were little things, details most would not catch unless they knew him well. But thanks to Aerie's lessons, I'd come to know Kirwan on a deeper level.

And this was not Kirwan. It couldn't be.

"Ah, yes," Kahlis called out, clicking his tongue. "Such an unfortunate series of events. Truly, I never meant for her to get hurt."

He uncrossed his legs, setting his teacup down as he leaned on his knees. "But let's not waste time dwelling on the past. I have a proposition for you, Hazlenn—"

"It's Hazel," I interrupted, hating the sound of that name on his lips. It had been the name my mother had called me, when I'd ventured into the Void in my mind to close the Rift. And I didn't want his voice tainting that memory—the only memory—I had of her.

"I know the power that you wield," he continued on. "It's a strong one, chaotic and unpredictable. And I know the company you keep. None of them are capable of helping you learn to control it."

"That's not true," I shot back. My eyes threatened to wander to the male beside me, remembering how Kirwan helped me call forth that power. I was learning how to use it. Slowly, but surely.

Kahlis' gaze swayed momentarily over to him as well, before landing back on me. "Perhaps they've been able to help some. But that is only the beginning, daughter. Accepting and controlling are two very different things. In order to truly master it, you need someone who is familiar with the origin of its source. Who was around when the Old World reigned. Who's not afraid of such a grand power as yours."

I leveled my gaze at him, fingers digging into the edge of the sofa as I leaned forward.

"I need *nothing* from you."

He waited a moment, running his lower lip between his teeth. Then he stood abruptly, sidestepping the table between the sofas and heading for the door. "Release it."

Kirwan rose, following suit as he gestured through the air. He brought his hand down, the world of luxury surrounding us melting away to reveal a grim reality beneath. The warm comfort of the room I'd been in moments ago was gone, leaving behind a rotting prison. I lifted my arms, feeling the weight of the shackles now around my wrists and throat, just like the servant girl from before.

Kahlis stepped through the bars of a cell, *my* cell, the metal disappearing as it allowed him to pass. "I shared my intentions. It is clear there's no reasoning with you today, so I'm not going to waste my breath. I'd hoped to do this amicably, but I can see now you have your mother's stubbornness."

"Don't you dare speak of my mother," I yelled across the cell.

He cocked his head towards me, watching through the engraved metal bars. "What do you know of your mother?" His words were careful, his features measured.

"*Enough,*" I ground out.

He hummed, his fingers tapping against the back of his hands, which were clasped neatly in front of him.

"I'll be back tomorrow." He backed up a step. His eyes darkened as he lowered his gaze to me. "My court is throwing a celebration in honor of your return, and you will be expected to attend—and *behave.* Use this time to think about my offer." He paused, chuckling deeply before adding, "And maybe familiarize yourself with your fellow prisoners."

Kirwan cut a quick glance to my left, my own eyes following the motion as I noticed something shifting in the darkness beyond. My breath turned rapid and heavy as I tried to make sense of what my eyes were seeing. The rhythm of my heart sped up, an all-too-familiar panic taking over.

Staring back at me between the bars were the same contrasting eyes as the male standing before me. Except this one was real—filthy, covered in dirt and dried blood, and what I was sure was most likely vomit, judging by the stench. His face was bruised and bloodied, his lip split and he wasn't using his right arm. But he was real.

"Kirwan?" I whispered, shaking my head as I recognized my friend.

"Hazel," he responded on an exhale, the word raw.

"What did they do to you?" I scrambled towards the bars, lifting a shackled hand towards him.

But Kahlis voice pulled my attention back. "Nothing he didn't deserve, I can assure you."

The false mirage of the being beside Kahlis transformed before my eyes, an entirely different male taking shape. I watched in horror as his fiery hair shifted to a hue as white as moonlight, revealing eyes dark as Kahlis', and tawny skin that glowed in the quickly receding candlelight.

"Come, Adonis," Kahlis called.

The white-haired male watched me only a moment longer before leaving to join his master on the other side of the bars.

"Your experience here will be directly linked to your cooperation during this time," Kahlis called out. "Obey me, and you will find my favor. But fight me—" He lifted a hand, gesturing to Kirwan's doubled over form on the other side of the bars. "And you will find out quickly just how short a temper I have." He clasped his hands in front of him as his head dipped, assessing me through hooded eyes. "Isn't that right, Kirwan?" Kahlis called out.

"I don't know, Dark One," Kirwan grunted with a hint of sarcasm. "I'd say so far it seems like you've been going easy on me."

I swallowed hard to cover my gasp, my eyes blowing out as I heard Kirwan's jest. The bastard must have had a death wish.

Kahlis hummed, a small grin playing on his lips. He looked down at the floor for a moment, fingers tapping against the back of his hand. "I'll have to remember that for your next session. Wouldn't want poor Hazlenn here to think we were going soft."

"No," Kirwan gritted out. "We wouldn't want that."

Kahlis tsked slowly, pulling my attention back even as I clung to Kirwan's hand. "So trusting, aren't you, little one?" I could practically hear his grin through the words he spoke into the darkness, felt the amusement he derived from whatever game he was playing. "But let me ask you this, why would he be here in the first place?"

My brows pinched together in confusion once more, head turning from Kahlis back to Kirwan. "What does he mean?" I asked. But even as the words rolled off my tongue, Kirwan's fingers stalled against mine.

"Hazel, I–"

"No lies now, Kirwan. I think it's time you come clean to my daughter. Let her know how deep your betrayal runs."

"Fuck. You," Kirwan growled.

"After all," Kahlis continued, ignoring the coarse words, "Hazel is my kin. And I only want what's best for her. And I could simply no longer stand by and watch those surrounding her poison her with their betrayal and lack of loyalty."

"Don't listen to him," Kirwan spat. His grip on my hand tightened, his words desperate. But I was honed in on Kahlis, watching the way his lips barely tipped up in the corner in the low light of the prison. Even now still holding back his upper hand.

"What are you talking about?" It was meant to be a demand, an insistence that he was lying. But it came out as more of a plea, because I knew in that wicked gleam in his eye that there was more. And deep down the answer already seemed to be screaming inside me. The reason Kahlis had found us when I'd closed the Rift; Kirwan's constant disappearing act, how even Nox couldn't always reach him through their connection. The truth behind Kirwan's guilt and rage. The guilt I saw in his eyes ever since Mirren's death.

"One of my many skills is being able to sense the magic in another," he mused. "It's why I was quick to pull Adonis into my employ, and how I sensed there were things Kirwan was hiding from me during the pesky little time period where he was spying on my kingdom." He paused, narrowing his gaze on me. "And precisely how I can no longer feel that meddlesome tether that has gotten in my way time and time again."

I froze, dropping my hand from the bars separating me and Kirwan. He called out to me, tried to grab my hand once more. But I could focus on nothing else besides my father.

"Seems like he left you too?" His smile was barbaric, sadistic. He lingered only long enough to make sure his words had hit their mark, before turning on his heels and disappearing down the corridor beyond my cell, Adonis following in his wake.

I brought my hand to my chest, clutching at the pain blooming in its center. The weeks of work Aerie had done with me—all of the healing and warding and mental shields we'd worked so hard to build—cracked with a deafening echo, releasing a torrent of emotion. The darkness of the Void in my mind swept over me, nearly taking me out as the monsters were set loose within me. The monsters Kahlis had once used against me—and surely would again.

CHAPTER 32
HAZEL

My body shook, my lungs incapable of filling up with air. My chest heaved, my gaze frantic as it darted around the small space. The walls began to move, the shadows slithering like snakes as they taunted me.

"No, no, no." I shrunk into myself, burying my hands in my hair and digging at my scalp in an effort to calm my racing mind. "Wake up. Just fucking *wake up*." I pinched myself, scraped at my skin, wincing at the sharp sting of pain with each effort to pull myself out of this nightmare. Because that's what it had to be—a nightmare. I couldn't accept that it was anything but.

Because if this was real, if I was physically here and Vander was gone and Kirwan had betrayed me... I couldn't put into words the fear that ravaged me. My stomach turned, my body heaving as I bent over and gagged.

"Hazel."

I closed my eyes tight, shaking my head vigorously at Kirwan's plea.

"Hazel, look at me. Focus on me. Please."

I forced myself to peer into the darkness, anger and confusion and despair fighting to win. Kirwan leaned slowly into the bit of moonlight filtering through from somewhere up above. A sob escaped my throat as I forced myself to look at him. Here, within Kahlis's prison. Here, as a captive who had supposedly betrayed me. I saw the friend who had helped build up my Divine power, who had shared laughter and tears with me. But within that image I was beginning to see the one who had betrayed me—even if Adonis had played the final part. The very reason I was trapped in this dark place.

"*Shh.*" He tried to reach a hand through the bars, but it jerked back at the movement, the chains around his wrist inhibiting him. "I know this is a lot to process, but please, love. Try to fight through it. I'll answer every last one of your questions, but I need you to come down from this first."

Another sob escaped my lips at the use of his and Nox's nickname for me. But I slammed my eyes shut, refusing to accept it.

"Well, this is going swell." Another voice. Not Kirwan's familiar one, but different, lighter.

"Knock it off, Finn," Kirwan called out to someone behind him. I was losing my mind. Hearing things, seeing spirits or visions or Fates knew what. This was more of Kahlis' magic. Maybe my mind had just finally broken.

My chest rose and fell in rapid succession as the panic intensified, my mind fully lost to its hold now. The reality of the world around me fell away—the only thing left the shadows closing in on me. They were hungry, famished, and desperate to consume. My face scrunched up with the effort it took to shut out those nightmares.

Gone. Vander was gone. Kahlis had confirmed it himself. And now I was alone.

"Hazel," Kirwan called out again. It felt more distant this time, as if he was slipping away. Or perhaps I was. "Focus on my words."

I tried to follow them, tried to hold on to the hope they offered. But only pain greeted me.

"Can you hear my voice?" he asked.

I nodded quickly, refusing to open my eyes.

"Good. Take your hands, put them on the ground beside you."

I did as he said, burying my hands in the loose dirt scattered across the stone floor.

"Do you feel that?"

"Yes." The sound of my own voice felt like a foreign entity, sharp and skittish and completely powerless.

"What does it feel like?"

I let the dirt stick to my fingers, rubbing them together to feel the fine grit. "Cold," I answered at last, my breath hitching as I spoke. "Damp?"

"Good, good," he repeated again. "And the air, can you place that smell?"

I tilted my chin up, inhaling deeply.

"It's shit," the other voice called out.

"*Finn*," Kirwan chided. His voice grew more distant as he muttered something I couldn't hear.

"Mildew," I answered at last. The scent evoked a new wave of nausea. But I welcomed it, somehow helping to bring me back to the present.

"Good job, love. Okay, last thing. Can you open your eyes for me?"

I shook my head, squeezing them closed even harder. If I opened my eyes, I'd have to face this reality I'd found myself in. One where Kirwan had betrayed me and Vander had left me and my father had won.

"I know you're scared, Hazel. I don't blame you, I'm scared too. We all are. Isn't that right, Finn?"

A snort sounded from somewhere behind him. "I'd have to be able to feel something in order to be scared. Lucky for me, they've stolen all sense of feeling from me."

I heaved again, a wave of tremors rolling through my body.

"Not helping," Kirwan ground out. "Ignore Finn," he said, his voice turning back my way. "She acts tough, but she's a kind soul underneath."

A grunt sounded from deeper within the prison, coming from who I assumed was Finn.

"Come on, Hazel. I know you can do it. Open those eyes for me."

I released a shuddering breath, nodding at last and slowly opening my eyes to the dark reality before me. The shadows were still there, but they no longer reached for me. My gaze darted around the small cell, checking my surroundings for anything still moving, still hungry for my blood. When I found nothing, my eyes landed finally on Kirwan.

I narrowed my gaze, Kahlis' words ringing through my mind. "How are you here, Kirwan?" My voice was wary, careful as I watched him.

Kirwan's jaw clamped together, the muscles in his dirtied neck flexing. But no answer came out.

I rose to my knees, hands gripping the bars separating us. "How did you get here? How did Kahlis capture you?"

Kirwan's eyes met mine, a secret battle happening within his mind.

"Out with it, lover boy," Finn sneered from beyond Kirwan's cell. Kirwan slammed a fist against the bars, cursing over his shoulder.

"I'm sorry Hazel." Kirwan turned his face back towards me, running his good hand through his matted hair and exhaling through his nose. "I should have told you a long time ago. Fuck, I tried to. But I couldn't."

"What?" I whispered, the anger melding with a swell of fear. "Tell me what?"

"It's my fault." His breath shuddered, trembling. "Mirren's death, Kahlis finding us at the Rift. You being here now. It's all my fault."

The rage I felt, the panic and confusion—it all fell silent. I stared blankly back at him. Even as he said it out loud, I couldn't accept it. Couldn't believe it to be true. How could he have done this?

"My time with Kahlis, it was complicated. Lennox got out when you returned. But I—Kahlis got to me long before I could." He braced a hand on the bars between us. "He held me here. He and Adonis tortured me for information on Talamh and Tir Nadaar. When I let it slip that Nox had told me of your return, they offered me a deal. They said they'd let me go if I would do what Kahlis asked."

"No," I gasped. My brow furrowed, my mouth falling open as I tried to comprehend what he was saying.

"They threatened Mirren and Lennox. He told me unless I accepted his offer and followed his orders he would take them both from me." Kirwan's voice cracked, his eyes glistening with unshed tears as he forced his gaze up to meet mine.

"He wouldn't have been able to harm them," I argued, pushing back. "The wards. Bastian. He wouldn't have been able to get to them."

Kirwan shook his head, pained. "He showed me, time and time again, what he would do to them if I did not comply. He had every detail planned out." Kirwan shuddered, as if recalling the faux memories. "How he would find a way to them. How he'd bring them back here, do all of the same things to them that he'd done to me. He even—" His voice gave out, rough with emotion. "He even showed me how he'd turn them over to the Daeomi, what kind of sick, fucked up shit he'd let them do for no other reason than pure enjoyment."

Silence fell between us. Subconsciously, I reached out, wrapping my fingers around his still gripping the bar. I couldn't imagine the images that haunted his thoughts, distorted his reality. But then again, I had been on the receiving end of Kahlis' mind games. So, perhaps I did, in some ways.

"I didn't know what to do, Hazel. I didn't know how to keep them safe," he continued on, his voice uneven with the effort it took to speak. "So, I said yes. He let me go, returned me to Talamh's border under the order to report back to Adonis with your movements. That's how..." He trailed off, stifling a sob. "It's my fault she's dead. My fault you're here now. And I know this is meaningless given everything you're going through now, but I am *so* sorry, love."

Tears spilled over my lashes, my body shaking once again. I'd never felt a betrayal so deep, the sting of its poisoned blade blacking out my vision. It had crested within me when I was with Kahlis, when Adonis wore Kirwan's face and pretended to be him. But I'd felt a rush of relief when I'd finally realized it wasn't truly him, convincing myself he could never be part of such a betrayal. Sitting here now, it was a double blow—tearing me apart as I experienced it all over again.

"Say something," he begged.

I fisted my hands into balls, letting my nails cut into the skin of my palms. Kirwan had been my friend. He'd helped me find the power of the Divine within me, had kept me company when Vander had gone off time and again. But now, every memory was tainted with this confession. Had he truly cared about me? Had he just felt guilty for spying on me? Or had he pretended to be my friend just to get close to me? To feed information back to my father?

I swallowed, jaw clenched tight as silent tears streamed down my face. Even with the anger staining my heart, I couldn't help but understand some small part of it. Kahlis' power wasn't like others. He infected the mind itself, making his victim believe in things that weren't even real. But as much as my empathy should have swayed my anger at Kirwan, I couldn't find the energy to let it.

Without another word I rose to my feet and retreated to the far side of the cell, where a bundle of moldy hay stretched out as a makeshift bed. I curled up on the hay, facing the stone wall, my back to Kirwan. It wasn't *just* his betrayal. Wasn't *just* Vander's sudden absence. It was a mounting accumulation of abandonment. And I felt it bone deep. There was no stopping its presence, no loosening its hold.

I was suddenly and fully alone.

"Feel better?" Finn's mocking voice called out.

"Shut the fuck up, Finn," Kirwan shot back. It was impossible to miss the emotion in his voice. I knew there was nothing I could say that would punish him more than how much he was punishing himself. So instead I let him sit in that self-loathing, refusing to even look upon his face. He didn't argue, didn't beg me to listen to his excuses or ask me to speak again. He just sat against the bars and watched over me as I cried myself to sleep.

I had no concept of time as I drifted between sleep and hysteria—the realms of the world around me and the world in my mind blending together till I couldn't tell them apart. When the panic became too much to bear, when my physical body spiraled as well as my mind, Kirwan would calm me down again.

I listened to his guidance, bitter at having to rely on his help after everything he had admitted. The logical side of me understood why he'd done it. If presented with the same situation, I would have done anything to protect Vander, Bastian, and Aerie. But the betrayal ran deep. I'd opened up to him, trusted him. And he'd sold me out—turned me over to darkness itself.

I should have known something like this was coming. Kahlis had gone too quiet. Yes, attacks were still happening across Tir Nadaar's borders, keeping both Vander and Bastian plenty occupied. And yes, I'd kept up with the tonics and wardings Aerie had made to protect me from his reach. But I shouldn't have trusted it, shouldn't have become so careless, so secure in my position.

Beside Vander, I'd grown to feel invincible. Safe. But now he was gone and I was here alone, at the mercy of my father.

I closed my eyes, reaching out through the tether for what felt like the millionth time. My body was exhausted with the effort, my magic draining as I tried over and over to get Vander to respond.

To prove my father wrong. I shuddered as I was met with nothing but more alarming silence.

"Fix it," I called out to Kirwan. I didn't know how much time had passed, but Kahlis had yet to return for me and despite the emotion that still ravaged my body, a new thought had begun to bloom in the recesses of my mind.

Kirwan cleared his throat, lifting his head to meet my gaze from the makeshift bed.

"Fix it," I repeated. "Figure out a way to get us out of here."

Kirwan watched me for a moment, shaking his head and letting out a shaky breath that could have been a laugh if in any other environment. "I must admit, when I'd first became a prisoner here, I was too filled with shame to use my connection with Lennox. I didn't know how to explain everything that had happened, was too scared of what he would say when he found out the truth."

He rose to his feet, tucking in closer to the bars that separated up. "But please believe me when I tell you that from the *moment* you entered this prison, I've been working on a plan to get you out."

I hesitated, somehow surprised to hear his truth. "And what have you come up with?" I asked after a beat of silence.

"The prison is set up like a sort of maze, a lot of winding hallways with dead ends and trick passages. I became somewhat familiar with it during my time as a spy here." He paused, looking out at the corridor beyond our cells. "I know how to get to the exit. If we're fast enough, we might make it."

I nodded, not meeting his eye.

"Of course, Kahlis and the Daeomi would be alerted right away if we escaped. That is, *if* our magic is even strong enough to get out of our cells." He paused again, chewing awkwardly at his bottom lip. "I'm sure you've sensed it since your arrival. That ill feeling. It's the wardings on the cell bars. The etchings create some sort of spell, a way to weaken your magic. Make it harder for you to heal, to fight back."

I lifted my head to look at the bars. Their black markings glimmered with a subtle glow I hadn't noticed before.

"But the first step is to get through to Lennox. To arrange some sort of meet up with him beyond the borders of Daravaana. Even if we make it past Kahlis' borders, we will need some help getting through the Dark Woods in our current condition." He sighed, rubbing at his temple.

"Do the wards affect the tether?" I asked after several moments of silence. I hated the hope that laced through my words. But I needed to know the extent of the truth Kahlis had voiced.

"No," Kirwan answered with an exhale. "It dims our magic, but those kinds of bonds are too strong to stifle with something as simple as that." He lowered his voice, shame leaking into his words. "I think my current struggle to connect with Lennox has more to do with my own strength levels inside this prison—and perhaps my brother's irritation with me as of late."

I closed my eyes, my lip quivering at what that meant. If Kahlis' wards weren't affecting the tether, then Kahlis' observation rang true. And I'd long since lost the self-control to contain the worst possible explanations for Vander's absence from wreaking havoc in my mind.

Footsteps sounded from somewhere beyond our cells. I sat up, putting my back against the stone wall as I watched the shadows beyond the bars. Kirwan mirrored my movements, backing away from where our cells met and retreating into the shadows of his own prison.

Moments later, Kahlis appeared in front of my cell, Adonis not far behind with what appeared to be a rather large bundle of fabric. Kahlis raised his hand to pass through the bars, a wretched smile plastered across his face.

"I thought you might like a change of scenery for the evening." Kahlis' voice echoed off the stone walls, too loud compared to the usual hushed tones used throughout the prison. "I told you of the celebration tonight? In honor of your return!"

I sat stone still, my teeth gritting together so hard I could have sworn they'd split in half. I couldn't believe the audacity of this male. The atrocities he'd done to me and those I loved, only to turn around and try to put some claim over me in front of his loyal subjects. It was pure delusion, thinking he held any claim over me simply because he sired me into this world.

"Of course, you'll need something more appropriate to wear," he went on, motioning back to Adonis and the bundle he held. The white-haired fae unraveled it, revealing an elegant black gown. It was beautiful, luxurious—midnight silk with a form fitting bodice and draping sleeves to match.

"What do you say?" He stepped forward, offering out his hand. The deep red stains on his fingers appeared almost black in the shadows of my cell. I turned my head to the side, refusing him.

He huffed a breath of air through his thin lips, his jaw setting firm as he stared down at me. He crossed his arms over his chest, tapping those dark red fingers impatiently against his upper arm.

"I thought you may have your objections." He lowered his gaze, shaking his head in disapproval. Without another word, Adonis retreated from my cell and entered Kirwan's. I sat up, on high alert as I watched Adonis make his way over to where Kirwan stood, bracing himself for what was about to happen. Adonis grabbed Kirwan by the hair, shoving him down and dragging him over to the bars separating our cells.

"Stop!" I shouted, my mind going frantic as Adonis dropped Kirwan on his bad arm. Kirwan's moans of pain filled the chamber. He leaned against the bars for support, cradling his elbow in his lap.

"If you're going to be difficult, then I have no choice but to incentivize you," Kahlis ground out. Adonis reached down again, lifting Kirwan's head so that I could see his expressions fully, caressing the side of his face with the glow of his magic.

"No, please," Kirwan whimpered as Adonis' magic took over. Unseen horrors unfurled behind Kirwan's eyes, his features twisting up in agonized pain. He didn't cry out, didn't give in, but I could see the torment written across his face at the invasion of Adonis' magic.

"Stop it," I begged again. "Leave him be."

"Then accept my offer. Spend the night amongst my court, without argument, and I will order Adonis not to harm him anymore."

"Don't—" The word was garbled, clipped, practically incoherent through the hold of Adonis' magic. I stared into Kirwan's eyes, his face pressed up against the bars as he fought through the terrors Adonis was setting loose in his mind. "Don't do it," he choked out again. Adonis tightened his hold, sending a new wave of magic into Kirwan's mind. This time, he couldn't help but cry out.

"Alright," I yelled, twisting back to face Kahlis. "I'll do as you ask. Just let him go."

Kahlis raised his hands, a smug look on his face as he helped me off the hay. Adonis pulled back instantly, a flash of something infiltrating his features as Kirwan fell against the bars. Before I could focus my attention on Kirwan, Kahlis led me to the gown—scooping it off the cell floor and holding it out for me to change.

I narrowed my gaze at him, rage rising within me as I realized he would not even allow me the privacy to change without an audience. I stripped down, holding myself in an attempt to cling to some modicum of modesty. Daeomi waited in the hall beyond, sniggering and exchanging lewd comments as I snatched the dress from Kahlis and pulled it onto my body.

Kahlis fixed the Daeomi with a glare that could burn through stone, and the chorus of commentary immediately silenced. I struggled to secure the gown on my own, pulling at the strings in the back for several moments before Kahlis stepped up.

"Allow me," he offered in a sickly sweet voice. Begrudgingly, I turned, offering him the back. The sooner I was dressed and out of this cell, the sooner I'd return to discuss our escape plan in greater detail.

Kahlis' fingers laced the back of my gown delicately, their soft and nimble touch shocking me. It was somehow worse than what I had expected, and it took everything within me to not shrink away from his touch.

"There," he said at last, grabbing my hand and spinning me around. "Now you look befitting of a fae court."

"He comes with us," I ordered, pointing to Adonis, who was still in Kirwan's cell. Adonis tore his gaze away from Kirwan, his eyes snaking slowly over my body and up to my face.

"You have no authority here," he sneered.

"That's enough," Kahlis ordered, holding up a hand. He didn't take his eyes off me, the hardened look on his face giving way to a small grin. "I keep my word, little one. Kirwan is safe... for now. But his safety is conditional to your behavior tonight. So I suggest you act accordingly."

He stepped out of the way, gesturing beyond the bars. I swallowed hard, stepping towards the first taste of freedom I'd had since being captured. Hope surged as I wondered what opportunities this would afford me, what information for our escape I may find laying beyond this cell.

I cut a nervous look back at Kirwan, still huddled on the stone floor. No matter what chances presented themselves tonight, no matter how deep his betrayal still felt—I wouldn't leave without him.

CHAPTER 33
HAZEL

Kahlis led me to a private chamber above the dark corners of his prison. It appeared to be some sort of dressing room. Another one of his female servants was there waiting for us with a wash bowl. He left me in her care, Adonis close by as she tended to me. She wiped down my face and arms with a wet cloth and pinned my hair back in a low, loose bun.

I tried to make eye contact with her while she worked, tried to use the time to learn anything I could of the world beyond my cell, but she disregarded me at every turn. Just like the servant on my first night here, her eyes were glazed over, her movements almost disembodied as she worked.

Everything about Kahlis' actions were intentionally offensive. He'd made me change in front of his Daeomi, all the while knowing he'd be bringing me here. He had his prisoner cleanse me, but only enough to appear proper before his court. He was sadistic, cruel, and I sat all the while stewing in my bitterness for the male.

When Kahlis returned, he offered me a box tied with a ribbon. Reluctantly, I opened the package to find a small metal wrist cuff inside. He showered me with compliments and praise, assuring me it was a gift from a doting father, something to compliment the gown he'd picked for me. But the familiar etchings on the metal told me otherwise.

It was nothing more than an extension of the wards surrounding my imprisonment, an added layer of assurance that I would act accordingly for his court. Apparently the chain corsets his other female prisoners wore were unbefitting for his daughter. The metal jewelry dug into my skin, its presence burning like acid as it worked to nullify my magic.

Kahlis led me down hallways, through more extravagant chambers and ghastly, oversized rooms until we were at last at the doors of what I gathered was his main hall. The look of satisfaction on his smug face had me wanting to run as fast and as far away from him as I could. But running would get me nowhere. Patience was the key to my freedom. Instead, I took his offered arm without objection as more of his servants opened the doors for us to enter.

The gathering within the main hall was anything but small. The sheer level of festivity shocked me. I was unaware he had so many members of his court. In my mind, Kahlis' kingdom had always been a barren, vacant nightmare, made up only of himself and his insidious Daeomi. But being here now, creatures both known and unknown to me gathered throughout the chamber, dancing and laughing and partaking in the celebration.

Dark, sultry music filled the hall. The middle was packed with bodies, writhing and swaying to the intoxicating rhythm. Thick smoke plumed from silk-draped alcoves on the outer perimeter of the party, the scent reminding me of the herbs Nox so often favored. Though, whatever herbs these were seemed to be quite a bit stronger. The smoke appeared to possess their minds, those partaking utterly lost to the ecstasy they were finding in one another.

I spotted several fae court members, more than I knew still existed in this world. I briefly wondered if Aerie knew so many of her kind still roamed the realms. They appeared to be the high-ranking members of the court. Their clothing and adornments matched that of Kahlis and my own, lavish in material and decorated with the most beautiful detailing. Some of his Daeomi and other creatures were in attendance as well, however their dress was much simpler and behavior louder, rougher, betraying their station.

Kahlis led me to a dais on the far end of the hall, motioning for me to take a seat on the steps. I obeyed begrudgingly, watching as he made his way to his throne and sat to observe his court. Adonis disappeared into the crowd, leaving me alone with the monster at my back.

For too long we sat there like that. It didn't take long for me to notice more of the female servants spread throughout the main hall. They were still donning their chains, but their gossamer strips had been exchanged for crimson silk. Regardless of the fabric, it still wasn't enough to cover their bodies, and I couldn't help but grimace as members of the court circled them like vultures.

The high-ranking fae fluttered about indifferently, picking and choosing whichever female they wanted like a tasting menu of delicacies catered just for them. Once they made their selection, they'd disappear behind the silk drapes of the alcoves. The select few Daeomi invited to the gathering seemed to be awarded that liberty as well. I found myself turning my gaze away whenever they approached one of the females, disgusted by the sight. Where the fae acted as if they were selecting from a carefully curated lineup, the Daeomi acted like bloodthirsty beasts as they dragged their chosen victim away.

A servant came by, offering me a goblet of a dark red liquid. I turned it down, not trusting anything available within the walls of Kahlis' kingdom. This wasn't Vesper's residence in Sgàil, where I could safely test my limits with fae wine. I needed my faculties tonight.

Adonis returned to the dais, snaking his way through the crowd with a female servant on his arm. She was draped in silken robes, decorated and adorned as if some prized possession worthy of showing off. Her blond curls fell down her back, complimenting the deep colors of the silk she wore. Her small form slinked up the stairs where Adonis had led her, and she casually perched on the corner of Kahlis' throne—as if she'd done so a million times.

Kahlis wrapped his arm around her waist. His stained fingers landed sickeningly high on the inside of her thigh, the silk robes falling to the side to give his hand access to her skin. She cut a fast glance down towards me, hardening her expression, before leaning into his touch and running her fingers through the white streak in the front of his onyx hair. I turned forward just as her lips landed on his neck, closing my eyes briefly and forcing down the vomit threatening to rise within me.

"My loyal subjects." Kahlis' voice boomed from behind me. I jumped, startled by the sudden interjection. "I have gathered you all here tonight in celebration. For my wayward daughter has returned at last!"

He rose as the crowd roared to life. Despite the noise, I could sense his steps descending the dais until he was directly behind me.

"Come, little one. They cheer for you."

I turned to find his outstretched hand behind me, the female discarded on the arm of the throne behind him. I hesitated a moment, debating the likelihood of denying him. But too quickly, Kirwan's pain stricken face flashed through my mind.

I took his hand and stood beside him on the dais steps.

"It is with great pleasure that I present Hazlenn, daughter of the Dark One. I understand that this may come as a shock to some of you." He turned his head to look at me as he spoke. "Our relationship has not always been an easy one." He winked at me, an utter lack of amusement in his dark eyes. "But I am hopeful that moving forward we will only continue to grow closer to one another and that she will find her place here, effortlessly."

I bristled at his false words, but tried to hide the furious trembles building inside of me. Any insight into Kahlis' home would give us a much needed advantage for our escape. Focusing on that single thought helped quell my emotions, as I smoothed a palm over the front of my dress.

"I understand that her previous alliances with Tir Nadaar may strike a nerve with some of you." A steady stream of hissed curses and jeers rose throughout the crowd. Kahlis held up a hand, silencing them. "However, she is here under my protection. Meaning that anyone who wishes to seek revenge on her is doing so against me as well."

In a perfect world, it would have been a sweet gesture. My father, standing before his court and claiming kinship to me, insisting on my safety amongst this array of nightmarish creatures and menacing fae. But this wasn't a perfect world. All I saw was a liar, a deceiver, spinning his story to a court of captive fools.

Kahlis motioned to someone in the crowd, and moments later Adonis came forward, leading the group of Daeomi in attendance towards the base of the dais. They knelt before their king, obedient soldiers.

"Earlier tonight"—Kahlis' voice rose—"these Daeomi accompanied me to fetch our guest for the gathering. I regret to report that their behavior was less than acceptable."

A scream tore from my throat as I jumped back in shock. Obsidian mist shot from Kahlis' hands, wrapping around the five Daeomi before him. It enveloped them, consuming them and swallowing them whole as they cried out in fear. The screams gave way to more disturbing noises, ones that turned my stomach as visions filled my mind of how Kahlis' magic must be tearing them apart within the shroud of his shadows. When the mist receded, nothing remained but pools of thick, black Daeomi blood and shredded piles of gore.

The crowd looked on in hushed whispers of disbelief and fear. But no one objected, no one dared to challenge the king's judgment. Kahlis didn't seem dismayed in the slightest by having lost his own soldiers—if anything, he seemed delighted to have an opportunity to show his court the full extent of his power. A promise that he could and would make good on his threats.

"Adonis." Kahlis inclined his head to where his second-in-command stood, just beyond the puddles of Daeomi remains.

"Yes, Your Grace?" he asked, pushing to the front of the crowd and bowing his head to his king. My muscles tensed as I watched him, suddenly wondering if he'd somehow find the same fate as the Daeomi. My stomach roiled with nausea, the stench of the bloodstained stone making me sick.

"When I call for your presence, you kneel before me. Before my throne, at my feet." A whip of Kahlis' magic lashed out across the room, wrapping around Adonis' throat and pulling him forward. "Or have we forgotten our etiquette, as well?"

Adonis choked as he fell to his knees, somehow forming a garbled apology despite the magic still restricting his neck.

"Better," Kahlis praised. "Did you or did you not raise your voice at my kin earlier this evening?"

I almost opened my mouth to dismiss Kahlis' accusations—to argue that Adonis' words hadn't been malicious enough to earn such a punishment. But logic kicked in, reminding me that I owed this fae stranger nothing. And despite how much I detested this needless violence, it served me better to keep my mouth shut and my head down.

"I did, Your—Grace." Adonis wheezed, using a significant amount of effort to answer his king. "And for that I am eternally apologetic."

Kahlis hummed, considering. He tightened the tendril of magic lingering around Adonis' neck for a moment longer before finally releasing it.

"For fuck's sake, Adonis. Get up. The noise of your strangled breathing is getting on my nerves."

Adonis stood slowly, running a subtly shaking hand over his dark tunic and vest—no doubt trying to brush off the humiliation of being so publicly punished.

"Let this be a lesson and a warning to all of you." Kahlis stretched his arms out to the trepidatious crowd. "No one is exempt from my wrath, not even my second-in-command. An attack against my daughter is an attack against *me*. Choose your path wisely."

And with that, he retreated up the dais, planting himself upon his throne and pulling the female back into his lap. With a wave of his hand, the music started once more and the party continued on as if nothing had happened. I stood at the bottom steps of the dais, at a total loss for words.

My eyes snagged on the pools of gore still marring the chamber floor. My body began to shake, my sanity slipping away with each passing moment. I stumbled blindly down the stairs, avoiding the blood as best I could as the crowd enveloped me.

"It's so nice to finally meet the daughter of the Dark One," a voice purred from behind me. I spun, not fully present, as a hand wrapped around me and landed at the small of my back.

"What?" I breathed, blinking up rapidly at an older fae male. My vision blurred as I tried to focus on his face.

"The King has been searching for you for quite some time now. I have to admit, it was too tempting to not see for myself what all the fuss was about." The angles of his face were sharp, his mannerisms like that of a fox. Simply being in his presence, beneath his touch, was unsettling. But between his sudden appearance in front of me and the violence I'd just witnessed moments ago, I couldn't gather myself enough to snap out of the daze that held me. Nor could I help myself from leaning into him.

I blinked and Adonis was beside me. "Fuck off, Erebos," he hissed. Without waiting for the fae's reply, he grabbed my arm and led me into the heart of the hall.

"What are you doing?" I asked once I finally got a grip on my bearings. I pulled my arm free, fighting to escape his hold.

Adonis grabbed my arm once more, pulling me in close so I could hear his hushed words. "The King expects you to mingle, but there are certain creatures within this court that you would do well to avoid. Erebos being one of them."

"I couldn't give two fucks what the king expects of me," I spat at the fae, yanking my arm hard.

"You will when he decides to take his irritation out on your friend down below." Adonis' eyes caught mine, a serious intent in his gaze. "Kirwan is worried about you, is he not? If not for the king, then do it for your friend." Something swam through those hardened eyes, but it was gone too fast to name.

"So what am I supposed to do?" I asked, giving in to my defeat.

"Drink, dance, fuck? Who cares as long as you're keeping him happy. But staying by my side will ensure you're interacting safely."

"And what do you get out of it?" I argued, still fighting his hold on my arm.

"I'd prefer to avoid another ridicule from the Dark One," he gritted out. "And he has pained me with the responsibility of overseeing your well-being this evening. So do the both of us a favor and *play along*."

I looked around slowly, shaking my head. "I can't," I answered at last, my voice shaking. "I can't pretend like this is all okay, that everything is normal." Tears swelled in my eyes, panic clawing at my chest.

"Hazlenn," Adonis called out, trying to hold my attention.

"Hazel," I corrected, even as my gaze swept over the rest of the crowded chamber. My breath grew frantic as bodies danced around us, the weight of their presence surrounding me becoming too heavy. The smoke thickened the air, burning my lungs. I was drowning in a sea of strangers, smothered by the unfamiliarity.

"Hazel," Adonis corrected. He reached out, a thumb stroking the side of my face. His touch was warm, and I leaned into the feel of it against my cold skin. The panic receded, a bright, invigorating feeling chasing it away as I finally found Adonis' eyes again.

"Enjoy your night of freedom," he whispered, the sound of his voice a melodic song. "Fill your belly, make your rounds. Because he will return you to that prison soon. And it will not be an enjoyable experience. Enjoy your freedom while you can."

The presence of his magic in my system was too inviting to question. There was no safety here, no familiarity or refuge. But for tonight, for one brief moment, I could pretend.

I no longer objected, no longer remembered what I had been so afraid of. I nodded, a smile growing across my face as I turned from him and made my way to the rows of food lining the far side of the chamber. A goblet of wine was handed to me and I drank deeply without a second thought. The room began to run together in waves of movement and light and shadow, but it no longer affected me. I gave in to the magic, letting it chase away the fear that had once consumed me.

I spun my way through the crowds, leaning into Adonis' touch and indulging in the libations of this vile court in hopes that soon I would wake up to find this all some sort of horrendous nightmare.

CHAPTER 34
HAZEL

I *was dreaming, diving head first into that blissful world of escape. I could tell because the pain was quiet. Not gone. But not burning as bright as it had been before. And for that, I was grateful.*

I blinked, looking down at my hands and trying to understand where my subconscious had taken me. My mother's journal was in my lap, my body cozied up in the armchair of my childhood cottage. It was empty, quiet, but the window on the far end of the small sitting room was open and I could hear a bluejay chirping somewhere within the trees just beyond.

I sighed in contentment, turning my attention back to the cracked leather journal in my hands. My eyes danced over the familiar twist and curves of the handwriting. I'd read her words countless times before, so much so that I had each entry practically memorized at this point.

My fingers splayed delicately over the aged paper as I read, following along with her words from another time and place.

My dearest Hazlenn,

I'm sure by the time you read this, you will have formed your own opinions of your father. Kahlis' reputation precedes him, even now. I'm sure nothing will have changed in the future. And my decision to hide your existence from him has probably done nothing to help cast him in a positive light. But I need you to understand, little one. We cannot help who we fall in love with, nor can we control the decisions of those who hold our hearts. I loved your father very much. It doesn't make much sense, and I often wonder how I could have loved such a monster, but I'd be lying to myself if I didn't admit that I left a piece of my heart with him when I walked away. I suppose that's life though, isn't it? It's messy, chaotic. And sometimes things don't make much sense, but it doesn't stop them from being true.

I don't want to try and change your opinion of Kahlis. He's done enough horrendous things in his lifetime to earn whatever feelings you have towards him now.

And he must answer for his transgressions. I just had to let you know, Hazlenn... there's another side to him. A softer, broken part. A small fracture of warmth in that cold black heart. And as hurt as I am by the path he chose, I'm not ashamed of loving that part of him. Even still.

I sighed, closing the book in my lap as I thought over her words. They should've bothered me, but nothing seemed to bother me here. I closed my eyes, feeling the wind whisper through the window and brush against my face. A roar from beyond startled me, my head whipping in the direction of the sound. It called to me, pleading for me to chase it, find it. But within the safety of my childhood home, I couldn't be bothered to try.

A muted cry pulled me from unconsciousness, pain ripping through my body as the floodgates opened and the realm of dreams faded away. My head hung between my arms, my shoulders screaming at the tension in their joints. I hung in the middle of my cell, returned to captivity after my night amongst my father's court. My toes scraped over the damp floor, trying to find a foothold.

I groaned as I pushed myself up with the tips of my bare feet, meeting bitter resistance in my shoulders at the sudden lack of tension. I was still dressed in the gown my father had picked for me, the taste of fae wine sour in my stomach. My vision spun, the remnants of whatever I had consumed last night evidently not happy with me. Another noise cut through the thick air, pulling my attention to my left. My muscles protested as I tried to turn my head.

"Kirwan?" I called out, my voice like gravel as the word worked past my dry tongue.

"I'm fine," he responded, not sounding much better than me. He grunted, and I forced my eyes to focus as I peered into his cell. He hung on his own set of chains, identical to mine. I cringed at the angle of his arm, remembering how he'd been unable to use it earlier. Now it was forced up above him, the shoulder joint at an obscene angle that had bile rising in my throat.

I leaned forward, heaving onto the stone before me. A rough, broken laugh broke out over the sounds of my dry heaving.

"Don't fret, love. It's nothing I'm not used to by now."

"Kirwan, I—" Emotion choked out my frail voice.

"No." Kirwan grimaced as he forced his gaze to meet mine. "Don't feel sorry for me, Hazel. Don't apologize." His breath was labored, his words slow and heavy as he shifted his weight to try and take pressure off his hurt arm. "How was last night?" he asked hesitantly. "Are you okay?"

Memories from the previous night swam through my mind in a haze of unfamiliar magic, and alcohol that had long turned bitter on my tongue.

"I don't know what came over me. I was so angry and scared, and then Adonis..." My voice trailed off, recognizing the feel of his magic still lingering in the recesses of my mind. It was chilling, how he could choose to inflict so much pain and darkness, or induce the same degree of deep-seated bliss.

"Don't be too hard on yourself." Though I couldn't bring myself to look at him, I could hear the slight amusement in Kirwan's tone. "Adonis' magic is near impossible to resist. He probably did you a favor by easing your inhibitions for the evening."

I swallowed hard, my mouth uncomfortably dry.

"Kahlis' gatherings are not for the faint of heart," Kirwan explained through strained words, the effort to keep up the conversation waning on him. "When he announced he was taking you to his court, I—" His voice broke. "I feared the worst."

"I'm okay," I reassured Kirwan. "Kahlis didn't hurt me." Even if I didn't truly believe it myself. I knew my night amongst my father's court was probably easy compared to what others must have experienced. But I couldn't deny the trepidation building within me. Like the worst was yet to come.

"But he *could* have," Kirwan argued. "And I would have never been able to forgive myself. I am the reason. My cowardice and stupidity is what brought you here. It's my fault, and as far as I'm concerned, every moment of torment you experience here will be as well."

I chewed on the corner of my dry, cracked lip. The truth of his betrayal still stung, the pain in Kahlis' words never far from my mind. But seeing the anguish Kirwan was putting himself through was too much to bear. "Hey," I called over to him, urging him to meet my gaze. He lifted his eyes to mine, glistening with unshed tears. "Get us out of here and we'll call it even." I softened my face in hopes that he would see the lightheartedness in my statement.

He offered me a kind smile, slowly shaking his head. "I already told you I'd do everything in my power to win your freedom Hazel, but—you and I both know I belong here. I won't sully your chances of escape by trying to free myself as well."

"No." I shook my head, surprising myself. "I won't go without you." I had been so angry with Kirwan that I refused to look at him just a couple days ago. But the thought of leaving him here, at Kahlis' mercy—I wouldn't wish that torment on my worst enemy. "Promise me," I swore, lowering my voice. "Promise me that if you get me out, you go with me."

Kirwan sighed, casting his gaze down to the floor. It took him a minute, but he reluctantly nodded his head in agreement.

"Alright," I said, exhaling in relief.

A door crashed open down the hall leading to our cells, abruptly ending our conversation. A Daeomi barged in, leading a prisoner back to their cell. I stiffened as he trampled towards us, dragging the prisoner behind him.

"Move it," he shouted.

"Make me," a familiar voice shot back. Judging by the thud that followed, that was exactly what the Daeomi did.

I perked up, my gaze cutting over to the shadows beyond Kirwan's cell. I hadn't noticed Finn's absence since I'd awoken. I wasn't even sure how long I'd been out. But I'd come to recognize the soft pitch of her voice, so at odds with her ornery attitude.

I shot Kirwan a questioning look, the rage in his eyes the only confirmation I needed. Moments later the Daeomi pushed Finn down the hall. She collapsed just in front of my cell, the first time I'd been able to see her.

My gasp was audible as I got a full view of her, only to recognize her as the female serving Kahlis at his gathering the previous night—still clothed in the silken robes. Her light blond curls splayed out around her, a shroud to cover her body. It reminded me of Aerie's, just a shade or two darker and much curlier. I retreated on reflex, shock taking over at the realization that I'd been sharing a prison with Kahlis' lover.

She whipped her head to the side, narrowing her gaze at me through her curls. My eyes were frantic, looking for a way to help her, despite the shackles on my wrists. The Daeomi came up behind her, grabbing her by the arm and heaving her up.

"I don't need your pity, *little one*," she sneered, using Kahlis' favored name for me like a slap to the face. Before I could respond, the Daeomi shoved her forward. She tripped, her head slamming into the bars of Kirwan's cell. He jolted forward, despite his restraints, snarling at the Daeomi. The creature only laughed at the faux threat, grabbing Finn roughly by the arm again and leading her deeper down the hallway. He stripped the robes from her body, revealing the same chained corset that Kahlis' other female servants wore, before tossing her into her cell.

"Better pray to the Fates you're not next," the Daeomi jeered as he passed my cell again. "There's a whole slew of us up there chomping at the bit to get our hands on the offspring of daddy dearest."

"Over my dead body," Kirwan gritted out.

The Daeomi's pitch-black eyes dragged from where they invaded my body over to where Kirwan hung. He chuckled darkly, licking his lips. "I'm sure that could be arranged."

Kirwan's magic slithered across the floor of his cell—faint, slow tendrils—but it was something. His eyes never left the Daeomi, his face wracked with the level of concentration it took to summon his power against the warding.

The Daeomi chuckled again but backed away into the shadows, retreating.

Kirwan collapsed once the Daeomi was out of view, his chest heaving and his muscles flexing against the pain.

"Kirwan—"

"I'm fine," he reassured me through labored breaths. "What about you, Finn?"

She took a moment to answer. I peered past Kirwan into the shadows beyond, finally able to make out the small shape of her cell thanks to the shifting position of the moonlight streaming in from above.

"No worse for wear," she answered at last, a little too perky for her usual tone as she huddled in the corner of her cell, digging something out of the shadows. Kirwan leveled his gaze at her back.

She turned to face him, pulling a large tunic over her still mostly naked form before meeting Kirwan's gaze. His muscles strained under the grime and dried blood covering his bare chest. I'd assumed at one point that Kahlis had been the one to strip him of his tunic, but seeing Finn in the oversized clothing and the protective way Kirwan responded to her now, my understanding was beginning to shift.

"Really." Finn's usual tone evened out as she leaned against the bars separating her and Kirwan's cells. "I'll be fine."

"Good," Kiwan responded at last, nodding his head. "Because we have a plan."

The skepticism cleared from Finn's face for a brief moment, an eyebrow raised. "We've been down this road before Kirwan. Escape is impossible."

"Not anymore," Kirwan shook his head.

"Oh yeah? And what's changed this time?"

Both Kirwan and Finn's gazes slowly turned my way.

"Me?" I asked, astounded. "What am I going to be able to do that you haven't previously?"

"You have unique powers, Hazel. Ones never tried before in this prison. The magic of the Divine—I think it'll be enough to break through the wards. At which point, Lennox will be waiting for us within the Dark Woods."

"I can't," I exhaled on a laugh. "Kirwan, I've barely been able to summon those powers on my own, outside of this prison. What makes you think I can summon them now, behind the wards and beneath Kahlis' hold?"

"Because," Kirwan's lips tipped up in an optimistic grin. "You have me here as a catalyst."

I shook my head in disbelief, unsure how I would ever be able to muster the strength to do what he was asking of me.

"We're getting out of here," Kirwan continued, seemingly oblivious to my doubt. "All of us."

CHAPTER 35
HAZEL

Despite my doubts, Kirwan worked with me for several hours in an attempt to call forth my power, testing it against Kahlis' wards. No matter what we tried, no matter how hard we worked, nothing changed.

Both Kirwan and I were still shackled in the middle of our cells, preventing us from connecting through touch as we had before. Kirwan assured me this was the reason for my inability to summon my power, but I felt it wouldn't have made a difference. He was too drained, too hurt, to be an effective catalyst as he had before. And as much as I wanted nothing more than to escape, knowing that our success relied solely on my ability to break the wards was a kind of pressure I didn't know I could overcome.

Finn had insisted we take a break when Kirwan's breath turned ragged and he'd lost the ability to hold himself up against the restraints above his head. I agreed, ignoring Kirwan's protests. It hadn't taken him long to drift into unconsciousness and as much as it pained me to see him so spent, it was a relief to have a moment of peace from his attention.

There were other prisoners being kept here; I could hear their mutterings drifting through the darkness. Finn was the only other in close proximity to our cells though, as far as I could tell.

"You still awake?" I called out to Finn. She didn't answer for several moments, almost convincing me she must have fallen asleep as well.

"What do you want?" The words were harsh, uninviting. I shut my mouth, chewing on my lower lip as I debated not responding.

"What does he do to you?" I asked at last. "When he takes you from your cell." The Daeomi's words had haunted me, his threats about taking me next. I could gather his insinuation, could read Kirwan's true fears at Kahlis taking me from mine. But I needed to hear it from her.

"Trust me, you don't want to know."

"I do if it is destined to be my fate as well," I shot back.

Finn sighed, coming up to the bars on the other side of Kirwan's cell, so I could see her better.

"He won't let them do that to you." Her words were meant to be a comfort, a reassurance. Instead they were laced with bitterness and hatred.

"I've been here for a long time," Finn continued. "And you don't serve the Dark One for this long without picking up some delicate insight along the way. He may harm you, torture you within an inch of your life and cause you excruciating pain. Even make you wish you were dead. But he has his intentions. And he cares too much about those intentions to jeopardize his plan by letting the Daeomi at you. He may hate you, but you are still his daughter—still the daughter of a fae king."

My blood went cold, a shiver raking up my spine as I forced myself to hold her gaze. Nothing but hardened, lifeless indifference met me there.

"And what of his intentions with you?" I asked, my voice barely a whisper.

"The Daeomi are not gentle creatures," she answered after several long moments, finally breaking her gaze away from mine. "I prefer to take the brunt of his attention over their rage any day. If that makes me vile in your book, then so be it. I've done what I had to, in order to survive."

I jolted at a sudden noise from down the hall, rousing Kirwan from his sleep. Footsteps echoing, making my stomach plummet as I slunk against my restraints in an effort to hide myself within the shadows. A quick glance to my left told me that Finn was doing the same.

Kahlis stepped into my cell moments later, a smug look settled upon his hollow, hardened face. "I quite enjoyed seeing you amongst my court last night." He paced haughtily at the entrance of my cell. He was alone today, no Daeomi or Adonis in sight. Kahlis must have noticed me peering over his shoulder, because he half turned to look down the hallway before facing me again. "So much so that I was eager to come see you before others in the palace had awoken. But don't worry, little one. I promise Adonis is safe and sound despite his punishment last night."

I could feel Kirwan tense in the cell beside me, his eyes glued to me—his concern at full attention.

"Why should I care what you do with your fae underling?" I hated the weakness in my voice, my thoughts moving through my mind like coarse, wet sand.

Kahlis grinned, hands clasped before him as his gaze fluttered to the dirtied floor before stepping up to me. "I noticed you could not stay away from him last night. Forgive me if I was presumptuous in thinking you had found some interest in him. An old male can be hopeful in his daughter finding persuasion to join his court, can he not?"

Despite my throbbing head, I raised my gaze to him and fixed him with an adamant glare. "I can assure you, the thought hadn't even crossed my mind."

"Yes, yes, you have your mate." Kahlis rolled his eyes and began pacing the small cell again. "But those kinds of bonds can be broken, if need be. After all, here you are alone. In your darkest hour." Kahlis leaned in, lowering his voice. "And where is your mate now?"

"You're wrong," I shot back, refusing to admit what I already knew. Visions flashed before my eyes, a conversation had in another time and place. The shadows of the Dark Woods, the stalking charm of a certain wolven shifter as he terrified me with his confession of wanting to break our bond. But I refused to believe Kahlis knew of that conversation, or that such a possibility existed.

The way his lips tipped up briefly as he caught my gaze had me doubting myself, though. His tongue clicked as he paced, looking over at me through a sidelong glance. "There are ways, little one. They may be difficult to carry out, but I assure you—there are ways. And if all else fails." He stopped once more just before me. "I can always claim his life. It's hard to honor a bond when half the connection no longer walks this realm."

The black pits of his eyes glimmered with delight, raising within me a vicious anger. I threw my body forward on an exhaled uproar. It was foolish, a desperate attempt to land my anger against this loathsome monster. But the chains held true; all I managed to do was cause myself more pain as Kahlis retreated a single step to escape my outburst.

My body gave out beneath the shackles, my chest heaving as I tried to recover from the blinding heat overtaking my body. No strength remained within me, my head lobbing forward so that my chin met my collarbone. Kahlis' polished boots stepped into my field of vision, and I rallied what little energy I could to spit at his feet.

White flooded my vision as he grabbed me by the hair and yanked my head up to meet his gaze.

"It seems that your mate has been influencing you. Acting like a wild animal will only cause me to punish you accordingly, *daughter.*" He produced a dagger from some hidden sheath, lifting my head up towards the ceiling so I could see as he brought the blade down across my left arm.

I cried out at the sharp sting as the blade split skin and sunk deep. I closed my eyes, guarding myself against the blood dripping down my upraised arm and onto my head. It invaded my senses, filling my nostrils with its metallic burn and seeping into the corners of my eyes as it rained down. He mirrored the punishment on my other wrist, invoking another cry from my throat.

I gagged immediately at my lapse in judgment, the hot liquid slipping past my lips and tainting my tongue. Kahlis held my head up for a few moments longer, letting the wounds bleed freely onto my face before dropping his grip and stepping away.

My ears started ringing from the whiplash, all of my senses drowned in crimson. My chest heaved as I spit a mouthful of blood onto the floor below me. I opened my eyes, blinking past the film of red. Kirwan was thrashing against his restraints, yelling at Kahlis—but I couldn't hear what he was saying.

I opened my mouth to urge Kirwan to stop. I didn't want my father's wrath landing on him once more. At least, for the time being, he was distracted by me. But before I could form a coherent thought, Kahlis had slipped through the bars and was receding down the hallway.

I spat again, desperate to get the taste of blood out of my mouth. Rubbing my face against my upper arm, I forced my vision to focus on Kirwan. He was speaking still, but all I could hear was an endless, nauseating pulsating in my ears.

"What?" I asked, cringing at the sound of my too-loud voice. I shook my head, trying to break free of the incessant buzzing. A warm sensation wrapped around me, starting at the raw pads of my toes and traveling up my body until it settled throughout my head. The ringing cleared, and I sighed in relief as I lifted my head.

"Thank you," I whispered, blinking my eyes as they followed the tendrils of healing magic, slipping like sunrays through the cell bars, over from Kirwan's open palms trapped above his head. I could tell by the creases burrowing into his face that it was taking considerable effort to summon the small bit of Auris magic. When he finally released the power, he stumbled, falling against the hold of his restraints. His chest heaved as he tried to catch his breath, but still his concern was focused solely on me.

"I can't stop the bleeding. The blade Kahlis used must have been enchanted, meaning he wanted you to bleed. But I can try and alleviate the effects of the blood loss."

"No." I shook my head. "You need to conserve your energy for yourself. For contacting Nox." Despite Kahlis' promise to leave Kirwan unharmed last night, his appearance was worrying me. His frame looked too thin, his arm still rendered practically unusable. He was three shades too light, the color depleting from him with each passing day. His magic must have been incredibly weakened after our attempts to break the wards. He couldn't afford to expel anymore energy on me.

"Kahlis said to tell you he'd return in a few hours. To start your lessons." Kirwan averted his gaze, shame filling his words.

"Lessons?" I echoed as I fidgeted with my restraints.

"To harness your power as the Divine, I would assume."

I pursed my lips together, looking up at my still bleeding wrists. The red ran down my arms, coating me in the sticky substance. It was not all that unlike Kahlis' own markings, staining my skin. I shuddered, lowering my gaze to find Kirwan watching me.

"The bond," I broached, lowering my voice. "What does Kahlis know?" I'd grown so confident that Vander had chosen to stay with me, that his sudden absence with the tether had to be explained away with some bit of information I hadn't figured out yet. I had believed him when he promised me he could never live without me. But Kahlis' confidence had rattled my own, his plan to get under my skin seemingly effective. After days of silence from the tether, I was starting to admit the possible truth in Kahlis' taunts.

"Hazel..." Kirwan started, dragging out my name.

"What does he know?" I repeated, my voice sharper than I'd intended. My arms were starting to go numb, Kirwan's magic already losing its effects. My vision was spotted as well, the edges vibrating with black dots as I focused a narrowed glare at him.

"He knows the truth," Finn called out from the other cell. "Kirwan won't tell you because he doesn't want to hurt you."

I looked past Kirwan into the shadows of the far cell, barely able to make out the shape of Finn's back where she leaned against the bars facing away from us. I cut my gaze back to Kirwan, whose own eyes were intentionally downcast.

"I, however, have no qualms about hurting you," continued Finn. "Kahlis may not know the finer details, but he's had his spies watching Talamh. The fact that no mysterious males have shown up to rescue you, and that he can sense the lack of connection between you and your mate doesn't bode well for your bond.

Besides—" Her voice grew softer, quieter. "You deserve to know the truth."

"What is it?" My patience was growing thin, the loss of blood going straight to my head.

"Kahlis wasn't lying. Your mate—"

"That's enough," Kirwan interrupted, looking over his shoulder to where Finn still refused to face us. "I should be the one to tell her."

"Tell me what?!" I yelled.

Kirwan sighed. "I was finally able to reach Lennox while you were gone with Kahlis. My magic hasn't been very strong the last few days." He gestured to his hurt arm, his slumping form. "I suppose the effort it's taken to try and continuously heal myself over the last however the fuck long I've been here has taken its toll on me. But I was finally able to muster enough magic to break through to Lennox. And he confirmed... Vander is gone."

"Gone?" I repeated, searching his eyes for what that meant. "Missing?"

"Perhaps." Kirwan nodded, but I could sense the reluctance in the word. "But—Nox shared that Vander had confided in him..." He trailed off, turning his words over on his tongue.

"Kirwan, I swear to the Fates if you do not tell me what the fuck is going on—"

"Alight, alright." He opened his hands trapped about him in surrender. "Some days ago, Vander confided in Lennox that he was debating breaking the bond. That he didn't want to hold you back from a life of happiness you could have—without him."

"I know he was considering it but—" I whispered, my voice drifting off. Vander had as much as said so that day in the woods. But the conversation had gone so differently, ending with him fully accepting the bond, rather than denying it. With him promising himself to me and I to him for the rest of our lives' threads. "It's impossible. We accepted the bond. He said there was no backing out."

"All we know right now is he isn't answering the call of the tether and he isn't within Talahm's borders. Once we escape we'll be able to find out for sure what's going on. The best thing for us to do now is continue working to break through the wards."

"No." I shook my head, squeezing my eyes shut. I reached out through the tether again and again. Banging, screaming, cursing at Vander to respond. To find me.

To save me.

"Hazel, I know this is a lot to process, but we're making progress. We just need to keep working."

"Can't you see," I cried, head spinning. "I *can't*. I cannot do it. We're stuck here and Vander's gone and I can't save us!"

Memories of that day played over and over in my mind. The feel of his fingers on my skin, the look of amusement in his eye as I yelled at him, lectured him, for his stupidity. How I used my ignorant show of power to tease him, to push him. It was nothing—all for nothing.

So then, you're not breaking the bond?

No, goddess. I'm not. I'm choosing you.

"He promised!" I yelled, tears running down my cheeks and mixing with the streaks of blood coating my skin.

"I know, but—"

"He promised he was choosing me." I cut Kirwan off. His words were once again unintelligible to me. They were drowned out by the darkness viciously circling my mind, screaming so loud that I could focus on nothing else.

Useless.

Worthless.

Not enough.

Never enough.

I wasn't enough for Vander, wasn't enough to save us from this nightmare. There was nothing I could do to become what they needed me to be. What they *all* needed. I thrashed against my restraint, blood pouring from my wrists once more as the wounds widened, deepened—the metal of the shackles shredding my already marred skin. The pain was bright, setting my skin ablaze with vicious hunger. I reveled in it, chasing the sensation with each crippling thought that whispered through my mind. One fed the other until I was nothing but blood and pain and hatred.

"Stop, Hazel. You're only hurting yourself more," Kirwan cried out, pushing against his own restraints as if he could do anything to stop me.

"I don't care," I sobbed, thrashing harder. Each cut was a plea. A desperate call for Vander's attention. "Where is he? Where are *you*?!"

An agonizing throb settled in my arms, my chest. I couldn't tell the physical ache from the emotional. All I knew was that with each moment the pain grew tenfold, consuming me until I was sure there was nothing left to take. And I turned every ounce of that pain down the tether, letting it act as a beacon for him to sense it, feel it.

To find me.

Or to haunt him in punishment of the cruel fate he'd damned me to.

CHAPTER 36
HAZEL

I had long since stopped responding to Kirwan, to Finn. All that existed anymore was the darkness I now resided in.

Without strength.

Without power.

Without Vander.

I barely registered when Adonis appeared in my cell, evaluating the wounds on my wrists—the once clean lines of Kahlis' blade now shredded. He pursed his lips, tapping his foot in an annoying rhythm that hurt my head before releasing me from the restraints and carrying me over to the pallet of hay. He stretched out a hand, the warding on the bars coming to life and lifting for the smallest moment to allow my own magic to heal my wounds. Without my consent. As the mangled injuries receded and the bleeding slowed, he lowered his hand once more.

"It is one thing for Kahlis to push your boundaries for the sake of finding your power," he lectured, an edge to his voice. "It is another for you to harm yourself recklessly."

My gaze landed past him, focused on nothing in particular as I waited for him to leave me be. I had no interest in his threats, nor Kahlis' plans for me.

His fingers tapped idly on his crossed arms, his invasive form still squatting on the ground beside me. "Do it again and Kahlis will not hesitate to punish you."

A huffed laugh slipped past my lips at the irony in his statement. "Hard to punish someone who is already punishing themselves, don't you think?"

Kirwan's eyes found mine, an understanding sorrow there that almost pulled me from the fog.

Almost.

Instead, I turned over, pulling my wrists to my chest and cradling them there as I let myself sink deeper into that darkness.

Adonis stood, taking his leave. "Kahlis will be back soon," he called out, pausing by the cell entrance. "I would suggest you do not let him know of this lapse in judgement or you will incur more of his wrath."

I closed my eyes, retreating within my mind. I hated myself for what I was about to do, only able to see the foolish desperation in the act. But despite the self-deprecation, I reached out through the tether once more—sending out a single word and a prayer to the Fates that it would somehow, somewhere find him.

Please.

Kirwan spoke to me every now and then, trying to cajole me to come back to him—to eat, to talk, to prepare myself for Kahlis' return.

But I couldn't. I couldn't explain the pain in my chest, as if my very heart was decomposing inside my body. He was my love, my *mate*, my best friend. And yet, he had left. And to make matters worse, I hadn't even come close to breaking the wards. My magic was meaningless here, void of the power everyone around me constantly promised I had. No one was coming for me, and I could not even save myself.

Guilt ravaged me as my thoughts turned to Aerie and Bastian. To Nox. They had all believed in me so much, had worked patiently beside me to help me find my power, my purpose. And it had all been in vain. I had failed time and time again, and even now I knew I was failing them once more.

Because if they were here, they'd be urging me to fight. To not give up. But my own darkness was too heavy, the weight of it smothering out their memories, their encouragement. Nothing existed outside of this prison for me anymore. So I'd decided there was no point in trying to escape. Better to rot away within these walls than face the reality that waited for me beyond.

Kahlis returned, his stoic indifference to my state obvious as he ordered his Daeomi to hoist me up and shackle me with my restraints.

"Tell me what you know about your power so far." He circled me as the Daeomi lifted me up, secured my bindings, then abruptly dropped my weight. The wounds had healed on my wrists, thanks to Adonis lifting the wards. But the familiar bite of the metal against my skin had me leaning into the shackles, testing their resistance and toying with the angle of the edges till I found the one that stung the most.

"Have you experienced its presence yet? Used its power?" He pressed on when I ignored him. "Can you pinpoint the feel of it pulsing through your veins?"

He came up in front of me, running his fingers over the length of my arm where it hung above my head. I let him, any fight I'd had left having bled out with the wounds he'd previously inflicted.

He fixed his gaze on me, dropping his hand as he exhaled deeply. "Hazel, you will give in to me. One way or another. And as much as I'm sure you won't believe me, I don't want to hurt you."

I turned my head to the side, disregarding him as I let my vision bore into a wet spot on the floor.

"But I will." He sighed, circling until he was behind me once more. His Daeomi reached out for me, one on each side, as they ripped the gown Kahlis had dressed me in to bare my back to their king. The dress hung off me, clinging to my arms by the draped sleeves—the smallest sliver of dignity hanging on me by a thread.

The energy in the cell shifted, not at all unlike it had at court when he'd punished Adonis before me. I stole a glance over my shoulder just in time to see him unfurl one of his shadows into a makeshift whip. My body shook in fear of what sort of torment I'd find at the end of it.

Kirwan was at the cell bars in an instant, eyes wild as he looked on helplessly. For the first time in days, I raised my gaze to him, shaking my head slowly as I watched the wheels of his mind working behind his eyes. He was looking for any way to intervene, any excuse to steal Kahlis' attention away from me.

A crack ripped through the air, the sound hitting my ears before my body reacted to the white hot pain exploding across my back. I cried out in shock, the sensation like nothing I'd ever felt before.

"Stop this," Kirwan pleaded, a fist banging on the bars.

The whip came down again, maiming the same spot it had before. Wet blood trickled down my back from where the skin had broken.

"If you will not work with me willingly, then I will force the Divine's power out of you. Through brute force." Kahlis paused only long enough to give orders to his Daeomi. One of them exited my cell, pushing his way roughly into Kirwan's and restraining him in his own shackles once again. Tears broke past my lashes as I heard him fight to get free, as he cried out in pain from the blows the Daeomi landed.

I tilted my head to the side, cringing at the pain that laced down my back at the movement. The Daeomi had been successful in his endeavors; Kirwan was strung up in his cell, blood running down the side of his face as a new, sickening red bulge protruded from his cheek.

Another crack echoed through the cell, another cry pulled from my lips. I couldn't control my reactions, the restrained cries turning into sobs as Kahlis wasted no time to bring his shadow whip down upon me again. It fell to his side, Kahlis' breath heavy as he leaned in behind me.

"Are you ready to answer my questions yet, daughter?"

I took my time, pushing myself up so that he could see me as I slowly shook my head no. He sighed, the disappointment in that noise a palpable energy. His magic filled the cell, obsidian mist crawling over my skin and invading my senses. I shivered in response, the feel of his shadows so drastically different from Vander's.

"Then we will continue." He raised his whip again, bringing it down in a threefold succession. My vision blurred as I lost my footing, the ground beneath me suddenly slick with my own blood.

"Show me the Divine," he ordered, bringing the whip down again. His tendrils sunk into me, invading my head, my heart. He was searching, probing for whatever secrets he thought I had tucked away within my subconscious. They were thorough in their exploration, leaving no piece of me unturned as they assaulted me.

"End this wallowing and let me see her," he ordered. "You have so much untapped potential. Use that darkness in your mind to fuel it! Not run from it. Not bury yourself beneath it."

I found my footing once more, lifting my body as best I could. "Get the *fuck* out of my head." My voice was raw, my jaw quivering.

I could feel his talons prying my mind open, desperate to find more than the agony and self-loathing that met him. I closed my eyes, focusing all of my energy on pushing him out. He chuckled, sensing the resistance.

"There's so much in here that you refuse to share with anyone else. So many deliciously dark thoughts." He stroked a tendril of magic through my mind, toying with that darkness he sensed inside me. "Oh, my child, the things you could do with this rage. If only you would let it out rather than turning it inward."

He came up behind me, grabbing me by the hair and tilting my head back so I could see him. "We could be great together, little one. An unstoppable force to rule this continent. Just show me what I need to know and I will give you everything you've ever dreamed of."

Kirwan's cries of protest gave way to grunts of pain as the Daeomi in his cell attempted to silence him. Kahlis gripped my hair tighter, holding my attention on his unsettling black eyes.

"All of this pain, all of this torment you are putting yourself through. And for what? A boy?" He scoffed, bringing his other hand up to my face and swiping my hair out of my eyes. "You are better than that, daughter."

"It seems we are in a similar position, then," I shot back, baring my teeth to him. That gave him pause, his brow furrowing.

"Explain."

"Two powerful entities left heartbroken by the love that abandoned us? Perhaps we do have more in common than I initially believed." I'd read my mother's journal, cover to cover, more times than I could count. Had I not, I would never have thought this monster capable of love. But I'd felt the tender care in her words, the way she talked about him, described him. It would have been impossible for her to stay for as long as she had if he hadn't reciprocated that love.

He tightened his grip, ripping pieces of my hair from my scalp. "You foolish girl. You know *nothing* of which you speak."

"I know enough," I shot back, smirking up at him.

He dropped my head, stepping back and bringing his whip down against my back again.

And again.

And again.

"Let the Divine free, you stubborn child. Let her flow through you so I can feel her power."

I set my jaw, refusing to give him the reaction he sought. I didn't know why it mattered to him that I owned this power within me. A gentle hum tugged somewhere deep in my mind, an answer almost within reach. But the pain was too heavy, the darkness too intoxicating to focus on it for long. All I could do was hang here as a silent passenger to my own demise as the shadow lashed my skin again—bloodthirsty and wicked as each blow took more from me. I could feel its magic infecting me, the darkness of his power poisoning me with each lash.

"Stop! You'll kill her!" Kirwan yelled. His words blended together, as if being spoken through a swollen mouth.

"She can end this pain as soon as she opens her mind to me and reveals what I want to know." Another crack broke through the air. Another jolt against my body.

"I will tell you nothing," I responded, although the words felt muddled, as if traveling through an impossibly thick mist. It was the last thing I had to cling to, the only element still in my control. And even if I had all but given up, I would carry that power with me to my grave.

He brought the whip down again, but I could no longer feel its sting. I was slipping away, the blinding pain making room for something else, something beyond this world. It called to me, pulled me towards it, beckoned me to join its tender fold.

"The Divine's power will never yield to you, Kahlis." Kirwan's words were desperate, frightened. "It will never recognize you as its master." I had half a mind to console him, to tell him it was okay to let me go. This wasn't a battle worth fighting.

"I'm not interested in wielding her power, *boy.*" Kahlis' words morphed into monsters within my cell, circling me. They were extensions of his anger, physical representations of his desperation to get his way. I blinked, and they were gone. The whip came down again, wrapping around my side and finding a new piece of flesh to tear open.

"Then why are you doing this?!"

"Because I need to see her!" Kahlis shouted back, spinning on Kirwan. Both cells went silent—the only noise, Kahlis' heavy breathing as his chest heaved between mine and Kirwan's cells.

Her. The word echoed through my half conscious mind.

Her. It felt too familiar, too obvious—invoking memories of distant days spent dancing in the sunlight of the meadows and reading beside each other on the sofa during thunderstorms. Memories I no longer had and couldn't possibly recall.

Her. Her voice echoed through my mind, never far but always just out of reach. Moments in Kahlis' presence flooded my mind—the way he touched my hair, skimmed my arm. His eyes were always on me, but he'd been looking for someone else.

"See who?" Kirwan finally asked. "The Divine?"

"My mother," I corrected in a raspy voice, the revelation hitting me all at once. Some small part of me had always suspected it, perhaps. I knew there had to be a reason he was so interested in me. It wasn't out of love or dedication as a father. Nor out of some twisted need to control me.

But a moment of clarity in the fog of death had revealed it to me, as I hung here in his prison—beaten bloody by his hand. It was because he thought I held the key, a path back to *her.*

His silence was all the confirmation I needed, the shock of my revelation causing his presence in my mind to retreat just slightly.

"Unfortunately for you," I sneered through slurred words. "She's dead." My body had taken too much, my consciousness slipping from my grasp no matter how hard I tried to cling to it. But I would fight every day, no matter how hard the battle, to prove Kahlis wrong.

"She's not." His words were ground through a clenched jaw, his delusions taking control. He stepped around where my body hung, leaning down to peer up at me.

"She is." I grinned back at him, finding entirely too much satisfaction in the bewildered look upon his face, the disheveled state of his hair and the blood—my blood—splattered against his pristine clothes. It was quite possibly the first time I'd seen him so out of control.

He stared at me a moment before shaking his head and standing. His whip of shadow evaporated as he released it, his hands smoothing out the black vest and tunic he wore. He stepped back, looking over my abused form. "Like I said, you know not of what you speak, daughter."

I thought him mad, a lovesick fool for clinging so desperately to a love that walked away from him. But even as he retreated from my cell, I couldn't help but acknowledge his pain, sensing the way it reflected my own.

"You told me to focus my power elsewhere, to not be consumed by the darkness eating away at me," I called out, raising my head to keep him in my field of vision, despite the near impossible effort. He turned back to me on the other side of my enclosure, peering at me through the bars. "Perhaps it's time you took your own advice. You're chasing nothing more than a memory, a spirit. I myself witnessed her passing. Believe me when I say she no longer walks this realm."

Kahlis lingered beyond my cell, one hand on the bars. His fingers tapped against the metal, the clank of his silver rings echoing down the corridor.

He lifted his gaze to me once more, leaning in. "Just because she does not walk this realm, does not mean she is dead and gone."

My brow furrowed, any hint of authority gone from my mind at the way he fixed that wicked grin on me, as if there was, even still, some vital piece of information hidden from me.

His glare cut over to the Daeomi still in my cell. "Get them down. I'll send someone to tend to her wounds." Those haunting black eyes remained on me, even as he backed away from my cell. "Can't have her giving out on us before she's served her purpose, now can we?"

The darkness swallowed him, leaving me confused and frantic for answers. The Daeomi obeyed instantly, releasing my shackles without warning. My body, too weak to stand, fell to the hard floor. A new flood of pain washed over me at the sudden movement, and without a moment's notice, I was lost to the world around me, slipping from consciousness as simply as the sun slips below the horizon.

CHAPTER 37
HAZEL

I existed within my mind, nothing but a bobbing weight in an endless sea of pain. Stormy skies rained down around me. Monsters from my nightmares reached up from below to pull me under. Water filled my lungs, burning me straight through. I cried out for mercy, for death, for anything other than this all-consuming ache.

But no one answered.

I blinked, and the shadowed silhouette of my cell came together around me. My body ached, the remnants of the lashings Kahlis had given me slow to heal, thanks to the warding of my cell. However, my back was bandaged and the torn gown had been replaced with a large tunic, not much more than tattered rags.

I lay there for what felt like an eternity, analyzing the space around me. Something felt different, out of place in this rotting oblivion. Kirwan and Finn must have been asleep. Soft sounds of their breathing whispered through the air. I didn't call out to confirm though; I didn't want to talk to either of them if I was wrong.

Instead I traced the shapes of the objects around me with my eyes as I searched the darkness once more. They snagged on a foreign shape in the far corner, by the bars of my cell. My body stiffened, freezing as I waited for the foreigner to make themselves known. What stranger would risk discovery to come down here and just stand in the corner, watching?

Just as I'd started to convince myself I was losing my sanity, that this silhouette was nothing other than my mind playing tricks on me, the stranger moved forward. I jumped, my body protesting in pain as I stifled a hiss.

The stranger was beside me in an instant, dark golden eyes staring down on me. With the moonlight on his back, his face was shrouded in shadow. I pulled away from him, but even as I did, I found myself leaning in to get a better look.

"Vander?" It was half a question, half a desperate plea for my eyes to not deceive me. He raised a hand, reeling in the shadows he'd cloaked himself in so that I could see his face once and for all. I knew it wasn't real, knew he was nothing more than a hallucination as my subconscious tried to cling to any semblance of sanity. But I didn't have the strength to fight it.

"Vander," I cried out again, this time more confident. He raised a finger to his lips, reminding me that eyes were always watching. I swallowed hard, nodded, and quickly scanned the cell beyond his shoulder.

When no Daeomi came to investigate my outburst, I scrambled up to my knees. "I thought you left me." Tears sprung freely from my eyes, my hands hanging in the air as they tried to decide where to land—too desperate to hold him everywhere all at once. "What happened?"

"It does not matter," he whispered in hushed, soothing tones. He lifted a hand to tuck my hair behind my ear, his fingers lingering before dropping back to the floor. He half knelt before me, balancing himself on the balls of his feet, as if prepared to run at a moment's notice.

"All that matters is I'm here now. And I'm going to get you out of here." He stood, reaching out his arm and offering me a hand. Relief flooded my veins, that ever-present darkness receding as I looked up at the future I thought I'd lost forever.

He wasn't just pulling me out of this prison—he was pulling me out of my heartache, my obscurity, and back into a life of hope and love and light. He led me to the bars of the cell, peering past them into the hallway beyond to make sure we were clear to escape.

"Why is he keeping you here?" Vander's words were hushed, rough. He didn't look at me as he spoke but rather continued peering down the hall as if in search for some unseen entity.

"I'm not sure," I answered in a daze, confused as to why it mattered in this moment.

Vander looked back at me over his shoulder. His eyes were harsh, hardened—but still golden, thankfully. He turned, gripping onto my arm and lowering his face to mine.

"I know you know, Hazel. Just as I know your Divine power is no match for the warding of this cell. Why aren't you escaping? Why choose to stay and live in this filth rather than free yourself?"

"I—you're hurting me," I pled, trying to pull my arm from his grasp as I took a step backwards. "What's wrong with you, Vander? Why are you acting like this?"

"Because I had to risk my neck to break into enemy territory and save your ass when you had every capability of doing it yourself." His jaw hardened as he voiced his truth. The words sliced through my skin, invoking more pain than Kahlis' whip.

"I—" I stuttered, stumbling over my words as I tried to find an explanation. "I thought you left me," I said at last, lowering my gaze. "I didn't want to fight for a life without you."

"So you were going to rot here forever then? Let all that power go to waste?" His grip tightened, pulling my eyes back to his. When I had once stared into those swirling irises, I had been greeted with love, passion, and tender care. Now, all that stared back at me was frigid indifference

"I'm sorry." My voice cracked, the sound jarring in the otherwise quiet prison. "I didn't know what to do, so I just... didn't."

"And you wonder why I desired to break the bond," Vander mumbled. "Your weakness sickens me. Perhaps I'd found it endearing at one point, but when you put the very lives of your loved ones at risk because of your foolishness..."

The darkness crept back in with each word he spoke, along with the vicious whisperings that refused to leave me alone. Vander must have noticed them too, through the tether.

He sighed, rubbing a hand through his hair before turning his attention back towards the hall beyond. "We can talk about this later, but right now I need you to lift the wards."

I gaped, brow furrowed. "What? No, Vander, I can't—"

"We don't have time for excuses, Hazel. Kahlis and his Daeomi will be back any moment. And you're the only one that can lift the wards."

"Why can't you lift them?" I argued.

"Because they don't respond to my magic. Kahlis is your blood, therefore they will respond to you more than they would respond to me."

"But, how did you get in here if you can't—"

Vander spun, cursing under his breath as he pulled me close. "I snuck in when the wards were open, while the healer was tending to the wounds on your back. Now, I told you we don't have time for this. Unless you'd like your father to return and find me here, in which case he will most likely kill me and Kirwan in front of you out of sheer amusement. Use your power and lift the fucking wards."

I nodded frantically, desperate to please him. Vander dropped my arm, allowing me the room to back up a few steps and lift my hands to the bars. Something brushed against my ear, making me roll my shoulders as I tried to focus on the task at hand. But no matter what I did, the wards wouldn't lift.

"Again," Vander ordered, nodding towards the bars. I sighed, licking my lips as I tried to focus my energy once more. He was so short, so angry. His eyes glowed a molten golden as he urged me to keep trying. I supposed I understood his temper. His presence here *was* a huge risk for him to take. The Mark had rather strong opinions at times, its influence not usually siding with things like joy and love. This was simply a window to his curse, something that would subside if I could just get us out from the influence of such a vile place.

"Fuck, Hazel, we're running out of time," he ground out. "You need to get this cell open now."

"I'm trying," I shot back. My hands shook before me; tears stung behind my eyes. Even if the Mark had been influencing him, I wasn't sure he'd ever been so angry with me. He felt so cold, so unlike himself. Another noise caught my attention, pulling my gaze over my shoulder and in the opposite direction of our exit.

"Hazel, *focus.*" Vander's hands were on me again, pulling me back to the bars before me. "Your magic isn't all that different from Kahlis'. Focus on your similarities, sense his magic in the wards and use those similarities to open them for us."

I nodded again, closing my eyes once more and lifting my hands. But as I let Vander's words wash over me, my hands fell to my side.

"What are you doing?" he urged.

"I have no similarities with my father," I choked out. Yes, I had darkness in me. Sometimes it felt like that was all that lived within me. If the past couple days were any example, it was a darkness so black, so bottomless, that it felt impossible to stay above it.

But my father's darkness was of a different breed.

Where I had found a family, a life, love—he had only inhabited hatred and pain. He thrived on vile, unspeakable acts, and didn't blink an eye at the evil that surrounded him. No, I was nothing like him. And therefore, I knew the wards would never open for me. As did Kahlis, or he would have never put me in here to begin with.

The buzzing started once more in my ear, too loud to brush off any longer. Vander was quietly shouting at me, pushing me to try again—telling me I was wrong, that the Dark One was my father, so there *had* to be similarities between us. Telling me I was foolish, scared, worthless. The words pelted against me like poisoned arrows, true to their aim as some part of me shriveled beneath their hold.

I took a step back, turning once more to look behind me. This time, another being greeted me. He took my hand in his, offering me a kind smile as he gently tugged me into the safety of his arms.

"Arlo," I breathed.

I buried myself against his chest, knowing this, too, was nothing more than a figment of my imagination. Some desperate defense mechanism in this nightmare I was trapped in. The two halves of myself battling for my sanity. He had always been my safe haven, my protector. And despite the fact he'd sacrificed himself, his memory was still here, still working to protect me. I didn't care if it wasn't real, didn't care if it was just further proof that I had truly lost my mind. I would cherish every moment with this version of my mate, for fear that he would be gone too soon.

"It's alright. I've got you, my darling divine." He ran his hand through my hair, petting softly as he held me.

"Hazel, what the fuck are you doing? Open the wards, we have to leave!" The other male's voice was desperate, angry behind me. But I understood now.

That was not my mate. Nor was it a piece of myself.

I finally refused to accept the vision before me any longer.

Arlo nodded at me, soft and encouraging as I closed my eyes and retreated into my own mind. Just as I'd done with Aerie countless times before. I'd forgotten the practice during my time here, but as I sank deeper into the recesses of my mind, the motions were second nature to me once more. For the first time in the last few days, I took the time to acknowledge the darkness that was consuming me—acknowledge, but not give it control. When I opened my eyes again, it was with the concentration and mental fortitude of the goddess that had come before me, not the hurting and frightened female that still lingered somewhere within.

I turned to face the male masquerading as my mate, determined to take back control. "I am not going anywhere with you," I seethed. "You are *done* fucking with my head, Kahlis."

The male's erratic eyes and furrowed brow slowly slipped away, revealing a devious grin as the corner of his lips ticked up.

"I suppose I should have known a simple glamour wouldn't work on you, little one. But after all of those revolting thoughts I unearthed earlier, I knew I had to try. It was too tempting an opportunity, your mind providing a delicious little playground."

The image before me shook his head in disappointment, and despite knowing it was not Vander, it made my chest lurch.

"What gave me away?" He gestured up to Vander's face. "The eyes? From what I could gather, their hue is ever-changing. It made it hard to decide which shade to go with."

I gritted my teeth together, facing him head on with the fabrication of Arlo's memory at my back. "Vander would never speak to me like that." I stepped forward. "He would never tell me I was worthless, never limit me to my bloodline or insist on similarities between me and the Dark One." I gestured towards my father in disgust. "And he would never push me past my boundaries for his own gain." I squared my shoulders, letting the truths wash over me in a baptismal cleansing that banished the darkness in my own mind. "He would have died beside me in this prison, trying to find a way out on his own, rather than push me past the point of breaking."

"Well, my child," Kahlis sneered. "Based on what I found inside that mind of yours, I'm not inclined to believe you. After all, if your male is so great, why has he not truly come to rescue you? Why would he choose to break your bond and put you through that agony if he truly loved you, as you say?"

I recoiled at his words, the sting of them like hot coals against my skin. But Arlo put a hand on my shoulder, another against my back, as he helped me stand my ground.

"You know not of what you speak." I repeated Kahlis' own words to him, letting them take their time as they rolled off my tongue. "You may have cared for my mother, but you cannot understand the love of a fated mate. Nor could you ever replicate that to fool me."

Kahlis hummed, the false image of Vander smirking and looking down to the ground as he clasped his hands behind his back. "You have so much to learn, little one. Starting with the very deities from whom you received that tether. The Fates."

I cocked my head towards him, waiting for him to explain.

"I, more than anyone, understand the Fates' magic. And you would do well to heed my warning to not fall into their deceit. Vander only loves you because he must. There is no deeper connection between the two of you than a Cosmic manipulation from an absent deity. Not true love."

"You're wrong." The words surprised me, echoed by Arlo behind me as the pitch of our combined voices rang through the cell. I had told myself that same lie countless times, had told myself that I wasn't worthy of Vander's love—that I hadn't earned it. I hated to admit how fully I had believed it, too. But seeing Vander's image before me, Arlo's memory behind me, after traveling to the dark depths of my soul within this prison—I could finally see it for what it was.

"I don't know where Vander is, or why he hasn't come for me." I stepped forward, Arlo's presence never leaving me. "But it doesn't matter, because you were right about one thing. I do have the power to save myself. Just as I have the power to understand that Vander's love, or lack thereof, doesn't change how I feel about him. Doesn't change how I feel about *myself*. And I'm done having my power stripped away by the lies and the doubt of my own mind."

"You need me, daughter," But even as he said it, he retreated a step, recognizing the intent in my eyes as I pressed forward.

"No, *father*. I do not need you. I never have. The Divine's power lies within me alone." The Divine's power had never hidden from me. I had hidden from *it*. But now, I could feel it burning rapidly through me, surging from a source that seemed to have no bottom, no limit of potential. And I didn't shy away—I reveled in the feeling. "And I alone will wield it." The image of Vander was the last thing I saw before I let that golden light blast forth.

Before, I had existed within my mind as nothing but a bobbing weight in an endless sea of pain. Stormy skies rained down around me once again. Monsters from my nightmares continued to reach up from below to pull me under. Water still filled my lungs, burning me straight through. Some part of me still cried out for mercy, for death, for anything other than this all consuming ache.

But this time, *I* answered. And I saved myself.

CHAPTER 38
HAZEL

Vander's likeness attempted to retreat in an obsidian mist—Kahlis sparing himself as he sacrificed his advantage. But my power was faster, bursting forth and enveloping him, along with the rest of the prison, in golden light. His glamour gave way to his true form as he crumpled between the now open bars of the cell, leaving the wards lifted just long enough to let my light through. The warding exploded around me, waking the rest of the prison.

I turned back just in time to see the image of Arlo fading away. He smiled, pride beaming from his honeyed eyes. It was the only goodbye we got before his image swirled in a cloud of pale blue magic and drifted back through the cells beside me.

Chaos had erupted within the prison beyond, the raucous hollering making it near impossible to hear anything else. I found both Kirwan and Finn collapsed in their cells as the pale blue light made its way to Finn, settling within her body.

I rushed out the still open bars of my cell, careful not to rouse Kahlis' body as I inched past. "What just happened?" I asked when I finally made it over to Kirwan's cell. I gripped the bars, testing their strength.

"We couldn't get through to you," said Kirwan. "I was trying to help you break his hold, but he had you pretty well trapped. That's when Finn suggested..." He trailed off, turning towards Finn.

Like Kirwan, she was hunched over on the prison floor. Her elbows rested on her knees, her chest rising and falling heavily. "Astral projection," she finished for Kirwan between ragged breaths. "Lucky for you, it's how my magic manifests. Unlucky for me, it's not the simplest thing to do, especially in this fucking place." She threw a hand out, gesturing to the bars surrounding us, typically humming with the energy of the wards. Their silence was deafening now, pushing me to break through the weakened metal.

"Astral projection?" I echoed. I took a step back, reaching out my palm and trying to call forth my power once more.

Kirwan nodded, pushing off the stone floor and rising to his feet. "Finn has the ability to—*assist* a soul to leave its body, to travel without the confines of a mortal form. She projected mine into your cell, in hopes that walking a different realm may make it easier to get through to you."

I paused my attempt to break open Kirwan's cell, my gaze finding his. "But I didn't see you, I saw—"

"Arlo. I know."

I shook my head, rubbing my fingers along my temple as my mind tried to make sense of everything.

"Hazel, you forget I spent time with Arlo. I'm the one who found him at the Rift, who brought him home to you. I knew the purpose he served in your life, how to use his mannerisms to convince you of his presence." He joined me at the bars, laying his hand over mine where it was once again clasped against the metal. "To calm your spirit. I knew what he meant to you. You haven't been on the best of terms with me, and another Vander would have just confused you further. But Arlo? He was the only way to break Kahlis' hold on you."

Silence fell between the three of us. The uproar of prisoners still rallied in the distance, but it was nothing more than a buzz in the background of this tender moment beside my friend. Despite the betrayal I'd once felt, he had continued over and over to prove his loyalty to me, his genuine love. Even when I'd given up on myself, he was still beside me, trying to fight my battles for me.

"Thank you, Kirwan," I finally whispered, letting go of the metal bar to lace our fingers together. He reached his other hand through the bars and squeezed my shoulder, grimacing at the effort it took due to his injury. I held his gaze for a moment longer before turning my attention past him to where Finn still sat on the floor, head hanging between her bent knees. "Is she going to be okay?"

"Yes," Finn called out, her tone doing nothing to hide her irritation.

"The warding is not an easy thing to combat. It takes a considerable amount of strength and effort to do what she did." Kirwan winked at me before turning his head just enough so that Finn would hear his next words. "I told you she was a kind soul."

Finn responded with an obscene gesture in our direction, never raising her head to look our way. Both Kirwan and I released a breathy laugh that died too quickly as the reality of our situation sank in.

"Step back," Kirwan warned, releasing my hand. "We have to hurry, before Kahlis comes to—or we're as good as dead."

I nodded, backing away from the bars as Kirwan raised his good hand and let tendrils of his power forth. They wrapped around the bars, bathing them in his contrasting shades of light and dark magic, until they pushed the bars away and let him walk through. He stepped up to me, pulling me into a brief embrace before turning and doing the same for Finn's cell.

"What about the other prisoners?" I asked in a hushed tone as Kirwan rushed us down another winding hallway of the prison. It was near pitch-black in these passages, no moonlight streaming in from above as there had been in our cells.

"We can't waste the time," Finn bit out harshly.

Kirwan slowed in front of us as another bend in the passage emerged. I hadn't noticed the change in his footfall and ran smack into him. I yelped, slapping a hand over my mouth as the noise echoed off the corridor. I couldn't see her, but I could feel the glare Finn was fixing me with.

Kirwan stretched out a hand, rubbing my shoulder reassuringly as we paused and knelt in the darkness. "She's right, unfortunately," Kirwan agreed. "As much as I would love to go release the innocents, this place is huge, and not every being captured here deserves to be set free. Kahlis' prison houses some true nightmares. It would take us too long to make the rounds and determine which cells to break open or which to leave undisturbed."

I pinched my eyes closed, my heart breaking at the thought of any innocent left behind. I reached for my power, but it was weakened after the encounter with Kahlis, so unaccustomed to being used. As much as it hurt, I knew they were right. At least for now, we couldn't save them.

"You left the wardings open," said Finn matter-of-factly. "The best we can do is hope they figure out the rest on their own, and move on." Her certainty effectively ended the conversation. She took over for Kirwan, leading the way through more passages and corridors. Eventually, torches started peppering the walls, letting us know that we were getting close to breaking ground.

Kirwan paused once more, grabbing one of the burning torches off the wall. "We should be getting close to the entrance now. Once we emerge from the prison, we will need to be as quick as we are stealthy."

I nodded, looking back and forth between Kirwan and Finn. It was clear that I was the only fearful one of the group. Finn was as hardened as ever, stone cold and focused on the task at hand. Kirwan, while possibly dealing with his own levels of worry, was mostly just making sure I was alright. His kind eyes found mine often, searching, questioning. He either kept his hand in mine or stayed at my back to ensure my protection.

Before we could move forward, a low rumble echoed off the stone walls surrounding us.

"What was that?" I whispered. Kirwan's gaze was transfixed on something behind us. Several painful moments passed as I watched him watch the shadows. The noise sounded again and Kirwan's eyes narrowed. We braced our bodies, waiting on bated breath.

Snaking tendrils of shadow crept down the hallway, bringing with them an eerie kind of quiet as they reached out for us. The rumbling subsided, seemingly quelled by the presence of the mist. We retreated a couple steps, staying out of its grasp, but the shadowy mist seemed nearly sentient, responding to our movements and adjusting to reach us still.

"Run," Kirwan breathed, almost silent.

"What?" I asked, spellbound by the mist closer than ever.

"Run!" he shouted this time, grabbing me by the arm and shoving both me and Finn in the opposite direction.

"What the fuck is happening?" Finn called out as the three of us ran through the torchlit passageways.

"Kahlis must have come to!" Kirwan shouted back. "He's calling the Daeomi, searching the prison halls and passageways, looking for us."

I sucked down hungry breaths of air, holding my side as I tried to keep up with the two of them. My bandaged back felt wet once again, reminding me of my fresh injuries. A healer had indeed tended to them, but thanks to whatever poison was laced in Kahlis' shadows, they were still apparently slow to heal, even after the prison wards had been broken. I could feel myself slowing, my energy quickly giving way to exhaustion. Kirwan could see it too, his grip on my arm doubling down as he continued to drag me along.

I lost track of how many turns we'd made, how many times we altered our route. The entire time, I could hear the echoing rumble of that mist chasing us, the distant noise of Daeomi around us. Their footsteps pushed us to move faster, the shouts and jeers reminding us of the penalty if we stopped, even for a moment. Upon what felt like our hundredth turn, Kirwan stopped short.

"There's an exit just beyond, to the left of this corridor. It's a single pathway up to the world above, a wooden door that empties to the exterior of the north wing of the palace. Beyond that are the Dark Woods. Once we get through the door, do not slow for anything. Make a beeline for the woods and take cover there."

Finn and I nodded, our heads on a swivel as the sound of the Daeomi echoed off the stone walls and came careening towards us.

"Finn, clear the path ahead. Hazel, stay a few paces behind her in case any Daeomi are lurking. I'll keep the rear." Our hurried steps slowed as the final corridor came into view. "Be quick, don't stop for anything. Alright?"

Finn's eyes narrowed on him, her head tilting ever so slightly. But she agreed nonetheless, giving Kirwan a single nod before shoving a hand towards him. "See you on the other side, lover boy."

Kirwan huffed out a sorry excuse for a laugh, taking her hand and pulling her in for a hug. He whispered something in her ear, squeezed her one more time, and then released her.

And like that, Finn disappeared into the nearby pathway, her small form jumping from shadow to shadow as she made her way towards the exit.

I followed suit, trying to match her movements and stay close to the stone walls and within the cover of the shadows. Kirwan was right behind me, a gentle encouragement. We were halfway to the exit, Finn just ahead, clearing the way, when the shadows enveloped us.

As if coming to life and jumping off the walls, they were suddenly all around us, trapping us in their darkness. The mist returned, growing tenfold and smothering us. I coughed, overtaken by the mist's aggressive invasion "Kirwan," I shouted through choked sobs, swatting away the darkness that filled my vision.

A hand grabbed me, pulling me from the darkness. Next thing I knew I was beside Finn. She slapped a hand over my mouth, keeping me silent as she snuck us into a hidden alcove between the suffocating mist and the exit beyond.

I watched in horror as the black finally settled into the stone floor, revealing Kirwan surrounded by a group of Daeomi and Kahlis' right hand, Adonis. My horror gave way to confusion as I recognized another body besides Kirwan. Slowly, I understood the point of Finn's tight grip on my arm, her need to hold me as she astral projected an image of me beside Kirwan, in an attempt to fool Kahlis' creatures.

I wanted to cry out, wanted to fight Finn off of me and run back to help Kirwan. There were too many of them. He'd never break through.

Kirwan looked at me, a smile hanging heavily on his lips—a million words passing with that one subtle glance. And suddenly, I understood.

He wasn't coming with us.

I whimpered against Finn's hand, shaking my head.

She pulled me back as the Daeomi circled Kirwan and the apparition of me. "Don't make a sound, I have to let go of your mouth to get the door open," Finn whispered into my ear. She waited for me to nod in agreement before she released her hand and worked silently at the door behind us. In a matter of moments she had it open and was darting into the night air, taking off without a second thought.

I looked back one more time, torn between my freedom and going back to fight with Kirwan. I couldn't pull my eyes away as I watched him fight off the Daeomi one by one. His gaze flashed to mine one last time, his chin jutting out as his words came back to me.

Be quick, don't stop for anything.

I swallowed hard, tears streaming down my face as I released a deep breath. I kept my eyes on him, even as I backed into the night—watching as the Daeomi enveloped my view of him and a furious-looking Adonis bent over the selfless, loving, too-good Kirwan.

CHAPTER 39
HAZEL

I turned and ran without looking back. I felt too exposed in the open courtyard of Kahlis' palace. I saw no one else, nothing standing in my path to the Dark Woods just beyond. But I'd learned to not accept things as they seemed within my father's court. The quicker I could get under the covering of the Dark Woods, the better.

I hoisted myself over the short stone wall that marked the end of the courtyard, my knees giving out from under me as I hit the ground hard. I rolled, resisting the urge to cry out in pain as the wounds on my back hit the rough ground. Using my momentum, I pushed myself back up to my feet and continued running.

Fear crept in as I kept my eyes on the tree line, trying to decide which direction to break for. I slowed, turning in circles. I couldn't see Finn anywhere. Kirwan had told us to break for the trees, but trees surrounded the palace—too similar to those of the

Dark Woods to be able to tell them apart. I couldn't even begin to understand which direction was the right one. He'd told me, I knew he had. But in the moment all I saw was a realm of endless possibilities and no inclination as to which way was the right way.

"You're not supposed to be out here." An obsidian mist gathered before me, a stray Daeomi taking shape. It smiled down on me with its pointed white teeth. I pivoted to miss the creature, but he was faster than I was. His slick black hand grabbed my wrist, pulling me towards him. "The whole fucking palace is looking for you, you know."

He twisted my arm, craning it behind my back so that my chest pressed against him. My stomach flipped at the feel of his oily skin against me. His wings stretched out around us, their presence caging me in. I squirmed beneath his grasp, desperately trying to pry my way out of his hold.

The Daeomi ran his free hand over the side of my face, letting a claw slip out to slice at my skin. I hissed at the sharp sting of it.

"Kahlis is going to be rather pleased—" His words cut off, replaced by a squelching sound as his grasp loosened and he stumbled backwards. My mind took a moment to catch up to what my eyes were seeing. A broken hemlock branch protruded from one of the creature's eye sockets. It released a gnarled cry as it fell to its knees, revealing a very angry and out of breath Finn behind him.

"What are you waiting for?!" she yelled, then turned and took off into the trees. It only took me half a second to follow, jumping over the crumbled body of the wailing Daeomi and sprinting to catch up with Finn.

The coverage of the sparse trees was a welcome relief, the first taste of hope I'd had since we'd left our cells. I found Finn quickly, her small form grabbing onto mine and leading me away from the palace.

"You saved me." It wasn't a question, but my words were full of shock.

"Kirwan made me promise to look after you," she responded matter-of-factly as we continued putting distance between us and Kahlis' palace. "I don't break my promises."

She left it at that, pushing us deeper and deeper into the Dark Woods. Each step felt like freedom, each pain and ache ravaging my body laced with promise and safety. And yet, tears streamed down my face to know who we were leaving behind.

We kept at the grueling pace, knowing we wouldn't be safe until we were back within Tir Nadaar's borders. We picked our way through the trees, our running giving way to a slower pace once we were sure we weren't being followed. Finn's skill set out here was shocking. She seemed to thrive in this environment.

I followed in her footsteps as she swung over fallen limbs, crouched behind thick trunks, and circled back to cover our tracks and make decoy ones. She let me know when she thought we'd made it far enough to stop for the night, and even offered to take the first watch so I could sleep. The trees had grown thicker here, and she boosted me up in a particularly curvy one to give us covering for the evening.

Hoisting herself up after me, she led us to the thick center of the tangled limbs and showed me how to wedge myself between the branches to ensure I wouldn't fall while I slept. It was becoming painstakingly clear to me that she was a gift straight from the Fates. I wouldn't have made it long out here without her. Pain bloomed in my chest, my mind wandering to what would happen to Kirwan, now that he'd stayed behind to secure our freedom.

"Thank you," I called out to her as she kept watch from her perch below, an arm's length away.

She cut a glance over to me, just for a second, before she continued her watch. "Don't mention it," she said at last. "I'm doing it for Kirwan. Not for you." At the mention of his name, she pulled at the tunic she still wore over the grotesque chains Kahlis had caged her in. Her wrists weren't secured to the chain around her waist, as they often were with the other female servants I'd observed, but she was bearing his shackles nonetheless.

"I'm sorry we had to leave him behind." I closed my eyes, tears pricking behind them—reliving the moment in my mind.

Finn scoffed, and I opened my eyes to find her shaking her head.

"What?" I pressed.

"We didn't *leave him behind*. He chose to stay behind, the idiot."

"You think he could have gotten away?" I asked, perking up.

A brief moment of hope bloomed inside me, dying just as fast as Finn sighed, her head slowly turning towards me. "He could have tried. But when Adonis showed up—the three of us staying there to fight him would have just complicated things. Kirwan knew the choice he was making."

I chewed on my bottom lip, trying to decide what to say. "What do you think Kahlis will do with him now?"

Finn fell silent, her gaze focused on something off in the distance. "Probably throw him back in that same rotting, Fates forsaken cell. I imagine he's too valuable an asset to kill off outright."

I swallowed, trying to ease the nausea taking root in my stomach. "Either way, I am sorry. Had I not been there, it probably would have been him in this tree with you."

Finn shifted, bristling. "We would have never gotten out of there without you breaking the wards. I never expected to see the light of day again," she answered after several moments of silence. "So I suppose it's I who should be thanking you."

"Thank Kirwan," I said instead. "He was right when he said you were a kind soul."

Finn winced, rolling her eyes. "Don't make me take it back. Now get some rest before I think better of it and decide to continue dragging your ass through the Dark Woods instead."

I could tell she had intended it with more bite, but it came out as the empty threat it was. I put my hands up in surrender anyways, shifting back on my tree branch and giving her some space. I needed it just as much as she did, still trying to scrub the image of Kirwan being overcome in that hallway from my mind.

"Goodnight," I said, turning over and burrowing into the tangle of limbs. The exhaustion consuming my body was so strong; I knew I'd have no issue falling asleep, even in this unusual circumstance. But as my heavy lids fluttered closed and my mind drifted, a deep sorrow resonated through me.

No matter if it had been Kirwan's choice or not, it destroyed me to leave him behind. He may have been the reason I was within Kahlis' prison in the first place, but he never stopped trying to protect me while I was there. He met me on the brink of darkness and led me back towards the light. No matter what waited for me back home, no matter how the others would react to the deception he'd hid behind, I would never forget that kindness.

"Finn," I mumbled, eyes still closed.

"What?"

"Why do you call Kirwan *lover boy*?" It had piqued my curiosity from the first moment I'd heard it. At first I wondered if it was because she suspected something deeper between me and Kirwan, but the longer we remained in that prison, the clearer it must have become to her that I was committed to another.

"That's not my story to tell," Finn answered after several moments of silence. There was sorrow in her tone though, and I now wondered if perhaps there was something deeper between the two of *them*. Surely not, or Finn would never have left him for my sake.

"Sleep," Finn ordered. "We can continue talking later." I gave a half nod, unsure if she was looking at me. I couldn't bring myself to open my eyes, their weight like stone as I let my mind drift further into unconsciousness.

When I awoke, it was because of a foreign sound. I peered through the darkness, trying to find Finn. She was crouched lower in the tree, poised at the ready as she got a closer look at the land below.

I couldn't tell where the noise was coming from. It was something between a hiss and a rattle, creeping through the branches around us and raising the hairs on the back of my neck. I remained stone still as I waited for it to end. Part of me wanted to climb down to where Finn was perched, but I didn't want to make any noise that could give away our location.

Instead, I closed my eyes and waited for it to be over.

When I opened them again, Finn was making her way back up to me. The sound was still present but less pronounced than before. I leaned in as she nestled herself on the branch beside me. "Is it one of Kahlis' creatures?" I whispered to her. Panic gripped my chest as I tried again to peer into the darkness and pinpoint the noise.

"Nah," Finn whispered back. "Just another creature of the Dark Woods. Nothing to worry about so long as we stay out of its way."

"How did you get so knowledgeable out here?" I was used to Vander's familiarity with this place, but I hadn't been prepared for Finn's comfort amongst the Dark Woods' shadows.

Finn shrugged, picking at the dirt under her nails. "I used to live out here, in another life."

"*Here*?" I asked, incredulous. I folded my arms over my chest, rubbing my fingers against the gooseflesh that had broken out across my skin.

Finn nodded, unfazed by my reaction. "It was another time, before Kahlis found me. I'd lost my family. I didn't have anywhere else to go. So I made the trees my home. In a lot of ways, these woods are what prepared me for my time with Kahlis. They hardened me, taught me what it meant to persevere against all odds."

I nodded. Vander had similar sentiments for these woods, and I found myself suddenly appreciating the safety the Dark Woods had offered me time and time again. My cheeks turned red as I realized the last time I'd been within its borders had been the night Vander and I had fully accepted the bond. Even then, something about its sentient presence had terrified me. But now, I was starting to understand the other side.

I looked up into the canopy above, taking note of the beauty in the shadows. It must have been early morning, dusk starting to peek through the thick foliage. It had been some time since I'd seen the sunlight; its presence made itself known by the lightening greys and sparse white light coming through the gaps in the leaves.

"We should get going." Finn interrupted my musing. "The others are probably not far out, and we don't want them traveling closer to Kahlis' borders than necessary. Better to intercept their path and redirect to Talamh's border than risk running into Daeomi out here."

Finn grunted as she dropped to a lower branch. The ease with which she moved through the trees was frustrating. I copied her path to my best ability, gritting my teeth as my body inched silently but clumsily down the tree.

Apprehension flooded me at the thought of reuniting with them. So much shame still lingered within me at the depths my darkness had reached within Kahlis' prison. Aerie had spent so much time working with me, helping to build those mental shields. And yet at the first test of their strength, I'd collapsed, retreated so far within myself that I'd given up on a life beyond that nightmare. Given up on *them*. And I couldn't help but worry things would feel... different with them now. Without Vander.

I dropped to the forest floor after Finn, standing to my feet and dusting my hands off. Finn stood there with crossed arms, waiting for me in silent judgment.

"What?" I asked, raising an eyebrow to her skeptical look.

"You were in a dark place just before we left the prison." She stated, seemingly sensing where my thoughts had ventured. I nodded. "Are you still there now?" Her composure didn't change as she stared me down, demanding an answer.

"No," I answered too quickly. "Maybe?" I lamented after a beat. I sighed, rubbing one hand over my forehead and resting the other against my hip. "I don't know where I am anymore. So much has happened that I'm just trying to keep up at this point."

"That's fair." She bobbed her head, allowing my response. "But it's also fair that I know where your head is at. We're out here together. I can't have you shutting down again like you did before. All that matters now is survival."

I nodded, understanding where she was coming from. "I have your back," I reassured her. "So long as you continue having mine."

She watched me for a moment, head tilted to the side. "Have you tried to contact your mate again? Since we left the prison?"

I stared back at her, surprised at her question as well as her knowledge of the extent of the bond. "No, I—I think I left that hope behind, to be honest."

She nodded, turning abruptly and starting off in the opposite direction. I scrambled into motion, jogging several strides to catch up with her.

"Why do you care?" I asked as we trudged through the thick foliage.

"Is it not believable that I care to know the mental state of my traveling companion?" It was so matter-of-fact, so devoid of concern. I bit down on my tongue, deciding not to respond.

The leaves crunched beneath our bare feet, the sound filling the space around us.

"I am no stranger to that dark place," Finn said in a low voice after walking in silence for several paces. "My life has been filled with so much bad, that sometimes it felt like the dark place was the only place that existed."

I nodded along, even though I knew she wasn't looking towards me. I stayed quiet, hoping she'd continue.

"I just—" She stopped walking, turning to face me. "I know how comfortable it can be in that darkness. But it's a lie. Nothing awaits you there but a life of loneliness and heartache."

For a moment, I thought she might reach out and take my hand. Instead, she waited a beat before turning back to our path to continue walking. I followed suit, stride by stride.

"I had the opportunity for a second chance at happiness. And I chose to remain in that dark place rather than open myself up to the world around me." She turned her head to look at me as we walked. "Don't make the same mistake I did."

I held her stare, shocked she was revealing so much. "I'm not sure what awaits me within Talamh's borders," I answered at last, turning my attention ahead.

"You don't know unless you try," she responded. "Unless you keep trying. Failure only happens when you give up." She slowed her pace as we came to a fork in the path. "Which way?" she asked, gesturing to the two options.

"Why are you asking me?" I furrowed my brow. She had already proven her familiarity within these woods. And I didn't have the slightest idea which direction was the right way.

"Because I'm teaching you. Now do as I say, look at the options. Take them in, and then tell me which one will lead us home."

I sighed as she turned my body to face the paths ahead. I took in each one, begrudgingly at first. But my apprehension slipped away as I evaluated the options. On the surface, they looked imperceptibly similar. But as I stood and waited for the truth of the Dark Woods to reveal itself, I noticed their small differences.

One had movement, a slight breeze, animals scurrying in the underbrush. The other was dead silent. Bones peeked through the grass, littering the path—an omen of ill fate.

"This one." I raised my hand, pointing towards the one promising safety.

"She can be taught, afterall." Finn smiled, the look on her face a mix between smugness and pride. I blew out a laugh, rolling my eyes and motioning for her to continue on our path.

In my heart, I knew it was the right way. The path leading me home. But the doubt still existed, the fear that even if it was the right path, it wouldn't take me to where I hoped to go. But there was little left to do besides trust in what I had left, to let the ones I still had around me guide me home. Regardless of who, or what, waited for me there.

CHAPTER 40
HAZEL

We walked for what felt like an eternity, pausing midday so that Finn could get a few hours of rest. She positioned herself safely within the tangled branches of another tree, and I kept lookout a few limbs below. While she slept, I took the opportunity to experience the beauty of the Dark Woods like I never had before.

It was like a veil had been lifted from my eyes, and I was able to see the wonder in the darkness of the trees for the first time ever. As if the Dark Woods themselves were finally accepting me as one of their own. I wondered if my bond with Vander had anything to do with this newfound appreciation. Perhaps being fated to the male that called this place his home, the one entity that the trees and the shadows bent to, had afforded me a glimpse behind the facade.

But even as my mind flipped through the possibilities, I felt the woods whispering to me, recognizing the power that flowed through my veins. Brushing against my skin with its own.

I leaned into its touch, relishing the way it made me feel closer to my mate. Kahlis and Kirwan had been so sure that Vander had left. His silence was still deafening. But what Finn had shared with me had been working away within the confines of my mind, convincing me not to give up hope just yet.

Soon, we'd find the others. A small piece of me was delusionally hopeful that Vander would be able to find his way back to me, that somehow this was all some large misunderstanding. And maybe even finding the others would be the key to that possibility. But the critical side of me, the darkness within me, was adamant that I give up that foolish hope. I let loose a breath, repositioning myself on my back as I looked up into the tree above.

I closed my eyes, breathing in the peaceful moment of the forest around me. I imagined a different day, a different situation. That I wasn't running for my life and escaping my father's wrath, but rather spending a sunny summer day with my mate at his favorite spot in the Dark Woods. He would be dangling from the tree limb beside me, drifting in and out of consciousness.

I let my hand hang off the branch I lay against, imagining his hand in my grasp. We would talk about our hopes and dreams for our life together, our family, the tribe. It was peaceful, blissful perfection.

If you're out there... The words were echoing through my mind before I knew what I was doing. *Please, give me a sign.*

I waited.

And waited.

And waited.

Birds sang in the distance, animals scurried through the decaying leaves. I squeezed my eyes closed, taking it all in, listening to the song of Vander's home. Vander's heart. When I opened my eyes again, my cheeks were wet from tears I hadn't realized I'd been crying.

My chest hurt so deeply, his absence an undeniable hole within me. He had once told me of the pain he went through being separated from me, that the ache he felt was soul deep. No matter how many times I'd heard him explain it, how many times I dreamwalked to him and witnessed the extent of that pain, I'd never fully understood it.

Now I could. And it made me hurt for my mate even more. No matter if he had truly left, no matter if I'd never see him again, my body ached from the thought of him experiencing this torment again. He had always been so convinced he deserved the darkness that stained his soul, but I knew the truth.

A goodness lived inside Vander. The kind of light that could only be forged in the darkness, just like mine. Because he understood what true darkness was, and he still chose to continue on, still chose *me*.

A deep howl broke through the silence of the woods. I sat up, wondering if I had imagined it. A fool's hope. I couldn't stop myself from surveying the land around me. My eyes monitored the trees, looking for any glimpse of that midnight fur.

It happened again, a far-off, distant but distinct howl. My heart leapt in my chest as I scrambled to climb up the tree.

"Finn," I whisper-yelled. "FINN." I reached out, shaking her arm.

"What?" she groaned, irritated.

The howl sounded again, slightly closer this time.

"I think it's him." I hated the excitement in my voice, wanted to bury it deep inside me and refuse to give it space to bloom. I looked back up into the tree, wishing Finn would understand the urgency in my voice. She sat up reluctantly, stretching and rubbing her back.

A third time, the howl echoed through the trees, finally catching Finn's attention. She didn't wait for me to repeat myself before she swung down the tree and onto the forest floor. I rushed after her, my dismount taking longer.

As soon as I hit the ground, we took off running. Neither of us needed confirmation from the other, no words of direction or explanation as we made our way through the Dark Woods.

We chased the howl endlessly, running in each and every direction as we tried to make sense of where it was coming from. Sometimes it sounded like we were getting closer, other times it was so faint I barely noticed it.

"I don't hear it anymore," I cried out in defeat, stopping short and doubling over to ease the pain in my side.

"Be patient," Finn bit back in a hushed tone as she slowed beside me. She knelt, one hand on the ground as she closed her eyes. "It will come again."

Before I could voice my disagreement, another howl rang through the trees. I whipped my head around in the direction it had come from. I didn't wait for Finn to confirm. I ripped past trees, jumping over logs and darting deeper into the thicket. Gone was the path we'd once been following, gone was any care of the dangers all around me. All that mattered was finding the wolf whose howl we'd been chasing.

I broke through a tree line, into a small clearing. The canopy broke apart in spots to let rays of sunlight stream down. I walked through their spotlights, shifting from darkness to light as I made my way into the middle of the clearing.

"Vander?" I called out. The forest had gone quiet once more. "Vander!" I pivoted, watching in every direction, eyes searching frantically for any glimpse of his fur, his golden glowing eyes, through the trees. I'd been so sure, so convinced it was him.

I closed my eyes again, listening for any sign of his presence. I tuned into the tether, dug my heels into the soil of this sacred land he called home. I would use anything to find him and bring him back to me once more.

When only more silence greeted me, I fell to my knees and wept into the grass. My tears rolled off my cheeks and onto the wildflowers beneath me, mixing with the dirt and turning it to mud. Even away from Daravaana and out of his prison, Kahlis' voice still echoed in my mind.

Those kinds of bonds can be broken, if need be. After all, here you are alone. In your darkest hour. And where is your mate now?

Something brushed against me. Something soft and warm and full of hope. My breath shuddered as I released it, reaching out towards the creature. Eyes still closed, I buried myself against the wolf in front of me. He welcomed me, letting me wail into his fur and cling to it with a fierce sort of desperation.

Because I knew. Without opening my eyes and seeing him for myself, I knew.

It wasn't Vander before me.

It was Bastian.

Bastian led us back to their camp, still in his wolven form, as Finn followed behind. My arm was draped over his shoulders as we walked, his attempt to keep me upright. My back ached, the wounds breaking open once more. My feet were torn up, bruised and bloody from running through the woods. But most of all, darkness stained my heart.

Bastian's silence was all the confirmation I needed that Vander was truly gone. He didn't try to end my sorrow, didn't offer any kind of explanation. He just let me hold onto him, took my tears and my cries as I mourned the confirmation I'd been dreading.

The sun was setting by the time we approached their camp. It had been a several hour walk, but the more distance we put between us and Kahlis' lands, the better. I could see the smoke through my swollen, puffy eyes. The first indication that we were almost home.

Finn had insisted on not foolishly giving away our position by lighting a fire. My family, on the other hand, was trying to make themselves known—so as to help guide me back to them.

When we broke into the borders of their camp, Aerie and Lennox were on me in an instant, taking over for Bastian. He slunk off somewhere in the distance, no doubt to find clothes as he shifted back to his mortal form.

Aerie held me at an arm's length, eyes dancing over my skin as she evaluated my wounds. "What did they do to you?" There were tears in her eyes, blood on her hands as she pulled them away from my back. I hadn't realized how much I'd been fighting the pain, the exhaustion. Being back in her arms now, I collapsed as it all came flooding over me.

"Lennox, go get my bag from my tent." Her words were short, clipped. Nox hurried to her aid. Aerie put her hands on either side of my face, cupping my cheeks and making me look at her. The sight of her kind, light blue eyes was my undoing.

"I'm so sorry, Hazel," she whispered as I fell against her, heaving with the weight of it all. "But you're home now. Let us carry it all for you."

I nodded against her chest as she stroked my hair. "I didn't think I would ever see you again." My words were garbled, tangled in shuddering breaths as I tried to regain my composure. Nox returned, kneeling beside Aerie. "So much has happened. So much

I need to tell you about. Vander, Kahlis. Finn and Kirwan—" My voice cracked, another sob taking over my body.

Nox's hands froze as he unpacked supplies from Aerie's bag, his gaze slowly lifting to me. "What about Kirwan?" He rose to his feet, eyes bouncing to the surrounding trees as he looked for his brother.

"I'm so sorry, Nox." I shook my head. I watched him retreat within himself, a silent conversation happening as he no doubt tuned into their twin connection.

"Finn?" Aerie asked, bringing my attention back to her. "Who's Finn?"

I turned, wincing at the pain as I tried to find where we'd left her. Bastian appeared from the trees a moment later, Finn in hand as he led her closer to the fire. Finn wasn't happy about it, judging by the way she squirmed under the chieftain's hold.

"Found her trying to sneak off. Figured if she was in half as bad a shape as you, I couldn't let her go just yet."

I eased my feet forward, rushing as best I could over to her and bringing her in for a hug. "Finn," I sighed in relief. "Promise you'll stay. At least so Aerie can tend to your wounds."

Finn froze as I pulled away, eyes on something over my shoulder. I looked back to find Aerie still standing where I'd left her, frozen in much the same way. Her hands were at her mouth, her eyes wide and filled with tears, as if she'd just seen a spirit.

"Serafina?" She exhaled a shaky breath.

Finn shifted nervously, wrapping her arms around herself. "It's—Finn, now."

Aerie rushed forward, wrapping the girl in a hug so fierce, I was sure she would break her. "I thought you were dead," Aerie cried.

"That makes two of us." Finn's eyes were wide with astonishment, her face pale.

"Hold on," Bastian cut in, finally releasing Finn's arm. "Serafina, as in, your sister?"

Aerie nodded, pulling back and swiping at the tears streaming down her face. I gasped. Serafina, one of the coven sisters Aerie had spoken so fondly of—the sisters who'd taught her their craft and danced in the moonlight together. Finn had mentioned losing a family, but never in a million years would I have thought she meant Aerie. I looked back at Finn, seeing her in an entirely new light.

"You got away?" Aerie asked, astounded.

"I wasn't in the cottage that afternoon," Finn breathed. "I'd gone out to collect more firewood. When I returned, I heard you and..." Her words faded away as she dropped her gaze to the forest floor.

"My father's attack," Aerie offered, voice quiet. "I'd returned home to the aftermath of his wrath, found their bodies—" She choked on a sob, pulling Finn into her embrace once more. "I couldn't make them out, couldn't even count how many there were." Her voice was shaky as she spoke against Finn's shoulder. "I'd just assumed you'd been with them."

Finn shook her head slowly, blinking back tears. "I'd ventured pretty deep into the woods. By the time I'd made my way back, there was nothing left. Except for you and your father." Finn's surety wavered, her words hesitating as a small moan escaped her throat. "I was scared," she admitted, barely audible as her voice was muffled by Aerie's steadfast embrace. "I'm sorry, Aerie. I was scared and I ran when I heard what he was doing to you."

Aerie shook her head, holding Finn tighter. "Don't you apologize, even for a second. You were smart to run." She pulled back just far enough to look down on Finn. "Had you stayed, he would have killed you too." The girls stared at each other, tear-stained and hypnotized at the reality that either were still alive. I clutched my chest, pushing back my own tears as I watched in astonishment.

Bastian ushered them to sit down by the fire in the middle of their camp, the conversation lowering to a distant murmur as they relayed their stories to one another. I waited a moment, wanting to give them the privacy they deserved before following them.

"As overwhelming as this all is," Nox whispered into my ear, wrapping a hand around my elbow and leading us to the campsite. "I need to know what happened to my brother."

I sighed, nodding, as I let Nox guide me to a fallen log. "We ran into the Daeomi during our escape. There were too many of them, surrounding Kirwan and cutting him off from us and the exit. He—he stayed behind to save us, to keep their attention on him and allow us a chance to get out."

Nox's jaw hardened, his throat bobbing as he swallowed. "But that's a suicide mission."

I shook my head, though my heart sank at the thought. "Finn thinks he's too important of an asset for Kahlis to kill outright." At my words, Finn bristled, her and Aerie's attention turning back towards us. "She was in the prison longer than any of us, so I trust her word. Haven't you heard anything through your connection?"

Nox's eyes flicked to Finn before shaking his head. "The connection is still there, but I can't get through to him. Maybe he's too weak to respond, or—" He stood abruptly, pacing in front of the fire for a moment before kicking a nearby rock, sending it soaring into the thicket of trees in the distance. "That damned fool!"

"Nox," I called, trying to calm him. "As long as you can feel it, Kirwan's still alive." The words sent a pang of pain straight to my heart, as I struggled to sense my own connection to Vander. I pushed the hurt aside, focusing on Nox as I continued. "Plus, I think," I paused, carefully considering my words. "I think he might be blocking you out intentionally."

Nox's eyes found mine, wide and wild in the light of dusk. "What do you mean by that?"

"He... he didn't want you to know the whole story," I tried to explain.

"What whole story?" Distress over his brother had turned Nox's words sharp, catching on to the conflict in my voice and losing patience.

Aeire paused beside Finn, her hand stalling where she'd begun cleaning her wounds. The whole clearing went silent, as if in wait for the words I was about to share.

"Kirwan was scared to talk to you," I said weakly. "He felt ashamed he was caught by Kahlis."

"Fuck that," Nox said after several silent beats. "He'd already contacted me for help. Why would he put the block back up when he needs us the most?"

I sighed, closing my eyes for a moment as I struggled with the right combination of words.

"He betrayed her," Finn responded before I had the chance. I spun my gaze to her, eyes wide as she shrugged indifferently towards me. "The were going to find out sooner or later. No use prolonging the inevitable."

"What the fuck do you mean, he betrayed her?" Bastian stood, muscles flexing in anger.

"It's not like that." I raised my hands. "He didn't have a choice. Kahlis was threatening you." My eyes met Nox's "He was threatening Mirren. Poisoning Kirwan with visions of what he planned to do to you if he didn't comply. So Kirwan did what he felt he had to, to ensure your safety."

"What he had to do?" Nox echoed weakly.

My eyes flickered between Nox and Finn, relenting as she gave me an asserting nod. "He fed information about me back to Kahlis, in order to keep both of you safe."

A sickening silence fell over the clearing, the others collectively processing what that piece of information implied. The only noise that rustled between the five of us as the truth washed over them was Aerie's movements as she tended to Finn's wounds and mine.

"And because of that, he sacrificed himself?" Nox asked at last. His face was twisted up in torment, brows furrowed as unshed tears threatened his eyes. "As if we wouldn't understand? As if we wouldn't have forgiven him? Sure, it would have taken time to rebuild that trust after he betrayed you, after his decisions led to Mirren's—" His words cut off, strangled on a stifled sob. "Fuck!"

Bastian moved closer to Nox, putting a firm hand on Nox's shoulder. "This is your call, brother. We will follow you, no matter what decision you make." Bastian's voice was so low, I almost didn't hear him. But I echoed the sentiment. Kirwan had sacrificed his freedom to get me free of Kahlis' hold. The least I could do was return the favor.

Nox shook his head, pushing off Bastian's embrace and pinching the bridge of his nose with his thumb and forefinger. "No. No, we remain on plan. Kirwan made his decision. We honor it, for now." He turned to face me, leveling his gaze. "We go back now and Kirwan's sacrifice will have been for nothing. I won't risk your safety trying to go after him while Kahlis is surely still hunting you down."

"Alright." Bastian turned away from Nox, looking at us from across the flames. "As much as I would love to give you girls some time to rest here for the night, we need to pack up and head out. We've been in one place too long, and even with the distance from Kahlis' borders, I don't think it's a good idea to linger here any longer than necessary."

"We are still outside Talamh's warding," Aerie agreed. "It's probably for the best that we push on a little more. When we return home I can fully address your wounds." She laid a hand on Finn's shoulder, causing her to stiffen. "Will you return with us? At least, long enough for you to recover. We can discuss plans once you've rested a few days."

Finn took a moment to respond, her eyes on the distant trees. She had told me they were once her home. I imagined it was hard to resist returning to their familiarity after all she had been through. But I hoped, perhaps for purely selfish reasons, she'd decide to come with us.

She dropped her gaze, nodding at last. Aerie sighed in relief, taking her hand and giving her a reassuring squeeze before returning to her work. Bastian brought both of us a canvas bag of dried meat and mugs of tea, hot off the fire.

"Go slow," he warned. "Your stomachs probably aren't used to the nutrients, and we don't want you getting sick on top of everything else."

Finn took the tea begrudgingly. Bastian handed me mine, throwing me a subtle smile as I took it. I offered him a small smile back.

I didn't want to admit how much I had missed them, or how close I'd come to never returning to them again. There was still so much left unanswered. So much we needed to address. But for this small moment, I relished in the relief of being amongst my family.

Even if it wasn't complete, even if the true extent of our future was unclear, I would count this as a win. Finn and I got away. We'd made it and were safe at last. And despite the sacrifices that were made to get us here, despite the heartache that still clung to our group, I would be grateful, at least, for that.

CHAPTER 41
HAZEL

I t didn't take us long to get moving. As much as I wanted to stay and rest, to relish in this feeling of freedom, I knew we weren't completely safe.

Not yet.

So we packed up and made our way back towards the Estate.

Aerie never drifted far from Finn's side. I could hear them whispering to each other, catching each other up on the journeys that led them here. Aerie had once told me her coven had died in a fire, at the hand of her father. Curiosity was eating me alive to know how Finn had ended up in Kahlis' prison, after surviving a horror such as Aerie's father—the mad fae king. But I wanted to be respectful of their space, and not encroach on this Fates ordained reunion.

Bastian led the way, never drifting far but staying ahead just enough to ensure the path was clear for us as we followed it back to Talamh. His gaze occasionally drifted behind, ever the subtle yet constant guardian for his mate. Especially given the shock she'd just received at Finn's return.

Which left Nox as my travel companion.

Both of us were quiet, gazes downcast as we made our way home—he without his brother, and I without my mate. I had so many questions I wanted to ask him about Vander, but I knew he was grieving. With each step in the opposite direction, he must have felt the resistance of a thousand boulders. Despite the horrors that had plagued me within Kahlis' prison, I felt the same way.

Kirwan had been my one light in that darkness, had helped me return from the brink of oblivion time and time again. It felt wrong to leave him there, even if that was the choice he'd made.

"Lennox," I whispered, risking a glance over to him.

"Hmm?" he hummed, lost in thought.

"I'm sorry."

"Don't, love. Kirwan is a grown male. He's free to make whatever decisions please him. And I'm forever grateful that he got you out of that monster's grasp."

"I know, but that's exactly why I can't help but feel responsible for his sacrifice. Perhaps if I'd fought harder, pushed my power further, I could have saved him too."

Nox let out a low sigh—days, if not months, of exhaustion weighing on him. He stalled his steps, tilting his head up to the canopy above. It was dark now, well into the night. Still, his eyes lingered above, as if searching for something.

He shook his head, bringing his gaze down to mine. "I'm glad he made the decision to save you" I looked up, my eyes wide with surprise and gratitude. "That was his role in the first place, to protect the people of Talamh. And maybe it'll be enough for him to get over the shame and come home to us. But don't for a second blame yourself. He did what he had to."

Nox pressed forward and put his arm around me as we walked. I winced, the weight of his arm against my back biting into the wounds there, but I didn't object. The physical presence of another being was worth the pain.

"Don't worry about him too hard. The asshole is nearly incapable of dying at this point," Nox added. "Knowing the kind of stubbornness my brother harbours, I doubt very seriously he will let that happen."

I laughed hesitantly, thinking about the poor shape he'd been in. I knew Nox was feigning confidence in his brother for my sake. I could sense the worry warring in his mind. But I pushed the feeling away, leaning into his embrace and pretending alongside Nox that Kirwan would find a way to stay alive until we'd return for him.

"Do you think Vander is truly gone?" I asked after a moment of silence. It had been the question on my mind since returning to them. He didn't respond at first, just pulled me in tighter as we continued our steps through the Dark Woods.

"We've been looking," he answered at last. "Me, Bastian—fuck, he's even ordered every sentry in Talamh to be on the hunt. So far, we've found no sign of him."

I dropped my gaze, watching the leaves crunch under our foot-fall. If I'd had any tears left to cry, they would have been falling now. But it felt as if I'd grieved every bit of energy I had left for my mate. What Nox shared wasn't news, not really. I should have guessed they'd be searching for him. I'd never seen a brotherly love as fierce as Bastian and Vander's. He wouldn't sit idly by while his brother was missing.

Had they found any inclination as to what happened to Vander, I knew Nox would have shared as much with Kirwan, and Kirwan with me. He wouldn't have watched me fade away into the darkness helplessly if he'd had a piece of hope to offer me.

"Hey," Nox said, hooking his free hand under my chin and bringing my eyes up to meet his. "We will find him." He held my gaze until he was sure I believed him.

"I know." I nodded in agreement. "It just feels so weird, not being able to sense him." I pulled my chin out of his hold, turning my head back to the path before us. My eyes searched the shadows of the Dark Woods, convinced if I looked hard enough, I'd find him slinking between the trees.

Nox leaned down, his breath on my ear as he whispered. "Anything you need, love, I'm right here. I'm not leaving your side."

I nodded again, surprised to find tears welling behind my eyes. I supposed there was more within me, afterall. Nox noticed them too, brushing a thumb over my cheek to whisk away one that had escaped.

"Let's just focus on getting you home, safe and sound. Then we can put together a plan to get our male back."

I let loose a breath of air, astounded by Nox's sarcasm that knew no limits. He grinned down at me, tightening his hold and pushing us faster down the path ahead.

When we returned home, the first thing Aerie did was drag both me and Finn into her greenhouse to address our wounds properly. My back had healed some on the journey home, thanks to Aerie's efforts and my own magic, which had been slowly returning as Kahlis' grip over it faded. I felt immediate relief as she applied a salve infused with her magic along the lashes. I sighed into her touch, thanking the Fates, the Cosmos, anyone who would listen for instilling Aerie with her magical abilities.

Finn was next. She perched on the edge of the daybed in the greenhouse, looking like a scared, wounded animal. I had never seen her so shaken up, and I was surprised being here of all things would break her stoic calm. Aerie offered her a fresh change of clothes, as she had me. But I knew the tunic Finn still wore had been Kirwan's. Judging by the way she eyed the stack of clean clothing, it was too large a burden to lift for her to shed those rags.

I stepped up, laying a hand on her shoulder. She jumped slightly, her shifty eyes darting up to me. "It's okay, Finn." I nodded towards the tunic, encouraging her to let me help. She reluctantly lifted her hands above her head, allowing me to peel the tattered fabric from her body and revealing the chains hidden beneath.

Aerie didn't gasp, didn't react at all. She was too kind, too seasoned to the harsh ways of fae kings, to be shocked by what she saw. Empathy radiated from her, though, as she approached Finn.

"May I?" she asked before touching. Finn nodded, turning her head to the side and focusing hard on a spot on the nearby wall. Aerie delicately ran her fingers over the chain harness, lips pursed in concentration as she evaluated how to free her from this bondage. "I know this is going to be hard for you, but I think I need Bastian's help to remove these." When Finn didn't respond, Aerie added, "Is that okay?"

Finn nodded, jaw tight.

"Alright," Aerie sighed, rising to her feet and retreating momentarily from the greenhouse to fetch Bastian.

"Finn, I—"

"Don't," she cut me off. "Like I told you before. I don't need your pity."

Aerie returned with Bastian before I could say more, so I took a seat beside Finn and laced my hand in hers. To my surprise, she let me.

"Because of the complicated nature of the harness," Aerie explained to Bastian as she led him over to the bed, "I need you to use your axe to try and break through the metal while I'm focusing my energy on the wounds beneath. The etchings should neutralize each other."

"Wounds beneath?" I asked, looking down on the metal contraption.

"Yes," Aerie answered hesitantly, watching Finn for a reaction. "Correct me if I'm wrong, Serafina, but the inside of these chains are lined with small spikes, yes?"

Finn waited a beat, reluctantly nodding but still refusing to make eye contact with Aerie. I stifled a hiss, imagining the discomfort Finn must have been in all this time. I knew the female servants were harnessed within the chains, the contraption acting as a sickening sort of corset to trap their upper bodies. But I had no idea they were being tortured by them relentlessly on the inside.

"And the spikes served as a way to—"

"Control us," Finn finished for Aerie, finally lifting her gaze. "An extension of Adonis' magic."

Images of the glassy-eyed females drifted through my mind, now understanding the immense pain they were bearing underneath. I had always viewed Finn as morose and disgruntled, without even realizing how much pain she was going through moment to moment. I understood now just how deeply she meant it when she'd assumed that being Kahlis' daughter would afford me certain mercies.

"I'm so sorry, Finn." I squeezed her hand.

"This should have never happened to you," Aerie added, running a hand down her other arm.

"Can you get it off, or not?" Finn pulled back from our touch.

Aerie looked up to Bastian in response. "What do you think?"

"The enchanted blade is probably our best chance to pop the clasps of the harness," he said thoughtfully. "But you need to be ready because those wounds beneath will be angry. How long has this been on you?"

Finn didn't answer, just hardened her jaw once more.

"All this time?" Aerie asked, lifting a hand to her mouth.

"Just get the damn thing off," Finn bit out. The urgency in her words set us all into motion. Aerie instructed Finn to lie flat on her stomach, arms stretched out above her. She had me hold her hands, urging me to stroke gentle circles against her palms in an attempt to sooth her.

Bastian positioned himself over Finn, with Aerie squatting beside her at the edge of the bed. He unsheathed the battle axe from his side, wedging the edge of the blade delicately beneath the lip of the chain clasped against Finn's back.

"I'm going to go slow and carefully, because I don't want to hurt you further," he explained down to Finn. "If we need to stop, just let me know. But the faster we can work, the better."

She nodded into the pillow. "Just do it."

And with that, Bastian started. It took him several minutes to break through the first clasp. Finn held firm at first, but as Bastian made his way up the harness, her stubbornness gave way to pain, the greenhouse filling with her muffled cries. But she never once asked him to stop, her determination a marvel to behold.

Aerie poured every bit of healing magic she could muster into the path Bastian was leaving for her. I reached into the Divine power within, surprising myself at the ease with which it came forth to aid Aerie's magic.

My chest eased as Bastian released the last clasps, and the rest of our magic flowed into Finn. Bastian moved out of the way, turning around to give Finn some privacy as Aerie removed the front of the harness.

I helped Finn into the clean tunic once Aerie had coated her wounds in more of the healing salve she'd used on me. The relief on Finn's face brought tears to my eyes, only rivaled by the nausea in my gut at seeing her abdomen covered in the tiny pinprick wounds.

When Aerie had finished and Finn was fully dressed, she backed up a step and took Finn's hands in her own.

"Better?" Aerie asked, searching Finn's features for any lingering pain.

"Much," Finn breathed out. It was the closest thing to happiness I'd seen from her.

"We'll have to keep using the salve for a few days, but now that the harness is off, your body should be able to heal the wounds quickly." Aerie helped Finn stand to her feet and led her through the greenhouse. "Let's get you into a room for the night. You need to rest more than anything else right now."

Finn nodded, letting Aerie guide her into the Estate and through the halls. Bastian and I followed, stopping in the kitchen to give them some space to get settled. My smile faded as Bastian turned his attention to me.

"How are you doing?" he asked, his words thick with emotion.

"I'm alright," I lied, not entirely sure how to sum up the gamut of emotions running through my mind. Instead, I turned into the kitchen to gather up supplies to make tea.

"Fuck," Bastian hissed. I froze, realizing the error in my movements. Aerie had removed the dressings on my back, leaving me in an open back tunic as a way to let them air out and soak up the salve.

"Bastian." I turned back to face him. "It's okay."

"No," he ground out through clenched teeth. "It's not. I was meant to protect you, all of you. And yet here we are, half the family immeasurably wounded, Vander missing, Kirwan gone, Mirren—" He leaned forward, his elbows on the middle counter as he buried his face in his hands.

I set the tea supplies down, moving through the kitchen to be by his side. "There was nothing you could have done, Bastian."

"That's bullshit. I could have protected you. I could have led better. I could have stopped Kahlis back when you first returned. Every day in this battle is another day I question why I was ever left in charge of this tribe."

I came up beside him as he stared straight ahead, still leaning on the counter. "You were given the responsibility of this tribe because not a purer heart exists." I nudged his shoulder. His jaw hardened, his chestnut eyes lined with pain. "Had you been able to do any of that, you would have."

Bastian shook his head, looking out the kitchen window as he tried to find the words to explain what he was struggling with. "It just feels like everything is a wreck right now. So many of us are hurting and bleeding, and I don't see an end in sight." He swallowed, a muscle feathering in his jaw.

"I can understand that." I sighed, turning to lean back against the counter and join him in looking out the window. It was dusk again, a whole day having transpired since Bastian found me in the Dark Woods and brought me back to their campsite. "And while I don't necessarily have a plan to get us through this, I know we'll figure it out." I elbowed him in the side, earning a sidelong glance my way before adding, "Together."

Bastian watched me for a moment, breaking eye contact at last as he chuckled softly. "Your endurance is inspiring, Hazel."

I mirrored his laughter, hoping it masked the darkness still threatening to pull me under. But I'd promised Vander a long time ago that I would fight, no matter what came our way, no matter how hard things got, I would continue to show up and fight. And now that he was Fates knew where, I needed now more than ever to keep my promise.

Bastian's gaze landed once more out the window. He opened his mouth to speak, but something beyond the Estate caught his attention. He straightened, leaning forward to peer past the murky glass towards the tree line.

"What is it?" I asked, reaching up on tiptoes to get the same vantage point as him.

"Something's out there," Bastian answered, his eyes briefly shifting to their wolven state. "Nox," he called out, his head spinning to the side as he tilted it to look deeper into the Estate. "Where is Lennox?"

"I—I don't know," I answered honestly. Aerie had taken us straight into the greenhouse when we returned. I hadn't had a chance to see where he'd gone.

Bastian was quick to move, his brawny form pushing hastily through the kitchen and out the side door. "Nox," he called again once he was outside. I followed him on quick feet, brow furrowed as I tried to figure out what was going on. "Lennox Raevynn!" Bastian's voice boomed over the rolling hills, causing a chill to creep down my spine.

Nox appeared moments later, coming from around the front of the Estate with a handful of summer berries. "What's up, Chieftain?"

Bastian's eyes rolled over Nox's form, inclining his head towards him before turning back to that distant spot on the tree line he'd been watching. Nox followed his gaze, eyes squinting as he leaned forward, looking for a moment as two blurred shapes stumbled out of the trees.

Berries fell from his hand, spilling over the tall grass. It was the only warning I had before both males took off running.

"What is happening?" I asked, sprinting to catch up to them.

"It's Kirwan," Nox called out over his shoulder. My eyes went wide as I turned my attention back to the woods, watching the shadows for the other twin. I caught glimpses of the body, two bodies perhaps, but the way my feet were pounding against the ground had my vision jostling with every step.

Bastian and Nox beat me there, looking out in brief, spellbound confusion at the sight before them. Someone was holding Kirwan up, bloodied and near unconscious at their side. It was a male, somehow recognizable—one I knew. I paused, trying to process the impossible scene.

Holding up Kirwan was the exact image of his twin brother, Lennox.

Bastian wasted no time in taking Kirwan's weight and laying him down in the grass. I rushed to his side, hands dancing over his bloodied, mangled skin as I tried to assess which wound needed the most immediate attention.

Nox, the *real* Nox, drew a dagger and held it to the imposter's throat.

"Who are you?" he asked, the tip of his blade teasing skin.

"Who's to say I'm not you?" answered the false Nox. "Perhaps you're the one that's not truly yourself."

Bastian raised his own axe in preparation for a fight. "I suggest you answer the question before you're robbed of the opportunity to speak again."

The imposter's hands rose, retreating a step. The movement granted him no advantage, both Nox and Bastian following suit.

"Lower your weapons," Kirwan croaked out. I turned my attention back to him, cocking my head to the side as I looked to him for some sort of explanation. Through bloodstained eyes and a fit of coughing, he offered me a shrug, squeezing my hand with what little strength he had left before finally giving me an answer.

"It's Adonis."

CHAPTER 42
HAZEL

Nox and I led Kirwan into the Estate, Adonis following at axe point with Bastian. He'd let the impersonation go now that he was safely within the wardings of Tir Nadaar, letting his usual features of long silver hair and black eyes slip back into place. We filed into the kitchen and deposited Kirwan onto one of the chairs. He didn't have enough strength to hold himself up, so I pulled a chair up beside him and let him continue to lean on me. Aerie joined us, quickly assessing the situation before disappearing to gather supplies.

As soon as Nox was free of his brother, he spun back to Adonis.

"Give me one good reason why I don't gut you right now," Nox spat, blade once again at Adonis' throat.

"Because I'm asking you not to, brother." Kirwan's head hung low, his chest rattling with a wet cough.

Nox looked back at Kirwan over his shoulder, raising an eyebrow to his twin. "Someone better start explaining what the fuck is going on before I start swinging blades."

"So you finally made it." Finn's curt voice broke through the tension of the kitchen. She'd emerged from her room, against Aerie's instructions to rest. "About time, lover boy." She crossed her arms over her chest, leaning on the doorframe into the sitting room.

"Lover boy," I echoed. Finn hadn't been exactly forthcoming with her reasoning for the nickname, nor did she seem all that surprised to see the two of them here before us. I'd thought perhaps it was her and Kirwan who had sparked something down in the depths of torment in that prison. But as my gaze fell to Kirwan, then swept over to Adonis, a wild thought bloomed within my mind.

"You and Adonis?" I asked hesitantly. Kirwan lifted his head from my chest only long enough for me to notice the way his eyes crinkled, as if stating an apology and standing by his decision all at the same time.

"No," Nox scoffed, turning back to Adonis. Adonis smirked, clearly amused by Nox's shock. "This is Kahlis' right hand. He *cannot* be trusted." As if to let the warning echo through the room, Nox twisted the blade, pricking the skin of Adonis' throat.

"Brother," Kirwan rasped, pushing off of me in an attempt to sit up. With some help from me, he managed to rise to his feet, stumbling forward and right into Nox. "Adonis betrayed the Dark One to bring me here. I would not be alive without him."

"You of all people know what dark, despicable things this bastard has done." Nox tightened his grip on his brother, urging him to see reason.

"Exactly. I know better than most. So if I'm saying he can be trusted, please believe me."

Nox searched Kirwan's eyes, a silent conversation passing between them. Nox sighed, helping his twin back to his seat beside me.

"Explain how you got here," Bastian cut in, not waiting to hear Nox's decision. "Last we heard, you'd been overtaken by Daeomi. Decided to take them on as an offered distraction to allot them a better chance at escape." Bastian nodded towards the far side of the kitchen, where both Finn and I waited.

Suddenly, I found myself wondering how much of Kirwan's plan Finn had been privy to ahead of time. Had she believed, as I had, that Kirwan was truly staying behind? Or had she known Adonis would come to his aid, even betray Kahlis to bring him home?

Kirwan nodded, or at least tried to. I put a hand to his chest to stop him.

"It's true. There were too many Daeomi, and I knew the three of us would never make it past them all. Once Adonis appeared, I knew I could take my chances against them—giving Finn and Hazel a window of opportunity."

Kirwan's chest heaved with the effort it was taking him to recount the story. Aerie finally joined us, pushing through the crowd of bodies to address Kirwan's wounds. She knelt before him, fussing over him as he went on, occasionally offering things to me to hold or motioning for me to help where I could.

"But why would he help you?" Bastian asked, tightening his hold on Kahlis' right-hand.

Kirwan chuckled, the sound turning into a ragged cough. Aerie pressed her lips together, concern etched on her features.

"Adonis grew a soft spot for me, some time ago," Kirwan said when the coughing had cleared.

Adonis rolled his eyes, but he didn't deny it.

"Perhaps we bonded through all of that one-on-one time." Kirwan smirked, his bloodshot eyes twinkling. Adonis met his gaze, returning the sultry look.

"This is all too bizarre," Nox interjected. "I fear I'm going to be sick."

"Why, because I found companionship in a male?"

"No, because you found companionship in the enemy!" Nox yelled as he loomed over me and Kirwan. I pulled Kirwan closer to me on instinct, flinching at the harsh tone of Nox's voice.

"Do not sit here and offer me the disservice of insinuating my lack of acceptance. I couldn't give two fucks who you fall for, Kirwan, so long as that someone isn't responsible for the pain and torment ravaging our continent. Do you forget who was there to feel your pain during your time within his prison? Whose blood burned alongside yours as I sat as silent witness to your torment—that is, when you *deigned* to let me in. You have spent years, *decades*, within their borders to gain information and bring Kahlis down." Nox huffed, wagging a finger at his brother. "Only to crawl into the enemy's bed and then bring him into our territory?!"

"I know this is hard to grasp, brother. But you will just have to trust my judgment here." Kirwan's words were clipped, concentrated with the effort it took to speak them.

"Trust your judgment?" Nox scoffed, retreating a couple steps. "Brother, you lost that right the moment you caused our sister's demise."

The room went silent. Aerie stiffened, tears threatening to spill over her lashes as she closed her eyes and gave herself a moment. Bastian didn't move, didn't argue either, his own features tainted with the emotions of betrayal.

Nox stared down his brother, breath heavy as he processed what he'd just said. He tore his gaze away, storming through the kitchen and scrubbing a frustrated hand through his hair.

Adonis attempted to step forward, no doubt moving to comfort Kirwan, but Bastian held him firm.

"I know that earning your trust will not be easy," Adonis said to Bastian behind him. "But I chose to betray the loyalty of quite possibly the most powerful male on this continent. For him." He nodded towards Kirwan's slumped form. "Besides, I did not come empty-handed. I am more than willing to share vital information to help your fight."

At that, Bastian perked up. "What do you know?" he asked in a rough voice.

Adonis responded only with a slight curl of his lips, before pursing them together as if to say he wasn't ready to share. Bastian pulled hard on the male, causing him to stumble back against the chieftain's chest.

"By the Fates, I swear if you don't start talking—"

"Adonis," Kirwan murmured against my chest. I laid a hand in his hair, brushing over the tangled mess with the tips of my fingers and willing some of my magic into the motion. Kirwan sighed with relief. Aerie looked up at me in surprise from where she still fussed over his larger wounds.

"Fine," Adonis relented, putting his hands up. "But this is my one bargaining chip, so I'm trusting you lot to honor your word and not throw me to the wolves the second you get your information."

"The wolves are already here, my love." Kirwan laughed, then coughed. I couldn't help but notice the way Adonis' muscles tightened at the sound, as if it was killing him to not be near Kirwan, to help in some way.

Adonis pulled his gaze away once Kirwan's cough had settled. His eyes flitted over the bodies in the room, taking each of us in one by one. Perhaps to evaluate the potential threat to his well-being, perhaps to plan an escape route should what he share not sit well with us.

"I came here to bring Kirwan to safety. I knew Kahlis would not let him live after helping his daughter to escape. He has worked tirelessly for years to get his hands on her, and this loss was crippling to him."

I turned my head from the male, hating how it felt like all eyes were now on me. I wasn't ready to talk about what cruel fates I met in that prison.

"But—" Adonis went on, rolling his bottom lip between his teeth. "That is not all. There have been developments lately, plans the Dark One has been making. As you know, his goal has always been to take back control of the continent. But I believe for the first time, he's starting to think wisely about how to achieve that. And possibly for the first time in many, many years, he may actually stand a chance."

"And why is that?" Bastian sneered, dropping his hold on the male to cross his arms over his chest and square his shoulders. As if to show how little he feared Kahlis—even if it was a facade.

"Because," Adonis turned to face Bastian. "For the first time since their fall, Kahlis has secured a treaty with another fae ruler."

Aerie, crouched on the floor and pouring her healing power into a large gash on Kirwan's leg, stiffened abruptly.

"In fact," Adonis continued. "He's entrusted the support of someone perhaps only worse than himself." This time, Adonis finally turned to face Aerie. "The mad fae king."

After Adonis shared his news, Aerie went deadly silent, focusing all of her attention on Kirwan's wounds. Eventually, when Kirwan could no longer hold himself up, Aerie insisted on moving him to the greenhouse.

A large part of me wanted to go follow them, to comfort Aerie and help however I could. But just one silent glance from her told me she needed space and time to process. And more than anything, to be out of the room for now.

I rose, finding the tea ingredients I had gathered earlier, before Kirwan and Adonis' abrupt arrival. If we were truly about to have this conversation, I figured a warm cup of tea would be needed all around.

"So why the sudden change of heart?" Nox wasted no time jumping into the questioning.

Adonis' head tipped up, eyes on the ceiling. "I've lost track of the reasons over the decades. I've been the Dark One's right hand since the uprising of the New World. My father was in Kahlis' court back before the fae kings were banished or killed. He lost my father in that war, but accepted me as a consolation prize." Adonis tucked a strand of white hair behind his tawny ear, revealing the pointed tip. "Perhaps I'm tired of taking the Dark One's abuse?"

"Or perhaps that male in the other room has thawed that frigid heart of yours, and given you something to live for," Finn quipped. She moved out of the doorframe as I handed out cups of steaming tea, taking the seat beside mine. I threw her a quick glance as I handed her a cup, noting the neutrality in her eyes as I returned to my own seat. She had no reason to trust Adonis any more than us. But her loyalties also did not lie with Talamh. I briefly found myself wondering what her opinion on the situation was.

Adonis leveled his dark eyes at her, jaw ticking. "Or perhaps that," he agreed at last.

"I don't buy it. Either of your reasons." Nox shook his head slowly.

"I saw Kahlis punish him myself." I spoke up, surprising even myself. "Adonis may have been his right hand, but it didn't spare him from the Dark One's wrath."

Bastian raised an eyebrow at me, assessing my words.

"Everyone faces the Dark One's wrath," growled Nox. "That doesn't make him trustworthy."

"There was another time too," I continued. "He helped me when he didn't have to, in Kahlis' court..." I trailed off, realizing he'd also been the one to care for me after Kahlis had left me to bleed out in my cell.

Adonis tilted his head to the side, watching me carefully, before raising his teacup to me and bowing his head in appreciation. My skin crawled at his sudden attention, remembering the hold his magic had on me at Kahlis' party. I averted my gaze quickly, burying my face in the warmth of my own teacup.

"*Helped* you?" Nox echoed, watching the exchange with a growing dismay. "Helped you, you mean, after trapping you in that prison in the first place? The same prison he evidently fell for my brother in between torture sessions?" Nox's voice was rising again, his anger barely contained. He stormed up to Adonis, pointing his dagger at his chest. "I do not trust you, snake."

"Lennox," Bastian chided on a low rumble. Nox's gaze shifted from Adonis to Bastian, appalled by his audacity to stick up for the fae.

"Don't tell me you're actually falling for this!"

Bastian raised a hand, stepping towards Nox. "I don't know what I believe yet. But I know the look I saw in Kirwan's eyes, I *listened* to the words coming out of his mouth. And if he is vouching for the fae, then perhaps that should be enough for us."

Nox fumed, his face turning red as he stared Bastian down. But he didn't fight back, because as much as it must have pained him to admit it, Bastian was right. Adonis was a stranger to us, but Kirwan was not. And we had to respect his word.

"More importantly, we need to address these rumors about a treaty with Aerie's father. If Kahlis is truly bringing him into this, trying to organize his efforts, then we are no longer dealing with merely a potential threat. He is starting a war, and we need to know so we can prepare."

"You already know," Adonis argued. "That's precisely why I am here. To warn you."

"Forgive me if I don't blindly take your word for it. I'd feel a lot better if I sent some of my sentries out to confirm your accusations."

"The warning," I said abruptly, the realization suddenly occurring to me. The fawn. The priestess' cautioning words. Adonis' presence here now. Bastian's gaze found my own, his eyes widening slightly. He nodded once, understanding the same thing I did. The Fates, the Cosmos, they were warning us once again.

He crossed the kitchen, hand poised on the doorknob. "For now, I suggest everyone get some sleep. It seems as if we may have some long days ahead of us, and we've just put many more long days behind us. As for me, I am going to go check on my wife." He paused just before leaving, giving Adonis a wary look. "And you come with me. We'll discuss where to put you with Kirwan."

Adonis bowed his head, following Bastian out the door and into the greenhouse beyond, leaving Nox stranded in the middle of the kitchen.

I rose to my feet, setting my teacup on the kitchen table behind me. "Nox," I offered, reaching out for my friend. "I know it's hard for you to accept. I don't quite understand it myself. But Kirwan did what he had to do to cope with the torment he experienced. And if he found companionship through that, then who are we to judge?"

"I know," Nox bit back too aggressively. I stifled the urge to jump, but Nox noticed my response. He raised his eyes to mine, softening his features and offering me an apologetic smile. "I know," he repeated, kinder this time.

"Your brother could do worse," Finn added, draining her teacup. "There weren't a lot of prospects in that prison. Suppose he'd decided to fall for the Dark One himself rather than his right hand. Then where would you be?"

"Not helping, Finn." My lips were tight as I reprimanded her.

Nox watched her for a moment, his chin dropping unexpectedly as he chuckled and shook his head. "I suppose you have me there.

I'll be thanking the Fates themselves for sparing my brother from that cruel destiny."

To my surprise, Finn's lips tipped up in a hint of amusement. She bowed her head, dismissing herself for the night and slipping off into the hallway to return to her room.

"Are you going to be alright?" I asked, lacing my arm through his as I led him into the sitting room. Nox allowed it begrudgingly, but made sure to stop by the carved out bar for a bottle of sunbeam whiskey.

"I'll be fine, love," Nox assured me, raising the bottle between us and waggling it in front of my face.

I rolled my eyes. "That seems healthy," I jeered. Nox laughed, popping open the bottle and taking a deep swig of the amber liquid. He handed it to me, raising an eyebrow in question. I pursed my lips together in disapproval, but took the bottle and drank from it anyway. The whiskey burned the back of my throat in a way that had me blessing the male beside me for thinking of the wonderful idea.

"Nevertheless, we persist," he sighed, leading me down the hallway. "I don't like it. I don't like *him*. But I suppose I will act civil for now. Until he gives me an opportunity to act otherwise."

I hummed, caught somewhere between frustration and amusement. "I know there's not much I can say for his aid, but he *did* help me. I didn't understand it at the time. Wondered if perhaps it was some lapse in judgment or some pathetic show of pity on his part. But Kirwan looked out for me at every turn in that deathhole.

Perhaps he somehow extended that request to Adonis, and he obliged."

"Perhaps," Nox agreed, even though the word sounded inauthentic on his lips. His eyes were focused ahead, as if not truly looking in this time and place. "Only time will reveal his true intentions here."

We stopped in front of my room, Nox offering me one last sip of whiskey as he pushed open the door. I peered into the darkness. Everything was just as I left it. No fire burned in the hearth, but my books were strewn atop the table by the fireplace. My bed was unmade from my abrupt leave of absence. Images of Vander and I in that same bed, on the floor in front of the fire danced through my mind.

I suddenly felt cold and alone, looking into this room frozen in time. So much had changed since I'd last stepped foot within its walls. And now that I was returning, everything felt suddenly less comforting, less sure.

I turned to face Nox, peering up into his contrasting eyes. "Would you mind—"

"I was already planning on it, love." He fixed me with that sarcastic smirk, but a genuine care shone in his eyes—the kind that only came from someone who understood my nightmares—as he stepped into the room and closed the door behind us.

CHAPTER 43
HAZEL

I *was back in my mother's cottage, watching a blue jay dance upon the branches of a hemlock tree just outside the window. It was mesmerizing, hypnotic. I found myself wondering what it would be like to fly, to spread my wings and disappear into the air. I could go anywhere I wanted to go, could be anyone I wanted to be.*

It was a beautiful thing, that level of freedom.

I sighed, turning away from the window and meandering through the cottage. I ran my fingers over my mother's trinkets, memories from another time and place. They were mine as much as they were hers, and yet they felt so foreign to me. It was a life I couldn't remember, even after the strides I'd made, even after the distance I'd traveled. It was a piece of me lost forever to my past self.

But that was okay. I wasn't that girl anymore. I didn't need her memories, her joy, her pain. I had my own now, and it was leading me to exactly who I needed to be.

A distant voice caught my attention. I bent my ear to the sky above as I tried to determine its familiarity. It sounded again, so far off yet so familiar. I toyed with what decision to make, the home around me offering a safety I wasn't ready to abandon. But the voice persisted, my curiosity getting the better of me, and I ventured out the front door to follow the sound.

In the clearing just beyond, forever marked by that nightmarish day, I could hear the voice clearly. It was unmistakably my mate's, my love's. I circled, searching high and low for its source, yet found nothing. I couldn't make out his words, but I heard the desperation in his voice.

"Vander?" I called out. "Vander!" I demanded more forcefully, when he did not answer me. He was so close. As close as he had been in days, weeks, years. And I wouldn't let him go this time.

Still, no response came. I ran to the trees, back into the clearing, through the cottage. I looked everywhere I could think of before falling to my knees in the very center of the marred meadow. This place was the source of his pain, the epitome of the darkness that marred his soul.

I looked up just as a creature stepped from the tree line. Its beady red eyes watched me, its joints moving in unpredictable ways as it shuffled just within the shadows of the hemlocks.

Discord.

"What do you want from me?!" I yelled. My throat was raw, my voice breaking.

The distant voice sounded again, murmurs on the wind.

Always present. Always warning.

"He's not even here," I cried desperately, throwing my hands out to the empty clearing. He was gone. Not even in my dreams could I find him. And yet here I was, trapped once again in his nightmare.

The murmurs trickled through the air once more, and though I couldn't understand them, my body responded without question.

I dug my hands into the ground.

Digging, digging, digging.

With no other direction to go but down, I plunged my hands into the soil and clawed my way to the abyss below.

"I'm coming, Vander," I cried into the dirt. My hands were bloodied, nails broken as they hit clay and rock and mud. But it didn't stop me.

Nothing could stop me.

Because I knew. At last, I knew.

And I would travel to the ends of the earth to find my mate.

When I awoke, a deep black sky greeted me from beyond my window. Nox's snores filled the room like thunder, pulling my attention over to where he'd made a bed for himself on the sofa. His overly long body was stretched out over the cushions. His mouth hung open, his limbs flailing in every direction.

But he'd stayed, just as he promised.

I rubbed my hands over my face, trying to bring my mind back to the present moment and out of the distant dream world. It had been so long since I'd dreamwalked. I wasn't sure if this event counted as that. It had been another dream about me in my mother's cottage. Just like the one I'd had in Kahlis' prison. Not another soul in sight.

I supposed it wasn't *just* like that dream. This one had its differences, if only I could remember what they were.

I pulled my hands away from my face, trying to concentrate on the world I'd just left behind. Suddenly, my face felt heavier, dirtier. My gaze fluttered to my hands in my lap, noticing for the first time the dirt beneath my nails, the dried blood staining my fingers.

"Nox," I called out, my body paralyzed with fear. I could do nothing but stare down at my hands. It had just been a dream, nothing out of the ordinary. Yet my hands were marred in this very real way, in this very real realm. From a dream I'd had within my mind.

Nox only responded with a loud snore, breaking me out of my daze.

"Lennox!" I yelled. He stirred, rubbing sleepily at his eyes.

"What?" he mumbled, turning over before he remembered he was on my sofa and not, in fact, in his own bed. He tumbled to the floor, all legs and arms and mumbled curses.

"Would you stop fucking around and get over here?" My voice was shaky as I tried to remain calm. But he heard the urgency regardless, popping up and surveying the room.

"What is it?" His voice was thick, groggy. He made his way over to my bed, pausing just before the mattress as he looked down at my outstretched hands. "Did a bit of midnight gardening?" he asked, brows furrowed.

"No," I exhaled on a frustrated breath. "I was having this dream about digging and then..." I trailed off, looking down at my dirtied hands.

Nox crossed an arm over his chest, resting his chin in his hand as he contemplated what to do. Then abruptly, he pulled me off the bed, not slowing as he made his way out the door and through the Estate. My body shook as he led the way, fear and confusion filling my blood as I tried to make sense of what was happening.

I blinked and we were outside. Nox was rapping hastily upon the greenhouse door. Aerie answered seconds later, her features looking haggard, exhausted, but very much awake.

"What is it?" she asked, her blue eyes poring over both me and Nox in search of injuries. Her gaze caught on the mud caking my hands and ushered us inside before Nox or I could explain.

She sat me down at the worktable, the daybed otherwise preoccupied with Kirwan's sleeping form. I made quick note of Adonis beside him, vigilantly watching over him in his sleep. Seeing the usually composed and stoic fae in such an intimate setting was jarring, and I turned my head away before feelings of sympathy had time to sneak in.

Nox had helped me onto the stool, disappearing toward the bathing chamber attached to the greenhouse. He reappeared moments later, setting a basin of water down and digging through Aerie's cupboards for some clean cloth.

"On the right, upper shelf," Aerie called out. She was bent over my hands, inspecting them carefully.

"Tell us about the dream," Nox said when he returned with a stack of white cloth. It wasn't a question, nor a command. Just a recognition that whatever this was held significance.

"I was in my mother's cottage," I recalled, closing my eyes to place myself back there. "I had a similar dream when I was being held by Kahlis."

Aerie's motions stalled, tension hanging in the air for a moment before she returned to her work. "What happened next?"

"I thought I... heard something. What was it though?" The noise echoed through my mind, just out of reach as I retraced my steps within the dream. It had sounded so familiar. "I had such a strong desire to chase it, to find it. When I had the dream in Kahlis' prison, I stayed put. But this time, I ventured out in search of its source. When I finally searched everywhere, there was only one place left to look."

I opened my eyes, sucking in a sharp breath as I pulled my hands back from Nox's grasp.

"Vander," I said breathlessly.

"Vander?" Nox echoed.

I nodded vigorously. "I don't know how, but it was him I heard. He was calling out for me, trying to find me. Or urging me to find him."

My body was still shaking, the chill of the night's air feeling utterly wrong for midsummer. Aerie let my hands go, wiping them down with a final wave of her magic before I tucked them into my lap, beneath the table and out of sight.

"What does it mean?" I asked, my voice a whisper as I tried to make sense of what he was trying to tell me. "Where is he?"

Aerie pursed her lips together, tapping a foot rhythmically against the wood floor as she stared down at the dirtied basin of water.

"You know, don't you?" Adonis' voice made me jump. He still sat beside Kirwan, still leaning tiredly against the wall. But his eyes were on Aerie's now, watching carefully. "Of course you do. You're fae, after all."

"What does he mean?" I asked, turning my attention back to Aerie. "What do you know?"

Aerie waited a moment, considering, before moving swiftly through the greenhouse and rummaging around in a distant cupboard. She reappeared moments later, pulling something from behind her back and laying it on the table before me.

I let my gaze drift slowly down to the tome before me. Before I even had my eyes on it, I knew what it was. Its familiar energy was impossible to miss.

"The Depths," Aerie shared, laying a hand on the tome. "Something mentioned in passing from time to time, a legend to the tribes, more than anything else. Folklore. But for those of us from the Old World—" Her eyes cut quickly to Adonis, then back to mine. "We know there's more to the myth than just a name, just an idea."

"Death is an ancient deity," Adonis explained, leaning forward and resting his elbows on his knees. "All that power, all that darkness. It has to be contained somewhere."

I tilted my head, brow furrowed. I didn't understand his insinuation, didn't see how this related back to my nightmare.

"Think about it," Aerie continued, opening the tome and flipping through the pages before turning it towards me. "Vander disappeared into the night, completely untraceable. Cannot even be reached by you through the tether? What within these realms has that strong of a hold on him? What within these realms would lead you back to that clearing still marked by the deal he made? Perhaps even marked by a portal to another realm?"

"No." Nox's eyes went wide beside me, realization setting in. "How?" he asked.

Aerie pushed the tome into my hands, guiding our attention down to the open page. A description of a dark, distant land, deprived of the sun's light or growth from the earth beneath one's feet. A nightmarish reality set in, a truth I'd been too reluctant to believe. But it had been right there before me, hadn't it?

I had known who Vander's deal had been with, had known other realms existed. I believed in the deities that ruled over all. Even Kahlis had told me that simply because a soul did not walk this realm did not mean they were gone. Why had I been foolish enough to believe Vander could only be one of two places—within Tir Nadaar or gone for good?

It had been staring me in the face the entire time, but I hadn't wanted to admit what it meant. There were breadcrumbs to this moment, details I'd overlooked for selfish reasons. Even as I reluctantly read the words, memories of another lifetime came flooding back to me. Of a different century in a different body that had traveled there. A goddess who had spent much of her time debating how to make such a dark and desolate place her home.

It was staring me in the face now, an undeniable truth that I could no longer ignore. *Would* no longer ignore.

"Vander... is in the Depths?" I asked, my voice cracking on the word.

Aerie nodded solemnly, taking my hand in hers and offering reassuring strokes against my newly healed skin.

But if that was a truth I could no longer deny, then another one followed. My mate was alive. I didn't care how impossible it felt, didn't waste time with fear of the unknown or doubt in my own abilities. I had sworn long ago that I would go to the ends of the earth for Vander. It appeared that my vow now stretched beyond those limits. Because I wasn't going to let a little thing like Death stop me from being with the one with whom my soul was woven.

I closed the book, letting the thud echo through the greenhouse as I met Aerie's soft blue eyes with my own.

"Then I'm going as well."

EPILOGUE
DEATH

A crack echoed through the Depths, an explosive sound as something new broke through the barrier between realms. I sat perched upon my throne after a millennia of waiting for this moment.

He appeared in my courtyard, a prisoner shackled in my chains. His shadows danced in my presence, desperate to be returned to their creator. I welcomed them, stretching and flexing as they wrapped around my skin, sinking beneath the surface.

I inhaled sharply, smelling her on him. I snarled, ready to tear into the male before me for claiming what was mine. But I withheld that anger, knowing even the smallest lapse in judgment would have the potential to ruin everything.

He lifted his head to me, confusion and terror washing over his features as he tried to make sense of where he was. I enjoyed the view, letting my lips tip up in amusement. It wasn't a real smile.

No, I hadn't felt one of those since I last held my goddess in my arms. But it was something, a step forward.

A sign that revenge was nigh.

I stood, grasping the chain from where it was attached to my throne, and jerked the being forward. He fell on his face, looking up at me in horror. I made my way down the stone steps, leaning over him as my shadows circled.

Desperate. Hungry.

"It's nice to finally meet you." My voice was low, raspy and dripping with sinister curiosity as I spoke to my captive kneeling before me. "Shadow of the Grimm."

Acknowledgements

With another book release under my belt, I just have to take a moment to praise the people that have surrounded me with their love and support during my journey as an author. As much as I love this work and have a deep passion for storytelling, none of this would be possible without the community I've found myself surrounded by.

First on that list, forever and always, is my amazing husband. My best friend. My soul mate. Thank you for always being at my side, for holding my hand during the hard moments and cheering me on during the wonderful ones. You are my number one fan, my forever personal assistant, and the best business manager I could ask for. Thank you for putting up with the late nights and the endless math questions. In the midst of my chronic illness diagnosis, you have gone above and beyond to make sure I am taken care of and still able to follow my dreams. Thank you for being the amazing man that you are. I love you to the ends of the earth.

To my artist, alpha reader, sounding board and bookish bestie, Myanna. You have been with me through so many different aspects of this journey, and I couldn't imagine a world where I am doing this without you. Your art brings my characters and books to life in a way I never imagined possible. Your continuous friendship, though... that's irreplicable. I am so incredibly thankful for all you have done and continue to do for me. Between countless crash outs, big wins, and the never ending anxious spiral, you have been such a blessing to my life.

To the rest of my alpha readers, thank you for sticking by my side through all the chaos. Y'all have been my pillars and I'm so lucky to have such an amazing team behind me. From the vague ideas to the insane questions and fangirling together over characters living in my head, y'all have been truly amazing. Thank you for being by my side through it all.

Sophie and Julia, the best editing and proof reading duo that ever lived, thank you for helping make my book shine. This one especially was a journey, with a super tight turn around time and a laundry list of questions and revisions. And y'all stuck with me, stride for stride. Thank you for caring so deeply about my books and always giving me your all during the editing process.

To all my beta and ARC readers, thank you so much for showing interest in my stories. I couldn't keep going without this community of people around me. Your continued support and love for my work is what inspires me to keep writing.

And to you, the reader. As always, thank you. This is, after all, for you! You are the reason I keep doing what I do. So, thank you for reading. Thank you for supporting. And I hope you enjoyed this story as much as I enjoyed writing it.

About the Author

Lindsey N. Rhoden is a mom to four crazy kiddos, full-time homeschooler, devoted wife, and a (sometimes more than) part-time writer. Located in the North Texas region, she has spent the last few years as a birth and postpartum doula and photographer, specializing in the art of Ayurvedic and herbal care. She enjoys nature, herbalism, and obviously lots and lots of reading. You can often find her cuddled up at home with a fantasy or dark romance book, a cup of matcha, and her cat by her side. And probably one of her four kids crawling on her.

Lindsey has been a writer from the time she could hold a pen. She dove into the world of literature during college and earned her degree in English with a concentration in literature from the University of Central Florida. Authors such as Ernest Hemingway, Agatha Christie, and Edgar Allen Poe inspired her to continue pursuing her own writing. Motherhood had other plans, though, and she took a long reprieve after graduation in 2018. In 2023, she decided to dive back into the world of writing and found out that apparently she had a lot to say.

To stay up to date on upcoming work from Lindsey N. Rhoden, be sure to follow her on social media @booktrovertbynature or check out her website at www.lindseynrhoden.com

IF YOU ENJOYED A BOND OF DARKNESS AND DISCORD

Be sure to check out the other books in *The Rift Series*